LINE
by
LINE

LINE by LINE

JENNIFER DELAMERE

BETHANYHOUSE

a division of Baker Publishing Group
Minneapolis, Minnesota

© 2020 by Jennifer Harrington

Published by Bethany House Publishers
11400 Hampshire Avenue South
Bloomington, Minnesota 55438
www.bethanyhouse.com

Bethany House Publishers is a division of
Baker Publishing Group, Grand Rapids, Michigan

Printed in the United States of America

Library of Congress Cataloging-in-Publication Data
Names: Delamere, Jennifer, author.
Title: Line by line / Jennifer Delamere.
Description: Minneapolis, Minnesota : Bethany House Publishers, [2020] | Series: Love along the wires ; 1
Identifiers: LCCN 2019055576 | ISBN 9780764234927 (trade paperback) | ISBN 9780764236327 (cloth) | ISBN 9781493425143 (ebook)
Subjects: GSAFD: Love stories.
Classification: LCC PS3604.E4225 L56 2020 | DDC 813/.6—dc23
LC record available at https://lccn.loc.gov/2019055576

Scripture quotations are from the King James Version of the Bible.

Other quotations reprinted from Myrtle Reed, *The Spinster Book*, G.P. Putnam's Sons (New York and London, 1901).

This is a work of historical reconstruction; the appearances of certain historical figures are therefore inevitable. All other characters, however, are products of the author's imagination, and any resemblance to actual persons, living or dead, is coincidental.

Cover design by Koechel Peterson & Associates, Inc., Minneapolis, Minnesota/Jon Godfredson

Author is represented by BookEnds, LLC.

20 21 22 23 24 25 26   7 6 5 4 3 2 1

I have heard of thee by the hearing of the ear:
but now mine eye seeth thee.

—Job 42:5

CHAPTER

One

London, England
Early March, 1880

Alice McNeil looked up at the London boardinghouse that had been her home for over a year. It was a lumbering pile of brown bricks that, to Alice, always gave the appearance of frowning. It was a humble place, no doubt about it, but it was reasonably clean and housed friendly boarders. The landlady who presided over them all was kind enough, if overly vigilant. Mrs. Reston kept watch over her brood of young ladies like a mother hen.

Alice knew she was lucky to have a good job and a place to live, but she was ready for a change. Unlike most of the women at this boardinghouse, she wasn't here as a stopgap before finding a man who would marry and support her. Alice had no desire for any of that nonsense; she wanted an opportunity to set up on her own. She wanted to make her own rules about when she could come and go and what she could do. This was no mere dream, for big changes were coming if—no, *when*—she got the job at Henley and Company, a firm that specialized in imports of wheat and cotton.

Alice had spent the past seven years as a first-class operator at London's Central Telegraph Office. The job was challenging and rewarding in its own way, but she was just one among hundreds of men and women who worked there like bees in a hive. Every aspect of their work, right down to the breaks, was strictly regimented. So was the pay. The telegraph service was a government entity, overseen by the postmaster general. While Alice enjoyed the work, she found the working conditions too stifling. She'd begun to look for positions at private companies that were large enough to rent their own private telegraph lines. They needed skilled operators, and the rumor was that most paid better wages than the government did.

Henley and Company had its own private telegraph line that was directly connected with its office in Liverpool. It also had a line to the Central Telegraph Office for reaching the wider world. They were looking to hire a new telegraph operator, and Alice knew she was perfect for the job. Her personal interview with Mr. Henley last week had gone quite well, she thought. He'd at least been willing to interview a woman for the position, which showed great acuity on his part. A few other places she'd applied to had declined to even speak with her. The interview had included sending a telegram on their wires to their Liverpool office—a test she'd passed with flying colors. At this point, all she could do was wait to hear back from them after they finished interviewing all the prospective candidates.

The door to the boardinghouse opened, and Mrs. Reston frowned at Alice from the doorway. "Tut-tut, girl, why are you lollygagging outside? The wind will blow you away if you're not careful!"

Yes, exactly like a mother hen, Alice thought, chafing a little. But she gave Mrs. Reston a smile and hurried up the steps.

She might be tired of this living arrangement, but Alice was heartily glad to be back in London. She'd spent the past few days at home in Lincolnshire, and it had worn her patience thin as paper. Alice always had mixed feelings about her family. She loved them all, but they exhausted her, too. They were all certain of the paths they'd taken in life, with no doubts as to whether another way might be better. Her three brothers all worked in the local village; two were married and had young children. Her only sister had just turned eighteen, and as of yesterday, she, too, was married. Alice was happy for them all, of course, yet she never quite felt in step with them.

She shrugged off these thoughts as she made her way upstairs, planning to unpack and rest before teatime. Opening the door to her room, she was surprised to see someone inside. It was Emma, the newest and youngest of the girls who boarded there.

Emma turned from where she was standing at the window, a small watering can in her hand. "Oh! You're back already. We weren't expecting you until after seven." She was a slight, quiet girl with a beauty many might describe as ethereal. Despite a hard upbringing, she was one of the sweetest and gentlest people Alice knew.

"I took an earlier train." Alice set down her bag. "What are you doing?"

It wasn't an accusation, for she knew Emma well enough to have no fears the girl was there out of mischief. She could easily guess the answer, though. It would have something to do with plants. Having grown up in the Kentish countryside, Emma was a natural-born gardener. Although she now lived in the city, she had done her best to bring a bit of the country with her. Her room was filled with plants of all kinds, and she'd even managed to coax a few flowers and shrubs to grow in the tiny patch of garden behind the boardinghouse.

Sure enough, Emma stepped away from the window, revealing four small potted plants arranged along the sill. "I hope you don't mind. These will thrive in the light you get from this window. Plus, it makes the room ever so much cozier, don't you think?"

Each of the plants had soft, lovely blooms. Their color even complemented the counterpane on Alice's bed. Even so, Alice gave her friend a mock frown. "Do you really want to keep them here? You know I am death to plants." It wasn't as though she held any malice toward growing things. It was just that she had no knack

9

for tending to them. Even the hardiest of plants never survived her forgetful oversight.

"I'll care for them. You needn't do anything but enjoy them. It seemed the least I could do, given all the ways you've helped me." Emma had recently graduated from the telegraphy school run by the postal service. Learning Morse code had been a challenge for her, but Alice had provided extra tutoring in the evenings to help her succeed.

There was a quick tap on the door, and Rose, one of the other boarders, came into the room. "Alice! So glad you're back. I've missed you, my girl."

"Have you?" Alice said with a teasing grin. Rose was among the least sentimental women Alice had ever met.

"Positively pining away," Rose insisted. "Primarily because that overbearing Miss Reed monopolizes the dinner conversation when you're not around."

"She does have a *lot* of interesting opinions," Alice agreed.

Rose scrunched her nose. "Interesting if you're a small-minded individual who cares only for fashions and gossip." She eyed the plants in the window. "Emma, I see you've been spreading your verdant joy to Alice's room."

"Yes, and you're next," Emma threatened with a smile.

"Fine by me. Just don't ask me to water them. I'd likely drown the poor things."

"I don't know why you two are so incorrigible about plant care. They add so much to a home. One day when I have a little cottage of my own, I'll fill it with plants and design the most wonderful garden."

Rose and Alice exchanged a look. Emma was always daydreaming about getting married and returning to the country. She was certainly beautiful enough to capture the heart of any man, but whether her life afterward would live up to her dreams was more doubtful.

"Yes, well, in the meantime, how are you getting along at work?" Alice asked. She knew Emma's first few weeks as a full-time telegraph operator had been difficult for her to adjust to.

Emma made a face. "I can't sleep at night. I keep hearing dots and dashes in my dreams."

"You'll get over that in time," Rose said. "That happened to me, too, in the beginning. But now I don't think a thing about it."

"Let's not talk about work right now," Emma said, turning to Alice. "I want to hear all about your sister's wedding!" Her face lit up at the thought of this happier subject. "Were there a lot of people? Was Annie's gown beautiful? Where did they serve the wedding breakfast? Where are they going on their honeymoon trip?"

Rose rolled her eyes. "I shouldn't be surprised that a wedding is uppermost in your mind."

"I love weddings," Emma said without apology. "They're always filled with so much joy and promise."

"Unfortunately, they're not always followed by the 'happily ever after' that's described in storybooks." Rose perhaps intended to tease Emma, but her voice held a note of pain that was evidence of her personal knowledge of the subject.

"I know there can be hardships," Emma replied, sounding chastened as she gave Rose a sympathetic look.

Alice and Emma didn't know all the details, but they were aware that life had not been kind to Rose. Although just thirty years old, Rose was a widow. Alice glanced at the mourning ring on Rose's left hand. Six seed pearls encircled a tiny diamond, all set on a black background. The delicate gold band was inlaid with black enamel, on which was inscribed *In Memory Of.* Their landlady, who had a better knowledge of Rose's past, had once whispered to Alice that the truth was Rose's husband had not been a good man, and few people lamented his early demise. Rose's general attitude toward men seemed to support that claim. And yet she wore the ring. Alice hoped that one day Rose might tell her why.

Seeing she had cast a pall on the room, Rose said, with what Alice suspected was forced cheerfulness, "You're right, though. Weddings can be marvelously fun. Come on then, Alice, tell us all about it." She took a seat in the room's only armchair. "What a wonder your sister was able to marry without your parents forcing you to marry someone first, like in *The Taming of the Shrew*."

"It's a modern miracle," Alice agreed with a smile. "Although I hope you are not comparing me to the tart-tongued Katherina."

Rose winked. "There are some similarities."

Alice made a pretend swipe at her before settling on the end of the bed. "Fortunately for me, in this day and age, it's not a requirement that the eldest marry first." Certainly not in her father's enlightened point of view. Alice was thankful for that. "It was a lovely wedding, despite the wind that threatened to blow off every man's hat as we walked to the church. March is not ideal for a wedding, but the lovebirds refused to wait even one month longer."

Emma sat beside her, all eagerness to hear more. Alice related as many pretty details as she could remember. It wasn't difficult to speak of the wedding in glowing terms. The bride and groom were very much in love, and everyone in the village had approved of the match. Even Rose looked misty-eyed as Alice described the heartfelt speech her father had given at the wedding breakfast.

Alice knew she was wiser in these matters than her friends, although she held nothing against them. She was not hardened and bitter about love, as Rose was, but neither was she naïve, like Emma, who dreamed of weddings and happily-ever-afters. No, she had found the better path, though she knew everyone had to make their own decisions in these things. One of her oldest friends, Lucy Bennington, had gotten married and done well enough, as those things went. Lucy was happy, or at least she thought she was, and Alice supposed that was more or less the same thing. Lucy shook her head over Alice from time to time, but no whisper of doubt ever settled in Alice's ears. Or her heart.

Long ago, Miss Templeton, the proprietor of Miss Templeton's School for Young Ladies, had shown Alice a better way. To make one's own way and live independently—Miss Templeton had relished that. Alice had seen that quality in her and admired it greatly, even as a young pupil. Miss Templeton had singled out Alice early on, inviting her to tea one afternoon in her chambers and sharing a thrilling vision for Alice's life that had permanently captured her dreams.

"My job is to polish up young ladies so they will be a fine catch for a gentleman," Miss Templeton had told her. "I am an expert at carrying out my duties, which is why this school has such a lauded reputation. However, I also keep my eye out for the truly extraordinary girl. One who is meant for better things."

Twelve-year-old Alice had looked at her with wide eyes. "Am I such a girl, Miss Templeton?"

"Indeed you are. You are clever and smart as a whip, and you prefer to work out your maths problems rather than pay one of the older girls to do it for you."

Alice's mouth dropped open in surprise.

"Don't think I don't know this," Miss Templeton said with a smile. "But I let them keep their little secrets while I look for the girl with pencil shavings on her frock and graphite smudges on her fingers."

Thus had begun Alice's apprenticeship with Miss Templeton, who had worked to get her accepted to the telegraph school and sent her off to London with the expectation of accomplishing many great things. The dream had begun with Miss Templeton, but Alice had fully embraced it. Her parents had been less sure. Alice had won over her father first. That hadn't been too difficult, given that he, too, was a telegrapher and treated her no differently than his three sons. Ultimately he'd helped her mother become accustomed to the outlandish idea. Alice's happiness was their primary aim, after all. As for a loving, homekeeping daughter who would care for them in their old age, her little sister was stepping into that role perfectly. With a stable home and a good husband, Annie could help her parents with whatever needs might arise.

In so many ways, her sister's marriage was a relief to both Alice and the rest of her family. Her new husband, Roger, was an earnest and hardworking man. He would love Annie and take good care of her. That was all Annie cared about. She wanted someone to admire and depend on.

Alice was made of different stuff. She relished the opportunity to strike out on her own, to prove her worth and value. She was glad the field of telegraphy was open to women. Most ladies only kept the job until they were married, but Alice intended to be one of the smaller number who made a career of it. What could be better than filling one's days with interesting and rewarding work, and to spend the evenings and weekends reading or walking in the park? She might even take up the new fad of bicycling. That would ensure she remained a spinster forever!

She wondered at herself sometimes, that such thoughts the world found peculiar seemed natural to her. But every time she sounded the depths of her feelings, the answer was no different. Her life had its unique rewards, and they were enough for her.

It was only after Emma and Rose had left her room so Alice could freshen up before tea that she noticed a letter sitting on her dresser—from Henley and Company! It must have arrived while she was out of town. She tore open the envelope and pulled out the letter.

She read it through at least three full times. Then, with a deep sigh, she sank into the chair Rose had recently vacated. She leaned back, her eyes closed, allowing her mind to fill with visions of all the things she would do in the days ahead. Everything in her life was unfurling just as Miss Templeton had said it would.

She had gotten the job.

Douglas Shaw sat opposite the desk of Mr. Pickens, a senior partner in one of the largest cotton brokerage firms in Atlanta. He leaned back confidently in his chair, waiting patiently while Pickens read through the details of the contract proposal Douglas had just handed him.

"'To load at Savannah, Charleston, or Port Royal . . .'" Pickens murmured aloud as he read, nodding in approval. "'Discharge at Liverpool or Bristol channel port, as directed at the time of the signing of the bill of lading. . . .'"

Douglas was confident Pickens would find nothing amiss. After four weeks of working with his company's business partners in New York and Charleston, Douglas knew the details of these contracts down to the last comma. Pickens's firm was a new client for Henley and Company, but Douglas had researched them thoroughly enough to know they were eager to improve their British trade.

Pickens finished the last page, took off his reading spectacles, and looked up at Douglas. "We may need to adjust these sailing dates. I'll confer with my manager about that. I'll also have to get his agreement to the terms for demurrage. Sometimes the trains can be delayed getting the cargo to port, which means it takes longer than anticipated to load the ship. We want to ensure any extra fees for this are reasonable."

"I feel confident we can work out the details to everyone's satisfaction."

"Yes, so do I." Pickens stood and offered Douglas his hand. "Congratulations, Mr. Shaw. We look forward to doing business with Henley and Company."

An hour later, Douglas walked the busy streets of Atlanta on the way back to his hotel, feeling quite proud and satisfied. He'd obtained a new and lucrative trading partner for his company. Tomorrow he'd be on a train to California to talk to grain merchants and build on his successes.

Seeing a telegraph office, he decided to go in and send a message back to his employer. Mr. Henley would be glad to hear the results of today's meeting as soon as possible. Douglas wouldn't be able to send confidential details over the public wire, but he could at least send the good news of this new deal.

After filling out the telegram form, Douglas waited in line for the clerk. He liked telegraph offices. The ones in America, especially in a big city like Atlanta, always seemed to be thrumming with activity. This one had four telegraph machines, all manned by operators who were busy sending and receiving the endless transactions that kept commerce moving. As a trained operator himself, Douglas could make out snippets of the messages coming over the wires among the cacophony of dots and dashes as the machines clicked away.

"Repeat that back to me, please," Douglas said, handing the form to the clerk when it was his turn.

The clerk looked it over to ensure the form was correctly filled out, then read the body of the message aloud. "'Meeting a success. Mystery sulfur minor tempest. Letter to follow.'" He gave Douglas a knowing grin. A less experienced clerk might have wondered at the string of seemingly random words in the middle, but this one had recognized right away that it was code. Every word in that odd sentence represented a whole phrase.

"Include the extra fee for return confirmation," Douglas instructed. "I'll wait while you send it."

"Yes, sir." The operator looked to be about twenty years older than Douglas. Perhaps he was content to remain a telegraph operator, but Douglas had always known he was destined for bigger things.

He'd come a long way since his days as a telegraph operator in Glasgow. An even longer way from his miserable upbringing in the poorest parts of that city. Yet today felt like just the beginning, for surely even greater things were to come.

CHAPTER

Two

Three months later

A lice disembarked from the omnibus and hurried toward the tall building on Leadenhall Street that was now her workplace. Although travel had been slow today due to heavy traffic, by walking rapidly, Alice was able to breeze through the door to Henley and Company's offices on the ground floor just in time. She greeted Mr. Dawson and Mr. Nicholls, the two bookkeeping clerks, and Miss Mavis Waller, who was the typist and filing clerk. Smiling, she took a seat at her desk and anticipated the day ahead. After three months, this had become her established routine, and she loved it.

Her desk was located in a recessed area near a window in the side of the building. Her view was of a narrow lane, used primarily by pedestrians, that separated her building and the one next door. The window did manage to catch some breezes, however, which was helpful on warm days. Alice opened it now to let in some fresh air. This bit of common sense was likely to bring a complaint from Archie Clapper, the other telegraph operator. His desk was next to hers, and he invariably objected whenever wind from the open window disturbed his papers. He wouldn't be here for another hour, though, so Alice decided to make the most of it.

Working with Archie was the only drawback to this otherwise enjoyable job. He was unfriendly and had a talent for ignoring his own laziness in order to criticize perceived faults in others. Alice could deal with him, though. She generally ignored any small barbs he threw at her and found pleasure in pushing back against his less subtle ones. At any rate, having an irascible colleague was a small price to pay for such interesting work.

As was often the case, the day turned out to be one when the telegrams were flying. There was a constant flow to Henley and Company's office in Liverpool, and from there, across the Atlantic Ocean to New York. Important deals involving sums of money so large they still made Alice's head spin were on the point of being finalized.

Sending these messages was more complicated than sending a standard telegram. Alice's first task upon starting work here had been to familiarize herself with the hundred-page codebook that had been developed specifically for communication with their clients and other offices. This was critical, since the overseas telegrams went through a chain of public telegraph offices before reaching their final destination.

This was the busiest day Alice had seen since coming to work here. The stream of messages was so constant that she didn't have time to bother about Archie's surly manner. On a normal day, she would occasionally send a pleasant smile his way even though she knew such friendliness irritated him. He usually turned away, as though determined not to allow any goodwill to penetrate his gruff exterior. Alice could not understand why he disliked her working here. It wasn't as though she might somehow steal his job and put him out of work. The volume of telegrams sent daily easily kept two people busy. Besides, if he was worried about that, he wouldn't allow her to do what was often more than her fair share. Most likely he simply didn't care to work with women. Alice had encountered that attitude before.

She had just sent off a particularly challenging telegram and poked the message onto the SENT spindle with satisfaction when she saw Archie glaring at her. She frowned back at him. "Is something amiss, Mr. Clapper? You appear . . . indisposed."

In truth, he looked as though he'd just eaten a particularly vile and indigestible meal. As much as she would have loved to have said so, Alice refrained. She generally tried not to sink to his level.

Archie motioned with his balding head across the office toward the door that led out to the main hallway. "I intend to tell Mr. Henley about the way you keep disrupting our work environment."

Alice turned in the direction he'd indicated, expecting to see the owner, Mr. Henley, standing there. Her question about what she'd been doing to cause a "disruption" was answered before she could ask. It was not their employer who had just come in the door; it was Lucy Bennington.

Alice suppressed a groan. Of all the days for her friend to drop by, today was probably the worst. Even now the telegraph was clicking away. Since Archie was working the incoming messages, he gave them both one more malevolent glare before turning his attention to answer it.

Catching Alice's eye, Lucy waved enthusiastically. By now, at least, Lucy knew better than to call out to her. That had gotten Alice into trouble before. Alice would have preferred her friend not come here at all, but Lucy was impervious to Alice's admonitions, insisting the office was not a prison. While that was certainly true, Alice was concerned about keeping up a professional image. She had not been here long, and she wanted to ensure no one could have a reason to let her go.

Alice sent Lucy an answering wave and a signal for her to wait. She had two more messages to send before she could take a break. Both required transcription into code. She worked calmly and deliberately to show Archie she had no plans to abandon her work before her scheduled time.

When Alice had finished sending the messages, she signed off and rose from her chair, not bothering to address Archie. This was her lunch break, and she wasn't going to waste a minute of it dealing with him. She hurried over to where Lucy still stood at the door, fairly wriggling with excitement.

"Lucy, what are you doing here?" Alice whispered. "You know it's difficult for me to get away while I'm at work."

"Yes, I know, but today there is a new shipment of ladies' goods at Drake and Sons, and of course, one must get there early, before the best items get snatched up. I was sure you'd want to join me."

Given that they'd been friends since the age of fourteen, when they had met as students at Miss Templeton's School for Young Ladies, Lucy was well aware that hurrying to buy a new item of clothing was the last thing on Alice's list of preferred pastimes. Lucy had been doing her best to change that. After marrying Mr. Clive Bennington, a well-to-do stockbroker, Lucy had become enamored with the joys of keeping up with the latest fashions. Ever since, she'd done her best to instill this love in Alice as well.

Alice took Lucy's arm and steered her out the door, away from Archie's disapproving gaze. "This isn't the best day for me to go out. There is a lot of work to do."

"You say that every time I come here."

"Perhaps because it is true."

"They work you too hard." Lucy's mouth twisted as she gave Alice a concerned look. "I worry about your health."

Alice did her best to tuck away her irritation at this remark. She might not live in ease with a husband to provide for her—something Lucy was always touting the benefits of—but she considered herself better off in other ways.

"I'll buy you lunch," Lucy added brightly, knowing this would sweeten the deal. "The tearoom at Drake and Sons has delicious sandwiches, and their cakes are like little pieces of heaven."

"All right," Alice relented, and not just because the offer of lunch did sound tempting. Perhaps it would do her good to get out for a while. Some days, Archie could really get on her last nerve. "Remember, though, I can't return late."

Lucy's joyful smile eased Alice's misgivings, even if it didn't lessen the burn of the disapproval Archie had sent her way. He wasn't her supervisor, she reminded herself. He had no authority over her—so long as she did not allow it.

◦◦◦

Douglas threaded his way through the crowd at the railway platform. Having gone on so many trips for his employer, he felt he knew every inch of Paddington by heart. He paused to allow a porter with a cart full of baggage to hurry by, and spared a quick glance upward to appreciate the giant arched glass roof overhead. Recent rain must have cleared it of its usual layer of soot, because today bright sunshine glinted through it.

Returning his gaze back to earth, he spotted a young lady giving him an appreciative glance as she walked in his direction. She was pleasant looking, an impression no doubt augmented by her tastefully flattering dress and an understated but elegant hat. He would gladly have tipped his own hat to her in response to her little overture, except she was on the arm of her father. So he settled for the merest hint of a smile and lift of his brow, which went unnoticed by the older man but not by the lady. There was a sparkle in her eye as they passed him.

This interlude added to Douglas's good mood. He felt invincible in all his dealings right now. This elation had been with him for the entire voyage home from America. He had spent six months there traveling around the country, from the East Coast all the way to California on the transcontinental railroad. It was the most ambitious trip Douglas had ever undertaken, and his employer, Mr. Henley, was more than pleased with the results. So many of Douglas's long-held dreams were becoming reality.

Mr. Henley stood waiting for him at the end of the platform.

"Welcome back, Shaw," Henley said, shaking Douglas's hand vigorously. "I don't expect you're surprised to see me."

He wasn't. He knew Henley would be anxious to get the particulars of the trip that could not be put into brief telegraph messages or even letters. "To be honest, I half expected a welcome band and maybe some banners," Douglas answered with a smile.

21

Henley looked perplexed. For a split second, Douglas wondered if he'd overstepped, sounding too pompous. But then Henley let out a robust guffaw. "That's a good one, Shaw! You deserve it, that's for sure." He motioned toward Douglas's bag. "I hope you won't mind putting off your return home until after you've come to the office?"

"I was planning on it."

"Very good. I knew we could count on you."

Yes, Douglas thought, as the two of them strode briskly outside and got into Henley's waiting carriage, things were looking good in every respect. The months he'd spent in America had yielded more than just good trading contracts for his company. Mr. Henley had hinted at generous benefits if Douglas made a good job of it. Soon there would be a promotion, along with the accompanying raise in pay, and introductions into the best society circles. Mr. Henley would even introduce Douglas to Miss Penelope Rolland, daughter of a wealthy banker and one of London's most eligible, rich, and well-connected young ladies. It was just another step in his rise to success.

Not bad for the son of a shipyard laborer, Douglas thought to himself as the carriage pulled away from the station. He smiled as he watched London unrolling before him, feeling almost as though he owned it. *Not bad at all.*

⁂

Although Alice could be irritated sometimes at Lucy's impromptu luncheon dates, she couldn't deny they were often enjoyable. She and Lucy sat in the tearoom in Drake and Sons, finishing up the tarts that had accompanied a truly delightful tray of little sandwiches. Lucy was regaling her with a story involving her sweet but mischievous lapdog, Bulwer, and a piece of beef that the butler had been horrified to discover behind the sofa.

Alice smiled, although it wasn't in response to Lucy's tale. A memory from their school days had surfaced in her mind. "Lucy, do you remember that time we took an unauthorized picnic by the stream that ran about a half mile from Miss Templeton's school?"

"I certainly do." Her mouth twitched in a playful smile. "I filched some food from the pantry and persuaded you to sneak away with me." She pointed a reproving finger at Alice. "As I recall, getting the goods past the cook was a lot easier than tearing you from your studies."

Lucy was right about that. Alice had always been a stickler for following the rules, and besides, she'd planned to spend those two hours preparing for an upcoming exam.

"I knew you'd been working too hard," Lucy said. "You have to admit it did you a world of good to steal those few hours of freedom and lounge in the sunshine."

Alice nodded. "The wonder to me is that we got away with it, despite showing up late for deportment lessons with dirt clinging to our skirts. I have no doubt Miss Templeton figured out what we'd done."

"Judging by the look she gave us as we stumbled in, I'm sure she did! But perhaps even that formidable lady realized an afternoon outside could do no harm."

If so, it was a piece of wisdom shared by Lucy and their former headmistress. Alice knew she could take life too seriously sometimes. Then, as now, it seemed Lucy's self-appointed job was to make sure Alice took a break from time to time for play. And really, as Alice popped the last bite of a strawberry tart into her mouth, she couldn't help but be grateful for it.

She finished her tea as Lucy signed for the bill.

"Right, let's get to the shopping!" Lucy said as they rose from the table.

They made their way to the ladies' clothing section of the department store. Lucy paused at a counter where a shop girl was laying out a colorful display of new scarves. "Aren't these lovely? Some of these would look stunning on you!"

"Do you think they'll be fancy enough to go with this?" Alice teased, indicating her plain gray frock. Wishing to look as businesslike as possible, she always wore gowns in muted colors with high collars and long sleeves.

"Well, they could certainly liven it up." Lucy draped a bright pink scarf over Alice's shoulders. "What do you think?"

Alice frowned as she studied herself in the mirror on the counter. "It's too bright. I don't think it's flattering at all."

"I suppose you think that dull gray frock is flattering?"

"I work with men all day. No one would take me seriously if I wore this to the office."

"Nonsense," Lucy scoffed. "Didn't you tell me there were eight hundred women at the Central Telegraph Office? I can't imagine all of them wore gray—especially as all women try to outdo each other in their sartorial choices."

"Well, there's only one other woman where I work now, and I'm not in competition with her."

"Even so, maybe it would be better to stand out—"

Lucy's protest died as Alice pulled out her pocket watch and flipped it open, pointedly checking the time. Alice was enjoying this outing, but she couldn't ignore her work commitments.

"All right," Lucy conceded. She took back the scarf and chose another from the counter. "What about this one? It's understated and elegant. No man could fault you for wearing this. Have you seen some of the brightly colored waistcoats they wear these days?"

The scarf was a rich purple, with threads of silver woven through it in a delicate pattern. Lucy draped it expertly around Alice's neck. "Look at how it enhances your overall appearance but not in a showy way. It's perfect!"

Alice had to admit it was pretty. Checking the mirror again, she felt an unusual stirring of vanity as she viewed the effects of the scarf. How could something purple bring out the green in her eyes? Somehow it did, and she liked the result. "Oh, Lucy, are you trying to turn me into a vain woman who cares about such things?"

Lucy grinned. "It's part of my nefarious plan."

It didn't take long for Lucy to choose two scarves and a pair of fine leather gloves for herself. She was free to indulge her fancy because her husband had given her credit at shops all over town. The shop girl wrapped up Lucy's purchases and entered the amounts in the store ledger. Lucy insisted that Alice should wear her new scarf out of the shop rather than having it wrapped. Since this would save time, Alice agreed.

Lucy's open carriage took them swiftly toward Alice's workplace. Lucy smiled with satisfaction, gazing up at the sunny sky. "Just think, if you were married, we could have all day for shopping trips together."

Alice was tempted to give her usual retort that Lucy knew full well she had no intention of ever getting married. She refrained only because she had no wish to quarrel with her friend. She had no time, either. They were at the door of Henley and Company, and she had to get inside.

"Thank you for buying me lunch," Alice said. She gave Lucy a quick peck on the cheek and got out of the carriage.

Their time together had been refreshing, but Alice was equally glad to be getting back to work. She loved the challenges and rewards of her job. As she went into the building, she took a deep breath, preparing to launch herself into what was sure to be a busy afternoon.

CHAPTER

Three

Mr. Henley and Douglas were just pulling up to the door of Henley and Company when a portly man in a suit and bowler hat, apparently recognizing Henley's carriage, raced across the street to meet them. In his haste, he misjudged where the carriage would stop and nearly got stepped on by the horse. Douglas recognized Mr. Sutherland, a proprietor at the banking house where their company kept its money.

Mr. Sutherland shook Henley's hand as soon as they'd gotten down from the carriage. "I've been hoping to run into you today, Henley."

"It's a good thing we didn't run into you!" Henley returned with a smile.

"Have you got a minute?"

"Of course." He motioned toward the door.

"Thank you, but I can't stay. I've got to be at the Royal Exchange for a meeting in a quarter of an hour. If we could just have a brief private word."

He sent a pointed glance at Douglas as he said this. It was his first acknowledgment of Douglas's presence. That was typical of Sutherland; he dealt only with anyone he thought was important. As an assistant to Mr. Henley, Douglas did not yet merit Sutherland's notice. *That will change one day,* Douglas thought. He was rising in the world, and that knowledge kept him from becoming irritated at the bank manager's dismissal of him.

Douglas could easily have removed himself by going into the building, but he thought it might be more useful to remain outside. That way he'd be within easy reach in case the men should decide to include him in the conversation after all. It would not be unusual for Mr. Henley to call him over, given that he was depending on Douglas more and more. In fact, that would be supremely satisfying. A sign to Sutherland that Douglas was trustworthy and astute enough to contribute to crucial business matters.

Tilting his head toward the building, Douglas said, "I might take a moment to enjoy a cigarette before going inside."

Henley nodded, and Douglas walked away, pulling out his cigarette case as he went.

The two men were swiftly engaged in conversation. Douglas struck a match against the brick wall and lit his cigarette. After a minute or two, he judged from the posture of the men that his presence wasn't likely to be requested. He was pretty good at reading his employer in these matters. He was tempted to be a little disappointed, but he shrugged it off. He knew where he stood in the company, even if Sutherland didn't realize it yet. He also had to consider that the conversation might be about another matter altogether. It could be something to do with Henley's personal affairs and have nothing to do with the company.

The day was hot—summer had arrived in earnest. Douglas took a few steps into the shade of the nearby pedestrian lane where it was cooler. He leaned against the wall and looked up. From here he could see the telegraph wires that ran across the buildings and into the offices of Henley and Company. He smiled as he contemplated the sight. Only large and prosperous companies could boast a private telegraph line. It was expensive—not only because of the annual access fee but also to keep a staff of telegraphers to send and receive the messages. Lots of people complained that the miles of wires running all over the city's rooftops were ugly. In some places, there were so many that they blocked out the light in the narrower streets. More and more, telephone wires were being added as well. Although the wires were not aesthetically pleasing, they were beautiful to Douglas. The telegraph had been an electric lifeline, pulling him up from poverty and on to better things.

The office windows were open. They were just above his head, so he couldn't see in, but Douglas knew he was standing near the window by the telegraphers' desks. He listened for the sounder. It was quiet at the moment. He could hear voices, though. Without the slightest shame, he moved under the window in an effort to hear what they were saying. He was so accustomed to gathering information via his ears that this sort of thing never felt like eavesdropping.

"I'm *so* glad you decided to return. We were about to send out a search party."

Douglas recognized the caustic voice of Archie Clapper. He shook his head in amusement. That man always sounded out of sorts. He was the type to see the downside to anything in life, no matter how good it was.

"I'm only two minutes late. You needn't make a case out of it."

This retort came from a woman. Douglas wasn't familiar with her voice. He could only presume it belonged to Miss Alice McNeil, the new telegrapher. He knew she'd been recently hired, but he had yet to meet her in person. Her manner of speaking was crisp and straightforward. This fit with the view he'd formed of her during a few telegraphic transmissions he'd sent from the company's Liverpool office after his ship had docked in that city yesterday. If she sounded more acrimonious than he'd expected, he would just put that down to the fact that she was, after all, speaking with Clapper. He would draw venomous words from a saint.

As the conversation continued, it devolved into something more akin to a battle of wits. This Alice McNeil was standing up for herself in a most interesting way. Douglas liked her already. He settled in and listened, the smile growing on his face as the conversation continued.

28

"I'm so glad you decided to return. We were about to send out a search party."

Despite his sneer, Archie's eyes lingered on Alice's scarf for a few seconds. Perhaps Lucy was right when she'd pointed out how becoming the color was.

Alice dropped into her chair and quickly stowed her gloves and reticule in a drawer. "I'm only two minutes late. You needn't make a case out of it."

"Look at the work that has piled up." Archie pointed to the basket that sat on the ledge between their two desks.

"Piled up in the last two minutes?" Alice raised an eyebrow. "Or am I now to be admonished simply for taking lunch?" She picked up the stack and riffled through it. There were perhaps a dozen missives, none terribly long. "Why, there must be nearly three hundred words here, all total." Alice was hard-pressed to keep from rolling her eyes as she spoke. As an accomplished telegrapher, she could send over forty words per minute. Getting through this stack would take no time at all.

"Mr. Henley left those before going out. I had no time to send them, as there was a lot of incoming." Archie pointed an ink-stained finger toward Mavis Waller's desk on the other side of the office. It did indeed have a pile of papers on it. Mavis's task, among other things, was to type up incoming telegrams, decoding them as she went.

Alice sent Mavis a questioning look, wanting to confirm Archie's assertion that they'd been busy. But Mavis kept her eyes down and continued typing as though oblivious to the conversation. Alice knew she was cowed by Archie, perhaps even afraid of him. Though how anyone could be afraid of that slothful lump of obstinacy was beyond Alice's comprehension.

"There will be more to come, now that the Americans are finally getting to their offices." Archie's deprecating tone suggested that the Americans were unforgivably lazy for keeping to their own working hours, given that eight o'clock in the morning in New York was one o'clock in London. Alice suspected that was why

Archie preferred to take the later of the two lunch hours. There was always a flurry of messages from the Baltimore office first thing. By taking lunch at that hour, Archie was leaving one of the busier times for Alice to handle.

Sure enough, the sounder began to click the opening salvo that someone was on the line. Alice sent back the reply *Ready* and picked up her pen. This message wasn't coming from overseas, however. Alice recognized the sender's initials, as well as his sending style: it was Jimmy Smith from the Liverpool office. He was a particular friend of Archie's, and they were often in cahoots. Alice had survived a hazing from Jimmy on her first day on the job. Also known as rushing, it was an attempt to show her up by sending the message so fast that she couldn't keep up and would have to "break" and ask him to repeat. But she had triumphed and been doubly rewarded by Archie's dumbfounded amazement.

"Of course, if you feel the incoming messages are too much for you to handle, I am happy to stay." Archie would have heard the initials of the sender as well and known it was Jimmy. He looked at Alice as though daring her to accept his offer.

He should have known better. "Thank you, but you needn't bother. Please don't let me keep you from going out. We could use more air in here."

Archie's face hardened. "I'll leave you to it, then." As he grabbed his hat, his lips twisted into a weird position that might almost represent a smile—if he had known how to accomplish that facial expression. Alice knew that look; he was up to something.

He went to Mavis, motioning with his hat toward the stack of papers on her desk. "Those are important messages from Liverpool. Mr. Henley will be back any minute, and he wants those waiting in his office when he arrives." He made as if to leave but then paused. It was obviously entirely for effect. "Oh, and by the way—be sure you get the decoding right. *Moustache* means there is no commission at port of shipment. *Movement* means there is a full five percent commission at port of shipment."

This was a reference to an error Mavis had made last month. It had nearly cost the company a lot of money. Even though they had gotten the matter straightened out, Archie wouldn't let her forget it.

Looking chagrined, Mavis nodded and kept typing.

Alice sent her a sympathetic glance. There was no time to do anything else, as Jimmy was sending the message full clip over the wire. The sounder was loud and insistent. Jimmy always sent messages speedily, but today he was transmitting faster than usual. Even after that first week, when she had proven her mettle, there were still times when Jimmy—usually goaded on by Archie— would see if he could best her. Most of the time Alice enjoyed rising to the challenge. Today, however, she would have preferred not to have to deal with this.

"Of all the days," she muttered under her breath. But she was determined not to break.

Several drops of sweat tickled down her neck. The room was hot even though she had persuaded Archie that they should keep the windows open.

With one ear, she heard Archie greet someone he apparently met coming in. "Good day, sirs." He only used that obsequious tone of voice around one person: Mr. Henley. He must be returning with Mr. Shaw. Alice would have turned around to greet them, but the incoming transmission was too fast.

She could hear Mr. Henley and Mr. Shaw speaking to Mavis behind her. Mavis had been with the company for over a year. Her voice changed to a shy warmth as she spoke with Mr. Shaw. Evidently he didn't intimidate her the way Archie did. Alice kept to her task. That was aggravating, because she had been keenly wanting to meet Mr. Shaw in person. They'd had a few exchanges yesterday when Mr. Shaw had sent some messages himself from Liverpool—in a much cleaner and friendlier style than Jimmy Smith was currently using. Alice was intrigued by this man who had risen from a telegrapher to the second in authority to the owner. Archie said Mr. Shaw was self-absorbed and full of himself, but

Alice knew to take anything Archie said with a very large grain of salt. Besides, coming from Archie, it was rather like the pot calling the kettle black.

"This is Miss McNeil, our new telegrapher," she heard Mr. Henley say. "Miss McNeil—"

Alice held up a hand to indicate she could not talk at this moment. She could tell this message was nearing its conclusion, and she wasn't going to allow the thread to drop.

"Miss McNeil and I have communicated over the wire." Mr. Shaw's voice was smooth, like butter—if butter had a sound. It was also brimming with self-assurance. Or was that a touch of ego she was hearing? Maybe Archie had been right about him.

Alice steeled herself to keep up with the sounder. This was no time to get distracted by a voice. She was a master at keeping up with any incoming message, no matter what might be going on around her. It was a point of pride with her.

But Mr. Henley would keep talking. "Miss McNeil has only been with us a few months, yet she has very nearly mastered that codebook and our other protocols for sending messages. For speed, she is as fast as Mr. Clapper. Quite astounding. Oh, but that's right, you learned Morse code as a child, didn't you?"

That last part was directed at her, but Alice didn't answer. She bit her lip and kept transcribing the message, pushing her attention to stay with the sounder. Finally, the message ended. She sent back the short confirmation just as rapidly, almost slamming the key on the last stroke. Then she leaned back in her chair and crossed her arms. That would teach that lizard Jimmy Smith not to try to show her up.

"Bravo, Miss McNeil," Mr. Shaw said. "Whoever was on the other end must have been sending better than forty words per minute. Yet you did not break."

Collecting herself, Alice turned.

And beheld the most handsome man she had ever seen.

Alice almost fell out of her chair. Not because she had turned too quickly and gotten unbalanced, but because she was shocked that this ridiculous observation about a man's looks had intruded itself on her brain. She carefully closed her mouth, which had somehow fallen open. She blinked a few times, as though by getting a clearer look at him she would realize that her first impression—that no man could really be the most perfect specimen since Adam—had been caused by a mere trick of the light.

It was a vain hope. He was still devastatingly handsome. Tall, with square shoulders, and dark hair and eyes. Neatly trimmed side whiskers. A clean-shaven face revealing a nicely formed chin. Nose, brows, forehead—everything in flawless proportion.

He was smiling at her. He had just said something. What was it? It really was too warm in this office. Maybe her brain was frazzled by the heat.

"I said, what you did was quite impressive," Mr. Shaw supplied, as though he could read her addled thoughts. His voice was pleasant, his accent hinting at Scottish origins.

Alice rose. Her legs were shaky—but that must be because she'd just spent a very tense few minutes keeping up with a racing telegrapher.

She breathed in, accepting his compliment and straightening with pride. She realized that since he was a telegrapher himself, he would know exactly what she'd just accomplished.

"How do you do?" Alice held out a hand to offer a handshake. After all, they were greeting each other as colleagues, even if his position in the company was higher than hers.

He looked momentarily surprised but didn't hesitate to respond. He grasped her hand with a warm grip that was neither too firm nor too weak, but which somehow made her legs wobbly again. "We've already had a few conversations, haven't we, Miss McNeil? Via the wire, I mean."

His eyes were as warm as his smile. His gaze lingered for a moment on her new scarf, but he seemed more intent on her face. As though he were trying to get to know her by studying its contours. Not that there was much to see, Alice thought. Lucy always told her she was too thin, and Alice was well aware that her angular face and straight nose were not the least bit interesting. Perhaps he'd noticed how the scarf highlighted her eyes?

Alice McNeil, do not *go down that path,* she told herself sternly. She was not about to become one of those vain and frivolous women who cared about such things. "Yes. The, er, wire."

It really shouldn't be this hard to breathe. Alice swallowed and tried to find air.

Mr. Shaw released her hand, and Alice turned, reaching for the paper on which she'd scrawled the telegram from Liverpool, intending to hand the missive to Mavis.

She was stopped by Mr. Shaw, who extended a hand toward the paper. "May I?"

Did he plan to check her work? He would have to know that, as a first-class telegrapher, she would find that insulting. But she wasn't in a position to object. "You already know what it says, I'll wager," she hedged.

He winked. "You're right."

Mr. Henley motioned for Alice to hand Mr. Shaw the paper, so she reluctantly did so.

Mr. Shaw read it over. "I see you filled in a few places where the sender dropped a letter in his hurry to send this. This *E* and that *T*, for example." He leaned closer to show her the words he was referring to. He was a good two inches taller than she was. There was a vague smoky scent coming from him, as though he'd spent his recent train ride in the smoking car. "Not to mention the terrible gaps he put between the words. As you noted, he meant 'to the train' although to my ear it sounded like 'tot he train.'"

"It was sloppy of him," Alice agreed, impressed at how much he had caught, especially as Mr. Henley had been talking the entire time. "You have good ears."

It was the usual compliment offered by telegraphers to someone who was adept at translating incoming messages by sound rather than by waiting for the Morse code to be printed onto paper by the machine. Why, then, did she find her eyes straying to his ears? Although partially obscured by his hair, she couldn't help but notice that they were perfectly shaped and lay at just the right angle to his head, neither too close nor sticking out too far. Of course.

"I've been doing this for nearly fifteen years," he replied. "And you?"

Was he really asking a lady to give a hint of her age? She narrowed her eyes at him, but he was smiling and seemed genuinely interested.

"As Mr. Henley mentioned, I learned it as a child. My father is a telegrapher. He worked for many years at the railway station in Ancaster. I spent a lot of time with him there." She paused, embarrassed that she had given out so much information without his even asking for it.

He didn't seem to notice her discomfort. He merely nodded. "That would go a long way toward explaining why you are so good."

He handed the paper to Mavis, who received it as if it were a special love note just for her. The stars in her eyes were so obvious that Alice was tempted to roll her own in response. It instantly brought her back to herself. She would never get foggy brained over a man. She could respect his talent and admire his drive to get on in the world, but neither of those things should be leaving her breathless.

The sounder picked up with another message. "Excuse me," she said, relieved for the excuse to turn away from his smiling gaze.

She took her place again at the telegraph. This message was coming from London's Central Telegraph Office. It was delivered in a smooth, competent hand that wasn't racing. As Alice worked, the two men went into Mr. Henley's office and shut the door behind them.

"Isn't he wonderful?" Mavis said as soon as Alice had finished receiving the message and was at liberty to talk again. "He's such a *nice* man. And so handsome, too." She leaned eagerly toward Alice over her typewriter. "Didn't I tell you he was handsome?"

She had. Many times. So had Archie—although in his case it had been in the context of insinuating that Mr. Shaw had risen in the company solely on account of his good looks and his ability to flatter potential clients. But the fact that Mr. Shaw had caught those specific details about the missing letters simply by ear *and* while talking with someone else at the same time, was extraordinary. A talent for telegraphy didn't necessarily mean he had business acumen, but it did indicate a sharp mind.

And there was no doubt that he was easy on the eyes. . . .

Alice cleared her throat and marshaled her thoughts. "I look forward to working with him," she said, putting no more emphasis on it than she would if discussing any other work colleague.

She wasn't going to say any more. Nevertheless, she couldn't deny she was glad that Mr. Shaw was so pleasant and competent. Mr. Henley could be terse and bark out orders, and Archie was, well, Archie. Mr. Shaw's presence could only improve the atmosphere here.

As for his being handsome, that was more likely to be a distraction than a help. It was best she got used to it as soon as possible so that Alice could keep her mind where it belonged—on her work.

<hr/>

"That can't be right." Mr. Henley looked up from his desk, where he was making notes as Douglas relayed details about his trip that had not yet been typed up for the official report.

Douglas stopped midsentence. "I beg your pardon?"

"You said, 'Two hundred bales of cotton from Ancaster.'"

Startled, Douglas shook his head. "Did I? I meant to say Alabama, of course. Two hundred bales of cotton from Alabama at four dollars per bale, in addition to the shipment from Georgia, twice the amount at the same price per bale. Shipping fees add twenty-five cents per bale. All total, I put the sum after conversion at sixty-four pounds, three shillings, and nine pence. We should easily make a profit by selling the cotton at the standard rate here in England, or perhaps even a little lower if we want to leverage our advantage over our competitors." For some reason this information came out unusually rapid. So rapid that he felt a touch breathless as he finished.

Henley studied him for a moment, his mouth quirking up in an expression Douglas couldn't decipher. He nodded and began scratching the numbers on the paper, totaling the sums himself to ensure they matched the totals Douglas had given him. Henley always did this. It wasn't that he distrusted Douglas's tallies; it was simply that he always double-checked the financial sums for everything in the business.

As he worked, Douglas thought over his verbal gaffe. *Ancaster.* That was where Alice McNeil said she was from. Somehow that tidbit had lodged in his mind. In one sense, that wasn't surprising. Douglas's memory was excellent. He retained a wide range of information from many sources. However, he was usually better at compartmentalizing it. How had Ancaster slipped into his discussion of business in America? He supposed it wasn't unusual that she would be on his mind. He had just met her, after all, and he'd been impressed by her ability to focus on the incoming message despite the distractions. He'd also enjoyed that taste of her sense of humor while eavesdropping on her conversation with Clapper. What other interesting things might he learn about her?

He smiled as he recalled the way she had given Clapper a dose of his own medicine—something that was greatly needed. Miss McNeil's predecessor was a mediocre telegrapher who tended to make mistakes under pressure. That had been bad for the company, if good for Clapper's sense of superiority. Clapper would have to work hard to prove himself better than Alice McNeil. From what Douglas had seen today, their competition was already underway.

It was a prospect Douglas was greatly looking forward to.

CHAPTER

Four

Alice found herself thinking a lot about Douglas Shaw as she rode the omnibus home after work. The whole tenor of the office had changed with his arrival. Alice suspected things were going to get a lot more interesting. In some ways, he was just as Archie and Mavis had described him, and yet they hadn't presented a full picture. She had found herself taken completely by surprise.

Perhaps it was simply her reaction to him that had surprised her. She had not expected to be so . . . well, *drawn* to him. She felt her cheeks go red from embarrassment even though no one in this crowded omnibus could possibly know what she was thinking.

She chided herself for her shallowness in admiring Mr. Shaw's appearance. Plenty of handsome men had never turned her head. Why was he different? She must have been drawn to that certain light in his eye, the kind born of confidence, and his equally assured bearing. She could admire anyone who was successful in life. Yes, that must be it.

Even after deciding this, she still found herself thinking about today's events long after she'd arrived home, eaten her supper, and fed Miss T, the cat she'd acquired shortly after moving into her small but comfortable abode in Islington on the northeast side of London. It was perhaps more accurate to say the cat had acquired *her*, for the creature had found its own way, via a tree, a brick wall, and an open window, into the rooms Alice was renting on the upper floor of a widow's house. The cat was friendly, and Alice was happy for the companionship. Besides, how could she refuse such an appealing creature who had shown so much determination to be there? She had named the cat after Miss Templeton. It seemed fitting, since living on her own in these pleasant lodgings was evidence she was living the life Miss Templeton had taught her to aspire to.

After dinner, Alice put on her hat and picked up her reticule. Despite having risen early and worked a full day, she still had too much energy to settle down for the evening. She decided to take a walk. On her way out, she took a few scraps of leftover fish to feed the two other cats who had gotten into the habit of lounging near the stoop of the house in hope of such kindness. They had not discovered Miss T's secret for coming and going from the house, which Alice considered a good thing. One cat coming inside was enough for her. But she was happy to give these others a bit of extra food when she had it.

After a stroll around the park near her house, Alice turned her steps toward the high street. There was still time to visit her favorite bookshop. Browsing the shelves could be just the thing to distract her thoughts.

⟡

Now that he was back in London, Douglas resumed his usual after-dinner walk with Stuart Carson and "Hal" Halverson, his friends and fellow boarders at the boardinghouse he called home for now. The walk was a good way to work off their landlady's meals, which were usually heavy on mutton and potatoes. It also gave him an opportunity to catch his friends up on what had happened during his American trip and about the benefits he was already gleaning from it. One such benefit was the prospect of an invitation to a dinner party where he would finally be introduced to Miss Penelope Rolland. Henley was working on a deal with Miss Rolland's father, a wealthy banker who had financed many shipping and import ventures. If Douglas was to begin courting Miss Rolland, it could make the deal even sweeter.

"I envy you," Carson said. "Not only is Miss Rolland rich, but the gossip in the papers is that she's a stunner, too."

"It'll be the perfect match," Hal added. "We'll miss you after you get married and move into a fancy home. But we'll anxiously await your invitation to dinner."

"Let's not put the cart before the horse," Douglas protested. "I haven't even met her yet."

"You can't be worried!" Hal snorted. "It's a sure thing. She's rich and you're handsome!"

The two men laughed, and Douglas joined them. However, he meant it that this match was not a sure bet. He was well aware he was a social climber, and he had to take care not to step on any toes along that ladder. The ebullience he'd felt on the trip home from America had begun to settle, and whispers of uncertainty arose in its place. Would he really be able to prove that his successes overseas could translate to the English social scene?

"Look at Douglas, acting so demure," Carson said with a smirk. "We know you always leave the ladies wanting more. Like that Miss Wilson who lives across the street from the boardinghouse. The way she bats her eyes at you whenever your paths cross on the street!"

"Which they seem to do quite often," Hal observed. He nodded and touched his nose—a habit he had whenever sharing what he considered a deep or clever insight. "I think she figures out how to make those accidental meetings happen on purpose."

"You flatter me," Douglas said. He wouldn't allow their words to go to his head. Although he hadn't met Miss Rolland yet, he was pretty sure that winning her over wouldn't be as easy as turning the head of the vapid Miss Wilson. Even if Miss Rolland were to fall head over heels in love with him, there were plenty of other obstacles to clear.

The men paused in front of a bookshop they often frequented. "Let's go in," Hal suggested. "I want to get the new issue of the *Illustrated Police News*."

Douglas frowned. "With all the enlightening and edifying books in there, you want to spend your money on stories of outrageous crimes?"

"There's valuable information in that paper!" Hal insisted. "Last week's issue had a story about two telegraph operators who got married, and three years later the woman killed her husband. Decided he wasn't good enough for her anymore, so she stabbed him to death—with a joiner's chisel!" He poked a finger in Douglas's chest. "There's a lesson in that, you know."

"Never take up woodworking for a hobby?" Douglas suggested with a smile.

"No! Never marry a telegraph operator! Working in a man's profession has hardened 'em. They'll never make obedient wives."

"I'll be sure to take that under advisement," Douglas said, nodding with mock seriousness.

He smiled to himself as they entered the shop. The talk of lady telegraph operators immediately brought to mind Alice McNeil. She was clever and not so hard to look at, although her hairstyle and clothing were rather plain—with the exception of that very feminine purple scarf. It seemed almost out of place on her, as though it hinted at another side of her that was not readily evident. He also knew she had a tart tongue and an ability to hold her own. But he was pretty sure she wasn't the sort of woman who would stab a man with a joiner's chisel.

Hal went to the newspaper rack to buy his penny paper while the other two men began perusing the bookshelves. After a few minutes, Douglas noticed that Hal's attention had been caught by a book after all. He was standing with the unread newspaper under his arm, reading the book and chuckling.

Douglas went over to him. "What did you find? A book of humorous stories?"

"I suppose you could call it that," Hal answered with a grin. As Carson joined them, Hal lifted the book to reveal the title stamped on its spine: *The Spinster's Guide to Love and Romance.*

Carson drew his head back in surprise. "Why would you want to read that?"

"There's a whole chapter in here that supposedly explains to women how men think!" Hal guffawed.

"I've never met a woman who wanted to know what we think," Carson joked, shaking his head in disbelief.

"The author of this book thinks they do. Listen here." Hal pointed to a place in the book and read aloud. "'Men are like cats; they need only to be petted in the right direction.'"

"What?" Douglas exclaimed.

"It gets even better." Hal turned back a page. "'There is nothing in the world as harmless and as utterly joyous as man's conceit. It is purely altruistic and springs from a desire to please others, for he is certain his numerous fine qualities enrich the lives of all he meets. The woman who will not pander to this belief will not get nearly so far as the woman who does.'"

"She's got a point, you know," Carson said, nodding sagely. "Hal, I think you might have found the most interesting book in this shop."

Alice hadn't meant to eavesdrop; that certainly was not her way. But seeing Douglas Shaw and two other men through the window of the bookshop as she'd approached, she couldn't resist. The streetlamps were not yet lit, but the lights in the bookshop shone brightly. From Alice's vantage point outside, the men were as clearly illuminated against the gathering dusk as if they'd been on a stage. Douglas's two companions seemed so different from one another that they made an odd trio. Douglas was the best dressed of the three, although one of the others, who was equally as tall, came a close second. The third man was easily five inches shorter—and wider—than the other two. He appeared to be reading aloud from a book, gesturing with one hand as he did so, and causing the other men to smile.

Alice had already formed a good opinion of Douglas Shaw, but now she liked him even better. Anyone who frequented bookshops was a decent gentleman in her book.

In her book. She chuckled.

The bell over the door jangled as Alice entered, but the men didn't seem to notice. They were too absorbed in the book.

Nellie, the daughter-in-law of the bookshop owner, was minding the store tonight. She had married Mr. Meyer's son last year. Her husband, being more interested in banking than books, did not wish to work in his father's business. Nellie, on the other hand, had taken to it like a duck to water. She'd begun by helping keep the place clean and organized, but before long she was involved in all aspects of running the shop. Tonight she was poring over what must be the account book, absently returning Alice's wave before turning her attention back to her work.

Alice made her way over to a tall bookshelf that stood between her and the men. There was no center board between the two sides, so Alice could catch glimpses of them between the books and hear what they were saying. She was curious what had them so intrigued. She guessed it was a book on history or politics, or perhaps an adventure novel. That was the type of reading matter most often favored by her father and brothers. She picked up a book and was careful to look as though she was intently perusing it, just in case any of them should notice her.

By now, the taller of Douglas's two friends was holding the book. "This one is interesting," he said. "'Woman has three weapons: flattery, food, and flirtation, and only the last of these ever weakens with time. With the first she appeals to man's conceit, with the second to his heart, which is suspected to lie at the end of the esophagus, rather than over among the lungs and ribs, and with the third to his natural rivalry of his fellows.'"

Alice took in a breath, stunned. This didn't sound like a political or history book. Neither would be likely to include an overly flowery version of the old saying that the way to a man's heart was through his stomach.

The shorter man plucked the book from the other man's hand, saying with a smile, "Let me show you this one." Flipping to another page, he began to read. "'When a man seeks a woman's society, it is because he has need of her, not because he thinks she has need of him. A wise woman who is an expert with the chafing dish may frequently bag desirable game, while the foolish maidens who have neglected this skill are still hunting eagerly for the trail.'"

"That is exactly how Mamie is drawing you in, isn't it, Hal?" Douglas said. "She has you by the invisible cord that leads to the chafing dish."

"I will admit that Mamie's chafing dish is a big draw," Hal said with a grin. "But our friend Carson here ain't immune, either. As it says here . . ." He cleared his throat. "'Food, properly served, will attract a proposal at almost any time, especially if it is known that the pleasing viands were of the girl's own making.'" He eyed his friend. "Isn't that how Miss Peters got you?"

"Nonsense," Carson replied, attempting to sound affronted even though he was laughing along with his friends. "I knew exactly what I was about. I sought her out. She was . . . er, auditioning."

Alice could hear the grin in his words. She wanted to snort in disgust. Auditioning, indeed.

Hal extended the book toward Douglas. "I'd say you're the one who needs this the most. After all, since you intend to enter the marriage market, you'll need some pointers about how women think."

"Hmm, maybe you're right." Douglas took the proffered book and turned to a random page. "'Married and unmarried women waste a great deal of time feeling sorry for each other. Each supposes her own state is best. At the same time, a paradox presents itself. There may exist hidden in each woman's soul a quiet touch of envy, a question about what might have been, had she traveled the other's road.'"

He stopped reading aloud, but his eyes remained on the page. Several long moments passed as he apparently continued reading. Finally, after giving a little huff, Douglas set the book back on the shelf. The hard cover thudded as it hit the wood, causing Alice to jump. She stepped back swiftly to avoid being noticed through the gaps in the rows of books.

But Douglas had already turned back to his friends. "I believe I prefer to wade into those perilous waters using my own common sense as a guide."

"Oh, that's always a good idea," Hal said. "Like going into battle unarmed."

"Why are we wasting our time on this nonsense? Let's find something worth reading."

"I've got mine," Hal said, pulling a newspaper from under his arm. It was the *Illustrated Police News*, a cheap newspaper filled with all sorts of lurid crime stories. This man might be a friend of Douglas's, but Alice hoped they didn't share the same taste in reading material.

The men moved to another part of the shop. The row where Alice was standing had only one outlet. The other end was a brick wall. She moved back to the wall and pulled out another book, affecting to be totally absorbed in it, in case they came around the corner and saw her there. But they never came her way. Before long they had made their purchases and headed for the door. The bell over the door jangled as they went out.

After they'd gone, the shop settled into an interesting, dusty quiet. Alice realized how much the presence of those men had filled the space. She remained where she was for another minute or so on the unlikely chance they returned.

Thinking it over, Alice was glad the men had seen that book on "feminine wiles" for the useless tripe it was. They had merely laughed and set it aside. On the other hand, Alice was angry that such a book even existed. How could someone think a book like that was worth printing? Of all the ways to use ink and paper . . .

There was one favorable aspect, she supposed. The men had acknowledged some parallels between what was in the book and what they'd experienced in their own lives. But that couldn't possibly mean there was truth to any of that nonsense, could it?

Alice closed the book she held and set it back on the shelf. She walked out from between the tall bookshelves and saw that she and Nellie were the only ones left in the shop. Nellie was still absorbed in her work. Alice was such a frequent visitor that Nellie knew she was glad to wander the stacks without assistance. Tonight Alice was especially glad of that, because her initial disgust about the spinster book was unfortunately growing into curiosity. She turned the corner and worked her way down the row where the men had been standing. She was going to take a look for herself.

CHAPTER
Five

Alice read the book titles along the shelf. She had not caught the name of the book, but she was fairly certain she'd know it when she saw it.

It didn't take long to find. The book was bound in bright red leather with the title in bold gold lettering: *The Spinster's Guide to Love and Romance.*

Naturally.

Alice frowned at it, not yet reaching out to touch it. The word *spinster*, which generally referred to any unmarried lady over the age of about twenty-three, was certainly applicable to Alice. She was rapidly closing in on her twenty-ninth birthday. Yet never in all her years had she wished for a guide to attract men. Why should she?

But then there was that bit Douglas Shaw had read aloud— about how the spinster and the married lady both felt sorry for each other, yet envied each other, too. Something about it had snagged in her mind.

Alice threw a glance over her shoulder to ensure no one else was nearby. She would not risk the embarrassment of being found reading this particular book. The last thing she wanted was to be mistaken for some dim-witted girl who was longing for romance. She was quite happy on that score, thank you!

However, there was no need to worry. The shop was quiet. Alice drew the book from its place on the shelf, running a hand over the smooth leather cover before opening it. The book was designed to look expensive, but Alice was familiar enough with better books to know the binding for this one was cheaper than it at first appeared.

She wondered which passage had caught Douglas's attention when he'd stopped reading. There would be no way to know. The book was fully an inch thick. How could the author have found so much to write on this topic?

Flipping to the title page, she found the name of the author: Mrs. Brindleworth. Presumably, the author had mastered the intricacies of male-female relationships so well that she was no longer a spinster.

The table of contents was amazing in and of itself, with whole chapters purporting to explain men, explain women, provide tips for widows, and detail the philosophy of love. There was also a chapter on the consolations of spinsterhood. Ha! Maybe Alice should start there. She turned to the page indicated.

The chains of love may be sweet bondage, but for the spinster, freedom is more enticing. The spinster, like the wind, may go where she will, and there is no one to say her nay. She may determine her own destiny and is not bound by the whims of a master.

Alice read on for several minutes, nodding in agreement at what was written.

Until she got to the last page.

There is only the troublesome end, which may not be considered until it is too late. The lavender and the dead rose leaves breathe a hushed fragrance from the heaps of long-stored linen; the cat purrs and the tiny clock keeps up its gentle rhythm, because they do not know their mistress can no longer hear. The slanting sunbeams of afternoon mark out a delicate tracery upon the floor, and the shadow of the rose-geranium in the window is silhouetted upon the opposite wall. And then, into the quiet house, steals the final, most infinite calm. Solitary in death, as in life—

Alice snapped the book shut so hard that the resulting rush of air raised dust particles off the nearby shelf. Irritated that her hands were shaking, she swallowed, closed her eyes, and took a deep breath. It was ridiculous that mere words in a book could affect her so intensely. It wasn't as though she were alone in the world. Nor was she lonely. She had the love of her parents and siblings and her whole extended family, not to mention plenty of friends. Surely that was enough to fill anyone's life! She would not die alone. And the mention of the cat—was that truly necessary?

The book was nonsense, and Alice hastened to assure herself that she was not the only one to think so. She recalled how the men had dismissed it. She saw Douglas Shaw as vividly as if he were standing here right now, the way he smiled at the foolishness of it and how his eyes crinkled at the edges when he did so. Alice was glad he'd seen the folly of it. That showed him to be a man of good sense. Something had caught his eye, though, something he'd found upsetting, just as had happened with Alice. She wondered again what that had been.

Alice had better ways to fill her time than by reading drivel such as this. Yet for some reason the book remained in her hands as she made her way to the front of the shop. She decided it was more than mere curiosity. She was going to read this book thoroughly, parse out all of its ridiculous assumptions, and prove its logic was flawed. Then she'd no longer be troubled by it.

Other patrons had entered the shop by this time, so Alice held the book with her hand over the title as she made her way to the counter.

Nellie must have finished her accounting tasks, for she was now sitting back in her chair, casually keeping an eye on the shop. There was a dreamy expression on her face, as though her thoughts were far away. Seeing Alice, Nellie smiled and straightened, her business-like demeanor returning. "Did you find something, Miss McNeil?"

Alice set the book on the counter. "I'd like to buy this, please."

Nellie flipped the book open to read the number written in pencil inside the front cover. Alice had forgotten to check the price, and now she gulped when she saw it. It was costlier than similar-sized books. But it was too late to change her mind. Nellie had already made the notation in her sales register.

As Nellie closed the book again, her eyebrows lifted when she saw the title. Alice thought she spied a hint of laughter in her eyes. "This is a good choice. I remember when it came in. It's a secondhand book, and the woman who sold it to me swears that it works! I might have tried a few of its tricks myself, but of course, it's too late for that, seeing as how my George and I have been wed nearly a year now." She grinned. "However, I'm glad to see you turning your thoughts toward finding a romantic connection."

"That's not the case, I assure you," Alice scoffed. "I had it pegged as a humor book. I anticipate being highly diverted as I chuckle over its contents, that's all."

"As you say," Nellie replied, still with a hint of a smile.

Alice pulled the required money from her reticule. "I'd like the book wrapped, please."

Nellie put the money in the till and expertly wrapped the book in sturdy brown paper. As she tied the string to hold the paper in place, she said, "I will say that finding true love is a wonderful thing." She gave the book to Alice. "Not to mention the additional joys it brings."

Her hands moved in a seemingly unconscious gesture to her stomach. Alice could see why. The evidence of a child to come was just beginning to make itself visible.

"How wonderful," Alice said, knowing this was the expected response. "When do you anticipate the happy event?"

"In October." Nellie smiled, her dreamy expression returning. It was clear she was thinking only of the joys of motherhood, not on its hardships. After the child arrived, and as others likely followed, Nellie would probably have to give up working in the shop. Alice thought that was too bad, as it was something she clearly enjoyed and excelled at. Thinking of babies brought on an uncomfortable sensation, as though Alice's insides had somehow twisted. Her mother had raised five children and lost two more as infants. The demanding work of running a large household had worn her out and brought her too quickly past her prime. The last child who died had been the youngest. Her mother's health, which by then had already been less than robust, had never fully recovered. Had those pains been worth it?

Nellie was looking at her questioningly. "Miss McNeil?"

Realizing she had impolitely retreated into her thoughts, Alice gave Nellie an apologetic smile. "I beg your pardon. I was wool-gathering. My felicitations to you and your husband."

Alice couldn't lose the uneasiness she felt, though. She gave Nellie a polite farewell and made for the door of the shop.

⌒⌒⌒

Hal and Carson were still lobbing jokes at one another as they walked home. Douglas didn't join in. He kept thinking about that spinster book. It seemed to put far too much emphasis on the romantic aspects of a relationship, speaking in flowery terms about how deep and passionate love must be in order for it to be truly real. *"Love is the bread and the wine of life, the hunger and the thirst, the hurt and the healing, the only wound which is cured by another."* He scoffed at the memory of that line. The whole idea of it bothered him because he considered marriage to be primarily a practical decision. He had no desire for emotional "wounds." It sounded painful and unnecessary. Although he hoped to win Miss Rolland's regard, he had no idea of falling in love himself. Now, though, he felt a touch of discomfort as he began to wonder: What would the lady be expecting?

He had noticed in the table of contents that there was a whole chapter dedicated to explaining women—including how to win their hearts. Douglas had joined his friends in deriding the book, but privately he wondered if there were any kernels of truth in there. Maybe this business of acquiring a wife and keeping her happy was more complicated than he'd imagined. It was a daunting thought. Maybe he needed some kind of training on the subject.

They reached the boardinghouse, and Hal and Carson went up the steps to the front door. They turned to look back at Douglas, who had paused with one foot still on the pavement.

"Aren't you coming in?" Hal asked.

"I still feel a little restless," Douglas answered. "I think I'll take another turn around the neighborhood."

He worried that one or both might offer to join him, but they merely shrugged.

"Suit yourself," Carson said.

They went inside, and Douglas turned back the way they'd come. It was a fine night to be out. He waved to neighbors he knew as he walked up the street and paused at the next intersection, a logical place to turn around and return home. But instead of doing so, he continued on, retracing his steps to the bookshop. If this book really explained how women thought, it could be valuable for helping his cause. After all, he'd never hesitated to read a book about any other aspect of life in which he'd advanced himself, from business to mathematics. Doing so had been instrumental in his success, despite a minimal education at a parish school. Why should this area of life be any different? It was true that people were not always so easy to explain as mathematics. Yet surely women had enough common traits that he could learn about and utilize to his advantage. He picked up his pace as he directed his steps toward the bookshop, anxious to get there before it closed for the evening.

He was a little breathless when he reached the shop door. As he pulled it open, a lady on the inside who'd just been reaching for the handle fell forward, put off-balance by the unexpected movement of the door. She gave a little cry of surprise and might have toppled over except that Douglas reached out to steady her by the arm.

"I beg your pardon, miss," he said. Then he drew back in surprise when he realized who it was.

Miss McNeil straightened, her arm falling out of his grasp as she reached up to adjust her hat. She looked just as surprised to see him. "Mr. Shaw! I thought you had—"

She pulled up, stopping midsentence.

"Yes?" he prompted. "You thought I had . . . ?"

She cleared her throat and clutched the book she was holding a little tighter to her side. As though if she dropped it, it would shatter into pieces like glass. "I meant to say, I never expected to see you here."

"I live not too far away."

"Do you?" She seemed genuinely surprised. "You live in Islington?"

"I'm a little more to the south, but this is an excellent bookshop and worth the effort to get here."

"I certainly agree with that." A smile broke through her flustered countenance, as though he had just complimented her instead of the shop. "Are you an avid reader?"

Douglas quirked a brow. "Do I look like such an uneducated lout?"

"Oh no!" she exclaimed, looking embarrassed. "It's just that . . . I come here often myself, and I've never seen you."

"It does seem odd that our paths haven't crossed before this," Douglas agreed. "But then, I've been traveling a lot."

Why did this conversation feel so awkward? She definitely looked ill at ease. Douglas realized he was holding the shop door wide open to the night. He couldn't close it, because she was standing in the way. To subtly rectify this, he turned as though just noticing his hand was still on the door. Her eyes followed his. Seeing his predicament, she moved to one side, clearing the way for him to close the door.

They both gave a nervous laugh, meeting each other's eyes. The lights in the shop poured through the window, illuminating the spot where they stood as clearly as if it were day.

It reminded Douglas that the shop would be closing soon. He really wanted to get that book. At the same time, he didn't want to pass up this opportunity to speak with Miss McNeil outside of the workplace. "I see you've bought something," he said. "A novel?" He'd always heard ladies enjoyed reading novels—the more sensational, the better.

Her head moved a little. Douglas wasn't sure whether this gesture was a nod, but her next words seemed to confirm that it was. "I like to read something diverting in the evenings." He waited for her to divulge the title of the book, but she merely added, "What sorts of books do you enjoy reading, Mr. Shaw?"

"Me? Oh, a little bit of everything, I suppose. I like anything that explains how the world works."

"Have you read *Electricity, Light, and Sound* by Dr. Appleton? It's a marvelous explanation of how electricity is being harnessed for light and telephones and all sorts of other practical uses."

"Why yes! Do you mean to say you've read it, too?" He was impressed.

This time her nod was unmistakable. "It's a fascinating glimpse into the future."

Her words were sincere, but she still looked uneasy. Douglas had the impression she wanted nothing more than to hurry off.

"Perhaps you need to be going?" he asked. "I don't mean to keep you."

She looked relieved. "Yes, I should be on my way."

Had speaking with him been such a chore? Douglas immediately chided himself for the thought. She simply had other things to attend to, that was clear.

He lifted his hat to her. "Until we meet again." With a grin he added, "I've a strong feeling it will be tomorrow morning at nine o'clock."

Her reaction to this pleasantry surprised him. She looked more worried than amused. Did she interpret his remark as some kind of order?

He tried to set her at ease with another smile. "I hope you'll have a pleasant evening with your, erm, diversion." He gestured toward the book. She still hadn't mentioned the title.

She clutched her parcel a little tighter. "I'm sure I will. Good night, Mr. Shaw." She at least managed a little smile, which Douglas returned.

He watched her hurry off, still holding the book close. Maybe it was one of those lurid romance novels. Maybe she enjoyed those as much as scientific works. If so, that was an interesting set of opposites, much like the lady herself. Although she was unmarried and at the age where some might use the label *spinster* or the less charitable *old maid*, Douglas found she was more pleasant to look at than such a label would imply. She had a crisp gait and looked about her as she walked, as though keenly aware of her surroundings. Douglas watched her until she turned the corner out of sight.

A man came out of the shop, tucking a newly purchased newspaper under his arm. He nodded to Douglas as he passed. It brought Douglas's mind back to why he was here. There were perhaps less than five minutes before the shop closed, so he needed to hurry.

He went inside and headed straight for the book. But when he arrived at the shelf where he was sure it had been located, he couldn't find it. He thoroughly checked the shelf again, as well as those around it, but the book was gone.

The shopkeeper approached him. "May I help you find something, sir?"

"Yes, thank you." He pointed toward the bookshelf. "When I was in the shop earlier this evening, I saw a book on this shelf. I've come back to buy it, but now I don't see it."

"I'd be happy to help you locate it. Do you remember the title or the author?"

"Yes, it was—" He paused, embarrassed. "That is, I believe the title was *The Spinster's Guide to Romance*, or something similar."

He waited for her reaction, expecting perhaps a smirk or grin of amusement. At the very least, she'd have to wonder why he wanted to read such a book.

However, she merely nodded and said pleasantly, "I know the book you're speaking of. However, I'm afraid it has been sold. I'm sorry I haven't another one to offer you."

Sold already! Douglas had been gone only half an hour. He

shook his head in amazement. "I expect books like that are very popular—especially with the ladies?"

"Oh yes, sir."

"Such as the lady who bought it tonight?" He cast his mind back to the book Alice McNeil had been holding. Although wrapped in brown paper, he thought it had been about the same size as the spinster book. Perhaps that was why she looked uncomfortable. She'd been determined to point out that she read serious books and hadn't wanted to tell him about the one she held in her hands. "The lady who was in here just a few minutes ago, for example?"

It was impertinent of him to ask, but curiosity had overtaken him. He held his breath, waiting for the shopkeeper's answer.

"That's the only lady we've had in the shop tonight, sir."

A touch of amusement stole onto her face, making Douglas certain he was correct. Perhaps this shopkeeper was familiar with Alice's reading habits. Was this out of the ordinary for her? Or was it entirely in keeping with her taste in books? Douglas couldn't imagine that Alice McNeil was the kind of woman who would want to learn how to attract men. But then, there were a lot of things he didn't know about women. That was precisely why he had wished to buy the book.

Another gentleman who'd been perusing a nearby shelf approached the shopkeeper with a book to buy. Douglas said good night and left.

As he walked home, he pondered the idea of a woman who clearly had a mechanical and scientific mind also buying something like the spinster book. It made her all the more interesting. In fact, if he hadn't been so determined to woo someone of higher station, he might even have fancied her.

He wished he had been able to buy that book and read more of it.

CHAPTER

Six

"Good morning, Miss McNeil." Douglas caught up to Alice just as she was about to enter the Henley and Company building.

She had wondered if she would see him on the omnibus this morning, since they would both be coming from the same direction. She hadn't seen him, though. He must have taken a different way in. She'd been glad for that, as she still felt uneasy about their meeting the night before. The last thing she needed was for him to discover she had bought the spinster book. On top of that, her brain still went gauzy when she looked at him. The vertigo she experienced in his presence was something she had to conquer—and quickly.

She took a steadying breath and murmured a greeting as he stepped ahead of her to reach for the door handle.

He held the door open for her. Forcing herself to look him full in the face, she gave him a nod of thanks as she passed through. Was there a twinkle in his eye? Or was she imagining it? He was definitely smiling. Alice's impractical heart sped up, despite her determination to remain unmoved. Mavis probably would have swooned right there on the steps. She chuckled at the thought.

"You seem to be in a good mood," Douglas observed. "Does that mean the book you bought last night was entertaining? What was it called? I never did catch the title."

A bolt of panic shot through her. Alice abhorred lying, but her determination to keep her secret held greater sway. "*An Elementary Treatise on Electricity* by James Clerk Maxwell."

That was as close to the truth as she could get. She had acquired that book recently from the same shop. Besides, she hadn't actually read any of the spinster book last night. She was still mildly appalled at herself for even buying it. She had placed it on a side table and instead spent her evening reading the other book in order to feel that she'd at least accomplished something profitable.

Alice pulled the book from her bag. "I brought it with me today, in fact. I thought I might sit outside and read it during my midday break. It looks as though the weather will be nice today and not too hot."

"You're reading Maxwell's work? How extraordinary."

"This is a collection of his lectures. I can't claim to understand all of it, but I do my best."

Her modest reply didn't seem to lower Mr. Shaw's opinion. He was still looking at her with undisguised admiration. This was distressing—especially in light of last night's foolish purchase, which only cemented her opinion that she wasn't as intelligent as he might assume. In her discomfort, she compounded her silliness by beginning to babble. "I was so fortunate to be able to find this secondhand at a price I could afford. What a shame that Mr. Maxwell has passed away, and far too young, too! But I'm confident his work will live on."

He didn't seem to notice anything amiss in her manner. He merely nodded. "He was a genius. Visionary too. I'm sorry you found the book before I did." He said that last bit with a smile to show he was only joking. "May I have a look?"

"Of course." Alice gave him the book but then immediately wished she hadn't. As Mr. Shaw flipped it open to peruse the pages, she realized it had a larger cover and was thicker than the book she'd been carrying last night. Would he notice? How closely had he observed the parcel in her hands?

He studied the table of contents with evident pleasure. "Yes, this looks very interesting." He closed the book and handed it back to her. "Perhaps you might be so kind as to loan it to me sometime?"

"I would be happy to." Alice returned the book to her bag. "And you? Did you find something? I don't believe you had much time to peruse the shelves."

She'd spent a lot of time last night trying to come up with reasons why Mr. Shaw would have returned to the shop. Her biggest fear was that he had decided, for some reason, to buy the spinster book after all. But she was equally sure that was unlikely. He'd dismissed the book out of hand, showing less interest in it than either of his friends had. Unfortunately, she couldn't ask him outright without admitting she'd been in the shop watching and listening to them.

"Yes, well, I . . ." Surprisingly, he looked nonplussed at the question.

If Mr. Shaw had returned for that spinster book, he would surely be as embarrassed as she was to admit it. That would be admirable, at any rate. But she repeated to herself that it was a ridiculous notion. Why would a man like him want to purchase a book like that? Based on her own reactions to him, she suspected he could win over any woman he wanted.

He cleared his throat. "In fact, I was looking for a particular volume on chemistry that I haven't been able to find anywhere else."

Yes, that made far more sense. He had mentioned last night that he was interested in books that explained how the world worked. It didn't explain why he hadn't asked for that chemistry book while he'd been in the shop the first time, but perhaps he'd been distracted by the conversation with his friends. "So you are interested in chemistry?"

It was an automatic question, more from politeness than anything. Yet he gave her a smile that would have pierced the heart of even the most hardened female. "Very much so."

Alice wondered if there was a chapter in that chemistry book on spontaneous combustion.

Chemistry.

Douglas had to laugh at himself for coming up with such an answer. While it was true he owned several books on the subject, his response cut too close to the bone. Not that he minded. At the moment he appeared to have Miss McNeil slightly off balance, and he was discovering he rather liked her that way. Although he hadn't known her long, he suspected she was the kind of person who had not been put off balance often enough. In Douglas's opinion, it was good to be shaken up once in a while. It helped a person learn to be more flexible.

They heard the sounder as soon as they entered the office. Someone was already trying to reach them.

"Everyone's up early today, it seems," Miss McNeil said. She was all business now, her composure returning. In a moment she was at her desk. Setting her bag out of the way, she tapped out the response indicating she was ready.

Archie wasn't there yet. He generally came in later and worked until seven. Douglas was surprised to see Miss Waller's desk unoccupied, though. She was usually the first person in the office. She always made a great show of being busy and having a lot to do, which Douglas didn't doubt was true. Yet she was terribly disorganized. Had she the cleverness to develop a better system, she might accomplish her work in half the time.

Douglas was about to walk to his office when he was stopped by Mr. Henley coming through the main doors at full speed.

He pulled up when he saw Douglas. "Shaw, I'm glad you're here. Listen, something has come up with that cotton shipment from Charleston. It was delayed a full month due to storms, and now the buyer is claiming we promised to reduce our fees if that should happen. Is this true?"

"No, sir. I'm sure we never put anything like that in the final draft of the contract, although I remember the buyer asking for it."

"We'll need to track down that contract. Where is Miss Waller?" Henley sent an angry glance at her empty desk.

"I don't believe she is here yet."

Henley blew out a breath. "Late again! That's been happening too often. If it keeps up, I'll begin stopping it out of her wages." He turned toward Alice. "Miss McNeil!"

She stood up, a telegram in her hand. "Yes, sir?"

"What is that message? Is it from Charleston?"

"No, sir. It comes from the post office in Camden Town. It was sent from a lady who says she rooms in the same boardinghouse as Miss Waller. She wishes to inform us that Miss Waller has fallen ill and will likely be out for several days."

"Of all the times for her to get sick," Henley said with a grimace. That was apparently the only sympathy he was going to extend.

"What do you need?" Alice asked. "I'd be happy to help in any way I can."

"Thank you, Miss McNeil. I appreciate you jumping in. I need to locate our file with the contracts for Manchester Textiles. It was signed last October."

She nodded. "I'll do my best."

"Keep an ear out for the sounder, though. I want to know if we hear from Southern Shipping in Charleston or from our insurance man in Liverpool."

"I'll help you look," Douglas offered, following Alice as she walked into the adjacent room used for file storage. When she looked at him in surprise, he added, "I have the advantage of knowing what the contracts look like."

"Right," she said with an appreciative smile. "Thank you."

The room was small and narrow, flanked on two walls by rows of filing cabinets. It felt more like a large closet, although it did have a window at one end for light. They began by sifting through the stacks of papers piled high on top of the cabinets. When this didn't yield what they needed, they began looking through the drawers. It took some time, owing to Miss Waller's inscrutable filing system.

At one point, Alice remarked, "This seems to be some odd

JENNIFER DELAMERE

mixture of chronological, alphabetical, and some other criteria that I can't identify."

Douglas shrugged. "Somehow Miss Waller always seems to find what we need when we ask her for it. Heaven knows how." He opened another drawer and began to thumb through the files. "Mr. Henley told her very specifically not to lose this information."

They both paused when they heard the sounder announce an incoming message. "I can answer that," Douglas said. He was always happy for an opportunity to keep his telegraphic skills sharp. He'd enjoyed telegraphy work, even though he was proud to have taken on a more important role in the company. "Why don't you keep looking?"

He thought she might object. It would be her right, given that it was officially her job. But she gave him a little nod and then pulled open another drawer. There was a look of grim determination on her face, and her brows were creased, as though she was trying to work out a complicated problem.

Douglas went to the telegraph machine and took down the message, perhaps surprising the sender—their clerk at the Liverpool office—when he identified himself as the receiver. The message was unrelated to the current situation, so he set it on the stack of messages to be typed up later. He returned to the filing room just as Alice was pulling a folder from a drawer.

"I believe this is it!" she said triumphantly, and handed it to him.

He opened the folder and perused the contents. "So it is. How did you find it?"

"It was filed among the items starting with V, naturally."

Douglas looked at her, confused. "Why do you suppose it was there?" He couldn't think of anything from the names of the companies involved that started with a V.

She smirked. "I assume that stands for 'Very Important.'"
They laughed.

Douglas said, "I never would have guessed that. I suppose it must take another woman to figure out how a lady's mind works."

Alice crossed her arms. "Not all women think that way, I assure

61

you. I was just guessing based on what I've seen of Miss Waller during my three months here."

Douglas leaned against the doorjamb, effectively blocking her exit from the filing room. He liked this conversation, and he wasn't in a hurry to move on. Whatever was going on with this contract could wait another minute or two. "So you're a student of human nature, Miss McNeil? Do you perchance make a study of men?" He was thinking about that spinster book, still trying to discern if or why she might have bought it.

She grimaced. "No need for that, I assure you. Growing up with three brothers, plus my father, I would say I know more about men than I care to." Her reply was tart, but Douglas could hear amusement underlying it.

"Three brothers!" he exclaimed. Perhaps this explained why she was able to hold her own with other men. It could also account for her unusual interest in scientific matters. "No sisters?"

"Just one." She frowned as though it were not an especially happy thought.

"And where are you in the order?"

"Somewhere in the middle. That's what my father always says when pressed. It's a joke," she added, perhaps misreading Douglas's surprised reaction as horror. "He has no trouble keeping track of who we all are."

"That's good to hear. And your sister?" He knew he was asking a lot of questions, but she didn't seem to mind answering them.

"She's the youngest."

"Is she also an expert telegrapher and file sleuth?"

Alice gave a little snort. "Hardly. She's my opposite in every way."

"Then I feel sorry for her."

It was a compliment, pure and simple. It was also, Douglas knew, bordering on flirtation, which was definitely not advisable. He did not want to jeopardize a good working relationship. But at least it was not false flattery. He meant what he said.

She looked at him wonderingly for a long moment. He noticed, now that he had a chance to really look at them, that her eyes were an interesting shade of dark green. There were hints of brown, but they were definitely green. He wasn't sure he'd ever seen that before. As the moment lingered, he began to worry that he'd been staring, and that his words had been too forward.

But then she smiled. "I thank you for the compliment. My sister probably would not."

"I imagine she has other admirable qualities."

"She's married." Alice said this in a derisive way that made it clear she didn't necessarily consider this an admirable quality.

"Is there a problem with that?" Douglas asked.

"On the contrary. It's a load off my parents' mind to have both their daughters settled."

Douglas shook his head. "I don't understand. Isn't there one still left to worry about?"

She looked at him blankly for a moment before catching his meaning. "Oh, they don't have to worry about me. I'm settled. I have work I enjoy and a comfortable place to live."

"Do you mean you don't intend to marry? You want to live alone forever?"

She drew back, as though Douglas's words fell too harshly on her ears. "I never feel lonely, if that's what you're driving at."

"But what about later in life?" he pressed. "What if one day you are unable to care for yourself, due to age or illness?"

Once again she gave him a blank look, as though he'd brought up an idea she hadn't even considered. A look that might have been worry crossed her face. It passed, however. She waved a dismissive hand. "I'll have a whole bevy of nieces and nephews for that."

"Miss McNeil, you seem to be living solely in the present."

"The present is the only place one can live, Mr. Shaw."

She spoke with such prim authority that Douglas could already picture her as an aging auntie, living in a corner of some relative's home and lecturing her little grandnieces and grandnephews about the proper way to behave. Or perhaps trying to relate some tale from her life that no one was interested in hearing.

It was not a comfortable feeling, to picture this vibrant young woman as old and feeble. He shook his head, trying to clear the image from his brain. "Nevertheless, a person must plan for the future. If you don't plan carefully, then your life will be decided for you, and not in a good way."

She frowned. "Are you speaking from personal experience?"

"If you count my parents and how their lack of industry and foresight affected my life and my brother's, then yes, I am."

"So you have just the one brother?"

After sharing her family details, it was only natural that she should question him in return. Even so, Douglas felt his good humor slip, much as Alice's expression had changed at the mention of her sister. "Yes."

Catching the troubled note in his voice, she raised her eyebrows.

Before she could ask more questions, he said, "My brother is currently in India. We don't hear from him much." He didn't add that Charlie had left under a cloud, having been estranged from the family for many years. That was a line of conversation he had no intention of embarking on. "Charlie's making his way as best he can. He and I are very different." With conscious effort, he changed his expression, trying to lighten it with a smile. "If you ask me . . ." He leaned in, as though to share something highly confidential.

"Yes?" Her attention was fastened on him.

"I'd say you and I got the best of the bargain, when the good Lord was handing out traits. But let's not tell our siblings. We wouldn't want to hurt their feelings."

As he had hoped, the remark brought a tiny smile to her lips. "A wise suggestion."

This moment of shared understanding seemed to be drawing them physically closer, too. There was less than a foot of space between them. Douglas loved the expression on her face just now. There was a light in her eyes and a playful quality in the way the corners of her mouth turned up.

It was over too soon for his liking. Alice took a step back, and a more businesslike demeanor settled over her. She pointed at the file in his hand. "I believe Mr. Henley is anxious to see that."

She made a move for the door, looking ready to push him aside if necessary, but there was still a smile playing around her lips. The kind of smile that told him this woman didn't mind sparring a little and wouldn't take umbrage at comments meant as harmless fun.

Douglas inched to the right just enough for her to get by. He couldn't deny that he enjoyed the sensation as she skirted by him, so close that she passed literally under his nose. He took a moment to inhale. She didn't smell of perfume, but he did catch a whiff of some mildly enticing scent. Perhaps she indulged in the finer floral soaps. It was a subtle feminine touch, like the scarf she'd had on the other day.

He followed her out of the filing room—and all but ran into her a moment later when she stopped short after two steps. It wasn't hard to guess what had surprised her.

Archie Clapper was watching them from across the room.

CHAPTER

Seven

Y ou're here early, Mr. Clapper," Alice said. She sounded breathless and, Douglas thought, guilty. As though she'd been caught doing something wrong. But then, Clapper could bring out those feelings in anyone.

"No laws against that, I believe." Clapper took off his hat and hung it on the hat tree. "Where's Miss Waller?"

"She's out sick."

He grunted. "It was bound to catch up with her sooner or later."

Alice had collected herself by now, and she walked toward him. "What's that supposed to mean?"

Clapper shrugged. "She's been stepping out with a fellow I suspect is . . . well, keeping her up too late."

He said this with a leer. His gaze traveled suggestively between Douglas and Alice, as though he suspected them of improprieties as well.

"Perhaps you might keep your ugly notions to yourself," Alice bit out.

"Right you are." But Clapper followed this statement with a deprecating look and added, "As we all know, interactions in the workplace should be for *business* purposes only."

Douglas could feel his anger rising, but he tamped it down.

JENNIFER DELAMERE

He was sure that jealousy motivated Clapper's words. Alice was clearly better at her job than he was.

Not that Clapper had anything to worry about. He was a cousin of Mrs. Henley. Douglas was pretty sure that was the reason he'd been hired and why he was likely never to lose his position. Even so, his actions often showed that he resented Douglas's success, as though he considered Douglas somehow beneath him because of his humble origins.

But none of those things had prevented Douglas's rise in the company, and Douglas intended to make the most of that fact.

He held up the file in his hand. "Thank you for your help in locating this, Miss McNeil. I'm very sure Mr. Henley will be grateful that you were able to successfully handle Miss Waller's duties without advance notice. He always looks favorably on an employee who goes above and beyond what is required."

Alice lifted her head with pride. "You're quite welcome, Mr. Shaw. If I may be of further assistance in this *business* matter, please let me know."

She and Archie exchanged mutually antagonistic glances as she passed him on her way to her desk. Douglas put this round at a draw.

As he walked toward Henley's office, he thought how much he'd like to tell Alice the truth about Archie's status in this company. Unfortunately, Henley had sworn him to secrecy. This was primarily to appease Mrs. Henley, who wanted to keep up the pretense that Clapper was here solely on his own merit. Sometimes she even hinted that he should be given more to do. That idea was laughable. At least Henley had been able to hold the line on that front. Even so, Douglas was unwilling to do anything to rile the owner's wife. She didn't much like him as it was. She couldn't deny how useful he was to the company, including the financial gains from which she benefitted. At the same time, she viewed him with a certain level of condescension, much as Archie did. They were peas in a pod in that regard. Douglas figured it was best to ignore them and focus on his work.

Mostly, though, he was irritated that Clapper had ruined what had been a perfectly friendly and interesting interaction between him and Alice. He could already see that she was a great addition to the office staff. She was clever, hardworking, and pleasant to be around. Too bad Clapper couldn't take a leaf from her book.

⌒⊘⌒

That afternoon, Alice ended up using her "superior sleuthing skills" to locate several other important documents. An enjoyable benefit of this task was that she gained a more complete picture of the company than she'd gotten from the telegraph work.

Everything was different today, and not just because of Mavis's absence. Douglas Shaw had boundless energy and optimism. Something he'd picked up from the brash Americans, perhaps? Whatever it was, it had infected the whole office. By the end of the day—and after some fascinating negotiations conducted by way of the telegraph—they'd sorted out the problem with the cotton shipment to the satisfaction of all the stakeholders. It had been easy to see why Mr. Henley was putting more and more trust in Douglas's abilities.

Their conversation in the file room that morning kept returning to her thoughts, even while they'd been busy handling other issues. Did Douglas really think all women had marriage as their life's goal? That was the only disappointing thing about him so far. She hoped that as they continued working together, she could enlighten his understanding on that subject.

For the rest of the day, Archie managed to keep his unsavory opinions to himself. Verbally, at least. He was still telegraphing them with his attitude and certain undertones in his remarks on unrelated subjects. It was clear he didn't like the idea of Alice and Douglas paired up to handle specific tasks. Why was it so hard for him to get along with anyone? Alice could not fathom why someone would deliberately try to poison their workplace environment.

Thinking it over after work as she walked to the street corner to catch an omnibus, she reminded herself that Mr. Henley approved of the job she was doing, and that was all that mattered. "You've been invaluable today, Miss McNeil," he'd told her before he'd left for the day. "You've done the work of two people, and I appreciate it." Alice even had the impression his words were more than simply a compliment to her. Given that they'd been within earshot of Archie, it might have been a subtle rebuke to him as well. But perhaps that was wishful thinking.

Clouds had rolled in with the afternoon. While waiting for the omnibus, Alice opened her umbrella as a light rain began to fall. She wished it had held off another hour. The omnibus, while never entirely pleasant, took on a distinctly sour odor when filled with damp people dripping on the straw-covered floor. She considered walking home. It would take about an hour and save her the threepence for the fare. It was a tempting idea, despite the misty rain.

Making up her mind, she set off. She hadn't gone fifty steps, though, before she was stopped by Douglas Shaw calling out to her. She turned to see him striding briskly toward her. He was carrying an umbrella, too, although it looked as though he'd opened it belatedly. His coat and hat were gleaming with fresh raindrops.

He brushed water off his shoulders as he reached her. "Are you planning to take the omnibus home?" he asked.

"No, I decided to walk."

"You're going to walk all the way to Islington in the rain?"

"It's only about two and a half miles. I've done it before." Alice had in fact often walked home while she worked at the Central Telegraph Office. The boardinghouse where she used to live was about the same distance away, and her saved pennies had added up and helped fund her move to her new place.

Douglas was still frowning over this plan. "Walking may be good for a person's constitution, but not when it's raining. I believe I'll take a cab home."

"What a fine idea," she replied, unable to keep the sarcasm from her voice. A cab ride would cost at least four times as much as an omnibus. It might be easy for someone like Douglas to casually spend all that money, but it was never an option for Alice.

He smiled at her caustic comment. "Yes, and I'd like to give you a lift."

Taken aback, she immediately shook her head. "I couldn't put you through the trouble."

"It's the least I could do after your heroic efforts today. Besides, it isn't out of the way. After all, we live in practically the same neighborhood. To be honest, I generally alight at The Angel and walk the last quarter mile from there because beyond that point it costs extra."

"How very frugal of you."

He laughed. "There's a cab rank on the next corner. Let's see if we can get one before everyone else decides on the same plan."

Relenting, Alice went with him. The rain began falling heavier as they walked up the street, making her glad she'd accepted. It was only as Douglas was giving her a hand into the cab that she had a moment of worry. In general, she considered herself too independent to mind the tut-tuts of old-fashioned people who got the vapors over a single woman riding in a carriage with a man. However, she would be irritated if Archie Clapper found out. Given his propensity to find wrongdoing where none existed, he would gleefully begin dispensing rumors. But he would be at work for at least another half hour. Surely there was no way he could find out about it. She might as well enjoy the unexpected treat of being taken home in a cab after a long day at work.

After giving directions to the driver, Douglas joined her in the carriage. An odd sensation ran through her as he settled into the seat beside her. It was uncomfortable and pleasant at the same time. She shivered a little, then stiffened in embarrassment, hoping he'd think it had been a reaction to the weather.

He didn't seem to notice. He leaned back in the seat and let out a sigh of satisfaction. "It was a good day today, wasn't it? We saved Henley and Company at least two hundred pounds. Nothing to sneeze at, even with the volume of trade we do."

"Thank you for including me in your assessment, but I feel my contribution was minimal."

He gave her a critical look. "You shouldn't indulge in false modesty, Miss McNeil. You've got a sharp mind and a willingness to think outside the normal channels. I believe you've got a real head for business."

"I should hope so, since I am employed at one," she answered with a smile. It was her usual reaction, to fend off a compliment with some sort of pleasantry. She was, quite foolishly, blushing a little at his praise.

Douglas shook his head. "I'm talking about a position beyond telegraphy. Beyond mere clerical work, too—even though you'd be a vast improvement over Miss Waller. In fact, I've been thinking over what you said this morning."

"Have you?" She was intrigued that their conversation had made an impression on him as well. He hadn't mentioned it again all day, and she'd assumed he'd not given it another thought.

"Yes. If you're serious about wanting to remain on your own . . ."

"I am."

"Then have you considered pursuing some type of managerial position? Something that actually involves you in the decision-making processes?"

"Me?" Alice was genuinely surprised that he'd even suggest such a thing.

"Are you averse to the idea?"

"No, not precisely. It's just that . . ." She wasn't able to finish the sentence. She would have said it wasn't a role typically open to women, but she could already hear Miss Templeton's voice in her head telling her not to downplay a woman's prospects.

"Tell me, why did you leave your position at the Central Telegraph Office? Mr. Henley told me you came highly recommended and that they were sorry to lose you. Were you unhappy there?" He was looking at her with interest, as though he truly wanted to know.

Alice tugged absently at her gloves, considering her reply. "The

CTO is a good place to work. The hours are regulated, the pay is reasonable, and the working environment is comfortable, especially compared to other occupations."

"Hmm." Douglas stroked his chin as though considering her words deeply, but a tiny smile lifted his lips. "That response does the exact opposite of answering my question."

She laughed. "True. Why did I want to leave if working there was so ideal? The truth is, I was tired of being one among eight hundred women."

"Eight hundred! I knew a lot of women worked there, but I didn't realize it was that many."

"Not to mention an even greater number of men. It was a factory, really. A very large message factory." She sighed. "I suppose by saying that, I'm dishonoring the unfortunate people who are forced to toil in the sweat and grime of actual manufacturing plants. I was thankful for my job—I just wanted to work someplace that was not so highly structured. With so many people, it was vital that everyone keep to a precise schedule, right down to the timing of breaks for luncheon and tea. There were detailed procedures for every aspect of the work, large and small. I chafed against the rigidness of it."

He gave an understanding nod. "You wanted to stand out."

"I suppose you could put it that way."

"Well, you have certainly managed to do that. I take it you enjoy working at Henley and Company?"

"Oh yes!" She said it too breathlessly, looking into his eyes, which were a nice shade of brown. Warm and welcoming. She held his gaze for several very pleasant seconds. Then, chiding herself for acting like a schoolgirl, she looked away. She tried to think of anything that might cool the sudden warmth she was feeling. The answer to that was obvious. "The only drawback is that I hadn't considered the possibility of working with someone like Mr. Clapper. He is a trial."

"Don't worry about Clapper," Douglas said. "He hates everyone, including me. Perhaps *especially* me. But ultimately, he can't stop either of us from rising in the company, even if he does not."

"I don't even think he wants to. I think he prefers just barely getting his work done and shirking anything that isn't absolutely necessary. So why is he upset if we advance?"

Douglas opened his mouth, then looked away and shrugged. "He has his reasons." Alice waited to see if any other explanation was forthcoming, but he simply said, "Look, we're nearly at The Angel already."

Sure enough, the carriage was on the main street leading to The Angel, one of the oldest public houses in Islington. Many omnibuses and other conveyances stopped here to drop off or pick up passengers. Alice could hardly believe the trip had passed so quickly.

Happily, it was no longer raining. The clouds had moved off to the southeast.

"Thank you so much for this bit of luxury," she said as Douglas helped her down from the carriage.

"It was my pleasure. Shall I accompany you the rest of the way home?"

"No!" It came out so fast, she worried that it sounded rude. But, as much as she enjoyed his company, having him walk her home felt too personal somehow. It wasn't as though she needed his help or protection. She took a breath. "That is, I'll be perfectly fine. This is where I typically get down from the omnibus every day. Besides, I'll be walking north up the high street, which is probably not the same direction as your home."

"You're right, my lodgings are in the other direction." He tipped his hat. "I look forward to further work adventures tomorrow—especially if Miss Waller is out again."

Relieved that he hadn't taken offense at her refusal, Alice gave him a nod and a smile. "So do I."

"But do think about what I said regarding career aspirations."

She lifted a brow. "Aren't you worried I might try to take your place?"

There was a glint in his eye as he gave her another of his impossibly appealing smiles. "Not if we grow the company enough to need *two* senior directors."

He walked away, leaving Alice pleasantly astounded. Here was a man who seemed to take her at her word and even encouraged her in further endeavors. It was so refreshing!

She blinked back the threat of happy tears and took a deep breath. "Careful, Alice, or you'll fall in love with him!" she joked to herself.

Then she laughed it off. There was no chance of that. He was merely an exemplary colleague, and she could see they were going to work well together. There was no harm in being pleased about that, surely?

Humming to herself, she decided there was no hurry to get home. She would take a turn around the nearby park. She could then stop at the fishmonger's shop. He was happy to give her the remains of fish that were too old to sell but which her cats found delicious. It would be an excellent ending to a very good day.

Only later, after Alice had visited the fishmonger and was walking along the high street toward home, did the buzz of happiness begin to wear off a little. It was dampened by her remembrance of a question Douglas had brought up that morning, regarding what she planned to do in old age. It honestly wasn't something she'd thought about. Those years seemed very far off, too distant to be even a speck on the horizon. Yet Douglas had spoken as if such decisions were critically important to make right now.

The answer she'd come up with on the spur of the moment—that she'd have plenty of nieces and nephews—still seemed reasonable. She was already blessed with four nephews and a niece, and that number was bound to increase now that Annie was married. Granted, the children were all under the age of seven. But Alice was young, too. She had many good years ahead of her. Everything would work out in due time. Besides, she might never even need their help. Miss Templeton had no family at all, and because she had made such a success of her school, she was living on her own well into a ripe old age. Alice could do the same with her career.

Despite the serious nature of her thoughts, the memory of her niece and nephews brought a smile to her face. The rest of her family might exasperate her sometimes, but Alice did enjoy being a doting aunt. She paused in front of a shop with a display of toys in the window. Among the balls and colorful wooden blocks, a complete train set was laid out. Her nephew Jack Jr. would love that. During her last visit, he'd spent a full ten minutes telling her the names of various types of locomotives and their attributes. He'd learned that from his father, Alice's brother Jack, who was fascinated by trains and knew endless facts about them.

On impulse, Alice went into the shop. Little Jack's sixth birthday was coming up soon. The large train set was too far out of her price range, but there was a smaller, single locomotive she could afford. It was five inches long and painted bright red. She could already imagine the boy "driving" it around the house, making steam engine noises as he pushed it along tables and chairbacks and windowsills. Her heart warmed at the image.

Yes, she would always want to be a part of those children's lives. That was enough for her. She set aside any worries about the future. The here and now offered plenty of interesting challenges to fill her life, not the least of which was Douglas's suggestion that she could advance her career in ways she hadn't yet considered.

With her thoughts returning to that happier subject, Alice purchased the toy and headed home.

CHAPTER
Eight

When Alice arrived at her lodgings, she was surprised to see Lucy's carriage standing in the street. Visits from Lucy were never unwelcome, but today Alice might have preferred to spend the evening alone. She was still mulling over all that had happened today. What a good thing she'd come home without Douglas Shaw as an escort. Lucy might have made assumptions that would be hard to dispel.

"There you are!" Lucy cried out in admonishment, coming down from her carriage. "I've been waiting for you for *ages*. Does that ogre Mr. Henley really work you so late?"

"I took a walk after work and looked in at a few shops. If I'd known you were here, I would have come straight home."

Lucy gave Alice a primly disapproving look. "Do you think it's wise to wander all over London by yourself?"

"Walking around in my neighborhood hardly counts as 'all over London.'" She added slyly, "Besides, I haven't yet got 'round to hiring a driver for my carriage."

This kind of jest about the disparity in their wealth normally elicited a pout from her friend. But today Lucy said, "Well, maybe someday soon, eh? Aren't you going to invite me in? I'm longing for a cup of tea."

"Won't your husband be expecting you at home?"

"Not today. Mr. B. has been called away to Manchester for a few days, so I'm quite at liberty to dine where I please."

"How refreshing that you are at liberty at last." This time, Alice's tone did elicit that frown. Lucy really did love her husband. That was something Alice still couldn't understand, given that she personally found him pompous and overbearing. She did not wish to disparage her friend, however, and so to atone, she gave her a welcoming hug. "I'm glad you're here. Come on in."

Lucy wasn't the only one who'd been waiting for Alice to return. The cats were sitting on the stoop, glaring at her. Lucy promptly sneezed, even though she was still ten feet from them. She claimed to be allergic to cats. Alice suspected the worst of Lucy's reaction stemmed from her dislike of them rather than from real physical causes. Lucy preferred her little dog, Bulwer, and the songbirds she kept in cages.

Alice hurried forward, opening the parcel of stale fish. She set the food several feet from the door in order to entice them away from it. "Here are some nice bits of mackerel for you. Aren't you going to thank me?"

The cats showed their gratitude by launching immediately into the proffered food and ignoring Alice completely. But at least they had cleared the path to the door.

Well, the doorway was *almost* clear. The cats had left a fresh mouse carcass on the doorstep. They had done a pretty thorough job of devouring the creature; all that was left were a few bones and the tail.

"Oh!" Lucy gave a cry of dismay when she laid eyes on it. "Oh! Oh!"

Lucy's eyes were so wide with horror that Alice was tempted to laugh. Although she was not fond of mice—dead or alive—she was not afraid of them.

"Don't worry. It's not in any condition to bite you." Alice picked it up by the tail and flung it under a nearby bush. Pulling her key from her reticule, she unlocked the door and ushered Lucy inside. "Come on, let's get that tea."

"How can you encourage those horrid beasts?" Lucy said as they took the stairs up to Alice's rooms.

"They're cats, not monsters. I rather like them. You'll be happy to know that Miss T is not as uncouth as the other two. She doesn't generally, er, supplement her diet."

Lucy gave an exaggerated shiver, to which Alice could only laugh.

Miss T, being more interested in dinner than in the guest, happily followed Alice into the kitchen for the last bit of fish. Meanwhile, Lucy made herself comfortable on the little sofa in the sitting room. Once Miss T had been fed, Alice set about making tea.

When she returned to the sitting room with the tea tray, she was surprised to see that Lucy had a book in her hand. To her dismay, it was the spinster book. She let out an exasperated breath. Lucy had never shown an interest in any of her books—until today. It would have to be *that* book that caught her attention. Perhaps something drew her to it instinctively. Words like *love* and *romance* were sure to pull Lucy in like a magnet. She was fully absorbed in it, nodding appreciatively as she read.

"I'm astonished you remember how to open one of those things," Alice teased, trying to hide her mortification.

Lucy gave her an impish grin. "I feel certain you never owned such an interesting book before."

Alice poured a cup of tea and thrust it toward her friend. This brought about the desired result of forcing Lucy to set aside the book in order to take the teacup, but it did not stop her from grinning.

"If you wanted advice on how to capture a man's attention, you need only have come to me."

"I have no interest in anything of the sort," Alice retorted. "I'm perfectly happy as I am."

Lucy eyed her in disbelief. "Then why are you reading this? It certainly isn't your usual choice."

"I haven't even begun reading it yet. I only just bought it last night. I noticed that there are chapters in there that purport to explain how men think, and I thought it might help me at work.

As you know, most of my colleagues are men. I thought perhaps, if I had a better understanding of them, we could work together more efficiently. . . ."

She faltered. Her explanation didn't sound very plausible, even to her. Her real reason for having bought the book—the urge to disprove its contents—no longer appealed to her, either.

"If you're speaking of that horrid Mr. Clapper, I don't think any book could explain him," Lucy said with a sniff. "As for other men, I've only read a few pages and have already seen some fairly accurate information." Setting down her teacup, she opened the book to find the place she'd been reading. "'He thought he had loved, until he cared for her, but in the light of the new passion, he sees clearly that the others were mere idle flirtations. To her surprise, she also discovers that he has loved her a long time but has never dared to speak of it before, and that this feeling, compared with the others, is as wine unto water.'"

She clasped the book to her heart with a dreamy smile. "Mr. B. was like that. There were so many other fine ladies of his acquaintance. Some had set their caps at him, and one or two had even turned his head a little. But the moment he saw me, a mere middle-class girl walking in the park, he fell in love. Every other lady he had known paled in comparison, and he would not rest until he had married me." She finished this last sentence on a sigh.

Lucy was a good-hearted soul, generous and unfailingly honest; this was one reason why the friendship they'd forged as girls had withstood the test of time. Yet their views of the world were very different. The passage Lucy had just read made Alice feel more queasy than entranced. She didn't want to think of men as passionate beings. She preferred to dwell on the fact that by and large they were rational, clearheaded, and concerned about things in the world that truly mattered.

"You said Mr. Bennington is out of town?" she prompted, wanting nothing more than to stop talking about that book. "How long will he be gone?"

"Nearly a week! That's one reason I'm here. I miss him terribly whenever he goes away. But this time I shan't be lonely. I'm going to have a dinner party the day after tomorrow, and you, my dear friend, are invited."

"A dinner party without your husband present? Are you sure he'd approve?" Lucy was usually more mindful about protocol—especially as she'd extended every effort to win the grudging respect of the upper-crust ladies and gentlemen who made up Mr. Bennington's social set.

"Nothing to cause scandal, I assure you. This is a very exclusive dinner party. Fred's ship is sailing the following day, so I thought we three could enjoy a fun dinner together before he leaves. Do say you'll join us. Fred will be ever so happy to see you."

Alice looked at her askance. "Are you sure about that?"

Fred was Lucy's brother. He and Alice had not enjoyed one another's company for years. It began with an incident when they first met, shortly after Lucy had begun attending Miss Templeton's School for Young Ladies. Being five years older than Lucy and already working as an apprentice, Fred had been sent by their parents to escort his sister home for a school holiday. Alice had embarrassed Fred—she'd bested him about some bit of knowledge in front of another schoolgirl he'd been hoping to impress. Alice couldn't even remember the details of what she'd said, but she'd sent the other girls into a round of dismissive titters. Fred had retained a grudge ever since.

It didn't help that, in addition, he had grown into a taciturn man with few interests outside of his work in the merchant navy. Like his sister, he hadn't bothered much with books after leaving school. Alice could think of many things that would be more preferable—not to mention less painful—than having to make conversation with Fred Arbuckle for an evening. She was pretty sure he felt the same way.

"Now you've got that look on your face," Lucy remonstrated.

"What look?" Alice belatedly attempted to rearrange her features.

"I wish you and Fred could get along. It would be so perfect if you and he were to—"

Alice held up a hand. "There's no use trying to play matchmaker between me and Fred."

Lucy looked affronted. "Why not? What's wrong with him?"

There was plenty wrong with him, in Alice's point of view. But to state those things aloud would only hurt Lucy's feelings. "As I said, I've no desire to get married. Even if I were so inclined, Fred has no interest in me. He never has, and I'm sure he never will."

Lucy set down her teacup. "If you want to know how to get along with men, I can tell you an important key—one that will be in that book, too, if it's worth the paper it's printed on. It's the wise old adage that 'one can catch more flies with honey than with vinegar.'"

"Perhaps." Alice wasn't prepared to concede the point.

"I know you and Fred haven't seen eye to eye for some time. But he is my brother, and you are my best friend. Won't you come to the party—as a kindness to me, at least?"

It was generally impossible to resist her friend's earnest appeals. Alice heaved a sigh. "Yes, I'll come."

"Oh, thank you!" Lucy threw her arms around Alice with such fervor that she nearly knocked them both over. She sprang up while Alice was still righting herself. "I must be going so that I can begin the preparations. Why don't you wear your new scarf to the party? It's ever so becoming."

"Yes, why don't I?" Alice echoed. It was pointless to argue.

After seeing Lucy out the door, Alice returned to her sitting room and plopped down on the sofa. Opening the spinster book, she began to sift through it. Maybe it had some advice for how to survive an evening with an incalculable bore.

Miss T wandered into the sitting room and jumped onto the sofa. As Alice reached out to pet her, she came across this line in the book: "*Men are like cats; they need only to be petted in the right direction.*"

Maybe that was the key. If she could get Fred talking about something he liked, she could simply smile and nod, and her mind would be free to think of other things. It wouldn't be as entertaining as being alone or in the company of someone who was truly interesting. But if it smoothed the waters between them, that would be a welcome change. One that Lucy would appreciate a great deal.

As she continued reading, Alice realized she hadn't once thought about this book today. Her interactions with Douglas Shaw, for example, had been easy and entirely natural. If only all men were as simple to get along with as he was—not dour like Fred or irritating complainers like Archie. This book must be designed for people who had no common ground on which to communicate. Otherwise, life was fairly straightforward, as far as Alice was concerned. Say what you mean and be friendly—or at least, make the jests in a good-natured way. That was exactly how things had been between Alice and her brothers. Aside from the occasional squabble that was inevitable among siblings, they'd all gotten along swimmingly.

Although she supposed, if she was honest, there had been a number of times when she'd had a more . . . well, *complicated* reaction to Douglas Shaw. The admiring looks he gave her at something she'd said or done, and the odd sensations she'd had while sitting so close to him in that hansom cab. Then there was that moment in the filing room, when she could have sworn he'd been flirting with her. . . .

In her distraction, she must have rubbed the cat the wrong way, for Miss T let out a yelping meow and tried to nip her hand.

Alice pulled back just in time to avoid the cat's teeth. "So sorry, my dear!" She gently smoothed the cat's ruffled fur. "Don't be angry. And don't worry, I won't forget what you taught me." She addressed the cat as if it were the real Miss Templeton. "I have no intention of going down that road. I enjoy working with him. That's all."

The cat rested her head on her paws and began to purr, as if in total agreement.

The best things about Douglas Shaw were the kindness he'd extended toward her by offering that cab ride and his genuine interest in her as a person. At work, he was clever in business and adept at solving problems. Those were the qualities she could admire in him. As for the rest, those had been mere physical responses, nothing more. She'd only known him for two days. Given time, those feelings would probably go away.

She had no plan for what she would do if they didn't.

Douglas arrived at his boardinghouse with time to spare before dinner. He checked the table in the foyer where the landlady set out the tenants' mail. One envelope of fine parchment with a wax seal stood out immediately. It was addressed to him. He took it into the parlor to read before going upstairs to his room.

Hal was also in the parlor, seated by the window and reading his copy of the *Illustrated Police News*. He lowered his paper as Douglas entered. "I see you've got mail." He waggled his eyebrows. "It looks *very* important."

Douglas sat in the overstuffed chair opposite his friend. "Care to take a guess what it is?"

Hal tossed his paper on the table next to him. "All I can say is, I'm exceedingly disappointed it does not smell of fine perfume."

"Naturally you took it upon yourself to check."

"It had to be done," Hal answered with a grin.

Douglas broke the seal on the envelope and pulled out the card inside. It was finely embossed with gold lettering. He read it, then met Hal's eyes.

"So when is the dinner party?" Hal asked.

"A week from Friday."

"Excellent!" Hal rubbed his hands together. "You're on your way now, Shaw. From here on out, you'll be hobnobbing with important people. I only hope you'll remember your humble friends from time to time."

Hal kept talking, but Douglas wasn't really listening. He was still marveling that he held this invitation in his hand, that it was addressed specifically to him. He'd been fairly certain this was coming, yet he still couldn't believe it was here. It represented a significant milestone.

To think that it had arrived today, after the very interesting time he'd had at work. Alice McNeil was such a pleasure to work with. He was looking forward to more of that in the days ahead. What a breath of fresh air she was, after dealing with Archie and the inept telegrapher Alice had replaced. Henley really had made the right choice in hiring her.

"Well, have you?" Hal asked.

"Have I what?" Douglas said, realizing he hadn't heard the question.

"Have you got a proper suit for the occasion? Carson knows a good tailor. Says the man works quickly, too."

"That sounds like what I need." Douglas stood up. "I'll have a chat with him about that tonight."

He went upstairs to wash up and prepare for dinner. A half hour later, he happened to meet Carson as they were walking toward the dining room.

"Hal gave me the good news," Carson said. He gave Douglas a friendly slap on the back. "You're a lucky man, Shaw, getting to spend an entire evening with the renowned Miss Rolland."

"Hmm? Oh, right." Douglas realized he'd spent the past half hour thinking through the logistics of the dinner party—reviewing what he would wear, what he knew about the men he was likely to meet there, and other such considerations. He hadn't thought once about the woman who was supposedly his primary reason for going.

But then, he hadn't even met Miss Rolland yet. He had no doubt things would change considerably once he had. Besides, he had no idea what to expect from her or how to prepare. He only hoped she would be as easy to talk to as Alice McNeil. That would make it a very pleasant evening indeed.

CHAPTER
Nine

I don't suppose you could give it a go?" Mr. Henley looked hopefully at Alice.

They were all standing next to the typewriter. Mavis was out again today, and Mr. Henley was growing anxious about documents that he wanted typed up and sent out to clients in America.

"I haven't been trained to use the typewriter, sir," Alice said. "Learning to use it properly takes some time. If I tried it now, I'm afraid the results would probably not be usable."

"That's disappointing," Mr. Henley said. "We've only had that machine for a year, but it has become indispensable. It's already the standard in American offices, isn't it, Shaw? We've simply got to keep up. Stay modern, and all that."

Douglas tipped his head in acknowledgment. "Yes, sir. By the way, if we're going to stay modern, let's look into investing in a telephone. I saw them in offices all over America. A new telephone exchange has just opened on this street, so getting a line to our office shouldn't be too difficult."

"Don't change the subject! Let's deal with one newfangled invention at a time."

"He always gets like that when I mention the telephone," Douglas whispered to Alice.

Henley looked across the office to the two bookkeeping clerks, who were still seated at their desks. "I don't understand why we could never get either of you to learn how to use this."

The clerks, Mr. Dawson and Mr. Nicholls, had both been with the company for over twenty years. They looked affronted at Mr. Henley's suggestion.

"Mr. Nicholls, as I recall, you got your start in the company by being our copyist," Mr. Henley pressed.

"Yes, sir, and I was the copyist for many years, until the growth of our company made my work in bookkeeping absolutely indispensable," Mr. Nicholls pointed out. "If you need me to hand-copy any documents for you today, sir, I will be glad to make time to do it," he added magnanimously. "But please do not require me to attempt at banging on that monstrosity."

"With all due respect, sir, we already have more than enough to do," Mr. Dawson added. "Keeping track of all the contractual requirements, legal requirements, monies, and fees for so many international ventures is an enormous task. You know yourself, sir, that accurate ledgers are the lifeblood of Henley and Company."

It was a testament to how well these two longtime employees were valued and trusted that they could essentially refuse their employer in this way.

"We received a note today from Miss Waller, stating that she will definitely be back in the office on Monday," Alice said.

"Given that it's Friday, surely we can wait until then, Mr. Henley," Douglas said. "Miss Waller's filing skills may be less than stellar, but she's an excellent typist. I believe we will be able to get everything completed by end of day Monday."

Henley nodded but still looked put out. "All right, that's what we'll do. Nevertheless, this is all very inconvenient. We ought to have more than one person in the office who can use that machine, especially for times like this."

"I nominate Miss McNeil," Archie called out from his desk.

Alice heard Douglas say under his breath, "Of course you do." She heard the censure in his voice, and she rather liked him for it. Typewriting was clerical work and was not considered at the same skill level as first-class telegraphers. Archie was signaling his pleasure at the idea of Alice lowering herself by doing that kind of work. She could see yet again why he had so often talked badly about Douglas: Douglas was hardworking, ambitious, and most importantly, a decent person.

Alice, however, was more interested in proving she was a valuable employee who was willing to put the company's needs first. "I'll be happy to take lessons, Mr. Henley, if the fee will be paid by the company."

"Yes, of course," Mr. Henley answered. "Thank you, Miss McNeil. I appreciate your willingness to step up."

Archie and the two bookkeepers exchanged smug smiles over this result. Douglas sent Alice a look of surprise, but there was respect in his expression, too. He, at least, seemed to understand why she had agreed.

Mr. Henley waved everyone toward their desks. "Let's get back to work, everyone. Shaw, we need to review the numbers for the Western Consolidated Grain deal. Can you get that information and bring it to my office?"

"Yes, sir. Be right there."

Henley went to his office.

Alice sauntered back to her desk. Wanting to take Archie down a few pegs, she said, "I really don't see why you couldn't learn typewriting, Mr. Clapper. Unless it's true what they say about not teaching new tricks to an old dog."

Archie responded with a sneer. "Better than lowering oneself to menial tasks in an effort to win praise from Mr. Henley. I certainly would never do that."

"No, you have no need to, do you, Clapper?" Douglas said. "You have other ways of keeping your position here."

The two men scowled at one another. Something was being said in that look, but Alice had no idea what it was. She only knew that if it had been put into actual words, it would have been ugly.

Archie looked as though a rude remark was on the tip of his tongue, but he was interrupted by the sounder. He shifted his attention to it, and Douglas strode off to his office. A few moments later, Douglas reappeared with a stack of papers in his hand. Alice watched as he walked into Mr. Henley's office and closed the door behind him. The most important work of the company was being done in that office. For a moment, she wished she could be in there, too, taking part in the discussion and helping to make decisions on weighty issues. Could she really ever rise to such levels, as Douglas had implied yesterday? It was a tantalizing thought—and, if she dared to admit it to herself, somewhat daunting.

For now, however, that was not why she was here.

She turned to her work. There was a stack of messages to be sent out. Refocusing her thoughts to the task at hand, she initiated the connection for sending the first message.

Douglas was so busy reworking the proposed contract for Western Consolidated that he didn't have time to think about the earlier conversation about typewriting. It wasn't until Alice came into his office with a handful of telegrams that he remembered his consternation.

He rose to meet her as she gave him the messages. Alice said, "Most of these were in code, so I went ahead and transcribed them longhand. I thought there were some you'd want to see right away, rather than waiting for Miss Waller to type them on Monday."

"Thank you." He sifted through the telegrams she'd brought, skimming their contents rapidly. "Yes, this is good. I can use this one especially right now." He pulled out a message from their agent in Chicago. "Is this everything?"

"There were several more from our Liverpool office regarding the insurance for that shipment lost in the hurricane last year. I took those to Mr. Henley. The lawyers are confident our claim will be paid by the end of summer."

Douglas could see she was gaining a personal interest in the company, and he liked that. "You've caught on quickly, Miss McNeil.

You've been paying attention to the details of the business. Even more than your particular tasks might warrant."

She beamed with pride. He noticed she wasn't wearing that pretty purple scarf today, nor really any kind of adornment. He thought that was a shame. Although she was no less pleasant to look at without it, that scarf had brightened her features. Douglas always felt that to succeed in any endeavor, it never hurt to make the most of one's attributes.

"The business of imports is really fascinating," Alice said. "I'm beginning to understand how all the elements work together, and I like that. When I worked at the CTO, I handled thousands of messages, all going to different places, and none of them had any context." She gave a little laugh. "At times I felt like a mere intermediary for messages going between distant stars, all mysterious in their meaning."

"An interesting flight of fancy," Douglas said. He liked her alert and inventive mind.

She smiled. "Not to mention that a lot of them used code words, which made the messages even more inscrutable."

"Ah yes. And now you're becoming initiated into those secrets."

"Precisely." Her eyes lit up.

Douglas thought back to this morning's conversation at Miss Waller's desk. "Are you really so keen to become a typewriter girl?"

Alice looked taken aback. "I wouldn't classify it that way. I'll be a telegrapher who happens to know how to use a typewriter. There's a big difference. I can't see Mr. Henley lowering my pay because I might do a bit of typewriting when needed."

"No, of course not. It will only make you more valuable as an employee."

"Besides, as we discussed this morning, typewriting has become the standard for business documents. I can only see this skill becoming more and more valuable, and not relegated only to clerks. It's already been added to the civil service exam."

"Has it?"

She nodded. Pointing a finger at him in admonishment, she

added with a sly smile, "As you told Mr. Henley, it's important that we keep up with all the latest developments."

He gave her an answering grin. "Right you are, Miss McNeil. I stand corrected." Her playful sense of humor was a refreshing change in the office, to be sure.

"We might also think about how we standardize our document formatting, what business terms we capitalize, and other such things," she went on. "I don't feel ready to tackle that just yet, but perhaps in time. I believe I should learn more about the industry first."

Here was a worker who was going out of her way to find more things to do! Douglas was more and more impressed with her. "Tell me, Miss McNeil, is this something that's been brewing in your thoughts for a while, or was it spurred by our conversation yesterday about getting into management?"

"A little of both, I think. There is one idea that has occurred to me since then. I noticed you and Mr. Henley both make a point of reading the *Shipping and Mercantile Gazette*. I wondered if I might read the issues when you're done with them?"

"That's a good idea. You'll learn a lot that way. I'd also recommend *Lloyd's List*." He picked up a copy from the corner of his desk and handed it to her.

She accepted it with a smile. As she looked down at it, Douglas realized it was still folded open to a particular notice that had caught his attention. He had even circled it in pencil.

She looked up. "Did you intend to keep this article about Mr. Andrew Carnegie? He's an American industrialist, I believe."

"Yes, that's right. He was born in Scotland, though. The article says he'll be in England for the next few months. I found another article in the *Times* that said he'll be touring the country with a group of companions in a coach-and-four."

"That sounds charming. Is there a reason it's of particular interest to you?"

"I'd love to find a way to meet him. We have some mutual business acquaintances in New York. According to the *Times*, he's in

London this week. Unfortunately, there was no mention of where he is staying."

"Perhaps he'll drive his coach-and-four in Hyde Park, like so many of our English gentlemen do."

She said it in an offhand way, but it struck Douglas as a very insightful comment. "What a brilliant idea! Perhaps I'll look for him this Sunday."

She beamed again. "Well, I suppose I'd better get back to work. Thank you for this." She indicated the newspaper in her hand.

"Happy reading. Oh, and Miss McNeil—"

She paused. "Yes?"

"I noticed you had on a very nice purple scarf the other day."

She gave him a sheepish look. "It was perhaps too frivolous to wear to work."

"On the contrary, it was most becoming. Not that you need it to do your job well," he hastened to assure her. "On the other hand, since you are striving to make a difference and to stand out, why not also present the very best appearance?"

For a moment, he was worried that he'd offended her in some way. Her eyebrows lifted, and then settled again. Overall, she looked perplexed.

In the end, she seemed to accept it as the disinterested advice that it was. "Thank you," she said, her smile returning. "I'll keep that in mind."

Alice paused on her way back to her desk, taking a moment to absorb what had just transpired. She was gratified that Douglas had encouraged her desire to learn as much as she could about the business. Given what she'd already seen of him, that was in line with what she'd expected.

What had truly surprised her, though, was his comment about the scarf. He found nothing wrong with the idea of wearing clothes to the workplace that flattered one's appearance. More interestingly, he'd noticed. This had stunned her and left her temporarily speechless. Perhaps she ought to take more heed of Lucy's fashion advice. Alice didn't think any man had ever complimented her on her appearance before—let alone a man like Douglas Shaw. Her pulse still sped up whenever she looked at him. She'd told herself she was getting better at ignoring those feelings, but for that moment in his office, she had been nearly overwhelmed by some heady mixture of happiness and pride.

She was still standing there, smiling to herself and feeling very pleased about everything, when Mr. Henley passed her. He gave her a nod of acknowledgment but didn't pause.

He went into Douglas's office. Through the open doorway, Alice could hear him say, "By the way, Shaw, I forgot to ask you earlier. Did you receive that invitation to the Rollands' dinner party?"

"Yes, sir, I did."

"Excellent! Rolland has been warming up to the idea of bankrolling our next venture. If you make a good showing at this party, his buy-in will be practically guaranteed."

It was another intriguing aspect of business that so much of it was carried out at social events, such as the one Mr. Henley was referring to. That seemed to be as important to success as official meetings in banks and offices.

Although Alice wanted to hear more, she was also aware that it was unprofessional to eavesdrop. She returned to her desk.

There was plenty of work to do, but she found it difficult to concentrate. So many ideas were keeping her mind otherwise engaged.

CHAPTER

Ten

On the heels of a pleasantly engrossing week at work, Lucy's "dinner party" was a bit of a letdown. It was turning out to be just as painful as Alice had anticipated. There was more food than the three of them could possibly eat, and Lucy was constantly burbling about one inane topic or another. By contrast, Fred said very little, although he ate quite a lot. A burly man, he seemed determined to do justice to Lucy's well-laid table. They were on the third course now, and he'd uttered perhaps a dozen words, mostly in answer to Lucy's questions.

"What's the matter, Fred—cat got your tongue?" Lucy joked after he had given another terse answer to one of her questions. She pretended to give a delicate little sneeze and said, "Oh my! I get allergic just thinking about those creatures!"

It was clear she was trying to lighten the mood. She wanted this to be a real party, after all. Alice could have told her this wasn't going to work, but it wouldn't have made a difference. Lucy was convinced, for some reason, that Fred could be jolly good company. Perhaps he was—when he wasn't around Alice. Maybe her presence was the reason for his sullen demeanor.

That was just silly, Alice decided. Thirteen years was too long to hold a grudge over such a minor matter. She might not particularly like Fred, but there was no reason they should act like mortal enemies.

After waiting until he had swallowed a mouthful of food and washed it down with some wine, she said to him, "I understand you are to be gone for several months. What will be your ports of call? It must be very interesting to visit so many places."

"No place is as good as England."

Lucy made a little tsking sound. "Now, Fred, Alice asked you a sincere question. Tell us where you'll be going."

He managed to look abashed at his sister's chastisement and set about answering Alice's question in a more cheerful manner. "We'll be sailing first to Gibraltar and then to Malta. We're taking a variety of goods to those places. Then it's on to India by way of the Suez Canal, where we'll be loading up on silk, tea, and indigo."

"That sounds fascinating," Alice said in all honesty. "What I wouldn't give to be able to travel like that!"

He seemed pleased by her reaction, although he downplayed her admiration with a little shrug. "I doubt you'd like the accommodations, though."

Was that an attempt at a joke? If so, maybe his gruff exterior could be breached after all. Always up for a challenge, Alice was now determined to get on this man's good side.

"It's a good living, too, isn't it, Fred?" Lucy piped up.

"Yes, we get a share of the profits. Not as high as them fancy gentlemen in the counting houses, of course, even though we do the real work." He finished off his last bite of fish, then sat back with a smile.

The footman removed his plate. Fred picked up his napkin and touched it to his lips. Alice could see he was trying to look cultured, but the effect was more like he was afraid his face might break if he pressed it too hard.

For some reason, the movement drew Alice's attention to his chin. As he set the napkin back in his lap, Alice noticed something she hadn't paid much attention to before. He had a dimple on his right cheek that became quite pronounced when he smiled. Perhaps she noticed it now because he'd had his hair and beard cut short in preparation for the voyage. Or because she hadn't seen him smile very often.

Or perhaps she was paying attention to it now because she had seen a mention of dimples in the spinster book. It was an amusing anecdote, highlighting the vanity resident in all men. If Alice said something about his dimple, would Fred fall prey to the same foible that had been described in the book? She had an irresistible urge to find out. The very idea of testing this theory made her smile.

Fred frowned at her. "Did I do something funny?"

Drat. She had let her amusement show. She didn't want Fred to think she was laughing at him. "I beg your pardon. I was simply smiling in surprise."

His wariness didn't lessen. "Surprise about what?"

"You have a dimple in your cheek."

"I do? Where?" He placed a hand precisely where the dimple was located, even though Alice had not specified which cheek.

She tried to quell a laugh. It was true!

"Maybe I shouldn't have cut the beard so close," he grumbled.

"Quite the contrary. It's good that it's more evident now. The dimple makes you look . . . er, very handsome."

"Do you really think so?" He looked suspicious.

"Well, of course she does, Fred!" Lucy said.

But coming from his sister, this remark had no impact whatsoever. Still fingering his dimple, Fred seemed baffled as to how to react.

"Alice, it's astonishing that you never noticed this until now," Lucy added.

"I suppose we all change over time," Alice said. "Wouldn't you agree, Fred? For example, don't you think it might be foolish to hold on to quibbles we had when we were children?"

"To attract a man, offer up a smile that is half-tremulous, half-trusting. It's a look he will find nearly impossible to resist."

This was a line from the book that Alice had found incredibly silly. However, now that she'd begun this little experiment, she would carry on. She offered Fred a smile that she supposed was half-tremulous, half-trusting, and hoped it didn't look as strange and wobbly as it felt.

Fred was staring fixedly at her. Alice knew he must be thinking back to that incident so long ago and comparing it to the way she was talking to him now. In one sense, it pained her to be the one to make this overture. It felt like giving in, because she still believed she'd been in the right.

"Blessed are the peacemakers." That advice came from a much more trustworthy book. Alice could at least take comfort in that.

"Do you really think the dimple makes me look handsome?" The furrow in Fred's forehead began to soften.

Alice gave him the wobbly smile again, and Fred beamed.

If he presses for an apology, this whole experiment will be ruined, Alice thought. That was the one thing she would not do. Nothing was worth giving up one's integrity.

"Reconciled at last!" Lucy exclaimed, clapping her hands together. "Old friendships forge a new path."

A flurry of unease skittered across Alice's stomach. She had been focused on the experiment. She hadn't stopped to consider that Lucy might want to give the results greater significance than they merited.

Lucy touched a hand to the base of her neck and gave the area a little pat as she sent Alice a smile. Alice frowned. Lucy was trying to relay a message of some kind.

The scarf. That was it. It must be something to do with her scarf. Was it slipping? Had she accidentally dropped food on it? Alice reached up to check it. Everything seemed to be in order, though.

Lucy said, "Fred you haven't said a word about how nice Alice looks tonight."

For a moment he appeared to be at a loss, but the motion of Alice's hands led his eyes to her scarf. "That . . . erm . . . that scarf looks . . . er, very becoming."

Lucy had set up their actions—and reactions—as expertly as

a puppet master. Alice felt her cheeks turning pink, but it wasn't a blush of pleasure.

A look of uncertainty entered Fred's eyes. Was he worried she wouldn't accept his compliment?

Oh well. In for a penny, in for a pound. Was there anything else in that spinster book she could use? She couldn't dredge up anything else from her memory, so she fell back on the wobbly smile. "How kind of you to say so."

Fred turned his attention to the next course being set down, and Alice breathed a sigh of relief.

"Fred, tell Alice about your prospects for this voyage," Lucy chirped. "And about your promotion."

He didn't need further prompting. He puffed out his chest in obvious pride. "I'm the chief cargo officer now. In charge of gettin' the goods on and off the ship. It's a very important job, as you can imagine. Especially for the unloading, keeping track of every crate and barrel. We have at least fifty kinds of items in those crates, and it's important to ensure that nothing goes missing."

That was all it took to get him talking. Alice hoped it was enough to take his mind off the romantic moment Lucy had been trying to conjure between them.

By the end of the evening, Alice was fairly certain she and Fred were now on good terms, even though she found him carefully scrutinizing her from time to time. She couldn't tell what that signified. Perhaps it was just his way of getting used to this new friendliness between them.

Nor was she overly worried when he offered to escort her home at the end of the evening. She kindly but firmly refused. She'd traveled home from Lucy's house by herself countless times, although Lucy always insisted she take her carriage.

What did alarm Alice, however, was that Fred placed a warm kiss on her cheek before she left. "That's for until I see you again. Six weeks isn't such a long time, you know. I'll look for some interesting trinket for you while I'm in Bombay."

Alice swallowed, unwilling to believe the glint she saw in his eye. Nor did she like the assumptions she detected behind Lucy's broad smile. Her friend was so radiant that she might have lit up an entire street.

Alice shook Fred's hand fervently, in a friendly, almost mannish gesture, to emphasize that they were simply friends. She hoped this was merely a precaution and that, despite his words, she would be out of his thoughts before his ship reached Gravesend.

Even with this potential danger, there was a kind of elation in Alice's heart as she rode home. Those tricks from the spinster's guide actually worked! A book with such a ridiculous premise did, in fact, contain useful information. Perhaps it was worth reading more, just to see what other gems it might contain.

⚬⚬⚬

"That's rather astounding, isn't it?" Emma said the next day, staring at Alice with amazement as she shared the story of what had happened at Lucy's party. Alice, Emma, and Rose were enjoying tea together, as they often did on Sunday afternoons since Alice had moved out of the boardinghouse.

"Astounding that a book could impart such hitherto unrevealed truths?" Rose scoffed. She held out a hand. "Let me see it. I daresay it doesn't contain anything I haven't known for ages."

"I daresay it doesn't," Alice agreed with a smile. She handed the book to Rose. She was still marveling over what had happened last night with Fred, and she decided to get their opinion, as it was not something she could discuss with Lucy. Lucy would interpret Fred's easy capitulation to a little flattery as evidence that he and Alice were destined for each other after all. She would insist that the book had merely helped Alice uncover the true love that had been right under her nose this whole time. Alice knew neither of those things were true. She was very sure she did not love Fred. But could his sudden change of demeanor be attributed wholly to Alice's cynical application of the book's suggestions?

"In some ways, I feel as though I played a joke on Fred and he didn't even realize it. I only hope there won't be any negative repercussions. What do you think?" Alice aimed the question at Rose, who was far and away the most knowledgeable of the three women in these matters.

Rose looked up from the book. "I think you were merely flirting." She grinned at Alice. "After all this time, you've finally learned how to do it."

"It's not a skill I ever aspired to develop, I assure you."

"Nevertheless, it can serve you well in certain circumstances, as you've seen. You said this greatly reduced the animosity Fred showed toward you. That's a benefit, right?"

"I hope so. I'm just worried about the possible cost."

Rose shrugged. "I wouldn't lose any sleep over it. Fred is a sailor. Plenty of women must have flirted with him at various ports of call. They would have other reasons for it, of course." She rubbed two fingers together to indicate money. Then, after a sidelong look at Emma, who was staring at her wide-eyed, Rose evidently decided to change tack. "Well, there are all sorts of reasons. I say merely that this can't be a new concept for him. He was simply reacting to your compliments with appreciation. That's a function of male pride, which is built right into them."

"That's what the book says, too," Alice said.

Rose flipped through a few more pages. "It's clear the author has a great deal of knowledge on the topic. Judging from the subtly negative remarks she has sprinkled among the protestations of how wonderful it is to be in love, I'd say she gained some of that knowledge the hard way. I might have written this book myself, after . . ."

Her voice trailed off. She must have been thinking of the way she'd been so ill-used by the man she'd thought had truly loved her.

"After what, Rose?" Emma prompted. She'd often asked for details about Rose's life before she came to London, but Rose had remained close-lipped.

Rose snapped the book shut and tossed it on the table. "Never you mind."

Emma immediately snatched it up and opened it. "I should

like to read it. After all, if it does describe how to secure a man's affections, I definitely want to learn more."

"And *I* should think we all have better things to concern ourselves with," Alice retorted. She began to wish she hadn't brought up the subject. She didn't want to encourage Emma's foolish notions of romance. "Emma, I feel quite sure that if you marry someday, it will be because you are lovely and kind and a genuinely good person, not because you had to resort to underhanded tactics."

"Not *if* I marry, but *when*," Emma murmured, her eyes scanning the pages. She began to read aloud. "'Love is the bread and the wine of life, the hunger and the thirst, the hurt and the healing, the only wound which is cured by another.'" Her voice got more and more dramatic as she read, swept away with the sentiment. "'It is the guest who comes like a thief in the night, the eternal question that is its own answer, the thing that has no beginning and no end. The very blindness of it is divine, for it sees no imperfections, takes no heed of faults, and concerns itself only with the hidden beauty of the soul.'"

When she was done, she gave a deep, dreamy sigh.

Alice was dismayed to realize that by bringing this book today, she'd given Emma an excuse to add more rooms to her castle in the air.

"That paragraph is nothing but overwrought nonsense." Rose tapped a finger on the page to get Emma's attention. "But this book does contain good information about how to manipulate men by appealing to their baser instincts. Alice, I believe you were on the right track when you asked whether this might be helpful for you at work." A devious smile lightened her expression. "You should try it on that horrible man you told us about—the one you said is the bane of your existence."

Alice looked at her, aghast. "You want me to flirt with Archie Clapper?"

"Let's not call it flirting. It's more like using certain strategies to get Mr. Clapper to change his attitude toward you. You've described your encounters with him. I know you are relentlessly honest and straightforward in your dealings with everyone. That's laudable, but it isn't always an advantage." Rose tugged on the book, and reluctantly Emma relinquished it. She flipped through the pages to locate a passage. "Take this example. It's too long to read, so I'll sum it up. It's about a young widow who knows perfectly well how to send a telegram, yet she suddenly forgets everything she knows while in the telegraph office."

Emma looked confused. "Why would she do that?"

"Because then she must ask for help from the promising gentleman standing nearby. He will immediately feel warmer toward her because she has fanned the flames of his masculine pride. He, of course, knows how to do everything the correct way, so he can deign to show her. The next thing you know, they have struck up a splendid friendship."

"Or maybe more!" Emma said rapturously.

"Let's just leave it at friendship for now," Rose answered, looking simultaneously amused and exasperated by Emma's one-track mind. "Alice, I think you should try something like that with Mr. Clapper."

"Why should I do anything to make him feel superior to me?" Alice objected. "That's the very last thing I want. I've fought hard these past three months to make him see that I am every bit as capable as he is."

"Here's what I think will happen. You ask him to show you how to do something, then praise him wildly when he does it. He will therefore want to do more of the same. If you play this right, he could end up doing more of his own work without realizing it instead of finding ways to lay it on you. He might even stop getting his chums to send messages at lightning speed just to trip you up."

Alice didn't feel convinced. "The truth is, I relish being able to show that I can handle whatever he throws at me."

Rose grinned. "I have no doubt about that. I'm not saying you should try to diminish anything relating to your skills as a telegraph operator. But there must be other areas where you might be able to apply this tactic."

"I'd have to think about it," Alice said doubtfully.

"You said yourself that you felt you had played a joke on Fred and he didn't even realize it. What if you did the same to Mr. Clapper? How delicious would that be? He might *feel* superior, but you would know that you *are* superior."

It was a tempting prospect. Maybe there was some truth to what Rose was saying. "Perhaps I will give it a try. It would be nice to have a more civil work environment."

Rose leaned back in her chair, raising her hands in a gesture of satisfaction. "I rest my case."

CHAPTER

Eleven

It was a fine day to be in Hyde Park. Douglas always enjoyed coming here. The gentlemen and ladies on horseback or in fine carriages presented a picture of what his life could be—and would be, if his successes continued to mount. Today, thanks to Alice's comment, he was here with an extra purpose in mind. He was watching to see if Andrew Carnegie's four-in-hand—a large coach pulled by four horses—would come by.

If so, he was determined to find some way to make an acquaintance with the businessman. On Sundays like this when the weather was good, people were rarely in a hurry. They would pause and chat with one another from their open carriages. All Douglas had to do was find a way to approach Carnegie and strike up a conversation, and surely the rest would take care of itself. They were fellow Scotsmen, after all, and both had worked their way up from poverty. Carnegie was further along on that road than Douglas, having earned his riches through steel manufacturing and railroads. But they had both begun their careers in a telegraph office. All these things could surely open the doors for Carnegie to consider the idea of a deal with Henley and Company. At the very least, it could yield other valuable contacts. And so, while strolling through the park with Carson and Hal, Douglas had been on the lookout for Mr. Carnegie's coach.

They had been in the park for perhaps an hour when Douglas

spotted the carriage he was looking for. He recognized Carnegie, who was driving, because he had seen him at a distance at that New York party. The plump, elderly woman seated next to him had to be his mother, and the friends he'd brought were in the coach as well.

"There he is!" Douglas said excitedly.

"Who?" Hal said.

"Andrew Carnegie, the steel magnate from America."

"How can you be sure?" Carson asked.

"I read in the paper that he is touring England with his mother and some friends. They are leaving for Windsor tomorrow and then traveling up the country all the way to Scotland."

"What a grand tour that sounds like," Carson said.

Hal smirked. "Even if he does have to bring his mother with him."

The carriage passed them without stopping, but to Douglas's delight, it began to slow as it reached the end of the park. "I'll lay odds they're planning to stop at Gunter's," he said.

"Why do you say that?" Carson asked.

"Well, look at his mother!" Hal answered for Douglas. "She looks very well fed. I reckon she likes a cherry ice as much as the next person."

"I was thinking mainly that it's dastardly hot outside today," Douglas said dryly.

Hal nodded. "I suppose the old lady does look a little wilted."

Douglas picked up his pace, and his two friends had to hurry to keep up.

"You're not thinking of going there, too?" Carson asked in surprise.

Douglas adjusted his hat against the breeze but did not slacken his pace. "Maybe I can speak to him."

"But you've not even been introduced!" Carson pointed out.

"Then again, he is an American," Hal put in. "They can be awfully casual about such things."

Douglas grinned. "Exactly. And he has Scottish origins, so it's for sure he'll be wantin' to talk wi' me." He said this with a thick brogue that caused the others to chuckle. Douglas had purposefully cultivated his speech to sound more English in order to better fit in among London's well-to-do. However, he knew how to play up the Scottish lilt when he wanted.

The coach had far outpaced them, but when they turned the street corner onto the square where Gunter's was located, there it stood. The footman sat on the box, keeping watch over the carriage and horses, but everyone else had gone inside.

"How do I look?" Douglas asked, straightening his cravat.

"Like the belle of the ball," Hal said.

Douglas gave him a little shove in reply. "Why don't you two wait here? The shop will be crowded."

"Sure, we'll just stand outside in the blistering sun while you cool yourself with a refreshing ice."

Douglas realized his friend was right. It would be unkind to leave them here. He struggled to admit it, though, because he really wanted the opportunity to approach Mr. Carnegie alone.

"Don't worry, we'll keep out of your way," Hal assured him. "No one wants your success more than we do. We want to be able to say our friend chums around with millionaires!"

"Indeed we do," Carson agreed.

They walked into the shop. By now Carnegie's party had been served. Douglas counted four women and six men in the group. They were seated at tables in a shady area behind the shop. Everyone except Mr. Carnegie. He was still at the counter, chatting with the proprietor, who wore a look of stunned surprise as Carnegie asked him about the costs and other details of transporting ice in the summertime.

Did the shop owner know who was addressing him? Or was his deference in response to the obvious wealth on display by the carriage and clothes of the whole entourage?

The shop owner paused midsentence when he saw Douglas and the others. Perhaps he was torn between the need to serve new customers and the fear of offending the wealthy one he already had.

Mr. Carnegie turned and met Douglas's gaze. Douglas judged his expression to be inquisitive rather than unapproachable. He took a breath and, offering up a friendly smile, closed the gap between them.

"Good afternoon, sir. I believe you are Mr. Carnegie of Pittsburgh? My name is Douglas Shaw. I apologize for approaching you without an introduction, but curiously enough, you and I attended the same charity ball in New York two months ago. I was there at the invitation of Mr. Pender of Allied Manufacturing. He wanted to introduce me to you, but with such a large crowd, we did not have the opportunity."

Douglas spoke in a rush, wanting to get the whole explanation out before Carnegie could stop him. He also made his Scottish brogue noticeable enough to ensure Carnegie would pick up on it. He finished by extending his hand to offer a handshake. It was a risky move. Douglas would look foolish if Carnegie brushed him off.

To his delight, Douglas's gamble worked, and Carnegie accepted the handshake without hesitation. "Pleased to meet you, Mr. Shaw. A fellow countryman, too, it seems. Where do you hail from?"

"Glasgow, sir. I'm a Lowlander like yourself, even though I grew up a ways from Dunfermline."

Mr. Carnegie's eyebrow raised at the mention of his hometown. He seemed pleased that Douglas knew this bit of information. "And why were you in America? I'm sorry I missed meeting you. I know Pender well. He's a client of mine."

"I was traveling on business for my employer, Mr. Josiah Henley of Henley and Company."

Carnegie looked at him with approval. "Henley must place a great deal of trust in you to send you all the way to America on business."

"I like to think I've earned it, sir. I've been working since I was twelve years old—first as a messenger boy and then as a telegraph operator." Douglas didn't elaborate on why he'd started working so early. Having come from poverty himself, Mr. Carnegie likely made the right assumptions. "I came to London ten years ago and started to work for Mr. Henley. I'm now his chief assistant, trusted with making new deals for the company." Douglas knew this sounded boastful, but he felt no remorse, because every word was true. When he was in America, he'd once heard a man say, "If you can jump over the barn, it ain't bragging to say so."

Carnegie was studying Douglas with interest. "Did you know I also began as a messenger boy? Started work for Western Union when I was a lad of five."

"Yes, sir, I know. Your story was recently in the *Edinburgh Evening News*, which I still enjoy reading even though I live in London now. The Scots are proud of your success."

"I merely made the most of opportunities afforded to me by living in America. I'm not saying it's impossible to rise in England, but it's a lot more difficult." He eyed Douglas. "I'll bet you believe you're the sort who could do it."

Douglas held out his hands and gave a little shrug, conceding the point. "I can't deny that's my aim."

Carnegie nodded. "No false modesty. Good. The fact that you were bold enough to approach me shows you're not cowed by your 'betters,' that foolish word they use over here. Does Henley and Company do a lot of business in America?"

"Indeed we do. Primarily shipping grain from California and, to an increasing extent, from Oregon. We also import cotton from the Southern states." Douglas almost felt a need to pinch himself. He was talking business with the great Andrew Carnegie! He spared a brief glance at his friends. They were seated at a table, grinning widely at his success.

"Is that so? I have a large share in the railroads out west—though I imagine an astute man such as yourself knows that already."

"Yes, sir. In fact, I was hoping you and I might arrange a time to meet and further discuss the subject. Perhaps we might even be able to broker a mutually advantageous shipping venture?" It was an audacious offer to make so early in their acquaintance, but Douglas had learned that Americans respected men who didn't waste time getting to their point.

Carnegie considered the idea. "That does sound interesting, but I'm afraid it won't be immediately possible. My friends and I are departing London tomorrow. We're traveling for the next few weeks, on our way up to Scotland. My mother and I have a hankering to see our hometown again."

"Will you be coming back to London before returning to America? Perhaps we could meet then."

Carnegie shook his head. "We're taking a ship from Liverpool at the end of next month."

"I would be happy to meet with you there. We have an office in Liverpool." Douglas persisted because he could sense that Carnegie was willing to see him if the details could be worked out. He did not think the millionaire was deliberately trying to put him off.

Carnegie smiled. "I can tell you are very interested in making this meeting happen. All right, I'll see what I can do. We'll probably get to Liverpool a day or two before the ship sails. We are making our travel arrangements on the fly, but I can telegraph you when I know the details. Have you a card?"

Douglas pulled a business card from his coat pocket. It contained his name and the address and telegraph information for Henley and Company's London and Liverpool offices.

Carnegie read it over before pulling out a small notebook and placing the card inside. "I shall look forward to further discussions. If for some reason we are not able to connect in Liverpool, here is the information for getting in touch with me in New York." He handed a card to Douglas. "Now, if you will excuse me, I should return to my friends. It was a pleasure meeting you, Mr. Shaw."

"I assure you the pleasure is all mine," Douglas replied.

As Carnegie walked off, Douglas looked again toward the table where Hal and Carson were seated. They both looked the way Douglas felt—like they were barely suppressing the urge to jump up and down with excitement. Douglas had spoken to many wealthy men on his American itinerary, but none so powerful as this man.

Before joining his friends, Douglas turned to address the shop owner. The man had not even tried to hide that he'd been listening to their entire conversation. He grinned appreciatively at Douglas. "Well done, lad. Good luck to ya."

"Thank you," Douglas answered, trying to sound as though he

spoke with millionaires every day. He bought three ices and took them over to Hal and Carson.

"Behold, London's next millionaire!" Hal exclaimed.

"What did he say?" Carson asked.

Douglas sat back in his chair. "I'll tell you about it later. Suffice it to say, things went very well. In the meantime, let us try to look like nothing so very out of the ordinary has happened." They were still within eyesight of Carnegie's party.

Hal chuckled as he downed a mouthful of his cherry ice. "Cool as a cucumber you are, Shaw."

They finished eating and left before Carnegie and the others. As they walked home, Douglas's mind filled with exciting plans. In a little over a month's time, he might be putting together a deal—possibly the best one Henley and Company had ever known! This could only bolster his career. Perhaps Henley would even make him a partner. When he got to the office tomorrow, he needed to thank Alice for her capital suggestion. What a boon she was proving to be. He was glad Henley had had the good sense to hire her.

They were still walking along the street when Carnegie's coach-and-four passed them once again. Carnegie gave a brief nod and a smile to Douglas as the carriage rolled by. Next to him sat his mother, looking a little less wilted and very satisfied at her position atop the carriage. She must feel on top of the world, to have gone from poverty to a life of such affluence.

A twinge of sadness nagged at Douglas as he watched the smiling woman seated next to her devoted son. He had never once considered taking his parents on holiday. Perhaps because he knew they'd turn him down outright. It wasn't as though he hadn't tried to help them, but he had to press them to accept any kind of financial aid, let alone something they would dismiss as a needless luxury. They were too stubborn and proud. The more Douglas rose in life, the more critical of him they had become.

If he could one day figure out how to make his parents proud of *him*, maybe then he would feel truly successful.

CHAPTER
Twelve

When Alice arrived at work on Monday morning, Mavis was at her desk. She was rolling paper into her typewriter in preparation for tackling the stack of documents waiting for her. She greeted Alice, then paused to sneeze into a handkerchief.

"How are you feeling?" Alice asked.

Mavis sniffled. "I've had the most dreadful cold. I couldn't eat or get out of bed for three days. I still haven't fully recovered, but I cannot afford to miss any more work." She rearranged her handkerchief and blew her nose.

"I'm sorry you're still not feeling well, but I'm glad you were able to come in. Mr. Henley certainly will be happy to see you."

"I knew the work would be piling up, but this is even more than I expected. Mr. Dawson and Mr. Nicholls have already told me what happened." She glanced toward the bookkeepers' desks, but they were both busy at their work. Turning back to Alice, Mavis whispered, "They are indignant that Mr. Henley asked them to learn typewriting!"

"It was amusing to see their reactions," Alice admitted. "But I can't really blame them for refusing. They are busy enough as it is."

"But so are you!" Mavis protested.

"Yes, but I don't mind learning. I'll look into taking a course.

It would only be for emergencies, though. If for some reason you aren't here."

"Well, I hope there won't be too many of those. Aside from feeling terrible and losing pay, there's Mr. Clapper making everything worse. Mr. Nicholls told me he was spreading terrible rumors about me. Is that true?"

Alice hadn't planned to bring that up, but now that Mavis had asked, she had to answer. "He insinuated some things, but I'm sure everyone here discounts them."

"I hope so!" Mavis shivered. "Horrid man. He sees something perfectly respectable and twists it in his mind. The thing is, there *is* a clerk from the marine insurance company on the third floor who rather fancies me. We've eaten lunch together a few times. I know Mr. Clapper has seen me with him. His terrible imagination has no trouble filling in other lurid details that simply aren't true."

"As I said, everyone here knows not to believe everything Mr. Clapper says."

Mavis shook her head, still worried. "If Mr. Henley hears those rumors and believes them, I'd be out of a job before I could say one word in my defense." She blew once more into her handkerchief.

Alice patted her shoulder. "Don't worry. I'm working on a plan that I hope will make Mr. Clapper a little less, erm, irascible."

Mavis looked up at her in surprise. "Really? How will you do that?"

"I'll tell you about it if it works. For now, you'd better get started on that typing. Mr. Henley is surely more concerned about that than about any dubious hearsay."

Mavis nodded. "Thank you for the kind words. I suppose we girls have to stick together, don't we?"

"Yes, well . . ." Alice wasn't comfortable with the idea that she should stick up for someone merely because she was a woman. She'd do the same for anyone. "We are work colleagues first, aren't we?"

"Right," Mavis said. She straightened in her chair, gave Alice another grateful look, and began typing.

Alice had barely made it to her desk before Douglas breezed

in. He wore a broad smile and had a definite spring in his step. He gave a hearty greeting to the bookkeepers and then made his way to Mavis's desk. He gave her a solicitous bow. "How are you today, Miss Waller? All better, I trust?"

"Oh yes, sir!" She gave a quick swipe to her nose, then set the handkerchief in her lap as she attached her starry-eyed gaze to Douglas. "Ready for work, sir."

It was a distinctly different answer than she'd given to Alice, but that was to be expected. Whenever Douglas was nearby, Mavis was so excited, it was as though she had an electric current running through her. Her obvious infatuation with Douglas made Alice feel sorry for that marine insurance clerk. The poor man would have a tough time getting her full attention as long as Douglas held her in thrall.

"Very good, Miss Waller! Carry on!" he told her brightly.

"Someone is in a good mood today," Alice called out.

"Yes, indeed! Miss McNeil, could you come to my office for a moment?"

Alice could not think what this was about, but she willingly obeyed his summons. Given his demeanor, she figured that whatever it was could not be bad. She saw Mavis watching them with a touch of envy as they went to Douglas's office.

Douglas tossed his hat and umbrella on his desk, then turned to face Alice. He was grinning at her in such a way that her heart rate seemed to triple. Perhaps she ought not to be so critical of Mavis's reactions to him. His pull was undeniably hard to resist. He really was too handsome. That made it difficult to focus on the important things, but Alice was determined to keep trying.

"Is there some sort of good news?" she asked.

"Yes, and I have you to thank for it. Do you remember the comment you made on Friday, about Mr. Carnegie driving his coach-and-four in Hyde Park?"

Alice remembered now. With everything else that had happened this past weekend, she'd forgotten all about it. "Was Mr. Carnegie there? Did you speak to him?"

Douglas plucked a card from his coat pocket and put it in her hand. It was the business card for Mr. Carnegie.

"That's wonderful!" she exclaimed.

"He was not able to talk for long, as he was with his mother and their friends. Although brief, our chat was friendly and productive. He's interested in learning more about Henley and Company. In fact, we're planning to meet in Liverpool next month, just before he returns to America." He smoothed his coat lapels with the self-satisfied smile of a man who has accomplished something extraordinary.

"I'm so glad." She handed the card back to him. "Mr. Henley will be happy to hear this, too, I'm sure."

"I'll tell him the moment he gets in." Douglas returned the card to his breast pocket and gave it a joyful little tap. "The best part about having the meeting next month is that it gives us time to prepare. I'll look at where his railway lines run and gather other important data. If we can put together a deal, we might make some very good money on that western wheat."

For a moment, Alice thought he was including her in that use of *we*. Then she realized he was talking about Mr. Henley and perhaps Mr. Dawson, who was a master at tracking down all kinds of financial information about other companies. But then, the telegraph generally played a role in all these things, and Alice would be a part of that.

"I'm sure we'll all do what we can to make this a success," she said.

"Miss McNeil, I really can't thank you enough. It may have seemed like a random comment to you, but bits of genius like that are exactly what we need more of in this company."

He took her right hand and shook it vigorously. He even looked as though he wanted to kiss her, but Alice hastily assured herself that was definitely not the case—not unless he was beside himself with elation. She felt her heart skittering stupidly just the same.

"This really means a lot to you, doesn't it?" she said, finding her voice once he'd released her hand from his wonderfully warm grip.

He sobered a little. "I've come a very long way in my life, Miss McNeil, and so has Mr. Carnegie. You could say he's been a role model for me. If the son of a dirt-poor Scottish weaver can become a millionaire, then by heaven, so can I. Some may scoff and say, 'But he lives in America, where opportunity is waiting at every turn for those who seek it.' And I say, Britain is the greatest shipping nation in the world. I will find my way, too!"

There was passion and determination in his voice. Underneath his affability and charm was steely ambition. Alice had always considered herself a person of resolve, but her goals had been aimed at building a career that she found personally satisfying, something that would prove she was a person of integrity and worth. It seemed Douglas was focused on gaining wealth and the status that went with it. Although such drive was admirable, Alice wasn't sure it was entirely healthy for one's soul.

She was still mulling that over as she left his office.

Mavis waved her over excitedly. "What did he say?"

Alice tried to downplay it with a shrug. "He shared some good news about a potential client."

"That can't be all," Mavis protested. "Why was he so excited to tell *you* about it?"

"Well, I . . . may have made a suggestion that led to it." Joy burbled up inside her as she said the words.

Mavis must have noticed the pink tingeing Alice's cheeks. "You're a little in love with him, aren't you?" she challenged, lowering her voice so as not to be overheard by the other men. "I know I am."

"Really? I'd never have guessed."

Mavis giggled.

"I admire how talented and hardworking he is," Alice said, which was true.

"And handsome, too, don't forget," Mavis said with a sigh.

No, there was no way Alice was going to forget that. However, by now she had plenty of other, more logical reasons to like him. And a few reasons why she ought to use caution—such as her uneasiness about his ambitions. For the moment, she decided not to allow it to dampen the happiness she felt at having played a role in his recent success.

Hearing the sounder announce an incoming message, Alice had the perfect excuse to end this conversation. She turned away from Mavis's dreamy smile—which was too much a reflection of how Alice felt on the inside—and went to work.

⌁

That week turned out to be a busy one at Henley and Company. Every day was filled to the brim with a multitude of tasks. The office settled into a new, more energetic version of the routine that had been in place while Douglas had been away—probably because of the many client prospects and resulting projects he'd brought back with him. There had been a convergence of deadlines, too, relating to legal matters and documents to file for customs and shipping.

Alice didn't see Douglas outside of work, either. He worked long hours, often shut up in his office or Mr. Henley's.

It wasn't until Wednesday of the following week that there was anything even approaching a lull. The first hour of the morning had been quiet, with few incoming messages. Douglas and Mr. Henley were out of the office, tending to other company-related matters.

Alice sat reading the issue of *Lloyd's List* Douglas had given her. She was becoming more and more absorbed in the shipping news, now that she was familiar with the companies and shipping lines referenced in the articles. She was just finishing an interesting article about the modern uses of bill of lading contracts to improve overseas trade when Archie came in to work.

After his usual curt nod that sufficed for a greeting, he set about sharpening the six pencils he always kept on his desk. It was one of his rituals. At some point during his first hour at work, he would methodically work through each pencil.

Sometimes the telegrams came in so quickly that stopping to ink a pen cost precious time. Alice always kept two or three pencils handy. Yet she had never seen any telegrapher approach this as Archie had. He carefully kept exactly six, always in exactly the same configuration in the pencil holder on his desk. It was the one area where he was overly vigilant, in contrast to his slovenly appearance and other work habits.

Maybe he simply took pleasure in the task. It certainly seemed so.

This was the perfect time to attempt the idea Alice had dreamed up based on the spinster book. The previous week had simply been too busy, but now she thought it might be worth giving it a go.

She took out a pencil-sharpening device, a fairly recent invention that Archie never used. He always used a short knife with a sturdy blade. Inserting one of her pencils into the sharpener, she gave it a few turns before murmuring, "Oh, dear."

Archie looked up at her.

She pulled the pencil from the sharpener. "I seem to have broken the tip."

"Well, of course you have. Those things never work as well as a properly sharpened penknife."

"I'm afraid I never quite got the hang of that."

"There is an art to it," Archie said, launching into this subject with the pride of an expert. "Most people try holding the pencil horizontally while sharpening it, but the better method is to hold it with a downward slant. You should try it sometime. Maybe you wouldn't wear your pencils down to the nub so quickly."

It was his usual sarcastic attitude, but Alice merely nodded thoughtfully. "I think you're right. I don't suppose you'd be willing to show me?"

He looked at her as though trying to gauge the sincerity of her question. Alice gave him that wobbly smile she had used to such good effect with Fred.

Something in her look and posture must have convinced him she was genuinely interested. He took out his knife and a pencil to demonstrate. "I always hold it at a forty-five-degree angle, like so. It yields a better point."

She picked up one of her pencils. "Like this?" She purposefully angled it at a more shallow angle, about thirty degrees.

"No, not like that." He reached out and pushed down the tip of the pencil. "Like that."

"Ah yes, I see."

"The angle of the knife blade is critical, too. Watch." He demonstrated with the pencil he'd been sharpening. "Have you got a knife?"

"I'm afraid not. Might I borrow yours, just for a moment, to see if it is something I might be able to do?"

Once more he paused, and Alice could see he was genuinely undecided about whether to agree to her request. It was probably the first favor Alice had ever asked of him. She knew it would put her in his debt, and a touch of worry crawled up her spine. She could only hope this plan would succeed instead of making matters worse.

"All right." He handed the knife to her. "But listen carefully. I don't want you dulling the blade."

He spent the next few minutes explaining the exact way to move her hand so that the blade didn't shave off too much.

Alice followed his instructions carefully and did, in fact, end up with a nice point on her pencil. "There." She set down the pencil and returned the knife to him. "Thank you very much. I shall definitely acquire a proper knife as soon as I can." Honestly, she could have done the job twice as fast and just as well with the pencil sharpener. In fact, she'd been doing that for the three months she'd been working here. But somehow Archie had never noticed. "Is there a preferred brand?"

"There are several kinds you can buy. There's a shop with a good selection near Charing Cross station on the Strand."

He gave her the directions and spent another ten minutes pointing out the features she should look for in a good penknife. As with Fred and his dimple, Alice had apparently hit upon the right way to get on Archie's good side. She was almost sorry she hadn't been able to try this sooner.

"Thank you," she said again, infusing her words with as much honesty as she could muster.

He looked pleased, although the look of superiority Alice had anticipated was there as well. "I'm glad to see you are not entirely unwilling to accept good advice."

Nevertheless, that was the last caustic remark he sent in her direction. From then on, Archie's attitude was almost in the neighborhood of friendly.

Alice smiled to herself for the rest of the day.

CHAPTER

Thirteen

Well, what do you think?"

Douglas surveyed himself in the mirror while Hal and Carson looked on critically. He was preparing to meet Miss Penelope Rolland tonight, and he wanted to give the best impression. He was wearing a new suit made at a tailor's shop that Carson had recommended. It was more than he could afford, but he'd decided it was necessary. One had to dress richly in order to get wealthy people to take you seriously. Besides, if a deal with Mr. Carnegie came through, it would lead to opportunities and promotions that would allow him to pay off the suit in record time.

"I don't think that cravat is tied correctly," Hal said.

"It's exactly right," Carson retorted.

Douglas was inclined to accept Carson's opinion in these matters, as Hal was a careless dresser. "I think it's the best we can do."

"Just listen to Shaw talking himself down," Hal said. "As if he weren't the most handsome gentleman in London. If I had your looks, I'd chat up every lady at that party and wait to catch them when they swooned."

"I'm sure that's exactly what I'll be doing," Douglas said with an answering smirk. "But first I've got to hunt down a cab to ensure I get there on time." He gave one last tug to his coat and reached for his hat.

119

As he rode in the cab toward the Rollands' home, Douglas reviewed everything he could think of in preparation for tonight's events. Mr. Henley would introduce him to Miss Rolland and her father, and then—

And then?

Douglas's collar suddenly felt too tight. If there was one minor chink in the armor of confidence he'd built up over the years, it was that he still felt nervous when interacting socially with people in the upper classes.

He'd overcome much of his rudimentary schooling through personal effort and reading. However, books were of no real help to him in society drawing rooms. Not even etiquette books. They could not instill the ease at such events that those born into money seemed to have innately. When Douglas was negotiating business deals, he'd discovered men could overlook the occasional *faux pas*. But well-bred ladies had a higher standard. They might not be swooning in his arms, as Hal had joked, but they would expect him to flawlessly know the right words to say and actions to take.

He reminded himself that he'd successfully navigated a number of parties and dinners during his American trip without any embarrassing mistakes. However, none of those had been at the same social level as he was approaching tonight. In any case, he thought it likely the Americans were more forgiving. Moving among the English upper classes was going to be more difficult. They had rules of their own—most of them unwritten. He would need all his powers of observation to catch important cues.

He alighted from the cab and paid the driver, then walked up the steps of the elegant townhome. Taking a deep breath, he rapped on the door.

⁂

"What do you think, Miss T?" Alice asked. Since the cat had just jumped up on the table, scattering a stack of letters and nearly tipping over the inkpot, Alice assumed the creature wanted to give her opinion.

Quite naturally, now that she had Alice's attention, the cat was content merely to sit on one of the envelopes and begin washing a paw.

Alice gently dislodged the letter from underneath Miss T. It was the note she'd received from her sister, Annie, urging her to come home for a visit in a few weeks' time. Their parents' fortieth wedding anniversary was coming up, and her siblings were planning a big celebration.

Alice smiled. Miss T might well want to hide that note, as she didn't like it when her mistress was away and she had to remain entirely out of doors. Not that the cat wasn't well fed during that time; Alice's neighbor Mr. Sacker, a retired fish merchant, always came up with tasty scraps for her. However, given that Miss T was proportionately as advanced in years as her namesake, she loved the comfort of sleeping on Alice's sofa.

"You are a prissy thing, aren't you?" Alice teased, stroking her cat's thick, soft fur. "Even so, I shall have to go." She sighed. "More's the pity."

She would have preferred to stay in town. It wasn't that she didn't love her family. She was heartily thankful to have grown up in such a loving—if somewhat disorganized—home. The problem was, now that her sister had made a happy marriage, the hints from her mother that Alice might do the same were growing more frequent and bothersome. Alice had hoped her mother's worries on that subject would dissipate once Annie was settled and had a good husband to provide for her. With two of her brothers and her sister now married, there were three solid households that could support her parents and provide any help they needed as they grew older. Instead, her mother had grown more fretful on the subject.

Alice might have been able to wave away the hints like a pesky housefly, were it not for the fact that her mother had begun to sway her father's opinion as well. That was very hard to bear. After all, he had taught her Morse code and had been proud to see her become an accomplished telegrapher in her own right. He'd encouraged her independent nature and been stalwart in supporting her decision to strike out on her own. The joke in their family circle was that after becoming father to three boys, he hadn't noticed the fourth child was a girl and had treated her just the same as the others. It wasn't until Annie had come along and grown into a proper, ribbons-and-lace sort of young lady that anyone else thought Alice ought to do the same.

Letting out another sigh, Alice absently scratched Miss T behind the ears. The cat rewarded this behavior by emitting a smooth purr, which vibrated against Alice's hand, causing her to smile. "You like our current setup just fine, don't you, my dear?"

Miss T bumped Alice's hand with her chin, encouraging her to keep going, but Alice gave the cat a final pat and rose from the table.

"You've reminded me that I ought to get this letter to your namesake down to the postbox."

Now retired from running her school, Miss Templeton resided in a small seaside village in Sussex. Alice wrote to her at least twice a month, sharing news about her work and other activities. There had been a lot to talk about in this letter! Alice was excited to report how well Henley and Company was doing and about her share in it. She'd even mentioned Mr. Shaw's return from abroad and how he'd been impressed with Alice and encouraged her to take on a larger role in the company. She knew Miss Templeton would be proud to receive that news.

Alice always looked forward to Miss Templeton's replies. While never long, her letters were usually filled with mildly acerbic anecdotes about the "old people" in her village, as though Miss Templeton were not to be counted among those elderly folk but was merely an observer, still a woman in her prime.

"Now, where did that letter get to?" Alice picked up the papers Miss T had so carelessly sent to the floor. "Ah, there it is."

She pulled the envelope from the stack and set it next to her reticule, which lay on a chair near the door. The rest of the papers went back on the table, which Miss T had now vacated. Sensing Alice was about to go out, the cat had jumped to the floor and watched as Alice donned her hat.

They went outside together. Miss T went off in search of creatures to stalk or other adventures. Alice set off down the street, knowing the cat would either let herself back in through the window or be waiting for her by the door when she got home.

At the street corner, Alice dropped the letter into the tall red postbox. As she did, it occurred to her that she hadn't heard from Miss Templeton in nearly a month. This wasn't so unusual, as her letters had been sporadic at times. Whenever that happened, Miss Templeton generally explained the lapse by saying she'd been busy with household matters or helping others in the town. She would never admit to being ill or otherwise indisposed. Alice felt a little worried. She prayed her old teacher was doing well.

The lamplighters were out, but the evening held a touch of pleasant coolness after a day of rain, and Alice didn't feel like going home just yet. She walked along the familiar street. Realizing her feet were taking her to the bookshop, she found herself thinking of Douglas Shaw. What was he doing this evening? Then she chided herself. Why should it matter where he was? What he did on his own time was his business.

Mr. Meyer was watching over the shop tonight. Upon seeing Alice, he said, "There's our best customer!"

"How is Nellie?" Alice asked after they had exchanged further greetings.

"Oh, very fine, very fine. She thought she might like some extra rest tonight. She gets tired so easily now, what with the baby on the way." Mr. Meyer took off his glasses and rubbed them on his shirt. His eyes were misty. "It will be my first grandson, don't you know."

"Grandson?" Alice repeated, pointedly emphasizing the last syllable.

"Ah well, a man can dream," Mr. Meyer replied with a wink. "Nothing wrong with a little girl, of course. We'll love having one of those, too. Perhaps for the next one." He put his glasses back on his face, beaming at the idea of being a grandfather.

Alice understood the thinking behind his words. First have a son, someone to carry on the family name. There was *nothing wrong* with having a girl, once the important goal of getting a son and heir was taken care of. She supposed she couldn't blame him, as men of his age generally held old-fashioned notions about such things. Even so, she felt a touch of indignation.

As soon as she could, she politely broke off the conversation in order to peruse the bookshelves. Occasionally she picked out a book and looked through it with interest. When she reached the row where the spinster book had been, she warmed with amusement at the memory of the night she'd bought it. That book had certainly provided some interesting ideas and experiences—even if Alice hadn't been using it to find *love and romance*. Thus far, she'd used it for *warming up irascible men to be not quite so irritating*. But that wasn't a book title that would draw a lot of buyers.

With a wry chuckle at herself, Alice left the shop and made her way home.

⚬⚬⚬

Miss Penelope Rolland was, in real life, somewhat less of a beauty than advertised. While not exactly stout, she was a trifle too filled out for her short stature. She had rather a wide face, too, and a short nose that turned up at the end. However, with the help of a first-rate ladies' maid and dressmaker, she managed to look pretty enough. Her gown was a flattering shade of blue, and her dark brown hair was braided and twisted so artfully behind her head that it was a veritable work of art.

These were Douglas's first thoughts upon meeting her, along with the suspicion that she had the self-confidence of a young lady who was constantly told she was beautiful because she was rich.

She greeted Douglas warmly, her blue eyes sparkling in the gaslight. Her gaze traveled over his well-tailored suit with an air of approval. That confirmed to Douglas that however long it took to repay the tailor, it would be worth it.

"So you are the Mr. Shaw I've been hearing so much about."

"Have you?" Douglas feigned surprise, though he was well

aware that Mr. Henley had already told Miss Rolland's father all about Douglas's successes and prospects.

Her father stood beside her, inspecting Douglas with what was probably a very different set of criteria than his daughter's. Mr. Rolland had come from a reasonably wealthy family, but he'd greatly enlarged his fortune through smart trading in stocks. He did not look like a man who would be willing to bestow his daughter's generous dowry on just any suitor.

Douglas met his gaze confidently, prepared for any type of interrogation Mr. Rolland might pursue, but for the moment, Mr. Rolland simply welcomed him inside and offered to introduce him to the other guests.

Now that Douglas was in the thick of it, he found his excitement was overcoming his earlier concerns. He'd breached an important threshold and was in the inner sanctum of London's upper classes. He shook hands with the gentlemen and repeated the requisite niceties to the ladies. He was not yet rubbing elbows with the aristocracy, as there were no titled persons at this party. But those things would come in time. Douglas noted the look of pleasure on Mr. Henley's face, a reflection of how well he thought things were going.

Mrs. Henley had come, too, and kept throwing worried looks at Douglas as though afraid he'd make some grave mistake. Even after all his years of working with her husband and the increasing ways Henley had been relying on him, her relationship with Douglas was still strained. Maybe her distrust of him was precisely *because* of his growing importance to the company. After all, her fortunes were bound up in Henley and Company as well. He suspected she didn't like having to rely on someone with Douglas's lowly origins. Mr. Henley never seemed to think twice about Douglas's background, whereas his wife never seemed to forget it.

Nor did it help that she was Archie Clapper's cousin. Clapper was bound to speak ill of him to her, as he did with everybody. Douglas had the feeling Mrs. Henley believed more of Clapper's bilge than she ought to. He would have to work hard tonight to impress her, but he accepted the challenge as a point of personal pride.

There were about twenty guests at the party, enough to fill Mr. Rolland's generously sized dining room without overcrowding it. As far as Douglas could tell, there was only one other person there who might be a rival for Miss Rolland's hand: a junior bank officer by the name of Edward Busfield. The first indication he was in the running was when he was designated to take Miss Rolland from the drawing room down to dinner. Douglas had the honor of escorting Miss Rolland's widowed aunt. Judging by the smile on the elder lady's face, she was quite pleased with this arrangement. By contrast, although Miss Rolland accepted Busfield's arm with a gracious smile, she allowed her gaze to rest on Douglas for a long moment before she was led off by her escort.

Busfield seemed respectable enough, but in Douglas's estimation, he was not a man who would stand out in a crowd. Miss Rolland exchanged pleasantries with him during dinner, but he did not command her full attention. She kept sending glances at Douglas. Although to be fair, she spent a lot of time looking at everyone, seemingly interested in what each guest was doing and attempting to catch snippets of all the conversations at the table. Collecting gossip to disseminate later with her friends? Or just naturally curious? Douglas didn't know her well enough to make a guess.

After dinner, the ladies left the room so the gentlemen could enjoy brandy and cigars. That was when Douglas's initial impressions of Busfield were confirmed. He came across as little more than a drone for his bank and added nothing of interest to the conversation. By the time the men got up to rejoin the ladies in the parlor, Douglas had reached the conclusion that despite the gaps in his social experience, he could be considered a better prospect for any lady's hand.

He was given greater reason to believe this when Miss Rolland made a beeline for him as soon as he entered the parlor. She was accompanied by her aunt, who suddenly had several urgent questions about banking and widows' pensions that she wished to address to Busfield. *Confidential* questions that had her taking Busfield by the elbow to another corner of the room. Had the two women planned this as a distraction so Miss Rolland could speak privately with Douglas? It was an idea he was happy to consider.

Miss Rolland smiled up at him. "I thought you all would never be finished with your brandy and cigars. Things are so dull without the men around." There was a coy smile playing around her lips.

"Tell me, Miss Rolland, what is it you ladies talk about while we are arguing over politics in the dining room?"

"The usual things, I suppose." She began to tick off items on her fingers. "The upcoming flower show, what we shall wear to Ascot, and—"

"Gossip?" he supplied, giving his voice a teasing lilt.

Miss Rolland's lips puckered into a mock pout. "Shame on you, Mr. Shaw, for thinking so ill of the ladies. I was going to say our plans for the week."

"Well, those sound like more important matters than politics."

"My aunt and I were discussing a little excursion to Finsbury Park in search of butterflies."

Here was a turn to the conversation he'd not been expecting. "Butterflies?"

"Are you interested in lepidopterology? I myself am a devoted lepidopterist." She sounded as if she thoroughly enjoyed the feel of those words rolling over her lips.

Given the vocabulary he'd heard her use so far this evening, Douglas had a wicked thought that these were perhaps the largest words she knew. "I must admit I don't know much about butterflies, although I certainly enjoy looking at them."

She smiled again, as though Douglas were flirting with her. Was he? Inwardly, he shrugged. He didn't know a lot about these things, but he could recognize when a person was enjoying his company.

"Well, they are a passion of mine!" she said. "I have a lovely collection. Perhaps I might show it to you sometime."

"I'd very much like to see it. Doesn't collecting butterflies require a lot of travel?"

"Oh, I've been all over England. But there are still a few specimens that I am told I might be able to find right here in London. In fact—" She paused for a moment to survey the room. Her gaze lit upon her father. He was on the other side of the parlor, and she seemed satisfied that he was too engrossed in conversation with Henley to be paying attention to her. "In fact, I intend to go to Finsbury Park tomorrow. This is the time of year when one can sometimes find the *Colias croceus*, the clouded yellow butterfly that migrates from the continent." She paused, focusing her gaze on him. "I don't suppose you ever go walking out toward Finsbury Park on a Saturday afternoon?"

It was an invitation, clear as if she'd written it on gold-edged paper. A park where perhaps not so many of the well-to-do might be found. How interesting.

"Why yes, as a matter of fact, I often go up there to, er, enjoy the view. I was thinking I might stroll out there myself. Perhaps around . . ." He paused. What was the best time of day for finding butterflies? He had no idea. "Perhaps around midafternoon?"

"I will be leaving for the park just after luncheon. Wouldn't it be surprising if we met?"

"Yes, very surprising indeed," Douglas agreed.

Breaking free at last from the elderly aunt, Busfield came over to join them.

Douglas had no further opportunities for private conversation with Miss Rolland. The rest of the evening was largely taken up with business talk between him and Mr. Rolland and Mr. Henley.

As he was leaving, Miss Rolland bade him good night with a warm handshake and a smiling look that seemed to confirm their "accidental" meeting for tomorrow. Although he had no way of knowing, Douglas was pretty sure Miss Rolland hadn't offered up any opportunities for an accidental meeting with Busfield.

On top of an evening that had gone well for his business, knowing he'd bested a bank officer in this regard made Douglas feel that tonight had been an unqualified success.

CHAPTER
Fourteen

I t's perfect!" Lucy enthused, draping the scarf around Alice's neck. "This shade of blue is exquisite. Perfect for your skin tone. I don't know why we didn't get this one before."

Once more they were in Drake and Sons department store, but this time it was Alice's idea. She had decided to take Douglas's advice and try to add more interest to her wardrobe. It was purely for business purposes, of course. She wasn't going to do anything out of vanity. *"A woman's vanity springs from her desire for love; by winning love, she thinks she has won power over the man."* So said the spinster book, at any rate—and Alice definitely did not desire either love or power over men. She was merely interested in expanding her potential for success.

"I'm so happy to see you taking an interest in fine things!" Lucy said as they left the store. "Shall we go to my dressmaker's next? I would love to see you fitted up with a pretty new gown."

"I'm afraid I haven't time today," Alice replied. "I have another errand to run."

While this was true, it was also a good excuse to avoid the dressmaker's shop. A new gown from the dressmaker Lucy patronized would be far out of Alice's price range. While Lucy would undoubtedly offer to pay for it, Alice could not in good conscience accept such an expensive gift.

"What could be more important than a new gown?" Lucy asked with innocent honesty.

"I'm going to the Strand. I need to buy a penknife for sharpening pencils."

Lucy looked less than impressed. "That sounds terribly dull."

Alice laughed at her reaction, all the more so because Lucy didn't realize she'd made a pun. "Don't worry, I'm not asking you to come."

"All right, but I shall get you to that shop soon!" Lucy threatened. She paused before getting into her waiting carriage. "Yes, I do like that color on you," she said, looking at Alice's scarf. Like last time, Alice had worn it out of the store rather than having it wrapped. Lucy added, "I like to think I'm the one who changed your mind about fashion, although I expect some other person may have been the reason for it."

"I beg your pardon?" Alice asked, startled. She could not think how Lucy could possibly have guessed that Douglas had put this idea into Alice's head. Alice rarely mentioned him to Lucy, and when she did, it was only in passing and relating generally to things at work.

Lucy gave her that knowing smile—the one that always meant she was wrong about whatever she thought she was right about. "I received a letter from Fred yesterday. He asked me to send you his very kindest regards."

"Ah yes," Alice said, choking back a grimace. "How very kind of him." She thought it best not to reveal that it had been a man at work who'd sparked her interest in improving her wardrobe. Lucy might jump to a new and equally wrong conclusion.

Was it better or worse for Lucy to make assumptions about Alice's interest in Fred rather than thinking something similar about a different man? That was too hard to decide—and neither, she told herself firmly, were correct.

She gave her friend a quick good-bye and set off toward the Strand.

Douglas had been walking around Finsbury Park for perhaps half an hour when he finally located Miss Rolland and her chaperone.

Given the size of the park, it might have taken much longer except Miss Rolland seemed to enjoy shrieking with delight as she waved her butterfly net in the general direction of her prey. Her chaperone, a plump, gray-haired woman, was more subdued, standing far enough away to avoid the wildly swinging net.

Douglas strode up the hill, calling out, "Miss Rolland! What a pleasant surprise to see you here!" He said this to keep up the ruse of the accidental meeting, not knowing whether the chaperone was in on the charade. He didn't take any particular satisfaction from these little games men and women were supposed to play, but it wasn't so bad if he thought of it as similar to the way businessmen would cut and parry during negotiations.

Miss Rolland paused midswing. "Oh!" She turned to face Douglas as he closed the distance between them. "Mr. Shaw! How wonderful to see you again."

"May I say you are looking quite lovely today." It was a line he had memorized, but he felt no guilt saying it. Miss Rolland's summer frock of white muslin edged in navy blue was very fetching, and the tinge of pink in her cheeks from the sun and exercise did her no harm.

"It's very kind of you to say so." She smiled sweetly at him as she placed a hand on her heart. "I'm sure the wind has blown my hair into a rat's nest." She gave a little laugh as she tucked a stray curl under her hat.

Was she fishing for another compliment? He figured a woman could never have too many of those. But if he was going to flatter her, he was going to stick to the truth. "You look charming."

She beamed at him in response. So far, so good.

Miss Rolland turned to her chaperone. "Mrs. Glover, it appears the sun is turning your nose quite red. I should hate for you to suffer a burn. Perhaps you might like to take a rest in the shade?" She indicated a park bench located under the trees.

"Thank you, miss. That's very kind." Mrs. Glover retreated to the bench—which, Douglas noted, was a comfortable distance away, giving them room to speak privately.

Once they were alone, Douglas asked, "Have you managed to find that elusive *Colias croceus*?"

She looked at him blankly.

He pointed toward her net, which now lay forgotten on the grass. "The clouded yellow butterfly."

"Oh." She shook her head. "No, only a few grizzled skippers. I already have specimens of those. But I am not discouraged. After all, the sport is in the chase, is it not?"

She took his arm as though he had offered to escort her somewhere, and began walking. Although taken by surprise, Douglas smoothly fell in step with her.

The spring breeze carried a bouquet of pleasing smells. As he took a deep breath to enjoy them, Douglas noticed some of the floral scents were emanating from Miss Rolland. He suspected she was adept at using every tool in her feminine arsenal for attracting men.

"It was Papa's idea that I take up lepidopterology," she said, smiling up at him from time to time as they walked. "He feels I should cultivate some intellectual interests in order to be well rounded. However, I like it because it provides plenty of opportunities to get outside. Much as I adore dinner parties and dances, there are times when life can be so stuffy indoors. Especially if there are too many people about when one wants to have a private conversation."

"A very astute observation."

She looked pleased at the compliment. "Isn't it nice that we should happen to meet like this, where we can enjoy the lovely day and get to know one another better?"

"Indeed it is." How interesting that she was keeping up the pretense about the accidental meeting even though no one else was within earshot. Douglas wasn't entirely sure how he felt about that. Did she actually believe her own fantasies?

She fluttered her eyelashes at him. "Tell me all about yourself, Mr. Shaw. I want to know *everything*."

"Hmm." Douglas allowed a hint of a teasing grin to warm his features. "That might take a while. Might we narrow down the topic?"

"I already know about your profession and your prospects." She spoke as though those were only minor details. Douglas knew just how important they were. They'd opened the door for him to meet her in the first place. Not to mention how crucial it was that she marry someone who could support her. She continued, "Papa has told me he believes you will go far in life."

"Did he?" This was gratifying news.

"He thinks highly of you. Everyone does. Except perhaps for Mr. Busfield." She giggled. "But I suspect what he said about you was prompted by envy."

It would seem Miss Rolland's brand of flirtation involved playing him against another suitor. Did she wish to stoke a competition between him and Busfield? Douglas was curious to know if the man had actually spoken ill of him, or whether Miss Rolland was misrepresenting his words. He decided to take a neutral stance.

He gave a casual shrug. "I'm afraid I don't know Mr. Busfield well enough to form an opinion of him."

"Let's not spend any more time talking about him," Miss Rolland chided, even though she'd been the one to bring up the subject. "I want to know about *you*. Which part of Scotland are you from? What was it like growing up there? It seems an exciting and mysterious place."

Of all the words to describe his early life, Douglas would never have chosen *exciting* or *mysterious*. "What makes you say that?"

"Why, there are so many interesting things! The mountains blanketed in purple heather. The men in kilts playing their bagpipes. The mist on the lochs." Her voice became dramatic. "The ruined castles, haunted by the tortured souls who used to live there."

Miss Rolland was imagining Scotland the way the guidebooks painted it. Or perhaps accounts written by the Queen herself during her frequent stays at her royal estate at Balmoral.

"Aye, Scotland has many beautiful places, although my experiences were perhaps not as *picturesque* as Her Majesty's." Douglas allowed his Scottish brogue to come forward, softening a comment that might otherwise have sounded caustic. Most of his childhood had been spent in a squalid row house in the poorest part of Glasgow, near the bleak industrial shipyards. He had not romped among the heather as a child; he and his friends had played with sticks and discarded bits of iron on a narrow, grimy street. The only royalty there were the men who were kings at hard drinking and fighting.

As a child, Douglas hadn't known a single person who wasn't struggling to keep the wolf from the door. At first, he had resented being taken out of school as a lad, forced into work to help support his family when his father had become unable to work. But being a messenger boy had shown him another reality: not everyone was poor. As Douglas shuttled telegrams between businesses and prosperous warehouses and the mansions of wealthy merchants, he saw a completely different side of Glasgow. Men in suits and top hats of the best quality, walking down the street as if they owned it. Homes filled with light and laughter. Fine carriages with splendid horses and footmen in their livery.

Once he had confided to a neighbor that he would one day work his way up to owning such fine things. The man had scoffed. "They'll ensure you don't, my lad. They're not interested in sharing the wealth, only in keeping us down and profiting off our backbreaking work."

But Douglas was proving that it could be done. He had come so far, and now he was on the verge of even greater advances. Even standing here in this meadow, talking with a wealthy young lady who was clearly interested in him, was proof of that.

"Mr. Shaw?" She was looking at him quizzically.

He gave himself a mental shake. How had it been so easy for those bitter memories to surface? He thought he had set those sorrows aside years ago. Other than sending money to his parents every month and the obligatory pilgrimage to their home a few times a year, he generally did his best not to think about them at all.

There was no way he could hide his humble beginnings, but he could at least downplay the grimmer aspects. Otherwise, Miss Rolland might think less of him. She might even worry that he'd be like the drunken louts in the slums who mistreated their wives and children. At least Douglas's father had been kind, if criminally lacking in ambition. He never rose above being a common laborer in the shipyards.

"Och, me lassie, I was just pausin' fer a moment to remember me dear home." He struck a pose with his hand on his heart and his gaze cast off in the distance.

Miss Rolland's face lit with amusement. "And where was that? In Edinburgh?"

Returning to a more casual stance, Douglas shook his head. "I grew up in Glasgow. While it is not as popular with tourists as Edinburgh, it is an important center for business. The shipyards provide the means for Great Britain to be the trading powerhouse that it is."

"Was your father in shipping?"

"Yes," Douglas said, allowing her to infer what she liked from that simple answer. "But London's my home now. I've come here, to the place Shakespeare dubbed the very 'forge and working house of thought,' to make my own mark on the world."

"My goodness!" Miss Rolland exclaimed. "Mr. Shaw, I hope you leave time in your schedule for leisure activities. As the saying goes, 'All work and no play makes Jack a dull boy.'"

"I'm here today, enjoying a lovely walk with a charming lady. I would say that is the very best use of leisure time."

She preened. "You're very kind. But there is even more fun to be had elsewhere. At the home of Lord and Lady Tilney, for example. Will you be going?"

"I'm afraid I don't know much about it. Can you enlighten me?" He was already intrigued. To rub elbows with the aristocracy would be another feather in his cap.

"You never know what famous personage might be there. The Tilneys know everyone! And of course, there is the dancing!"

Douglas felt his stomach lurch. He swallowed. "Dancing?"

"Yes! It's their annual charity ball. There will even be some Scottish country dancing, as Lady Tilney's father is a Scottish baron."

"Do you enjoy dancing, Miss Rolland?" Douglas asked, though the answer was painfully obvious.

"Why, naturally! Doesn't everyone?" She scrunched her nose.

"Except for my father, and perhaps a few stuffy men of his acquaintance. But Mr. Busfield is quite an accomplished dancer."

There she was, bringing up that name again. Douglas didn't think she sincerely favored the bank officer over him, but he couldn't be sure. It was just that level of uncertainty that she was doing her best to instill in him. And in this case, Busfield probably did have the upper hand. Perhaps it was time for Douglas to have another try at lessons from that dancing master—or better yet, find one who was more capable.

His throat constricted, but he forced himself to speak, keeping the greater goal in mind. This was an opportunity to meet titled and well-connected people. "It sounds lovely. Perhaps you might secure me an invitation?"

"Yes, I'm sure I can. Lady Tilney's sister is a particular friend of my aunt." Her eyes were shining with excitement. "How wonderful it will be! My favorite dance is the waltz. Do you have a favorite dance, Mr. Shaw?"

"Oh—well, I, er, I enjoy so many of them." He patted her arm. "Why don't you tell me more about this butterfly-collecting hobby of yours?" He tried to sound relaxed and carefree, as though the weight in the pit of his stomach at the thought of dancing were not becoming heavier by the moment.

"I have a secret to tell you," Miss Rolland whispered.

"Oh?"

"I don't actually collect the butterflies myself. I secretly buy my specimens from a man in Kent. I know it's terribly naughty to mislead my father about this. However, he likes it so very much that I have this hobby. I keep up the pretense because I've decided that as long as he's happy, that's the important thing. Wouldn't you agree?"

"It's hard to fault that logic," Douglas answered, painfully aware of the irony of his words. In a sense, he had a similar goal with Miss Rolland. Unfortunately, he didn't think there was any way to keep her happy without actually dancing with her himself.

CHAPTER

Fifteen

I t is a conundrum," Carson said as he and Douglas talked over the situation in the boardinghouse parlor. True to her word, Miss Rolland had secured Douglas an invitation to the charity ball.

"What's the conundrum?" Hal asked, coming through the door in time to hear Carson's remark. He was carrying a small pork pie, which he began eating as soon as he'd plopped down in one of the chairs. Hal often frequented the pie seller whose cart was located at the end of their street. Sometimes Douglas thought his friend single-handedly kept the vendor in business.

"Don't let Mrs. Taylor see you eating that in here," Carson cautioned.

Hal took a moment to enjoy a bite of his pie, his mouth turned up in a satisfied smile, and then swallowed before answering. "Today's Thursday. Our dear landlady always goes to her friend's house for tea on Thursday. Besides, if she fed us properly, I wouldn't be needin' to look elsewhere for more food, now, would I?" He took another bite. "What's the conundrum?" he asked again, his mouth half-full.

"Shaw has to learn to dance in order to successfully woo Miss Penelope Rolland," Carson said, summing up the problem.

"Has to *finally* learn to dance," Hal corrected. "It's not like we haven't been trying to teach him these past two years." He pulled a handkerchief from his coat pocket and wiped a pie crumb from the corner of his mouth.

Douglas groaned, rubbing his forehead. He'd overcome so many challenges that were harder than dancing. A veritable mountain of them. Why was this one thing so impossible for him to master? He'd even taken dancing lessons for six months. That had ended when the dancing master finally declared there was nothing he could do for Douglas, saying in a rather supercilious tone that some men were simply born without the capability to dance. He'd suggested that Douglas only attend parties where suitable excuses were available for not dancing, such as billiards or card games.

Douglas had a feeling, though, that even if such pursuits were available at Lord Tilney's ball, Miss Rolland wasn't the type to take no for an answer. Visions of treading all over her feet filled his thoughts. What if he broke one of her toes? That would put an abrupt end to his chances with her.

"Don't lose heart," Hal said between more mouthfuls of pie. "How much time do we have?"

"The ball is in two weeks," Carson answered. Douglas was still shaking his head, wondering how he was going to get out of this.

"We're in luck, then," Hal declared. "There's a tea dance at Ally Pally on Saturday. There's always a congenial crowd, and the music's good. Plus, my Mamie's a right good dancer. I'll bet she could teach you what you need to know."

"No!" Douglas blurted.

The Ally Pally, or Alexandra Palace, was in fact an entire entertainment complex. Located on an expansive hill just north of London, the "palace" housed a theater and other meeting rooms. The grounds also boasted a race course, cricket and bicycling grounds, a lake, and a pleasure garden. Hundreds of people flocked there daily. There was no way Douglas was going to subject himself to dancing lessons in the middle of a crowded dance floor.

He had spoken with such vehemence that his friends sat looking at him in surprise. He cleared his throat. "It wouldn't do any good. Six months with the dancing master proved that."

"Ah, but sometimes the ladies can teach you something you might not learn otherwise," Hal replied, speaking with the air of a sage.

"Aren't you worried about me dancing with your ladylove?" Douglas teased.

"Not at all. She's too sensible to fall for the likes of you—a handsome bloke on his way up in the world. She has no delusions of grandeur. She knows she's better off settling for me."

Douglas raised his brows. "That's some compliment."

Hal grinned. "I give her those kinds of compliments all the time. She likes it." Having finished off his pie, he wiped his hands with his handkerchief. "So what do you say?"

"Absolutely not. Thank you for the offer, but it couldn't possibly work. Besides, I have something else to do that day."

"Which is?"

Douglas scrambled for an excuse. "Well, there's . . . work. Mr. Carnegie has agreed to meet with me in Liverpool in a few weeks. I need to be prepared."

"What are you going to do about the dancing?" Carson asked.

"I'll make up some excuse." He thought back to the dancing master's remarks about finding a diversion. What could he do or say to avoid dancing with Miss Rolland without disappointing her? He snapped his fingers. "I'll say I twisted my ankle while riding and the doctor says to rest it for a few weeks. Perhaps even a month." By then, perhaps, he might have secured her undying regard. After that, the rest would take care of itself.

"You're going to lie to her?" Carson said, looking appalled.

Carson was the sort of chap who never strayed from the belief that honesty was the best policy. Typically, this described Douglas, too. But desperate times called for desperate measures.

He said with grim determination, "I'll deliberately fall off that horse if I have to."

⁂

"Is that your new penknife?" Archie asked.

Alice had placed the new knife on the edge of her desk closest to Archie's to ensure he saw it. She'd noticed his gaze on it several times, but he hadn't said anything until now. Alice had been waiting for him to mention it.

Nodding, she picked it up. "I bought it at that shop on the Strand you told me about. The man was very helpful, just as you said he'd be." She held out the knife. "Would you like to see it?"

Archie took it and looked it over. "It's a good brand," he said, reading the name painted on the metal handle. "May I test it?"

"Yes, please do. I'd like very much to get your opinion. I believe he sold me a good knife, but I don't know enough about these things to be sure."

To Alice, her words sounded like pandering, similar to that story in the spinster book about the widow who suddenly forgot how to send a telegram. But in fact, it was true. This was one area where Alice did not have much experience. At least she could be honest about it, and the words still had the desired effect. Archie looked pleased that she'd consulted his expert opinion.

"I can tell you if it's any good." He opened the blade and scrutinized it, then tried it out on one of his pencils. "It's acceptable," he said, setting his pencil carefully back in the holder with the others. He gave the knife back to Alice. "I might have chosen one with more weight in the handle, but this is good for a woman, I think."

"That's what the shopkeeper told me," Alice said, trying not to roll her eyes. The clerk had had the same condescending attitude toward women that Archie had.

Alice considered this the end of her experiment with Archie. Hopefully the goodwill she'd gained from it would remain, which would make the whole endeavor worth it. She was unlikely ever to use that knife, except perhaps from time to time when Archie was watching. She'd just have to be careful to use her pencil-sharpening device only when he wasn't around.

One sign that Archie's agreeableness was going to last—at least for today, at any rate—occurred a short while later when Alice prepared to go on her lunch break.

"You can leave those with me," he said, pointing toward a stack of messages to be sent out. "There hasn't been too much incoming today, so I'll probably have some time."

Alice thought her jaw was going to hit the floor. Archie *never* volunteered to do extra work. Especially not outgoing messages. Many of them needed to be encoded before sending, and he was generally too lazy to go through the extra effort of thumbing through the codebook to find the needed words. That was why he preferred to work the incoming messages. With those, he could simply write down verbatim what came in and give the messages to Mavis to decode as she typed them up.

"Are you sure?" Alice said, blinking in surprise.

He frowned at her. "Do you think I'll get something wrong?" he accused. The business with the pencils had eased some of his surliness, but it hadn't changed his basic nature. He still got testy far too easily.

"No, no, of course not." Alice handed him the messages. "Thank you."

Still marveling, she collected the food she'd brought for lunch and the current issue of the *Telegraphic Journal and Electrical Review* that she planned to read while eating. She glanced at Douglas's office as she walked by, but the door was closed. He'd only been out twice all morning, and those times he'd seemed distracted about something. Alice thought he might be worried about a complicated legal issue that had arisen with a shipment in customs. Perhaps when she got back from lunch, she'd check to see if there was anything she could do to help collect the required information to take to the customs house.

As she passed Mavis's desk, Mavis put out a hand to draw her over. "How did you get him to start being nice to you?" she whispered, pointing toward Archie.

"Always appeal to their conceit," Alice said. Smiling, she went out to enjoy her lunch.

Realizing he'd been reading the same sentence for a quarter of an hour and its meaning still hadn't registered in his brain, Douglas finally dropped the paper onto the desk and leaned back in his chair. He rubbed his eyes as though they were somehow to blame, when he knew the problem went deeper.

With the amount of work he had to do, it was foolish to allow something as simple as a dance to derail him. Realistically, he'd always known that if he aspired to rise in society, he would have to conquer this issue. Now he was at the point of do or die. He had to find a solution.

Despite his earlier declarations to his friends, he was still undecided about what to do. Feigning injury was the coward's way out. On the other hand, attempting the dance would have as much chance of success as the Charge of the Light Brigade.

As he generally considered himself to be a man of integrity, Douglas also contemplated the more honest route of simply admitting to Miss Rolland that he couldn't dance. Perhaps he was overestimating how she would react to that news. Maybe it would make no difference to her. On the other hand, even if she snubbed him, it would be a setback but not the end of the world.

"No," Douglas said. He stood up and began pacing his office. If there was one thing he hated, it was admitting defeat. He wasn't ready to do that yet.

He paused at his window, which opened onto the street behind the building. He noticed Alice McNeil coming out of the little lane that ran alongside the office. The lane where he'd overheard her berating Archie Clapper. He chuckled at the memory. It provided a much-needed bit of cheer after the morning he'd wasted fretting.

Alice had a newspaper tucked under her arm, and she carried a small oilcloth parcel that probably contained food. He wondered if she was planning to eat her lunch at the nearby church, which had a small park attached. Workers in the area often sat on the benches under the trees to eat their midday meal. Douglas had sat out there himself a number of times, especially if he was mulling over a problem. It was a rare and pleasant little patch of green in the city's maze of brick and stone.

Maybe a touch of fresh air would be good for him, too. It might clear his brain. He grabbed his hat and went out.

He bought a hand pie and an apple from a street vendor, then made his way to the church park. Sure enough, Alice sat there, absorbed in her reading as she munched on a piece of cheese.

"May I join you?"

She looked up, surprised, then smiled when she saw the food he was holding. "I see you are eating a clerk's lunch today, Mr. Shaw," she teased.

"Never hurts to economize." He took a seat next to her on the bench. "What are you reading?"

"It's the *Telegraphic Journal and Electrical Review*."

By now, Douglas knew enough about her reading preferences that he wasn't surprised at her choice. The journal was filled with technical articles, mostly about advances in machinery and other updates in the field of telegraphy. He liked that Alice had a hunger to learn new things. He was the same way. Even so, he found the journal could be dry reading sometimes, aside from an occasionally humorous anecdote. "That doesn't seem terribly suitable for light lunchtime reading."

"Oh, but the article I'm reading is fascinating!" she replied. "It's about the future of telephone service in England. I think you'd be interested to read it—especially given the number of times I've heard you mention to Mr. Henley that we ought to get one installed."

"Have I been that obvious?" he joked, and they shared a smile. He really did like how Alice picked up on things at the office. "One day I might actually get him to agree to it. I'm certain the telephone will be hugely important to our business in the future."

"The article discusses how the government will be taking over licensing and operation. It's going to be run by the postal service, like the telegraph service is now."

"So I've heard." He frowned. "I believe that's a terrible idea.

It will cause England to lag behind. There are so many technical issues yet to be worked out. Private industry always solves those problems faster than the government."

"Yes, there's been an ongoing debate about it." She grinned. "The letters section of the journal has gotten quite heated."

Douglas noticed the pleasant way her face lit up when talking about something that interested her. She looked particularly nice today. Perhaps it was due to the pretty blue scarf she was wearing. A gentle breeze ruffled the nearby trees, and he thought about how refreshing it was to be sitting outside on such a nice day, discussing a topic that was intriguing, relevant, and potentially vital to their business.

He sat back on the bench and began to unwrap his pie. "Care to tell me more about it?"

"Certainly," she replied, looking pleased that he'd asked. As they ate, Alice shared highlights from the article. After summing up the main points, she added, "The article notes that there is an upcoming lecture in London on this very topic. The speaker has been involved in the installation of telephone exchanges all over England, almost from the beginning. I definitely plan to go."

"That lecture is bound to be filled with useful information. I believe I'll go, too." Douglas said this without hesitation, genuinely enthused at the idea. He turned toward Alice as he spoke. Their eyes met, and suddenly there was a moment of silence. A *long* moment of silence. The ease with which they'd been conversing stalled into something unexpectedly awkward.

Sometimes he forgot that Alice was a woman—which was absurd, because he never *really* forgot it. It was just that so often it didn't seem to matter. But of course, in other ways it *did* matter a great deal. He couldn't just casually offer to go with her someplace, as he would with Carson or Hal.

"I'm not trying to intrude on your plans, by any means," he hastily assured her, leaning back to put more distance between them. "I didn't mean to imply—"

She blinked and turned her head, breaking their eye contact.

He waited, unsure what to do next, while she seemed to be collecting herself.

After a moment she shrugged and said casually, "It's a public lecture. Open to anyone. I think it's important that we stay current with all technical developments when it comes to communications. After all, that is critical to a firm such as Henley and Company. Wouldn't you agree?"

"So it is." He took a breath, relieved that she hadn't gotten the wrong idea.

"My friend Mrs. Bennington will be going with me," Alice continued. "She's interested in the telephone, too, although strictly from a user's point of view."

She said this last part with a smile, which seemed to indicate that the discomfort of a moment ago had cleared. Douglas still felt there was something different in the air between them, but it didn't necessarily strike him as negative, only as, well, different.

"I take it Mrs. Bennington is not employed as a telegrapher?"

"Oh no. She's not employed at all. She's supported by a rich husband."

There was a note of dismissal in Alice's voice, the same he had heard that day in the filing room when she'd talked about her sister's marriage. She really did seem dead set against the idea.

"Does getting married generally stop a woman's interest in learning?" he inquired with a smile.

"Well, I do get Lucy to go with me to the monthly lectures at the Ladies' Improvement Society in Bloomsbury, so there's that."

It was another playful dig at her friend's expense.

"That sounds like a lofty title for an organization," Douglas said.

Alice shrugged. "It covers topics of general interest but nothing terribly advanced or technical. I'm hoping this lecture on the telephone will have more detailed scientific information."

"Where is the lecture to be held?" he asked.

"It's going to be at the Alexandra Palace on Saturday afternoon."

Douglas gulped. *Of all the places for it to be. And on the very day of the tea dance.* It brought him back to the reason he'd stepped outside in the first place—to forget about the problem of the Tilneys' ball. Amazingly, he *had* forgotten about it. Until now.

For a few panicked moments, he thought about changing his mind. But then he reasoned that he wasn't likely to run into Hal. After all, Saturday was the busiest day of the week there, as thousands of Londoners made the most of their half holiday. The lecture would be held inside, while the tea dance would be at the outdoor pavilion on the other side of the grounds. It would be simple enough to come and go without getting anywhere close to the dancing.

"If I happen to see you there, perhaps the three of us can sit together," Alice suggested.

"Yes, that's a fine idea."

That solved the problem. They were going together but *not* going together. It was very simple, and there was nothing at all untoward about it.

Gathering her things, Alice rose from the bench. Douglas followed suit, preparing to go with her, but she paused, saying hesitantly, "Perhaps we shouldn't return to work together. I wouldn't want the, er, office gossips to get the wrong idea."

She'd used the plural, but Douglas was sure Alice was referring to only one person: Archie Clapper. It was wise of her to exercise caution. He nodded. "In fact, there is an errand I need to do at the bank. I may as well take care of that now."

They parted ways, with Douglas heading toward the bank while Alice went toward the office. Even if nothing had changed in regard to his problems, he was grateful for this time with her. It had been a pleasant and much-needed diversion.

Unlike the dance at the Tilneys', he was certain the lecture at Ally Pally was something he was going to enjoy.

❧

When Alice returned to the office, she noticed that Archie's previous good mood seemed to have evaporated. Also, the stack of outgoing messages was back on her desk.

"Did you not have time to send these after all?" she asked.

"No," he said, giving her a dark look. "Too busy."

From the way he said it, she guessed the real reason was simply that he'd changed his mind. "Well, thank you anyway for the offer. I'll get to those now."

"Did you have an enjoyable lunch?" He said it like an accusation.

"Yes, very enjoyable!" His attitude couldn't dampen her enthusiasm.

The half hour she and Douglas had spent conversing had been . . . well, electrifying. There was no one outside of her father and brothers with whom she could have had such a stimulating conversation. Given that they were in Ancaster, her opportunities were few and far between.

Her smile had the effect of deepening Archie's frown. What had caused the change? In an effort to distract him from whatever was bothering him, she said, "I was reading the *Telegraphic Journal*. There is an interesting article about telephones in there. On my way back, I even paused to look into that new telephone exchange they've just opened up on our street."

That was true. She'd had a brief but interesting conversation with the manager there and was looking forward to telling Douglas about it later.

Impulsively, she extended the journal toward Archie. "Would you care to borrow it?"

He accepted it with a nod, although he was still looking at her with suspicion. When he left for his lunch break a few minutes later, he took the journal with him.

Once he was gone, Alice went over to Mavis. "Were there a lot of incoming messages while I was away?"

"No," Mavis said, confirming Alice's suspicions. "It's too bad, because Mr. Clapper was acting strangely the whole time and having work to do might have helped."

"What do you mean by 'acting strangely'?"

"After you left, he got up and looked out that window to the lane. Did you walk that way?"

Alice nodded.

"Mr. Shaw left a few minutes after that, and I saw Mr. Clapper get up again and look out the window. Then he just sat at his desk and glowered for the rest of the hour."

Alice let out a sigh of frustration. Her efforts to thwart the office gossip had been to no avail. She went to her desk and began sending the messages, trying to take her mind off Archie Clapper and his penchant for seeing the worst in everything.

She was surprised, therefore, that when Archie returned, he seemed to be in much better humor.

He gave the journal back to her. "Thank you. That was very interesting." He gave her a smile that she gauged was sincere, though it looked so odd on his face that she was tempted to avert her gaze.

She went back to work, still puzzled, but deciding things had somehow turned out all right. Even if Archie's brand of friendliness made her instinctively cringe.

CHAPTER
Sixteen

Alice, are you running from a fire?" Lucy teased breathlessly as she tried to keep up.

"I'm sorry." Alice forced herself to walk more slowly. "I don't want to be late for the lecture."

Lucy wiped a bead of perspiration from her forehead. "Why are you so excited about the telephone? People are already saying it could replace the telegraph one day."

"Do you think I should ignore it and hope it goes away?" Alice smiled. "I say that's all the more reason I should learn what I can. If my occupation is in jeopardy, I want to be informed of it."

These things were all true, but the real reason Alice was in a hurry was to ensure she had time to meet up with Douglas before the lecture began. Getting to the Alexandra Palace grounds had taken longer than planned, and now they had to hurry to reach the lecture hall on time.

"Mr. B. wants to have a telephone installed at our house," Lucy said. "He says it will be a mark of distinction to have one. But he also teases me that he worries I shall enjoy having a telephone far too much. He says I shall ruin him by running up exorbitant fees by constantly making calls to my friends!"

Alice took in little of her friend's ramblings because her attention had been arrested by a surprising and unwelcome sight:

Archie Clapper was standing outside the lecture hall. Alice got the impression he was looking for someone—and she didn't want to guess who that person might be.

The knot in her stomach tightened when he caught sight of her. He gave a quick smooth to his hair, straightened his coat, and began walking toward her. "Why, good afternoon, Miss McNeil," he said, taking advantage of a brief pause in Lucy's stream of words. "What a surprise to see you here. Although I suppose it's not such a surprise, is it?"

"No?" Alice said, at a loss.

"It was in the *Telegraphic Journal*. I couldn't help noticing that the information about this lecture had been circled. *In pencil*," he added, as though that point were somehow significant.

While Alice was still digesting this, Archie gave Lucy a little bow. "Good afternoon, madam."

Lucy was as dumbfounded as Alice. Her surprise was probably a reaction to Archie's greeting. Although Lucy had only seen him from a distance, she knew from Alice's descriptions that his manner was not normally so polite.

Utter dismay took over Alice's surprise when she grasped the meaning behind Archie's words. He thought that by circling that information and then handing the paper to him, Alice had left him a hint. In other words, she'd unwittingly followed another key in the spinster book: *"The method of communication is so easy and so unsuspect. You have only to put faint pencil marks against the passages and lend the volume to him, and he will respond."*

Archie stood looking at her expectantly. Was he waiting for some sign that he'd correctly deduced the meaning of the circled passage?

A few stragglers rushed by, intent on getting to the lecture hall.

"I believe the program is about to start," Alice croaked.

She said this in some vain hope that she might find a way to break free, but unfortunately Archie took it as confirmation that he should join them. He nodded. "Yes, we should go in. We wouldn't want to miss anything."

When they reached the door, Archie opened it for them. As Alice passed him, she caught a distinctive smell. He'd put bear grease in his hair. To impress her. It was almost too much. The very last thing she needed was Archie's attentions. She realized now that she preferred him when he was rude and distant. In fact, any kind of animosity short of attempted murder would have been preferable to this.

Lucy said nothing. Clearly, she was as stunned by these events as Alice was.

Alice was still desperately trying to think of a way to separate from Archie when she saw Douglas. He was standing at the end of a row of chairs near the front. He lifted a hand to get her attention, then frowned when he saw Archie. Archie didn't look any happier to see him. Looking irritated, Douglas walked forward to meet them.

"Your attention, everyone!" bellowed a man standing at the lectern. "Please find your seats! We'll begin in five minutes."

At this announcement, many latecomers who'd been milling about began to scramble to find a place to sit. Now swimming upstream, Douglas skirted the crowd in order to reach them.

"I've got three seats saved in the second row," he said. "My apologies, Clapper. I didn't realize there would be a fourth person."

Douglas didn't sound the least bit sorry. The two men stared at one another, sizing each other up.

Archie's face twisted into a sneer. "Don't bother about me. I'll just take a seat in the back." He tossed a sour look at Alice. "It's my fault for being *too late*."

Douglas's eyes narrowed as he caught the insinuation behind Archie's words. Evidently deciding to let it go, he turned to Alice and Lucy. "Right. Let's go, then."

Alice breathed a sigh of relief as they moved away with Archie making no further objection. She knew she would pay for today's events later, though. It wasn't a happy prospect.

"It's very kind of you, Mr. . . . ?" Lucy said as Douglas ushered them forward. She must have been confused as to why this man was saving them seats. They hadn't been introduced, and Alice hadn't told her he would be here. The smile on Lucy's face indicated she was finding Douglas more than acceptable as company, however. Compared to the alternative of Archie, who wouldn't? Even so, Lucy's admiring gaze made Alice recall her own reaction upon meeting him. If she, who never paid attention to such things, had been bowled over by this handsome man, she had no doubt Lucy would be even more susceptible.

They paused at the row where Douglas had saved them seats, and Alice quickly made the introductions.

Lucy gave a nod of recognition when she heard his name. "So nice to meet you, Mr. Shaw. Alice has told me about you, although she didn't mention that you were so—" She paused, catching herself just in time, and started again. "That you were so, er, interested in telephones."

Alice was grateful that Lucy refrained from what she'd evidently wanted to say, but it didn't stop her cheeks from burning in embarrassment. She ought to have prepared Lucy a little better. "We'd better find our seats," she reminded them.

They made their way to the chairs Douglas had saved, which were in the center of the row. Alice ended up seated between Douglas and Lucy.

"Clapper didn't come here with you, did he?" Douglas said once they were settled.

"Of course not!" Alice answered vehemently. "We happened to meet on the way in." She wasn't ready to admit her unintended role in bringing about the meeting.

"I'm glad to hear that."

"Thank you for saving us," Lucy said. "My heavens, it appears all the employees from Henley and Company have come to this lecture today." She caught Alice's eye, and her expression transmitted loud and clear how impressed she was with this particular employee.

"Was Clapper being rude to you?" Douglas asked with concern.

"No," said Alice. "He was being nice—which was far worse."

This statement brought a gleam of amusement to Douglas's eyes, and the corners of his mouth moved as he seemed to suppress a smile. Alice returned the look, pleased he'd understood her so perfectly.

There was no time to say anything more. The director returned to the lectern and began to introduce the speaker, giving a long list of the man's qualifications. Alice heard, rather than saw this, as she was still looking into Douglas's eyes. They were filled with friendly good humor that was so inviting. . . .

Lucy tugged at Alice's sleeve.

Dragging her gaze from Douglas, Alice turned and said, "Yes?"

"I can already tell from the introduction that this is going to be terribly technical," Lucy whispered. "I'm sure I'll need to ask you for clarification." As she spoke, she sent a brief glance toward Douglas that conveyed—to Alice's surprise—a hint of worry. But that made no sense, given Lucy's initial pleasure at meeting him. Alice decided she must be mistaken.

Over the next hour, the speaker presented a breathtaking vision of what the future with telephones would be like. Perhaps she ought to be worried for her job after all. In a world where people could speak directly with each other, even over long distances, there would be no need for the telegraph operator as an intermediary.

However, that reality was still a long way off. It paled in comparison to her current problem. Even as she listened intently to this lecture, Alice could not forget that Archie was seated somewhere behind them. She imagined him watching them, making assumptions about why they had obviously decided to meet here today. As if there could be any other reason than that they were colleagues with a mutual interest in the newest forms of electrical communication.

Lucy's actions disturbed her focus as well. She kept finding reasons to whisper comments to Alice, and her gaze frequently moved between Alice and Douglas as though assessing a doubtful situation. Something was going on in her friend's mind. Whatever it was, Alice knew she would have to address it later.

After a lively question-and-answer session, the program came to a close. As everyone stood, Alice turned to see if she could find Archie in the crowd, wanting to know if he was watching them.

He was. He gave her a long, cold look that actually made her shiver. Then he turned and walked out of the hall.

Since they were near the front, it took a while to exit due to the crowd. By the time they made it outside, there was no sign of Archie.

Alice saw many people making their way down the path that led to the park. She would have loved to go there, too, but she hesitated to suggest it since they were with Douglas. She was unsure of the protocol of this situation. So they all stood where they were.

Douglas appeared to have forgotten about Archie. He was smiling. "That was an excellent presentation, wasn't it?" he said to Alice. "He really knows what he's talking about. What did you think of his explanation regarding the possibility of a transatlantic telephone cable? It seems almost too fantastic to contemplate, doesn't it?"

"Yes, but the way he explained it, I believe it will happen one day. After all, it's only been about fifteen years since we succeeded with the transatlantic telegraph cable. Many people thought that would be impossible, too." Alice quickly became swept up in Douglas's enthusiasm as they imagined what it would be like to actually talk to a client who was on the other side of the ocean and how it would impact business.

They'd talked for perhaps ten minutes when it became evident that Lucy was not saying anything. This was not surprising, as they were speaking of things outside her friend's knowledge and interest. Although Alice felt guilty about this, she also hoped it truly was the reason Lucy had grown quiet, and that it wasn't because she worried about this time they were spending with Douglas. Was she harboring the idea that it was somehow wrong for Alice to spend leisure time with someone from work—and someone who was technically her overseer? Perhaps she worried there might be negative consequences for such fraternization.

Alice decided she could not be responsible for whether a person attended a public lecture. After all, Archie had been there as well.

The thought of Archie sent another chill down her back, despite the heat. She was glad he hadn't tried to press his company on them. And yet, was that really a good thing? Archie had sent hate-filled glares at her before today. Plenty of times. But that was before the pencil incident. And she'd never seen the stark malevolence he'd shown today just before he walked away. So much for any ground she might have won by being nice to him. It was all gone now—and then some.

Nearby, an ices vendor stood next to his cart, calling out, "Ices! Ices! Raspberry! Strawberry! Lemon! Halfpenny only! Halfpenny only!" He wore a bowler hat, a red kerchief around his neck, and spoke in a thick Italian accent. "You there! *Signore!*" he called out to Douglas. "You buy nice ices for the ladies, yes? Don't leave them suffering in the heat when they could be cooled down with a sweet treat!"

"Would you like one?" Douglas asked them.

"We couldn't ask you to buy us anything," Alice protested.

"It's but a trifle. I insist." He tilted his head and studied Alice. "You look like a lemon, I think."

"I can't say I've ever been told that before," she replied with a laugh.

"I meant to say that you look like the sort of person who enjoys lemon-flavored ices," he clarified with a smile. "Because they are tart on the tongue. Am I right?"

She wanted to say no, just to tease him, but she couldn't bring herself to do it. She was too amazed that he'd read her that well. "How did you guess?"

"It's a talent. It cannot be learned." He turned to Lucy. "You are strawberry, I think."

"Right you are, Mr. Shaw."

"Perhaps you missed your calling," Alice joked. "Being so good at divination, you might have gotten a job at a carnival."

"Och, no, me lassie. I'm thinkin' higher than that." Douglas

155

slipped into his Scottish brogue, perhaps to add a touch of levity to his words. "I intend to use it to succeed in business, for you see, 'tis a skill that can be used to win over customers as well." His eyes lit up with pride. "Mark my words: if I'm not the owner of Henley and Company someday, it'll be because I own somethin' bigger."

Alice heard the ring of conviction beneath his lighthearted delivery. Once more she reflected that, despite a measure of hubris, there was something impressive about his unwavering intention to rise in the world. She hadn't heard him use the brogue so heavily before. For some reason, it did fluttery things to her stomach. But then, she did have Scottish ancestry. Perhaps he was connecting with some deeper part of her. . . .

"You certainly are ambitious, Mr. Shaw," Lucy observed.

Her statement pulled Alice from the reverie she'd almost slipped into. "Humble too," she added, trying to bring him down a notch—and settle her skittering thoughts.

Douglas grinned. Dropping the brogue, he said, "Wait here, ladies."

They waited in the shade of the building's portico while Douglas went to acquire the ices.

"Mr. Shaw seems very personable," Lucy said.

"Yes, he is. As he said, he uses it to good advantage in business."

"I see."

Having no idea how to respond to that cryptic remark, Alice said nothing.

Douglas was on his way back when Lucy said, "Oh, Alice, I nearly forgot!" She pulled a small envelope from her reticule. "I got a letter from Fred yesterday. He's reached Bombay. He sends his kind regards—and he enclosed this note for you in his letter."

Lucy said this precisely as Douglas came within earshot. The way his eyebrows lifted slightly told Alice he'd heard. Mortified, she took the note and thrust it into her bag. "Thank you. I'll read it later."

Lucy gave a sniff of irritation at Alice's hasty dismissal.

"This Fred seems to be a world traveler," Douglas remarked as he handed them their ices.

"He's my brother," Lucy said. "Oh, and Alice, he also mentioned that he bought you a little present. He's eagerly anticipating his return so he can give it to you."

Douglas looked at Alice as if seeing her in a whole new light. "You seem to have many admirers, Miss McNeil."

Did he think she was dangling after men—or worse, that she had a beau? Although he spoke with ironic amusement, she thought he seemed disappointed, too. Perhaps he thought she hadn't been serious about her goal of remaining single and pursuing a career. Perhaps he thought she'd lied to him. That bothered her most of all.

Lucy ate a bite of her strawberry ice and smiled with satisfaction. "Thank you, Mr. Shaw. This is delicious."

Then Alice understood. Lucy saw Douglas as a rival to Fred! She had chosen that exact moment to bring out Fred's letter in order to ensure Douglas didn't try to court Alice. The whole idea would be laughable except that it was too unsettling. In too many ways.

Honestly, the entire situation was impossible to fathom. With Archie, Fred, and Douglas showing interest in her, she suddenly felt like Lewis Carroll's Alice, finding herself in a topsy-turvy world.

"I . . . that is . . ." Alice sputtered, trying to find words. "Fred is merely a friend, you see. We've known each other since we were children, and—"

"Shaw! Is that you?" A man's voice interrupted Alice's ramblings.

Alice immediately recognized the man approaching them. It was one of Douglas's friends, the one named Hal. He was escorting a vivacious-looking young woman in a brightly colored gown.

Douglas's reaction was not what Alice would have expected. Instead of looking pleased, he closed his eyes, deflating the way a man did when he heard very bad news, and turned to face the newcomers.

CHAPTER

Seventeen

H o, ho! You decided to come after all!" Hal said.

Douglas grimaced, swallowing a few choice words before he could utter them. Hal had found him. In the midst of thousands of people. Of course he had. Because there hadn't been enough bizarre things happening this afternoon already.

"Hard at work, I see," Hal said. He tipped his hat at Alice and her friend. "Tell me, which of you ladies is the dance instructor?"

They both looked understandably surprised.

"Neither of them," Douglas said. "We came to hear a lecture about the future of the telephone." He indicated the Alexandra Palace behind them.

"A lecture? That's how you want to spend a lovely afternoon like this?"

"It just ended," Alice said, jumping into the conversation with a smile. "Why does Mr. Shaw need a dance instructor?"

"Didn't he tell you?" Hal looked at him askance. "No, I don't suppose he would. After all . . ." He paused, giving Douglas a cheeky grin.

Douglas knew what he was thinking—that he was here in a social capacity. Maybe Hal thought he was planning to court one of the ladies. Or both, even. He had to disabuse his friend of that notion right away. "This is Miss McNeil and her friend Mrs. Bennington. Miss McNeil works as a telegraph operator at Henley and Company. That's why we are here today. It's . . . er, research."

"Is that right?" Hal looked skeptical. Or perhaps he was disappointed that Douglas wasn't trying to court two women after all.

Douglas completed the introductions, then added, "Mr. Halverson is a fellow boarder at the same house where I live."

"Please call me Hal—it's simpler," Hal insisted to the ladies. "And this is Mamie." He indicated the dark-haired woman clinging to his arm. Douglas had not met Mamie before, but she matched the image he'd had of her based on Hal's descriptions. She wore a bright red-and-blue-striped dress and matching hat that edged dangerously close to garish. There was an obvious touch of man-made color to her cheeks and lips. Apparently she had a lot of natural energy, for she fairly bounced on her toes, even as they stood there talking.

Mamie released her hold on Hal long enough to pump both ladies' hands enthusiastically. "I'm so pleased to meet you. We're just on our way to the tea dance. Won't you join us? It will be loads of fun!" Her accent placed her origins firmly on London's poorer east side.

"Is this why Mr. Shaw needs a dance instructor?" Alice asked, looking distinctly amused.

"I am not good at dancing, so I end up turning down a lot of offers to attend dances. That's all." Douglas looked at Hal pointedly, trying to transmit his desire that they keep the subject of the upcoming ball and Miss Rolland out of this conversation. It would be too embarrassing to admit he was a would-be suitor with a fatal flaw. Alice only knew him as a successful man of business, and he wanted to keep it that way. He didn't want to allow his private life to seep into his relationships with work colleagues. On the other hand, he thought grimly, he ought to have thought of that before coming here.

Hal gave a nod and a wink, as if to say, *Your secret is safe with me.*

"I'm surprised you should have trouble dancing," Alice said, turning her gaze to Douglas.

"Why is that?"

"Because you're a telegrapher, and a good one to boot."

159

He shook his head. "I don't follow."

"Some years ago, while I was still living at home, my older brother had the same problem. It was hindering his ability to woo a particular young lady in our village."

Douglas started in surprise. Had his problem been that transparent, despite his effort to keep it vague? "That's . . . er, too bad," he mumbled.

"It was a problem," Alice agreed. "But then I reminded him that he was a highly proficient telegrapher. Soon he had conquered the issue. He's now happily married to that lady."

"What does telegraphy have to do with dancing?" Douglas asked, unable to make the connection.

"When you send a message in Morse code, the rhythm is critical, right? You've got to ensure your dots, dashes, and pauses are clearly defined and follow a set pattern. The space between letters is different from the space between words. If you don't keep that distinction, the message can become garbled. Dancing is similar. All you have to do is find the rhythm—the meter underlying the music. Don't think of it as trying to attach a particular step to a particular sound; think instead about listening for that underlying pattern and moving with it."

"But isn't that the same thing?"

She shook her head. "You'll see the difference if you put this advice into practice."

"You seem very sure of yourself on this subject."

She laughed. "I have three brothers, all of whom had to be taught to dance. Believe me, if my brothers can learn, anyone can."

"So you're saying you enjoy dancing?" Douglas blurted in amazement. Perhaps it sounded rude, but he would never have pictured this serious-minded woman enjoying such a frivolous pursuit. Especially as she was so determined to remain a spinster. He honestly couldn't believe that Fred fellow was a serious contender for her affections. Nor any man, for that matter. He thought he would sense somehow if that were the case.

What was dancing for, if not to woo someone? Douglas couldn't imagine that anyone did it simply for enjoyment. If a person wanted physical exercise, there were plenty of other pastimes that were far more interesting. Squash or lawn tennis, for example.

"Oh yes, I love dancing," Alice said, smiling. "In fact, I feel sorry for people who don't. I think their main problem is that they put too much pressure on themselves. Either they feel they must be perfect, or the corollary to that: they fear that if they make a mistake, they will lose the regard of someone who would otherwise love them passionately."

"That fear might be substantiated," Douglas said, thinking of Miss Rolland.

"For silly schoolgirls, perhaps," Alice answered dismissively. "Or debutantes with their heads in the clouds."

"But you were a schoolgirl once," he persisted.

"Yes, but I was never a *silly* one."

"I can vouch for that," Mrs. Bennington interposed.

"Enough talking!" Hal said. "Let's get to that dance. Shaw, I believe Miss McNeil has shown you the way forward. Now all we have to do is give it a go." He looked at Alice. "I assume you can be talked into showing him how to apply this information?"

Alice turned to her friend. "Lucy, what do you think? Do we have time to stay?"

Lucy frowned. "I've already given my staff instructions to expect us for tea."

"But it wouldn't be the first time you've done something else instead. They are very good at changing course with no notice."

She was trying to talk Lucy into staying. Heaven help him, Alice *wanted* to teach him to dance.

"I couldn't impose on you," Douglas said, trying to hide his panic. She'd put forth an interesting hypothesis, but he wasn't going to risk making a public fool of himself. He was already kicking himself for taking the chance of coming out to Ally Pally today. "You've made other plans, and I can't allow my friends to derail them. Besides, Mr. Bennington might not wish his wife to be at such an event without him."

"He's out of town," Alice said.

"Nevertheless, perhaps another time would be better—"

"It's now or never, I expect," Hal said. "Don't you want to be ready for—"

"Hal!" Douglas interrupted sharply. "Wait here," he told the others, then took Hal's arm and dragged him out of earshot. "Don't mention Miss Rolland or that charity ball," he hissed. "That's something I wish to keep private."

Hal smirked. "I won't say a word about it. Wouldn't want to make Miss McNeil jealous."

"That's not what I mean," Douglas said in exasperation.

"Look, friend, this sounds like your best chance to get it right before the ball. Miss McNeil clearly wants to stay, and the other lady looks like she can be swayed easily enough."

"But I work with her! I can't be dancing with her." Douglas felt a measure of alarm over the idea that, if he allowed himself to examine it, was not entirely due to his inability to dance.

"She seems like a level-headed young lady. Perhaps if you swear her to secrecy, she'll not tell anyone else in the office—especially not in the event you fail!" Hal indulged in a guffaw at Douglas's expense. "But she seems pretty sure of herself, so I'm betting you might get somewhere. Come on, the dance is already underway. I can hear the music from here."

Hal strode back to the others before Douglas could launch any further objections.

Whether Alice succeeded or failed in teaching him to dance, Douglas was filled with a terrible sense of foreboding.

⚜

"I don't think this is a wise idea," Lucy whispered to Alice as they walked toward the dance.

Alice was beginning to have doubts, too, but now that they were committed, she wasn't going to admit to it. "We don't have to stay long. It should only take a few dances to show Mr. Shaw what I'm talking about. Then he can practice with other ladies."

Judging from the way Mamie's appreciative gaze kept straying to Douglas, Alice was certain she would be more than happy to take a turn in his arms. If Mamie and Lucy—and herself, unfortunately—were any indication, every woman practically fainted at the sight of him. He certainly looked handsome now, even though his forehead was pinched and perspiration dotted his brow. He even tugged on his collar. Poor man, he really was terrified of dancing.

Alice rather enjoyed knowing that. Until now, she'd thought there was nothing this man didn't excel at.

Although it was still early, the electric Chinese lanterns were already lit, sending a warm glow along the path through the garden. Up ahead they could see a pavilion, on which was seated the band providing the music. The area all around the pavilion was open for dancing. Tables and chairs were set up farther out, along the edges of the clearing. Plenty of people were already dancing to the lively tune, although the place was not filled to capacity.

"I see an open table over there," Douglas said and steered them all toward it. "Why don't we take time to enjoy the music first?"

Hal snickered, seeing his friend's ploy for a few minutes' delay. But no one objected.

They sat down, and as they listened to the music, Alice found her toe tapping to the rhythm.

"Mamie, let's you and I get this started," Hal said as a new tune began.

Mamie jumped up eagerly, and the two of them went off to find a space on the dance floor.

Alice realized that in order to dance with Douglas, she'd have to leave Lucy seated alone at the table. Because she didn't want to do this, she didn't press him to dance. She would have to wait until Hal and Mamie returned.

They watched the dancers for the next few songs. "Hal and Mamie dance well together," Alice observed. "They must do this a lot."

"They've been sweet on each other for some time."

"Why don't they get married?" Lucy asked.

"Hal can't afford to keep a wife yet. But he thinks by next year he might be able to manage it."

Alice found herself growing fidgety. "We can still begin the lesson while sitting here," she told Douglas. "Are you ready?"

He gave her a crooked smile. "Ready as I'll ever be, I suppose."

"Just relax!" She reached out to reassure him, placing a hand on his arm. It was warm, and as he moved under her touch, she felt a little jolt, a sensation not unlike touching a live wire. She quickly withdrew her hand, although it took another moment to gather her wits. "Think about how you tap out Morse code. A dash is longer than a dot. There is a short pause between letters, and a longer pause between words. Now, this song is a waltz. Just listen to it."

"One, two, three. One, two, three," Douglas intoned, clearly drawing up a memory from some previous dance class.

"Right. But the *one* is longer than the *two* and the *three*. Think of a dash followed by two dots. Dash, dot, dot. Do you hear it? Dash, dot, dot."

"Dash, dot, dot," he repeated obligingly. "Is that to be taken altogether, which is Morse code for the letter *D*?"

"Let's say one dash for the letter *T*, followed by two dots for the letter *I*," Alice answered. "That way the space between the two dots aligns more closely with the music."

"*T, I*," Douglas repeated. "Dash, dot-dot." He frowned. "Dash, dot-dot."

Alice could see he was still finding it difficult to make the connection between the code and the music. "Try closing your eyes to block out distractions," she suggested. "Listen carefully to the music."

He followed her instructions. "Dash, dot-dot."

With his eyes closed, he looked vulnerable, in an appealing sort of way. Alice found herself admiring the fine curve of his dark eyebrows and the sweep of his lashes along the lower lids. She watched the way his lips moved as he said the words. Even the little beads of sweat on his forehead were charming.

Lucy gave a little cough. Alice turned to her friend and got the impression that Lucy's cough had been intentional, as though she saw and disapproved of the way Alice had been studying Douglas. Alice grew uncomfortable under Lucy's critical gaze. She had to be careful not to give Lucy the wrong idea about her regard for Douglas. She could admit to a growing friendship between them, but there was nothing more.

The music came to an end. Douglas opened his eyes and looked at Alice. "How was that?"

"Very good," Alice said, trying to sound like a disinterested instructor. "Did you feel it?"

"I . . . think so." The uncertainty in his voice contradicted his words.

The band launched into the next song. Alice listened for several bars until she had identified the tune. "This one is trickier. It's a schottische." She thought about the best way to translate this one to Morse code and decided on the single dash for *T* and a dot for *E*, and then worked with Douglas on it. "*T, T, T, E; T, T, T, E; T-E-T-E-T-E-T-E.* You'll notice the second half of that string has a quicker pace than the first half. That's because the *E*s in that set represent hops."

"Right," he said, one ear cocked toward her as he listened carefully. He repeated the phrase after her. After several more repetitions while watching the dancers, his mouth broadened in a smile. "I think I hear it!"

Hal and Mamie returned to the table. "Did you watch us to see how easy it is?" Mamie exclaimed, giving Douglas a light poke in the arm. "Now it's your turn!"

Alice sent Douglas a challenging look. "Ready?"

A sudden wild look in his eyes provided the clear answer. Alice half-expected him to back out. He was made of sterner stuff, though. Taking a deep breath, he resolutely stood and offered her a hand.

As he helped her up, Alice found herself experiencing a few jitters of her own. That was absurd, of course—why should she be nervous? It was only a dance, and one she knew well. Perhaps she was merely tense on his account, knowing how apprehensive he was to try this experiment in public. Yes, that must be the reason.

It accounted for everything except the odd sensations generated by his warm hand holding hers.

The park had been steadily filling with people, and the dance area was now very crowded. Douglas led Alice to an area on the opposite side of the pavilion from where they'd been seated. She assumed he didn't want to practice under Hal's amused gaze, because there weren't any fewer people over here.

Douglas frowned as he looked around. "How can people dance if they can't even move?"

"Let's go over there," Alice said, pointing to an area at the fringe of the dancing.

Once they'd reached the spot, they turned to face one another. Douglas lifted his hands and paused, clearly wondering if or how he was supposed to hold her.

"Let's not worry about that just yet," Alice told him. "Let's stand here and listen to the music, just as we were doing at the table."

Throughout the song, they continued repeating the letters together. Eventually, she began to see his body make small, tentative movements to the music. It really was irresistible, she knew, once you connected with the rhythm. It told her Douglas was ready.

"All right, let's try it," she said just as the band began to play a waltz.

He must have felt the time was right as well, for the fire of confidence lit his eyes. Seeing the return of his usual fearless bearing caused her normally reliable heartbeat to stumble out of its usual timing. He took her right hand in his left. When his right arm came around her waist, it felt warm and electric. The attractions of this man were hard to resist. Their pull on her was stronger even than the music. Alice swallowed a nervous gulp.

"I see you remember that much from your previous lessons," she managed. "Now, let's try moving. Don't worry so much about what your feet are doing. I'll do my best to follow."

Douglas was amazed to find himself filled with the sensation of actually *wanting* to move to the music. More astounding than that, however, was the discovery of how good it felt to hold Alice in his arms. She looked thin and angular, but as he set his hand on the small of her back, he found that holding her was comfortable. No, it was more than that: it was delightful.

This woman who had proved herself adept at so many things was now stealing into his heart as well. He swiftly warned himself that that was the *last* thing he should be thinking about right now. He had to keep his mind on the dance.

They began to move. Still trying to find his way into the music, Douglas made several missteps. His confidence began to flag. Seemingly undaunted by his repeated mistakes, Alice kept bringing him back to the right movements. He doggedly continued on, repeating the letters aloud.

Then, unbelievably, came a breakthrough. He knew Morse code so well that its rhythms were practically a part of his soul. As he concentrated on the ebb and flow of the dots and dashes, somehow the connection was finally forged between his brain and his legs. The steps his dancing master had tried to drill into him finally made sense!

He must have begun doing it correctly because now Alice was following *his* movements. His confidence surged. He didn't try to dwell on his feet so much as the rhythm of the *dash, dot-dot*. He could do this. He *was* doing this.

She met his gaze, beaming with pleasure. It was a look he'd never expected to see on a dance partner. Nor did he ever think he'd find himself wanting the music to continue for as long as possible, rather than being desperate for it to end. He even managed to breathe a little, although not to speak, as he was too busy repeating *dash, dot-dot* to himself, picturing an endless row of *T*s and *I*s flowing along the wires into infinity. He focused on her lips murmuring *dash, dot-dot* to help him, and he swept her along the wires he'd conjured in his imagination.

167

When at last the song did end, Douglas came back to reality still buoyed by elation.

He had done it!

The woman who had just eased him over a seemingly insurmountable obstacle was still smiling up at him. She said breathlessly, "That was . . . very good!"

"Alice, you are a miracle worker. If you weren't such a cracking good telegrapher, I'd suggest you open a dance school! Thank you. Oh, thank you!"

Impulsively, he took hold of her upper arms and drew her close, intending to plant a thankful kiss on her cheek. But just at that moment, the band started up again—a rollicking new song that started with a loud clash of cymbals. Her head turned toward the sound. Instead of meeting her cheek, Douglas's lips connected squarely with hers.

He ought to have pulled away—and really, she ought to have done the same. He relaxed his grip to signal that she could easily break free if she chose. But her shoulders softened, and she tilted ever-so-slightly toward him, encouraging his embrace. The mistaken kiss became incredibly and wonderfully real.

Her lips were soft and warm, more appealing than he would have guessed—if he'd ever allowed himself to consider it. He realized now that this was what he'd wanted for ages. Her lips had been tantalizing him all along; the keen intelligence lighting her eyes had been drawing him in. Holding her in his arms felt exactly right. It was like arriving at a destination that was new and yet long beloved. She kissed him back with equal fervor, a surprise that made the wonder of it even greater.

The drums and cymbals and some kind of horn seemed to be playing what was going on in his heart. It was a joyous melody with a touch of dissonance, and it perfectly reflected his exhilaration. All around them, people were dancing energetically. Yet they seemed distant, like the background of a painting. His senses were wholly taken up with the joy of kissing Alice McNeil.

The impression that there was distance between them and the

dancers was broken when one of the couples bumped into them, forcing them to break apart.

Alice stumbled back, but her gaze remained on Douglas. She appeared dazed and breathless. Her lips were parted, and her face was flushed deep red. In short, she looked absolutely stunning.

"Beggin' your pardon," the gentleman said. He gave Douglas a wink. "That rousing polka can get people movin' in all sorts of ways, can't it?"

His partner giggled at his joke, and the two of them moved away.

Once more, Douglas took hold of Alice—this time to gently pull her out of the fray.

"What . . . just happened?" she asked, her words unsteady.

The happiness that had been lighting her face was gone. Worry had replaced it. Douglas could see she was already regretting what she'd done.

It was a shock to be taken down from his euphoria so quickly. Worse than plunging into cold water. But he had to face the fact that his actions had been foolish, and they might well have hurt her. He swallowed, his mouth dry. "Alice, I apologize. I should not have presumed—that is, I never intended—"

"I understand." She placed a trembling hand to her chest and breathed deeply, as though she were still trying to find air. "It was a mistake."

Her gaze darted around nervously, and he knew what she was thinking: Did anyone in their party see them? Douglas did the same. They were standing by the bushes at the edge of the shadows. The dancers in their proximity were too busy enjoying themselves to pay any attention to them, and there was no one among them that he knew. He could only thank heaven they were not within eyesight of Hal and the others.

"Perhaps we should go sit down," Douglas offered.

"No, give me a moment, please." She added with a nervous laugh, "I need to compose myself."

Had he upset her that much? "Alice, I want you to know that I have only the utmost respect for you. I would never presume to force my attentions on you. You are a respected colleague and, I hope, a friend, too."

His words did not have the effect he'd hoped. Her chin drooped, and her eyes squeezed shut. He realized he had addressed her by her given name. A sign of familiarity at odds with his words.

She took another deep breath and straightened, squaring her shoulders and meeting his gaze. "There's no need to apologize, Mr. Shaw. That was a silly thing to have happened. I'm sure we can put it out of our minds. I'm so glad I was able to help you with the dancing."

She said this with a smile that seemed to wobble, drawing his eyes to the lips that had been pressed so fervently against his just moments ago. Heaven help him, he wanted to kiss her again. He wanted to throw all common sense to the wind. Of all the things he planned to accomplish in this life, falling in love with a determined spinster was most definitely not among them.

Nor did love appear to be in her plans, either. She turned her head, her gaze once more scanning the crowd. She raised a hand to check her hair, although everything was still firmly in place. "We should be getting back. They'll be wondering what happened to us. I don't want to leave my friend alone, which might happen if Hal and Mamie get up to dance."

She turned and began to walk off, but Douglas reached out to stop her. She looked at him questioningly as he took hold of her hand.

He couldn't let her go without impressing on her how grateful he was. "You did me a great favor tonight."

She reacted with a little intake of breath, searching his eyes. Douglas thought he saw a glimpse of the woman who had so ardently returned his kiss. It was quickly gone. "You're welcome." She removed her hand from his. "I'm sure you agree that we ought not to speak of this at work. Of any of this, I mean. If anyone there should overhear us—"

"Understood." She was right to be thinking of her reputation. His, too, he supposed.

He could agree not to *talk* about what had just happened—the dance and that impetuous kiss—but not *thinking* of it was an entirely different matter. It had been the stuff of dreams. And now, like a dream, it had vanished into the night. As they made their way through the crowd, Alice walked a full arm's distance away, not looking at him, pressing firmly ahead. She seemed determined to put the kiss behind them. He had too much respect and esteem for her not to honor her wishes.

The disappointment he felt must surely be nothing but a stray bit of manly pride. He was no womanizer, but he wasn't used to being turned away, either. He ought to be glad of it, for she was obviously the only one of them who was thinking clearly.

Buck up, lad, he thought, *and put on the smile.* It was time to don a carefree countenance in order to prevent the others from guessing what a terrible misstep he'd made tonight.

CHAPTER

Eighteen

Not for her, this silly idea of romance. Alice cringed inwardly as she recalled how superior she'd felt about the naïveté of others. Who had truly been the naïve one? She was astonished at her response, body and soul, when Douglas had kissed her. Why had she not believed a person could feel something as powerful as that?

And yet, from the first moment she'd seen him, standing in the middle of the office looking impossibly handsome, she had known. *She had known.*

Granted, it had been far back in the unconscious portion of her mind, but somehow she'd known that one kiss from a man like this would be so shattering, it would obliterate everything she knew about the subject. That was why she had spent every day since meeting him doing her utmost to ignore the unreasonable feelings he ignited in her. Telling herself they were mere fantasies, the kind instilled into little girls by way of fairy stories.

Now she could not deny that this was something very real. It was utterly unnerving.

They reached the table to find their friends drinking bottled lemonade. Hal was entertaining the ladies with a magic trick. He was pulling a penny from Mamie's ear. She laughed with delight as though she'd never seen this done before.

"You are returned at last!" Hal said, tossing the coin onto the table as he stood up. "Did you have success? I couldn't see what you were doing. You seemed to have disappeared behind the shrubbery."

"We were on the other side of the pavilion," Douglas answered. "Miss McNeil is an excellent teacher. Her advice about using Morse code worked like a charm."

Surprised to hear Douglas speaking so casually, Alice turned to give him a disbelieving look. He looked flushed, but in a way that could easily be put down to the exertion of dancing on a warm evening.

"Do you mean to tell me your toes are intact?" Hal aimed this remark at Alice.

"Indeed they are." She tried to smile as she said this, but she wasn't able to shake off the powerful effects of that kiss as neatly as Douglas had. Her lips still felt the ghost of his touch.

Hal clapped his hands. "That's wonderful news! It should bring great happiness to Miss Ro—er, to the ladies."

Douglas grimaced. Alice supposed he must be tired of his friend's teasing. She sank down gratefully on the chair Douglas pulled out for her, which brought her to eye level with Lucy.

Lucy studied her with a frown. Unfortunately, Lucy was usually able to read Alice's emotions with surprising accuracy. To deflect Lucy's intent gaze from her burning cheeks, Alice pointed toward their drinks. "Is that lemonade?"

"We got one for you," Hal said, extending a bottle toward her. "I imagine you're thirsty after all that exertion." He took a seat across the table from her. Although his manner was casual, he, too, had a sharp gaze. Alice suspected that, like Lucy, he didn't miss much.

Alice accepted the bottle, taking a moment to enjoy its chill against her sweating hands. Then she took a sip, thankful for the refreshing cool liquid as it slid down her throat.

Hal lifted a bottle toward Douglas, who had remained standing, since there were no more chairs. "I treated the ladies, but you owe me a sixpence," he said as Douglas accepted the bottle. He accompanied this remark with a smile and a wink that showed he was joking.

"Why don't we just subtract it from the two shillings you owe me?" Douglas answered with a grin.

"Done. So, tell us all about it. I still can't believe Miss McNeil managed to cure those two useless feet of yours."

This time, Douglas seemed to take his friend's teasing in stride. "It was amazing, really. There was this moment when it finally clicked in my mind, like a key turning a lock. In the end, there's not much to it, is there? I mean, there is, but it's not so hard to piece it all together." He was speaking with almost unnatural rapidity, and he must have realized it, for he paused. He smiled at Alice. His warm eyes gleamed, but she was drawn to his appealing smile and the full lips that had been pressed to hers. . . .

Alice gulped. She pretended to take another sip of lemonade in an attempt to hide the fact that she was unable to breathe.

Hal sat back in his chair. "Would you two care to show us what you learned?"

A brief shadow crossed Douglas's face. Alice didn't know what he was thinking, but she knew she could not trust herself to be in his arms again. Certainly not in front of Lucy and the others.

Douglas tugged Hal up from his chair. "Why don't you and Mamie take a turn? It was kind of you to wait on us, but I can see Mamie is tired of sitting here."

"That's a brilliant idea!" said Mamie. "Come on, Hal. My feet are itching to dance!"

Hal didn't need persuading. "Watch us for a few pointers," he said and took Mamie off to join the other couples. They were soon caught up in a sprightly polka. Mamie's laugh was audible above the music as Hal twirled her energetically around the dance floor.

Douglas took the chair Hal had vacated. He gave a deep sigh and pulled out a handkerchief to wipe his brow. Alice realized the upbeat demeanor he'd displayed moments ago had been primarily for Hal's benefit. Perhaps he was as worried as she was that the others might guess the two of them had shared more than a dance. The thought set her cheeks burning so hotly that it took all her strength of will to keep from pressing the cool lemonade bottle against her face. She didn't want to draw attention to her discomfort.

Douglas looked unsure what to say next. His gaze rested briefly on Alice, and it seemed to transmit many things—above all, a sincere tenderness that made her heart gallop. Not trusting herself to speak, Alice took another sip of lemonade. She expected Lucy to fill the void, but her friend merely frowned and said nothing.

Douglas turned his gaze to the dancers. With a crooked grin, he picked up the penny and began to idly tap it on the metal table. After a moment, Alice realized that the sounds were not as random as his posture indicated. He was sending her a message in Morse code. *T-H-A-N-K Y-O-U.*

She took in a breath as impudently happy feelings ran around her heart. Douglas glanced at her to see if she'd caught on. She gave him a brief nod. She was sure that if she were to tap out her response, Lucy would notice what was happening. Alice wanted to keep this just between herself and Douglas.

Lucy finished off her lemonade and set the empty bottle on the table with a decided *clink.*

"I apologize if we left you too long with Hal and Mamie," Douglas said, noticing Lucy's obvious irritation. "It can be trying to spend too much time with them."

"Nonsense, it has been a pleasant afternoon," Lucy answered, although her voice was strained. "Nevertheless, Alice and I ought to be going home. It wouldn't do for us to be out on a Saturday night, what with Alice a single woman and I without my husband present. There is a good reason society has these strictures in place. If women are out and about by themselves, it is easy for them to fall prey to unscrupulous men."

There was a time—right up until an hour ago, in fact—when Alice would have scoffed at this notion. Although she had always been careful not to place herself in potentially dangerous situations, she'd never been overly concerned about whether being out and about on her own was "acceptable." Now she saw only too clearly that there could be truth behind the dire warnings of prim matrons. Just thinking about how easily she'd succumbed to Douglas's kiss—and in a public place!—showed Alice that she could be just as vulnerable as more weak-minded women.

She could understand Lucy's agitation, but she did not think it was entirely justified. Lucy was neither Alice's mother nor her guardian. Since her marriage, Lucy had often fussed over Alice's determination to remain single and "unprotected." Yet never before had she acted like an overbearing chaperone.

"I understand." Douglas nodded to signify he was in full agreement with Lucy's words. "Perhaps I might escort you home, in order to ensure no one attempts to bother you along the way?"

He either hadn't caught on that Lucy had implied he was one of those "unscrupulous men," or else he was doing an excellent job of pretending otherwise.

Lucy gave a firm shake of her head. "I thank you for the offer, Mr. Shaw, but there is no need. We shall take a cab home, rather than the train, and I'll ensure that Alice gets home safely."

She pushed back her chair, and Douglas quickly rose to help her up. "Then I'll accompany you to the cab rank." He gave her a diffident smile. "I'm not much of an escort, but I'm afraid I'm the best you have at present."

Lucy looked up at him, appraising his words. Alice could see another refusal on the tip of her tongue. Was Lucy really so angry that she'd turn away this polite offer? But after a moment, she gave a nod. "That's very kind of you, Mr. Shaw."

Alice was glad her friend had relented. The worst possible thing would be to end this evening on a sour note. Lucy could sit firmly on her high horse when it came to Douglas, but Alice had to work with him every day. She couldn't afford to antagonize him—not if she wanted to maintain a productive relationship at the office.

The walk to the cabs was mercifully short, yet not nearly long enough. Alice continued to battle contradictory emotions. The current atmosphere between the three of them was far removed from the earlier friendliness of the afternoon. She was sorry for this.

On the other hand, would she change anything about what had happened? Would she prefer not knowing just how wonderful his kiss could be? She was not prepared to answer that question. Not now, at any rate, while she was in the heat of it. Not while she felt so intensely aware of the man walking next to her, as though every nerve were trying to imprint the sensation of his closeness into her memory.

Douglas helped Lucy into the cab first and then Alice. Once she was in, he gave her hand a little squeeze before letting go. A subtle gesture, but filled with meaning. The problem was that Alice had no idea what it meant. She heartily wished she could decode that message as easily as the dots and dashes that flooded her ears every day.

"I will see you bright and early on Monday, Miss McNeil," Douglas said.

"Yes," she answered, gazing into his eyes. It came out as a breathless sigh. *No, no, that's completely wrong.* She straightened and cleared her throat. "I'm sure it will be busy, what with the contract details being hammered out for the Portland deal. Not to mention keeping up with the progress of the shipments from Savannah."

That sounded better. Crisp and businesslike.

"Indeed." Douglas nodded seriously. "There will be plenty of work waiting for us."

There would be more than merely work to face on Monday, Alice thought gloomily. There would also be Archie Clapper.

From the moment Hal had invited them to the tea dance, Alice had not thought once about him. Now she recalled the events at the lecture hall with a heavy sense of dread. What would be the ramifications of what had happened there today?

"Where to?" asked the driver, ready to get on with his fare.

Alice gave him the address of her lodgings. She leaned back in her seat, determined not to seek another glimpse of Douglas as the carriage rolled down the drive toward the London road. She did send a quick glance at Lucy, who was looking straight ahead, her mouth closed in a thin line.

After they'd been traveling for several minutes, Lucy finally spoke. "You need to be careful, my dear. That man is not to be trusted."

Alice shook her head. "What makes you say that? I believe he is honest and straightforward." She meant this, despite all that had happened.

"You may change your mind about him," Lucy replied.

Alice turned toward her. "Why are you so upset that I danced with Douglas?" Too late, she realized she'd used his Christian name.

Sure enough, Lucy's eyes narrowed. "I feel sure you did more than simply dance with him," she challenged.

"No," Alice said, the bald lie rolling off her tongue before she could stop it.

Lucy cocked a disbelieving brow. "I know it's easy to become enamored with such a handsome and engaging man. I won't deny he turned my head when I first saw him. However, I learned something very interesting from Mamie while you two were off dancing. Something I think you should know."

This grim announcement threatened to do more damage to Alice's tattered emotions. She swallowed. "What is it?"

"Hal went off to buy the lemonade, leaving Mamie and I alone at the table. Mamie said she hoped Douglas was successful in learning to dance, as there was so much riding on it. I asked her what she meant. She looked embarrassed and then asked me point-blank if you were in love with him! I told her certainly not."

"Quite right," Alice said, although she couldn't put any feeling into the words.

"Mamie looked relieved," Lucy went on. "She said that was good, since Mr. Shaw has been courting the daughter of a wealthy banker."

This information should not have been surprising. A man like Douglas would naturally have an interest in courting. It would explain why he was so determined to learn to dance. Why, then, did this news hit her with the force of something completely unexpected? She said shakily, "Is that so? Well, I . . . certainly wish him well."

She hoped this came out in the positive spirit in which she

intended it and not as sarcasm. Douglas was determined to rise in business and society. Alice was well aware that building his net worth was of primary importance to him. Who better for him to marry than the daughter of a wealthy banker?

Sighing, Alice sank back against the worn carriage seat and absently fingered a tear in the leather.

Lucy reached out to pat her hand. "Men like that are masters at toying with women. They get what they want, and then they move on. In your case, it was—"

"Learning how to dance," Alice supplied firmly. "I taught him to dance, and for that he is grateful. I'm sure neither of us expects more."

She was glad that Lucy didn't argue. They rode on in silence as Alice pondered the day's events. Had Douglas been dishonest with her? Had he been untruthful, simply because he had not revealed the specific reason for his desire to conquer dancing? Had he deliberately misled her?

"There could be any number of reasons why Mr. Shaw didn't mention this lady," she said finally. "For one thing, it isn't any of my business. For another, we planned this outing merely as colleagues interested in learning more about technical advances in the telephone. The dancing wasn't planned at all, remember? I had to persuade him to dance. He had no way of knowing I enjoyed dancing, much less that I could help him learn."

Lucy sniffed. "Whatever the reason for how things played out, it's clear to me he's had quite an effect on you. Don't try to deny it."

"I don't deny it," Alice said quietly. "We were both so elated at his success that it . . . well, it drew us together."

"Just remember that he may not have your best interests at heart. Not like old friends do. Friends like me." Lucy pointed toward Alice's reticule. "And Fred, too! He thought enough of you to send a note from halfway around the world."

"Let's not discuss Fred right now, if you please," Alice snapped.

"Hear me out," Lucy insisted. "Fred is a good man. He earns good money on these voyages, you know. The officers keep a percentage of the haul, and his ship has been very successful. He may not be as handsome as *some* people"—she gave a little sniff, as though she found it insulting that Douglas should be better looking than her brother—"but Fred will never do you wrong. You won't have to worry about anything. All your needs will be met."

"They are met now," Alice said. "I have work that pays well, and I take care of myself."

"Yes, but a job is never guaranteed, is it?" Lucy persisted.

"By that kind of logic, neither is Fred's. And then how would he support me?"

Lucy pursed her lips. "You didn't used to be so contrary."

You didn't used to try to marry me off to your oaf of a brother, Alice thought. But to appease her friend she said, "I promise I will read his letter, and I will spend some time with him when he returns from India."

Lucy gave Alice a tiny smile. "Well, that's good enough for now, I expect."

Alice was glad to get home. She needed time alone to sort out her thoughts. She sat on her sofa for a long time, too worn out from the emotional highs and lows of the day to even prepare for bed.

Noticing that the spinster book was within arm's reach, Alice picked it up and opened it. Maybe now was a good time to review that chapter on the consolations of spinsterhood, she thought grimly.

Instead, she came across the passage that had so enthralled Emma:

Love is the bread and the wine of life, the hunger and the thirst, the hurt and the healing, the only wound which is cured by another. It is the guest who comes like a thief in the night. . . .

The words seemed to stab at Alice's heart—or rather, to expose a hollowness that had already existed without her even realizing it. That a single kiss could bring on such a surge of longing . . . This discovery shocked and stunned her. She had thought herself immune to such things; now she knew it was only because she'd never truly been exposed to them. No man had ever kissed her like that. It had been intoxicating.

Her newfound knowledge would do her no good, however. She would have to set it aside, if she was going to continue on as she had been. What other choice was there? Or ought she to look for another job? No, surely that was an overreaction.

"My emotions are high, that's all," Alice said to herself. "It's a common failing for women." She sighed. It might be common to other women, but it had never happened to *her*. The memory of the kiss and the feelings it evoked coursed through every part of her being.

Miss T jumped up beside her on the sofa, stepping onto her lap and nuzzling her chin. "Thank you for the comfort, my dear," Alice said, even though she knew the cat's actions were merely a shameless bid to be petted. Alice obliged, taking solace in this tiny measure of companionship, and turned the pages of the book to the passage she'd initially been seeking.

> The spinster has no need of the man's name, nor his troubles. Her career lies before her! She has only to choose the thing for which she is best fitted and work her way upward. . . . That which is obtained by personal effort is by far the sweetest in the end.

Now the book was finally making some sense! This was Alice's calling and her goal—to be free to live her life unencumbered. With this frame of mind, it was easier to remind herself of the cold, hard truth about Douglas Shaw—he was actively seeking another woman, someone who would advance him in society and enlarge his bank account. How could she waste even a minute of her time mooning over someone like that? Clearly his primary goal in life was to get ahead. To that end, Alice had been useful to him tonight. The rest was of no consequence to him, and it ought not to be for her, either.

Holding firmly to this resolve, Alice got up and prepared for bed. She'd been soundly shaken, but she would recover.

CHAPTER

Nineteen

Alice's steps slowed as she approached her workplace on Monday morning. Today she could not muster her usual enthusiasm. Despite her resolutions, the effects of Saturday's events had been hard to shake. She was still nervous about seeing Douglas again, worried about keeping her professionalism firmly in place, and dreading her next encounter with Archie.

As she entered the building, she saw Mavis by the stairs on the opposite side of the lobby, having a quiet chat with the clerk from the insurance company. They were standing very close, and Mavis was looking up at him in a way that told Alice the clerk had a greater chance of winning her heart than Alice had initially surmised.

Averting her gaze from the couple, Alice went into the office. She noticed that neither Mr. Henley nor Douglas had yet arrived. Perhaps that was why Mavis felt emboldened to spend a few extra minutes with the clerk.

Alice got to work. There were several messages on her desk, waiting to be encoded and sent. She picked one up and read it, sighing at the sight of Douglas's now-familiar handwriting. She knew that, driven as he was, he often worked outside of normal business hours. It was likely he'd been working on Saturday morning and left these messages before the two of them met for the lecture.

Mavis came in a few minutes later, her eyes shining with happiness. Alice pretended to be absorbed in her task in order to discourage conversation. She couldn't bear the idea just now of listening to Mavis's romantic chatter. After another minute or so, she heard the clickety-clack of the typewriter, indicating Mavis had settled into her work.

Over the next half hour, Alice dragged out what little work she had, trying to focus on anything except Archie's impending arrival. She could not guess whether he would conduct their future interactions with anger or with his patented brand of deprecating remarks. Either way, it would not be pleasant. There was nothing he liked better than having excuses to be snide—and Alice had provided him with more than enough.

Archie was not the next person to enter the office, however. Alice knew the moment Douglas stepped through the door. She felt it in every cell of her body, long before she heard Mavis's chipper, "Good morning, Mr. Shaw!"

She could feel him looking at her, too. She was certain she was the first person his gaze had sought as he'd come through the door. But she kept her eyes on her work.

She desperately wished she had some telegram to send or that the sounder would announce an incoming message! She didn't even have the option of *pretending* to be transmitting a work message while really sending a friendly greeting to Rose. It wasn't unusual for telegraphers to chat over the wires during slow periods. But Douglas, understanding Morse code by ear, would know what she was doing.

With no other options, Alice settled for picking up a few messages that had come in earlier, intending to take them to Mavis. They were not critical, and Mavis had other work to do at the moment, but it was the best excuse Alice could come up with. She was embarrassed that she was trying so hard to avoid talking with Douglas. It was an indication of how much she was still bothered by what had happened. A sign of foolishness and weakness. But it was either that or risk showing the real emotions she was trying to suppress.

She stood up, messages in hand, and began walking toward Mavis, but Douglas went out of his normal route to his office in order to intercept her.

"Good morning, Miss McNeil. How are you?" He smiled at her in the casual, easy way he always had. Alice thought she could spot tension in his eyes, but nothing that marred how handsome he was. Nothing to prevent the way her heart sped up, especially now that she knew his kisses surpassed even his looks. Nothing to indicate *he* had lost any sleep over a stray kiss.

"I am tolerably well, thank you." She tried to brush past him.

He moved again into her path. "How was your weekend? Did you have an opportunity to read more of Maxwell's book on electricity?"

Was he flirting with her? He wasn't aware that Alice knew about Miss Rolland. Maybe he was the sort to pursue two women at once. That roused her anger—but not *jealous* anger, she insisted to herself. More like intense disappointment. She wanted to think better of him.

They had agreed not to discuss the weekend's events at the office, so how did he expect her to respond? She decided she could be forgiven for throwing him a look of utter disbelief, as if he'd just asked whether she could confirm the moon was made of green cheese. If he truly thought nothing had changed between them, she could add insensitivity to his list of offences. "I'm afraid I didn't have time. I had other commitments, although I'm sure I would have found more enjoyment reading that book." It came out frosty and hard. He frowned, looking at her in obvious surprise.

This time he didn't stop her as she continued to Mavis's desk and handed over the telegrams for typing.

"I had some time, so I've already decoded these for you," Alice told her.

"Thank you, that's very kind," Mavis replied. She attempted a smile, but Alice could see she was troubled. She had to have noticed the tension between Alice and Douglas.

184

"Miss McNeil, I wonder if I might have a word with you in my office?" Douglas said, his voice now curt and businesslike.

This was the very last thing Alice wanted to do. Especially as Mavis was still watching them with concerned interest. A private chat in Douglas's office would only fuel her curiosity and speculation. That was something Alice had specifically hoped to avoid when she'd asked Douglas not to talk about this at work. He seemed to have decided not to keep that promise.

Unfortunately, she had no choice in the matter. Douglas had spoken in a manner that did not allow for refusal. He motioned her toward his office, and she reluctantly complied.

⸎

Douglas had seen Alice glance at Miss Waller before following him to his office, and he'd seen the typist's troubled look in return. Had Alice told her what happened? Douglas couldn't think of a worse thing she could do. Why had he not considered any of these possibilities when he'd casually invited himself to join Alice at that lecture? Why hadn't he listened to the voice warning him that Hal would find him, even among so many people?

Self-recrimination did no good, however. Here they were. He thought they had ended the evening on a reasonably good note. Apparently he'd been wrong. She was clearly upset. He'd thought they had an understanding to forget what had happened and move ahead. That had turned out to be an immensely tall order. He'd spent every waking moment preparing his mind to accomplish it. Now he wasn't sure what she expected of him.

He closed the door and turned to face Alice. "Miss McNeil, I hate to think the events of the weekend are still troubling you."

She stared him down. "What makes you think I'm troubled about it?"

"How about that thinly veiled insult out there?" Frustration sharpened his words.

Something that might have been guilt flickered briefly in her eyes, but she didn't answer. He could imagine she was mentally

185

falling back to reload a fresh round of biting remarks. Douglas didn't want to continue on that way. He might never be able to tell this woman how he felt about her, but he was going to do all he could to keep their relationship on good terms. If that was even possible. He hoped with all his might that it was.

Aiming for a more neutral tone, he said, "When we parted, I had the impression we agreed to put that incident behind us."

"And *I* believe we agreed not to talk about it at the office," Alice hissed. "Do you want to risk the gossip and possible damage to our reputations by asking me in here?"

"We've had many conversations in my office before," Douglas pointed out.

"About business matters!"

"No one will know the difference with the door closed. Although they might start guessing, based on how you were acting out there a moment ago."

She took in a breath. "I'm sorry, Mr. Shaw, but I'm finding it very difficult to act as if nothing has changed. What I don't understand is how it is so easy for you to do so. It seems very"—she paused just long enough to clench her fists—"callous."

Yes, he had been wrong. Very wrong.

She'd been so adamant about remaining single that Douglas had spent hours convincing himself that was what she truly wanted. He thought she had been better at walking away from that kiss than he had been. She hadn't. Without meaning to, he'd found a vulnerable spot in her heart. What was he to make of that? He tried to reconsider his position, but it was impossible to do on the fly while she was staring at him with hurt and anger.

He swallowed, wondering how in the world he was going to make this right. "You have every reason to think me a heartless cad, and I'm truly sorry. If it's any consolation, I never intended to take advantage of you. I was beyond thrilled at how you'd helped me understand dancing, and, well . . ."

You were irresistible.

No, he couldn't say that. Not now. It must have somehow shown

186

in the way he was looking at her, though, because she softened—ever so slightly—as though tempted to melt into his gaze.

Clearing his throat, he took a step back. "It was a mistake, you see. The way you turned your head at that precise moment—well, it took me by surprise, and—"

She stiffened, all trace of vulnerability disappearing. "You needn't make excuses for kissing me by mistake. I'm quite sure we both regret the action."

She spoke with utter distaste. Surely it was a cover for hurt pride? Douglas had always prided himself on being an expert at dealing with people, but that was in business. Clearly he had no idea how to talk to women. Now he'd insulted her, when that was the last thing he wanted to do. He shook his head in agitation. "That's not what I—"

Alice put up a hand to stop him. "As I said, there's no need for further apologies. We have both agreed that we must put this behind us. However, I must request that you not ask to speak to me privately again. Mr. Clapper has seen us together outside of work. If we are seen going alone into your office, there will be gossip. He'll make sure of it."

"I won't allow that contemptible man to dictate my actions!" Douglas had always disliked Clapper, and now his loathing was unmeasurable.

"I am leaving now," Alice said coolly. "But I have one more thing to ask before I go. You didn't want me to know about Miss Rolland, did you? You kept trying to stop Hal from mentioning her. But Mamie must not have gotten the word about keeping quiet, because she relayed all the information to Lucy."

So that was it. Now Douglas understood why her attitude toward him had changed so drastically. But her response only confused him more. "Are you jealous? That doesn't mesh with your insistence that you want us to be nothing more than work colleagues."

He regretted the words the moment he spoke them. He saw real pain in her eyes now. Had she begun to care for him? Whatever her feelings, he seemed an expert at trampling on them.

Alice sucked in a breath. "You're right, Mr. Shaw. Why you did not wish to discuss Miss Rolland is absolutely none of my business. It is my fault for allowing emotions to direct my words instead of common sense. I won't allow it to happen again."

With that, she turned on her heel and stalked out, pulling the door shut behind her with such force that it was only marginally short of an angry slam.

⟐

Alice pulled up short just outside Douglas's office. Mavis was staring at her in alarm, her fingers poised above the typewriter keys.

Also observing Alice carefully, albeit with a completely different expression, was Archie Clapper. He was early again, as though he couldn't wait to begin tormenting her about Saturday.

He leaned back in his chair and gave her the look—a half smile, half sneer—that always rankled her. "What's the matter, Miss McNeil? Did you and Shaw have a lovers' spat?"

Alice walked toward her desk. "Your twisted imagination is working overtime again, Mr. Clapper. I'll thank you to keep your rude comments to yourself."

This wasn't how she'd wanted this conversation to go. She had even considered offering an apology of some sort, although she knew the mix-up had not been her fault. Now she could see that approach was out of the question. She returned his look with a dark stare, wanting him to back off, then took her seat at her desk.

Archie being Archie, her blunt retort did nothing to remove the superior expression from his face. "I know what you're after, Miss McNeil. But I think you should know that he's merely toying with you. It's no use setting your cap at him. He'll never be within reach of a mere telegraph operator. He's chasing loftier game—the daughter of one of Mr. Henley's cronies. It's one of those alliances where everyone comes out richer."

"I'm well aware of that, thank you. Not that it is any business of ours," she added pointedly. "Nor does it matter one bit to me.

188

I've no intention of 'setting my cap' at anyone." Alice shuddered. She hated that phrase.

"You could have fooled me, the way you've been making eyes at him and, well, *everything else.*"

Alice glared at him. "Are you referring to something in particular, or are you merely indulging in your usual coarse insinuations?"

It was a rebuke, but it was also a question she truly wanted the answer to. She had a lingering fear that Archie had seen her dancing with Douglas—or worse, their kiss. She'd seen no sign of him at the dance, but she suspected Archie could be adept at lurking in the shadows if it suited his purpose.

Archie allowed her comment to bounce off him, his skin as thick as an elephant's. He fiddled with the pencils on his desk as he gave her a self-satisfied smile. "It's rather ironic, really, seeing as how his origins are lower than yours. Do you know Shaw's father couldn't even read? Just one of the ignorant louts who work in the shipyards by the legions."

"Don't be insulting, Mr. Clapper."

"It's true! Just ask him. Although you may have to pry it out of him. He's rather loath to talk about his family, as you might imagine." He tapped one of the pencils on his desk. "Now I, on the other hand . . ." He pointed his pencil at himself for emphasis. "I've got a fine family lineage. We can trace at least one branch back to the Domesday book. That's what really matters, you know."

"Perhaps Mr. Shaw doesn't care about such things." Despite all that had happened, Alice still found herself coming to Douglas's defense. She realized now that he'd said very little about his background, though he'd asked plenty of questions about hers. Maybe he *was* ashamed about coming from the lower class. Maybe he was trying to hide it, believing that if those details were known, it would hinder his acceptance into society. But unlike Archie, she was going to give Douglas the benefit of the doubt. "Perhaps Mr. Shaw doesn't talk about his family because he understands that in this day and age, what matters more is hard work and industry."

"Yes, I'm sure that's it," Archie drawled. "If one defines 'industry' as the need to marry a dim-witted debutante to seal one's success."

There wasn't much Alice could say to that. She dismissed the underlying misogyny in the phrase *dim-witted debutante*, as Archie would immediately assume the worst about any woman. It was doubtful he had any personal knowledge of Miss Rolland. For all either of them knew, she was clever and sophisticated, and surely well bred. What bothered Alice, though she'd tried not to give credence to it, was the idea that Douglas could be the kind of adventurer she considered to be the very worst.

Douglas's plan was far from novel, of course. It had been the English way for centuries. Even so, Alice realized she'd been nurturing the idea that Douglas was above that kind of coldhearted calculation, where an offer of marriage was no more than a business deal. He took a great deal of pride in having advanced in life on his own merits, not beholden to anyone. If he aligned himself with someone for the sake of a large dowry and social position, those benefits would surely come with a father-in-law who would expect Douglas to do his bidding in return. It just didn't fit what she had seen of him. Had she been mistaken, perhaps blinded by his good looks, intelligence, and business acumen? Such things could easily turn the head of anyone. *Even sensible-minded me,* she thought ruefully.

Whatever the case, right now Alice wanted nothing more than to wipe the supercilious smile off Archie's face. He'd dropped an unintentional clue when he'd said that *at least one branch* of his family history was illustrious. She would lay odds that he came from the branch that *didn't* stem from greatness. Otherwise, why would he be working as a telegraph clerk? It was a respectable occupation, and one Alice was proud to call her own, but it was far from lofty.

"Is that why you don't put forth the slightest effort to improve your own situation, Mr. Clapper? The mere fact of having worthy ancestors makes you content to toil away in an office, expending the most fair-to-middling effort possible?"

This remark brought a flash of anger to Archie's eyes. She braced for an onslaught—which, to be honest, she probably deserved. What she'd said might be true, but it had been rude to say it. Sucking in a breath, she charged herself to stop allowing Archie to bring her down to his level.

Surprisingly, though, Archie's irritating smile returned. He smoothed back his hair and shrugged. "Mere conservation of effort, Miss McNeil. Why beat myself up in the impossible task of trying to get ahead, when in the end it all comes down to who your relations are?" Tossing his pencil on his desk, he leaned back in his chair. "I've got a proper inheritance coming soon, when my wealthy old aunt finally passes on to that realm where she no longer needs it. I'm simply biding my time. In the meantime, I've got a tidy little stipend that keeps me from having to pinch my pennies until they scream—as I suppose *other people* who work at this job must do."

Did he think Alice's salary was insufficient? He couldn't know that Mr. Henley was paying her a fair wage, one that was higher than normally offered to a woman. Alice was getting by just fine. She had almost no savings to speak of, but she was working hard to rectify that.

Archie leaned forward and eyed her in a way that was bolder than his usual laconic stare. "So if you'd like to step out with me sometime, I can take you to some nice places. A restaurant, maybe, or the theater. You wouldn't have to settle for a six-penny lecture at a recreation ground designed for the masses."

It was another thinly veiled insult, this time aimed at Douglas. As though her meeting him at a lecture hall for educational purposes was some kind of romantic interlude. Of course, if Archie had seen the two of them dancing, he could easily get that idea. Alice attempted to squelch that fear. He'd only mentioned the lecture. That was surely all he knew regarding what had transpired between her and Douglas that day—although it was too easy for his warped imagination to fill in the rest.

Walking out with Archie—the very thought made Alice's stomach turn. "You can set that dream aside right now, Mr. Clapper. I am sitting here next to you because we are forced by circumstances to work together. But don't dare to think you can approach me outside of work. Not in *any* capacity."

She spoke fiercely, no longer caring if she drew equal fire in return.

Archie tensed. An ugly expression crossed his features, making him even more repulsive than normal. He appeared to be considering several things to say, all of them undoubtedly filled with vitriol. But then he sat back, his shoulders relaxing, and gave her a smile as if he knew he'd won. "As you wish, Miss McNeil. Don't expect the offer to come again."

It would have been laughable if it had not sounded so sinister.

CHAPTER

Twenty

The rest of the morning was no more pleasant, even if it was free of direct altercations. Alice did her work and spoke with Archie as little as possible. The telegraph wire picked up its usual Monday morning pace with incoming messages. Mr. Henley and Douglas were busy on a new project that required a lot of outgoing messages as well. Whenever Douglas came to talk to her about a work-related issue, she kept her manner formal and businesslike.

Keeping a calm exterior, when so many thoughts and emotions were still roiling within her, had been a severe test of her will. There were moments when she thought the strain would do her in. After what had seemed an interminable morning, her lunch break finally arrived. Alice collected her hat, gloves, and reticule, and quickly left the building, eager for a few minutes of peace.

On the sidewalk, she paused to take a deep breath. Somehow, she had to find a way to make her work tolerable. She could not allow Archie to get under her skin. Not at any cost. Nor could she permit what had happened between her and Douglas to linger in her mind, affecting her so deeply. Even now, memories of that kiss could make her face grow warm and her pulse race—

No.

Alice was not going to dwell on one incident that had become more personal than it ought to have been. She was not in love with Douglas Shaw. She'd merely had her emotions put in a tumble by a very pleasurable kiss. It would be foolish to confuse those two things. Despite what happened at the dance, Alice was fully aware that Douglas had no intention of pursuing her. He had far different plans for matrimony, and it didn't matter in the least what Alice thought of them.

Nor would she be pushed around by a boorish colleague who resented her presence simply because she was a woman. From now on, she would be extra careful to keep her mind on business only. She would pursue her well-planned objectives, which were only tangentially tied to Douglas Shaw through their work at the same company.

With these resolutions firmly in her heart, Alice strode down the street with her head held high.

❦

Douglas came out of his office just in time to see Alice leaving the building. Everything about her movements signaled that she couldn't wait to get out. He couldn't blame her. The morning had been difficult. Tougher by far than he had expected. Keeping his mind on work had been nigh on impossible when he was busy berating himself for how he'd mishandled the situation.

Douglas regretted many things about what had happened, not the least of which was losing the easy camaraderie that had existed between them at work. He wanted more than anything to find some way to get that back. Whether that could happen after the line they had crossed remained to be seen. He had only himself to blame.

He had come out of his office with the intention of conferring with Mr. Henley over a shipping contract he'd been reviewing, but through Henley's open door, he could see that the bookkeepers, Dawson and Nicholls, were already talking with him about another matter. Miss Waller was not at her desk; she must be at lunch.

Douglas crossed the room and went to the window that faced

the street. He could just see Alice near the main entrance. She stood there, clenching and unclenching the gloves she held in one hand, having apparently forgotten to put them on. Douglas had just about made up his mind to go out and speak with her when she squared her shoulders and walked off. She passed the window where he stood, but she was looking ahead and didn't see him. He watched until she was no longer in view.

"Be careful around that one," Clapper said.

Startled, Douglas turned from the window to see the telegrapher standing not five feet behind him. Always too quick to notice details that might be to someone else's detriment, he had observed Douglas's gaze following Alice down the street.

Douglas decided it wouldn't do any good to pretend he hadn't been watching Alice or that he didn't know whom Archie was talking about. "Do you have some complaint about Miss McNeil?"

Clapper grunted. "Do I? She's a first-class flirt. She's ruining the work environment here."

"Don't be ridiculous."

Undeterred, Clapper continued his accusations. "I know she acts straight-laced and proper most of the time, but she's still a woman. And like all the rest of 'em, she's not above using her feminine wiles to advance herself—whether at work or in *any other* aspect of life, if you take my meaning."

"Are you referring to the events of last Saturday?" Douglas worked to keep his anger under control. Clapper was always trying to goad him, always acting superior despite the fact that he occupied a lower rank in the company.

Clapper took a step closer to Douglas. "It began long before then. She's been trying out her artful ways on me, too."

Douglas eyed him in disbelief. "How so?"

"She was effusive in her praise of the way I sharpen my pencils." Clapper said this with the air of a barrister presenting irrefutable evidence of a crime.

Douglas very nearly laughed outright. "You think that qualifies as flirting? Perhaps she was being sincere."

"Granted, she was only pointing out the truth," Clapper conceded with a sniff. "But it wasn't so much *what* she said as *when* she said it. And *why*. Before then, she'd been nothing but disparaging in her dealings with me, ever since she began working here."

Clapper was surely exaggerating, but Douglas didn't press him on it. If Alice had acted negatively toward him, it was because he'd brought it on himself. "Why do you suppose Miss McNeil's demeanor suddenly changed?"

"Simple. You came back to London."

Douglas shook his head. "Why should that matter?" But he already knew what Clapper was going to say. He was starting to have a terrible feeling about all of this. Clapper had witnessed their meeting outside of work. He'd drawn exactly the kind of conclusions that came naturally to his suspicious mind. The worst part was that he wasn't entirely wrong.

"She's set her sights on you, of course. And she's using me as a pawn in her games." Clapper's eyes narrowed. "Did you tell her about my family connection to this company?"

"Certainly not. Look, about last Saturday—"

"Yes, let's talk about that," Clapper interrupted. "How do you suppose she lured us both there?"

Lured? Douglas stared at him blankly.

Clapper began ticking off points with his fingers. "First, she starts being nice to me, as though trying to get my interest or butter me up. Then she offers to loan me a copy of the *Telegraphic Journal*. The information about the time and place of that lecture is circled in pencil. How much larger of a hint could she drop?"

"And what would be her purpose for 'luring' you there, if she had set her sights on me?"

Clapper looked at him as though he were daft. "That's obvious! Women always think they appear more enticing if a man knows he has competition. She planned for the two of us to see each other there, both thinking she had invited us."

"So you're saying she's trying to turn us into rivals?" The thought was ludicrous in so many ways that Douglas could barely keep the derision from his voice.

Clapper grunted in disgust. "I'm not so stupid as to think she ever considered me a true contender. Certainly not now that I've had my eyes opened to the kind of woman she is."

He was speaking for all the world like a spurned lover—which was probably how he saw himself.

It was too outlandish to believe. Alice, a conniving, scheming woman? It wasn't possible. Except he had seen her that night coming out of the bookshop—and he was certain the book she'd been carrying was that spinster book. Even his brief glance at its pages had showed Douglas there was a lot in it about how to manipulate men. Was she trying to find an underhanded way to ensnare him? It just didn't make sense.

He couldn't say why Alice had suddenly made an effort to get into Archie's good graces. She might have had a good reason. But in her dealings with Douglas, there had been no artifice. At least, none that he could recognize. Except for that pasted-on smile she'd given him before the cab had driven away. That had been after their dance and the wondrous kiss that had followed. . . . Douglas shook his head. Judging from her behavior today, she wanted to distance herself from that moment, not capitalize on it. Unless that was some sort of ploy as well. . . .

All these possibilities clashed in Douglas's mind, making his head hurt.

Clapper was watching him as though he could read the succession of thoughts parading through Douglas's mind. Perhaps he could, given they were largely planted there by his insinuations—which made it glaringly obvious how poisonous they were.

Douglas said coldly, "Thank you for the warning, Clapper, but it isn't necessary. If there is some problem between you and Miss McNeil, I suggest you work it out between yourselves. As for the rest, I can assure you that if 'trapping' me was her aim, she has failed."

This was supposed to be a rebuke, but Clapper didn't take it that way. He merely gave Douglas a smug smile. "I'm glad to hear you're not falling for her tricks. After all, you've got bigger fish to catch, eh? It could be quite embarrassing to Mr. Henley if you threw over the daughter of his closest friend because you were dallying with an employee."

Douglas advanced on him. "Are you trying to threaten me?"

Clapper stood his ground, his expression as oily as his slicked-back hair. "As you said, I'm simply warning you. Women like that can be bad for business."

"So can unfounded, malicious gossip. You think your position in this company is unassailable, but I can ensure that changes if need be."

It was clear from Archie's smirk that he thought Douglas's threat to be an empty one. However, Douglas fully believed his words, even though, if pressed, he had no idea how he'd make good on them.

"I'd suggest you get back to work," Douglas ordered as the sounder announced an incoming message.

"Certainly, sir." Clapper gave an obsequious bow of his head before returning to the telegraph machine.

Douglas returned to his office. He sat thinking for a long time. In Clapper's comments, there had been an indirect but unmistakeable reference to Miss Rolland. That Clapper should be aware of her was no surprise, given that he was in frequent communication with his cousin, Mr. Henley's wife. Mr. Henley and Mr. Rolland had been friends for a long time. They belonged to the same club and frequented the same social circles. Douglas suspected that if the Henleys had been able to have a son, they would be pushing him to marry Rolland's daughter. It would be advantageous from a business standpoint, but it would mean something personally to them as well.

Was Clapper interested in Douglas's possible alliance with Miss Rolland because it would benefit the company, which was his livelihood? Or had he simply realized he'd made a fool of himself for thinking Alice might fancy him, and now he was determined to slander her in retribution? Both possibilities seemed equally likely.

Eventually, Douglas decided two things. First, whatever happened, he was going to ensure that Alice's reputation was preserved. Archie couldn't be allowed to besmirch someone's character. If Douglas had to go toe-to-toe with Mr. Henley over this, he would do it. He couldn't believe she was playing games with any of the men in this office, even though Clapper's warped suggestions had briefly tempted him to consider it. He was going to treat her with the respect she deserved.

Secondly, he was going to put forth his best effort at that charity ball—not because of Clapper's threats, but in spite of them. He was already committed to attending the event. It had been his goal for months. He could not allow anything to deter him from pursuing what was best for him and for the company.

Not even a wonderfully fervent kiss from a self-professed, confirmed spinster.

⁕

A brisk walk often helped Alice calm her thoughts, enabling her to analyze thorny problems more effectively. Today, though, it wasn't working. The clatter and bustle of the city streets, which normally invigorated her, only further jarred her frayed nerves.

Realizing she was approaching the street where the Central Telegraph Office was located, she decided to visit the little park next to it. Many an overtaxed worker sought refuge there for a few minutes of peace on a busy workday.

As she turned into the park, Alice was pleased to see a familiar face among the men and women seated on the benches lining the path. Emma was just tossing a morsel of bread to a pigeon when she caught sight of Alice. Immediately she smiled and waved a greeting. Alice realized what she needed most right now was a friend to talk to. Someone who wasn't Lucy. Someone who could listen sympathetically without judgment.

Emma rose from the bench, hurrying to meet Alice. "It's so lovely to see you!" she exclaimed after treating Alice to an enthusiastic hug.

"How did you guess this was the hour when my pitiless overseers allow me a few minutes of freedom?"

Alice shook her head. "You make the CTO managers sound like wardens. Or dog trainers."

"To be honest, it's tempting to apply either of those analogies," Emma replied with a playful grimace.

"In fact, it was mere chance that I found you here," Alice said. "Serendipity, if you will."

Emma's face lit up. "Ah, that makes it even more special." She was a firm believer that daily life was woven through with many events that were *meant to be*. She studied Alice for a moment. "You look like you could use some cheering up."

Alice gave her a wry smile. "Is it that obvious?"

Emma laced an arm through hers. "Let me show you something." She led Alice to a rosebush near the bench where she'd been sitting. "Look at these," she said, pointing to the profusion of pink blossoms. "I noticed last week that this plant wasn't doing well. Whoever tends this park must not have given it proper food. So I brought some fertilizer I had made at home. I also put in minerals that discourage beetles."

"Why would you spend your effort tending to a bush in a public park?" Alice asked in surprise.

Emma shrugged. "I sit out here nearly every day. I feel attached to these roses now. And in any case, isn't it lovely? They smell wonderful, too." She leaned over to catch their scent, indicating that Alice should do the same.

Alice followed her example. There was something relaxing about taking a moment to admire their beauty. She breathed in their soft fragrance, then let out her breath in a long sigh. "Yes. They are lovely."

This simple act of appreciation for a tiny piece of nature made her unexpectedly teary. Evidence her emotions were still too overwrought.

Emma gently squeezed her arm. "Would you care to discuss what's bothering you?"

Alice longed to unburden herself, but she didn't know whether she should. And in any case, time was short, given they were on their lunch breaks. "I'm afraid it's rather a long story."

"The abridged version, then." Emma led Alice to the bench. It was clear her curiosity had been piqued.

When they were seated, Alice took a moment to formulate her words. "Several men have suddenly begun showing, shall we say, a certain level of interest in me."

Yes, that certainly was the abridged version.

"Men at your workplace?" A twinkle came to Emma's eyes. "That happens to me a lot."

"That's because you're beautiful," Alice said without hesitation.

"And you are . . . ?"

"Not interested in marriage," Alice answered flatly. "I want to continue my career in telegraphy."

Emma didn't appear surprised at Alice's response, but she knew Alice pretty well. "The answer is simple, then. Put them in their place. Say you are there strictly to work. You set the example, and they will have to follow."

"Simple," Alice repeated, without conviction. In her heart, she knew it *would* be simple, if only her heart would cooperate.

Emma's expression turned serious. "Are these men interfering with your work? Are they coercing or threatening you in any way?"

"No," Alice assured her. For the most part, it was true. Archie's comments were disturbing, but if they contained any veiled threats, she didn't think they could amount to anything. "It's distracting more than anything else."

That was abridging a *lot*. Archie was annoying, but Douglas aroused so many kinds of feelings that Alice couldn't catalog them all. That was quite a few steps beyond mere distraction. The worst part was that she missed the way things were before that kiss. She had enjoyed the friendly warmth between them and how easy and pleasant it had been to work together. Would they ever be able to get back to that? Would her own heart allow it? Did she even *want* to, now that she'd seen Douglas's more unscrupulous side—that he was willing to marry someone purely for material gain?

Emma's eyes widened. "This wouldn't have anything to do with the spinster book, would it? I remember Rose suggesting you try it at work."

"Yes, that's part of the problem. You might say it worked too well."

"Interesting." Emma tapped a finger against her cheek. "Will you loan me that book sometime?"

"After all the trouble it's gotten me into?" Alice said, aghast.

"Of course! It's clearly potent."

"Potent?" Alice arched a brow. "Like bombs or dynamite?"

"I expect the key is learning the best ways to apply what's in there," Emma replied, undaunted. She gave Alice's hand a reassuring pat. "Whatever you may have unleashed at Henley and Company, I'm sure you can handle it. You're the best at what you do. Keep taking the high road, and you will be successful there."

Alice gave her friend a grateful smile. "I do feel better for having talked about it. May I ask for an additional favor? Please don't tell Rose about this. She already distrusts men, and this will only lower her opinion of them even more."

Emma crossed her arms and smirked. "With all that has happened, you are concerned about not increasing anyone's anger toward men?"

Alice knew she was teasing, but it was an interesting point. "The situation is frustrating, to be sure. Yet I can't say I'm not at least partially to blame. Besides, men don't have a monopoly on doing bad things to people."

"You are certainly correct about that," Emma agreed. "I work among hundreds of women, so I should know. Oh!" She reached into her pocket, pulled out a small watch, and flipped open the cover. "I've got to hurry back or I'll be late, and then my supervisor will be impossible. Her scoldings sting worse than lye soap." As they rose from the bench, Emma added, "I hope you're feeling a little better, at least."

"I am." Alice meant it. Her heart was still bruised, but her burden was lightened.

Emma flashed another gentle smile and hurried off.

There wasn't much time left to Alice's lunch break either, given that she still had to walk back to the office. She looked around the park one last time, watching the telegraph workers coming or going from their breaks. Despite the difficulties, she was still glad she'd left the CTO to work at Henley and Company. All she had to do was concentrate on her work and not allow any personal issues to interfere, and she would be fine. She left the park and hurried down the street.

She turned the corner onto Leadenhall Street five minutes late. Given that Archie would be glaring at her no matter what, she didn't care. She would continue to face him down and stand up for herself.

As she approached her workplace, she hesitated when she noticed Douglas standing in the narrow pedestrian lane next to it, smoking a cigarette. If there had been any way to enter the building without directly passing him, she would have been tempted to do so. However, there was not.

The sight of him still did odd things to the rhythm of her heartbeat. She supposed she might as well get used to ignoring it. There seemed to be nothing else she could do.

Douglas crushed his cigarette and came over to her. "May I talk with you for a moment before you go in?"

Alice nodded, not wanting to speak before she heard what he had to say.

"I wish to apologize again for all the misunderstandings last Saturday and for the hurtful things I said this morning. Please know that I have nothing but the highest respect for you as a person and a fellow colleague." He paused, waiting for her reaction, looking worried she might not accept his apology.

In truth, Alice was gratified to hear his words. Douglas was as concerned as she was about keeping things genial between them at work. Despite how it might *feel* at times, they were both after the same thing.

She took in a breath. "You're right. I believe that, as mature, sensible adults, there is no reason we can't continue working together as productively as we did before we—er, before Saturday."

His relieved smile almost made her want to take back her words, because whenever he looked at her like that, she hardly felt able to function. She had to look away in order to keep her thoughts coherent.

"There is one other thing," Douglas added. "Mr. Henley has told me time and again how impressed he is by your work. I have repeatedly confirmed to him that he is correct to have such confidence in you. And as for Mr. Clapper, I've told him in no uncertain terms that he is not to spread malicious gossip of any kind, or he will absolutely find himself out of a job. I will not have anyone maligning your good name."

"Thank you," Alice said. His concern for her reputation raised him even higher in her estimation. He might have some goals in life she could not understand or agree with, but he was not a ruthless cad. At least, not toward her. But what about toward wealthy debutantes? "May I assume you extend such gentlemanly courtesy to *all* women of your acquaintance?"

It took him a moment to understand the meaning behind her words. Alice knew when he made the connection because his brow furrowed. Maybe he didn't like being called out as a fortune hunter. Maybe he was simply angry that Alice should revisit personal matters when they'd just agreed to keep things businesslike. That anger would be justified. Why had she brought it up? She could only blame her addled thoughts.

"I'm sorry," she said. "Please disregard that question. It truly is none of my business. Thank you for your kind words just now. I should get back to work—"

"No, wait." His words stopped her as she was turning away.

Alice stilled, feeling foolish and wishing she had left matters where they were.

"I strive to be honest in all my dealings, Miss McNeil." He spoke with quiet earnestness. "I make no apology for being an ambitious man, but I would never use anyone merely to get ahead. I would never marry unless there was genuine affection between me and my bride. I hope you can believe that."

Alice looked into his eyes, seeking evidence that he was telling the truth. What she saw was a hint of vulnerability, as though he had shared a small piece of his soul. Heaven help her, it still made her breathless to look at him. No, she was *not* in love, she hastened to assure herself, but she genuinely liked this man very much. "I believe you have always been honest with me, Mr. Shaw. I have no reason to think you would treat others any differently."

His face broadened in a smile, and he visibly relaxed. "I can't tell you what it means to hear you say that."

If Alice allowed herself to be ruled by emotions, she would have said this moment made her very happy. Since she didn't, she would merely acknowledge that she and Douglas had reached an equitable middle ground, and she was going to endeavor to keep it that way.

"Speaking of work," Alice said, "I'd better get back to it."

This time he didn't stop her, although he gave her another smile that warmed her insides so intensely, she might have melted right there on the sidewalk. She hurried inside, fanning herself as she sat down at her desk. She cared not one whit that Archie berated her for being late. In fact, she hardly noticed.

CHAPTER

Twenty-One

You can do this.

Douglas kept repeating the words to himself as the hansom cab approached the mansion where the ball was being held. It had been easier when he'd first gotten into the cab and pulled away from his boardinghouse on the other side of London. Now, as they joined the slow line of carriages on the drive, Douglas found his confidence waning.

Each vehicle paused at the main entrance while men in fine suits and silk hats alighted and then handed down bejeweled ladies in sumptuous gowns. Douglas watched them closely, aware they'd been born and raised to this well-heeled life. How to act and what to say at such events came as naturally to them as breathing. The dinner party at Mr. Rolland's home was nothing compared to this. Douglas knew he wasn't going to be accepted into this world simply because one of its daughters enjoyed flirting with him. There would be so many things to remember tonight and pitfalls to avoid. He had no qualms about facing any of them—except for the dancing.

He had been practicing every day, pairing the steps with the telegraphy trick he'd learned from Alice. He had not said anything about it to her, though. In fact, they had both spent the past week carefully avoiding mention of anything outside of work. Douglas had to admit it was probably for the best. Things at the office seemed to have returned more or less to normal. Clapper was still Clapper, but he had confined himself to his usual grumblings and not stepped over the line Douglas had drawn.

Alice was still Alice, too. He loved her energy and diligence more every day. He was sorry only that she was obviously keeping a careful distance from him. He wished he could have talked to her in preparation for this evening. He wished even more heartily that he could have danced with her again. But that was the line over which *he* could not go.

So he had done his best to prepare on his own. Now that he thought of everything else he'd have to do correctly in addition to the dancing, he wished he'd stuck with his original plan of limping in with an unfortunate "injury." But he had promised Miss Rolland a dance tonight, and he would do it. His sense of honor kept him from ordering the cab driver to turn around.

Honor.

Douglas gave a little grunt. He was honor bound to all sorts of things now. Alice had effectively asked him if he was the kind of man who would marry solely for money. He had insisted he wasn't, and she'd believed him. The truth was, until that point he hadn't thought about it all that deeply. He had figured he'd marry Miss Rolland if he found nothing objectionable in her and if she would have him. The idea of love hadn't entered his mind. When cornered by Alice's question, he couldn't even say the word. *Affection* was the best he could come up with. Now he found himself hoping he could garner a real affection for Miss Rolland just so he would not have lied to the woman he truly did care for. This ridiculous paradox was so unsettling that Douglas knew he must put it out of his mind if he was going to make a good showing tonight.

The cab came to a stop. Douglas got out, paid the driver, and entered the fray.

Once he was inside the ballroom, it took a few minutes to locate Henley. Douglas finally spotted him standing with his wife and another couple in a small grove formed by six potted trees.

Mrs. Henley was chatting with the other lady as they surveyed the crowded ballroom. They were probably gossiping about the other attendees. Or perhaps critiquing the ladies' dresses. Meanwhile, their husbands pretended not to look bored.

Henley brightened when he saw Douglas. "Did you just arrive? You'll have to hurry if you want a chance at Miss Rolland's dance card. There's a rumor it fills up quickly."

"A rumor put forth by the lady herself, I'll wager," joked the other man.

Henley introduced him as Mr. Warner. Douglas recognized the name. Warner owned several successful factories located just to the east of London.

"I've heard from Henley that you're a valuable asset to your company," Warner said, shaking Douglas's hand. "I'd give my eye-teeth to find someone who can combine ambition with a genuine talent for business. Most men I've worked with have too much of the first quality and surprisingly little of the other."

"I'm glad to hear Mr. Henley speaks highly of me," Douglas answered. "I won't deny that I work hard to earn his good opinion."

Warner gave him a pleased smile. "I admire a man who manages to sound self-effacing while still acknowledging his high worth."

"Don't get any ideas about stealing him from me," Henley said to Warner.

Warner held up his hands. "Wouldn't dream of it." But the glint in his eye said he wouldn't mind trying.

It was mere jesting, but Mrs. Henley gave Douglas a look as if he'd just said he planned to abandon the company tomorrow. "You'd better go track down your prospect," she reminded him. "You don't want to miss your chance with Miss Rolland."

Mrs. Henley didn't seem to realize that she and Douglas were on the same side—they both wanted success for her husband's business. Why did she persist in treating him like the enemy? It was as though she feared he would fail the company in some way. It was true that, with money and society bound as closely as they were, there was a lot riding on Douglas's successful courting of Miss

Rolland. Had Clapper been talking with Mrs. Henley, poisoning her mind with ugly gossip about Alice? If he ever had proof of that, Douglas didn't think he'd be able to restrain himself from doing Clapper bodily harm.

Tonight, however, he could do little besides act as though he and Mrs. Henley were on the best of terms. "Right you are, madam. Do you by chance know how I might locate Miss Rolland among all these people?"

"I believe she's holding court near the mirrors along that far wall," Mr. Warner put in.

Douglas excused himself and headed in the direction Warner had indicated. As he threaded his way through the crowd, he could feel the gazes of Mrs. Henley and Mrs. Warner on him, tracking his progress. Perhaps they were discussing his chances of success with Miss Rolland. It was a nice irony, albeit one Mrs. Henley would never be aware of, that his odds were better tonight because of the help he'd gotten from Alice.

Douglas reminded himself yet again that he must set aside all thoughts of Alice. He was here to court another young lady. This plan had been in place long before he'd met Alice. He must remain committed to it.

It was marginally easier to pull his thoughts into line when he finally laid eyes on Miss Rolland. She looked quite fetching. As usual, she'd made the most of her assets, from a flattering hairstyle to a gown that was just the right shade for her complexion.

You see, this is not so difficult. She is attractive, and she is attracted to you. Her father is Henley's friend and an important business associate. Everybody wins. He repeated this to himself several times as he approached her.

She was talking with three other young ladies, coyly pretending not to notice his approach until he stood right next to her. He gave her a bow. "Good evening, Miss Rolland. I hope I may intrude upon your notice for a moment?"

She turned toward him, eyes wide in a show of surprise. "Mr. Shaw, how lovely to see you again!"

"How are you getting on with your butterfly collecting?"

She opened her fan with a playful snap and viewed him over the top of it. "I have no new specimens to speak of. But I hope to collect one very soon."

"I have every confidence in your success," he said with a wink.

The other ladies tittered with delight. Miss Rolland introduced him to Miss Travers, Miss Lawson, and Miss Brenner. Given the way Miss Rolland presented him with a certain flourish and a nod to her friends, he could almost hear an undertone of *This is the man I was telling you about!* They looked him over with warm appreciation.

"But you mustn't ask them to dance," Miss Rolland told him, punctuating this order by poking him lightly with her fan. "Their cards are already full."

The way Miss Brenner's eyebrow lifted signaled that perhaps Miss Rolland wasn't being exactly truthful about that.

"Please tell me you've reserved at least one dance for me," Douglas said, mustering all the fervor he could at the idea of dancing.

Miss Rolland studied her card as though she didn't already know precisely what was on it. "Why yes, it seems there is still one opening. It's for a waltz."

Douglas breathed an inward sigh of relief. If it had been any of the other dances, such as the quadrille with its intricate patterns, his ship would have sunk before it even left port. "Perfect."

He watched as she wrote his name in the spot she had indicated. From his viewpoint, the writing was upside down, yet he easily discerned that several of the other slots were filled by Busfield. Interestingly, it made him think of Archie Clapper's remark about a woman playing two men against each other as rivals. Miss Rolland was the kind of woman who would do that. Not Alice.

"You arrived just in time, Mr. Shaw," Miss Rolland informed him. "The dancing is about to begin. It opens with a grand march. Who will be your partner for that—if I may be so bold as to ask?" She looked at him with wide eyes that held a hint of teasing.

Her question took him by surprise. He looked at her friends, but they gave him disappointed smiles, indicating they were already taken.

A great musical flourish sounded. This signal unleashed a buzz of activity across the ballroom. Gentlemen began circulating through the room to find their partners. It wasn't long before Miss Rolland's friends had all been whisked away—but not before each one had given her prettiest smile to Douglas.

Busfield walked up and, with only a cursory greeting to Douglas, offered his arm to Miss Rolland. She laid one hand on his arm and gave Douglas a little wave with the other. "Remember, it's the waltz after the second lancers!"

As he led her away, Busfield spared Douglas a sneering glance, as though he'd bested him somehow.

"Enjoy it while you can," Douglas said under his breath once they were gone. He smiled to himself. This was all just another form of negotiation, and he was an expert at that. If he thought of it that way, his natural competitive instincts took over and increased his enjoyment of it all.

For the moment, he was in a situation that he ought to have anticipated. He felt he should make an appearance at this opening march. There were no steps to worry about; one simply escorted a lady around, following the leader. However, he'd have to be suitably introduced to any young lady before he could ask her to dance. He certainly did not want to inadvertently cause a scandal by committing a crime against proper etiquette. That would be worse than not dancing at all.

A short distance off, he spotted a woman standing by herself. Judging by the wisps of gray threaded through her dark hair, she was perhaps around fifty years old. She was tall and somewhat broad. Given that her gown, which was not in the latest style, fit rather too snugly, Douglas guessed she hadn't always been so stout.

What really caught his attention, though, was that her foot was tapping in time with the lively music calling people to the grand march. Her wistful expression as she observed the couples lining up to begin made it clear she wanted to be a part of the proceedings.

Douglas didn't think she was one of the more important matrons at this ball. She was someone's aunt, perhaps. Or a cousin.
Whoever she was, she wore a dance card around her wrist, so she
must be open to the idea of dancing. He took in all these details
in a moment. This unlikely combination of things told him he
should take a chance.

He approached her. "I beg your pardon, madam. My name is
Douglas Shaw. I hope you won't think me too forward, but . . ."

He paused. He knew he was considered handsome. He'd done
his best to avoid allowing that knowledge to make him vain, but
tonight he was heartily glad he'd been blessed with good looks.

The woman's eyes grew wide with happy surprise at being thus
addressed. She said tremulously, "Yes?"

He could almost feel the way she was hoping against hope as
her gaze locked on his.

"I recently had the honor of becoming acquainted with the
Misses Travers, Lawson, and Brenner. Would you be among their
party? If so, then you and I might say we have already made an
acquaintance—in a manner of speaking." Douglas had guessed
that she was related to one of those young ladies largely by her
proximity to them.

She nodded. "Why, yes. I am Mrs. Andrews, Miss Lawson's
aunt. I am chaperoning her this evening because her mother—my
sister—is under the weather. But I don't like to hover too closely,
as I believe young people should be allowed room for a bit of fun."

"Fun should not be reserved only for the young," he countered
cheerfully. "I don't suppose you would honor me by allowing me
to escort you for the march?"

She looked as though she could hardly believe what she'd heard,
but she lost no time responding. "I'd be delighted, Mr. Shaw."

They found a place in line just as the march got underway. The
primary purpose of the march was to provide an opportunity for
the gentlemen and ladies to observe each other. This was especially
important for the ladies, as they had the important task of judging
one another's gowns. The men were a more homogeneous group,

dressed in black coat and tie, with the exception of the occasional officer in uniform or Scottish gentleman in a kilt.

The couples stood side by side in a long line, following the lead couple as they walked toward the top of the room. At that point, the men split off to the left and the women to the right. Douglas had practiced this with a smaller group at one of his dancing lessons, but tonight he was astounded to see how it looked with hundreds of people. Still leading their respective rows of men and women, the head couple circled back to the place they'd begun and then rejoined. Everyone following did likewise, reconnecting with their partners. Then they split up again. This time the rows of men and ladies passed each other as they followed the lead of the top couple. As Miss Rolland breezed by Douglas, she gave him a brilliant smile. She wasn't the only young lady to send lingering gazes in his direction. Douglas basked in the knowledge that he was making such a good impression.

The march was surprisingly energetic. They were moving swiftly and covering a lot of ground. The lead couple each wound their way separately around the room, creating ingenious patterns as the long lines of people followed in their wake. At last the couples were brought together once more. As Douglas took Mrs. Andrews's arm again, she looked so ecstatic that he was glad he had asked her to dance.

When the music ended, everyone was out of breath and yet laughing, too. After many thanks to one another, Douglas and Mrs. Andrews parted with amicable good wishes. The lady presumably went back to her nonhovering oversight of her niece, while Douglas found a spot where he could watch the dancing. He watched carefully, noting how the couples interacted with one another, how the ladies were led off the floor by their dance partners, and how they reconnected with new partners for the next dance. This was all information he could use.

Several times he caught sight of Miss Rolland. She clearly enjoyed dancing. She constantly wore a delighted expression and seemed to flirt with every partner. Most men simply accepted it with gracious good humor. Busfield was different. Whenever they danced, he spent a lot of time whispering in her ear, looking very serious. She did not seem to mind, and several times she gave a sly smile, as if he were saying something scandalous. Was he really a serious contender for her hand? Douglas would have to find out.

Douglas had watched five or six dances when he was joined by Mr. Henley.

"I'm glad we found you," Henley said. He was accompanied by a tall, elderly man who was impeccably dressed, right down to the diamond stud in his cravat. Henley introduced him as Viscount Pennington.

Instantly, Douglas forgot about the dancing. Here was his first introduction to a member of the aristocracy, and it couldn't be better. The viscount was active politically and known to promote laws favorable to trade.

Douglas gave him a bow. "It's a pleasure to meet you, sir."

The viscount studied Douglas through gold-rimmed spectacles. "Did I see you in the grand march with Mrs. Andrews?"

"Yes, sir," Douglas said. Had that been a mistake after all? He exchanged a worried glance with Henley.

The viscount smiled. "Well done, young man. Mrs. Andrews is the sister of an old school chum of mine. She was quite the dancer in her day. It was good of you to take her around."

"Thank you, sir. It was a pleasure. She is a charming lady."

Henley looked proud enough to bust the buttons off his shirt. He was too good a businessman not to realize that Douglas had just pulled off an important maneuver for getting into the viscount's good graces.

"I had the honor of making his lordship's acquaintance just this evening, and he was kind enough to agree when I asked him if I might introduce him to my right-hand man," Henley enthused. "I told him you are an admirable gentleman as well as quite astute when it comes to business," he added, implying that Douglas had just proved his point by dancing with Mrs. Andrews. Turning to the viscount, Henley said, "Sir, I wonder if we might take a few minutes of your time to discuss a bill that's just been sent up to the Lords from Parliament, regarding international trade contracts and liability."

The viscount acquiesced, but as Henley began to lay out a case for supporting the bill, his interest seemed to fade rapidly. "It sounds very intriguing," he said, although his attention was focused on some friends he'd spotted across the room. He gave them a quick wave before saying to Henley, "Why don't you pop round to my solicitor tomorrow and fill him in on the details. That will help me decide how to approach the debates."

"Thank you, sir. I'd be delighted."

"And now back to the fun, eh?" the viscount said and left them to join his friends.

"That went well," Henley said.

Douglas frowned. "Do you really think so? He only seemed concerned about how it would affect his own interests."

"I've never met an aristocrat who approached life any differently, to be honest. But we do what we can. You pulled off quite a coup with that grand march. It's gotten us in the door with his lordship's solicitor. That's a good start."

Perhaps, but Douglas found it disappointing. The viscount wasn't interested in socializing with them, only in discussing business—and even then, only briefly. That invisible barrier was still firmly in place.

"Have you danced with Miss Rolland yet?" Henley asked.

His question brought Douglas's mind back to the next order of business. "Not yet. I believe it's coming up."

"Well, have at it. I'm off to find some refreshment."

The dancers were finishing up the lancers. Miss Rolland was escorted from the floor by a man Douglas didn't recognize. Apparently Busfield was only in for the waltzes.

Douglas walked over to her and gave a little bow. "I believe we are next?"

"Oh yes!" Miss Rolland's face was flushed with happiness as she accepted his proffered arm.

As Douglas led her out to find a spot among the other dancers, he could feel beads of perspiration break out on his brow. Here was the test he'd been dreading. He placed his hand on the small of Miss Rolland's back. She was shorter and rounder than Alice, but he figured that shouldn't matter when it came to the dancing. He could compensate for her shorter step. He took a deep breath and led off as the music began.

One, two, three times around. The letters flowed in his head, buoyed by the underlying dots and dashes. He and Miss Rolland moved smoothly together. Douglas wanted to bless Alice for her help, but he didn't dare allow his mind to wander too far from the task at hand.

Unfortunately, he hadn't counted on the talking.

Miss Rolland said, "Are you enjoying the company this evening, Mr. Shaw?"

Her question disrupted the mental stream of dots and dashes that allowed him to keep time with the music. "I—I beg your pardon?" It was all he could get out, and he tried to say it in rhythm with his steps to avoid disaster.

"I was highly amused to see you paired with Mrs. Andrews in the march. Of all people! I would have thought it ridiculous, except you looked so utterly charming, leading her around as though she were the most elegant woman in the world and not some old cow sent by Mary's mother to keep watch on all of us."

"I don't think you're being charitable. She is very nice." Again, his words came out very singsong, matching the one-two-three of the waltz. He wanted to say more, but he had to keep his mind on the steps. As it was, he narrowly missed stepping on Miss Rolland's toe.

"If you say so," she replied dismissively, then immediately launched into another subject. "There are so many interesting people here tonight. I danced the polka with Baron von Halberstadt, who was once a school friend of Prince Albert! He is old, of course, but amusing nonetheless. And I danced the schottische with Lord Stanford, whose cousin is that notorious earl who eloped with an American heiress. . . ."

Douglas vaguely heard her words, but he allowed them to roll over his head. He smiled down at her, his expression frozen in place as he concentrated. For a while, she seemed content to do all the talking. But then she paused and looked at him expectantly. He realized she'd just asked him a question.

"Well?" she pressed. "What do you think of him?"

"Who?"

"Viscount Pennington." She said his name in nasal, clipped syllables that mimicked upper-crust speech. "I saw you talking with him. He's rather a bore, don't you think?"

Douglas stopped midstep. Taken by surprise, Miss Rolland stumbled ungracefully, then glared up at him. They bumped into another couple as he tried to help Miss Rolland recover her balance. He was rewarded with their offended scowls.

Sending apologetic smiles to everyone in the vicinity, Douglas pulled Miss Rolland out of the stream of dancers so he could gather his wits. "I was just thinking that I'd so much rather look at you than talk just now. Your eyes are positively sparkling, the way they perfectly match the color of your dress." He paired these words with the ardent gaze of a suitor.

She tapped him lightly with her fan. "You are incorrigible, sir."

"Let's dance now and talk later, shall we? Perhaps over a nice glass of punch?"

She gave him a coy smile. "Why do you think I saved you the dance that's just before the break?"

Douglas raised an eyebrow. "Now who's the incorrigible one?"

She giggled. Clearly the crisis was past.

They resumed dancing. Miss Rolland continued to make comments from time to time, but Douglas merely nodded and smiled. When at last the waltz ended, they came to a smooth halt on the final note. A massive feeling of relief and triumph rolled over him. He felt his chest expand in pride. They passed Busfield as they left the dance floor. The bank officer said nothing, but he regarded Douglas with narrowed eyes.

Jealous, Douglas thought. He smiled down at Miss Rolland. "Now, about that punch?"

"Yes, indeed!" she replied enthusiastically.

He began to lead her toward the refreshment room. It was easy to guess which direction it was in, since many others seemed to be going the same way.

Miss Rolland paused and looked up at him. "I was just thinking—there are bound to be a lot of people crowding the drink tables just now. Why don't we wait a bit?" She tucked her arm tighter around his. "In the meantime, I know a quiet place where we can cool down."

Douglas had a good idea where this was going. He hadn't expected her to do something like this so soon. The dancing had been a major challenge, but he suspected he was about to navigate even trickier waters.

He gave a quick look around, judging who was near them and who might be watching. There was no sign of her father. During her monologue while they'd been dancing, she'd mentioned that at social events, he generally preferred to spend his time in whatever room was designated for men to enjoy a cigar and a glass of whisky. Nor did Douglas see the Henleys anywhere.

He did see Busfield, who was watching them from a short distance away. His attention was forcefully diverted, however, by the three young ladies Miss Rolland had introduced Douglas to earlier. They approached Busfield from behind, so that he was forced to turn his back on Douglas and Miss Rolland in order to speak with them.

Douglas also noticed Miss Rolland's smile of satisfaction. "This way," she said, tugging on his arm. It had all been beautifully choreographed.

He had expected to step onto a terrace or into one of the little groves of potted trees for the few moments of privacy Miss Rolland had obviously planned. Instead, she led him down several hallways. He grew more worried the farther they got from the noise and lights of the ball. Flirting was one thing, causing a scandal was quite another.

"I hardly think all this walking will cool us down," he pointed out nervously.

"Almost there." She paused, pointing to a closed door farther down the hall. "That is a small parlor. Hardly any of the guests would know about it. I'll go in first, just to ensure it's not occupied."

"All right." At this point he had to go along with her plan, although he was determined not to spend too much time here. He would not risk damaging either of their reputations.

Miss Rolland slipped down the hall and into the parlor. Almost immediately she came back out and waved him forward. As soon as he was inside, she shut the door. The room was in shadows, illuminated only by stray beams from the streetlamp outside.

"Well, this is cozy," Douglas murmured. "Miss Rolland—"

She took hold of his hands. "Please call me Penelope," she commanded in a breathless voice. She lifted her face to his. "You will no doubt think me scandalously forward. But from the day we met, I knew we had a certain connection. Don't you feel it, too?"

At the moment, what Douglas felt was supreme uneasiness as she pressed herself closer to him. It was clear what she wanted. He dislodged his hands from hers and gently grasped her upper arms. The sooner he kissed her, the sooner they could extract themselves from this potentially dangerous situation.

"Yes," he said. "I feel . . ."

It didn't seem to matter that he couldn't finish the sentence. Her dreamy gaze showed that she accepted this as proof he was too moved to put his feelings into words.

Then he kissed her. Or she kissed him. He wasn't sure which of them moved first. But did it matter? He told himself it should not matter that she had orchestrated this moment. Why shouldn't he be pleased with a woman who didn't hesitate to go after what she wanted? He certainly would never be content with a shrinking violet.

Nor was the kiss entirely unpleasant—although he found himself oddly aware that this time there were no clashing cymbals in the background. Then he felt like the worst kind of cad for even thinking about that right now.

Miss Rolland reached for his lapels and pulled him closer in an effort to prolong the kiss. Douglas obliged. When at last he felt like he could step back without insulting her, he did.

She raised a hand to her cheek, her dreamy, happy expression returning. "Oh, my heavens!" she said softly.

"Miss Rolland—Penelope—I feel we shouldn't stay here. I have too high a regard for your virtue—"

"I understand." She gave him an adoring smile "You are a true gentleman."

He was glad she had accepted his excuse at face value. "Thank you for your trust. Let's get you back to the dancing." He pointed toward her dance card. "Those gentlemen will be quite angry with me."

"None of them hold a candle to you," she breathed.

Douglas shifted in discomfort. He did not deserve such praise. "Let's get going," he repeated. She clung to him, and he gave her a last kiss before they left the parlor.

Was Miss Rolland in love with him or merely infatuated? The question seemed vitally important in light of the conversation he'd had with Alice. As for his own sentiments, he had to admit he was no closer to being in love with Penelope Rolland than he'd been before. He wasn't sure how he was going to manage it, or even if he was right in trying to force feelings that simply weren't there.

They made their way back to the ball without incident and were able to get a glass of punch before it was time for the next dance partner to take Miss Rolland away. She parted from him reluctantly, but Douglas felt only relief.

He had, to varying degrees, accomplished what he'd come here for. In so many ways, though, it seemed like only the beginning of a long and uncertain road.

CHAPTER

Twenty-Two

Archie picked up a stack of messages he'd received that morning, dropping them onto the typing desk as he headed for the door. As he was going out, he passed Mavis, who was just coming back from her lunch break. "Late again, Miss Waller?" he said with a deprecating smile.

After he was gone, Mavis huffed to her desk, throwing down her gloves.

"Don't pay any mind to that surly windbag," Alice said, going over to her.

"Why must he always be so hateful to me?"

"He's like that with everyone."

Mavis shook her head. "He seems worse than ever lately. Didn't you have some sort of plan to make him be nicer?"

Alice grimaced. "Unfortunately, that didn't work out so well."

"I *have* noticed that things are always, well, tense around the office these days." Mavis eyed Alice. "Have you taken a disliking to Mr. Shaw for some reason?"

The question took Alice off guard. "Not at all," she stammered, looking away. "I can't think why you should think so."

In the week since she and Douglas had talked in front of the building, Alice had strived to keep a cool and professional demeanor, but being around him still unsettled her. Mavis was probably picking up on the fact that Alice and Douglas no longer interacted with the same ease they'd had in the beginning. Regaining it had not been possible. Aside from her own conflicting emotions, there was also the fact that Archie was watching them like a hawk.

Alice was aware, because she'd overheard Henley speaking to Douglas about it this morning, that Douglas had recently had a successful evening with Miss Rolland. One that included dancing. He must have been able to take what Alice had taught him and apply it effectively. Would he mention it to her? Or did he consider that too sensitive a topic to bring up again?

Her eyes dropped to the messages Archie had left on Mavis's desk. She noticed Douglas's name as the recipient on the top message. She picked it up, not hesitating to read it. After all, it could just as easily have been received by her.

"Is it something interesting?" Mavis asked.

Alice found it very interesting. It was from Andrew Carnegie. It appeared Douglas's meeting with him in Hyde Park was going to pay off. The message stated the days Mr. Carnegie would be available in Liverpool next week. "It's a request from an American industrialist to meet with Mr. Shaw."

"That sounds like it could be good for Henley and Company, doesn't it?" Mavis said, brightening. This news seemed to make her forget about her trouble with Archie.

"Yes, it does." Alice couldn't help but be elated for Douglas. She remembered with satisfaction that it was her comment about Hyde Park that had ultimately led to this meeting with Carnegie. Since then, Douglas had been working hard to put together proposals for potential deals. Alice had helped with that, too.

Work had been hard for Alice since the tea dance, it was true. She'd continued daily to wrestle with her heart's illogical stirrings whenever she was near Douglas, as well as her frustration with a churlish colleague who wished ill on everyone. Yet here was a victory worth celebrating. For this moment, she was proud of her part in it all.

Douglas walked back to the office after a meeting with Henley and Rolland at their club. The other two men had remained at the club for luncheon, but Douglas had decided to forgo the meal.

He was glad to get away. He'd been nervous about seeing Rolland again, worried that somehow word of Douglas's intimate tête-à-tête with his daughter at the ball two nights ago might have reached him. Apparently it had not. Rolland would surely have acted like an outraged father if it had. Instead, he was warm toward Douglas, and the three of them had spent a profitable hour discussing business matters.

That had eased Douglas's mind, but then pressure came from a different quarter. Rolland had accompanied Douglas to the door of the club while Henley went to wash up before luncheon.

"There's something I think you should know," Rolland had told him. "Mr. Busfield came to see me yesterday. He wished me to know that he was interested in seriously courting my daughter—with my permission."

"And what did you tell him?"

"I told him I had no objection."

"I see."

"I also said I'm aware that my daughter has a number of interested admirers. When the time comes—and I imagine it will be soon—I will allow her to make her own choice." Rolland gave him a penetrating look. "Provided the man in question meets my high standards."

"That's very wise, sir."

"I like you, Shaw. I believe my daughter has taken a fancy to you. But I would advise you not to dawdle or try to string her along, or you may find another man has won her over."

"Thank you, sir. I will take that under advisement."

Even now, as he walked briskly along the street, Douglas could think of a hundred things he ought to have said. Perhaps he ought to have been effusive in his praise of Miss Rolland. But his mind had been scrambling, torn between the need to best his competitor and uncertainty about whether he was doing the right thing. Uncertainty he'd not been able to shake. Uncertainty that Alice had put into his heart.

He took a slight detour in order to pass the little church park where Alice sometimes ate her lunch. It wasn't the first time he'd looked for her, although he felt foolish for doing so.

She wasn't there. It seemed she'd found someplace else to enjoy her midday meal these days. Could she be purposely avoiding him? Sadly, he knew it was a distinct possibility. Perhaps it was just as well. What could he say to her?

When he reached the office, he found Alice and Miss Waller having an animated discussion. He loved the way Alice's face lit up when she was excited about something. He hadn't seen that look since they'd chatted about that lecture while eating ices. And when she'd smiled up at him during their waltz . . .

He sent a worried glance toward Archie Clapper's desk despite knowing that, whatever else that man was, he was no mind reader. Happily, Clapper wasn't there. Perhaps that was why the women were in such good spirits.

He gave them a smile as he removed his hat. "Good afternoon, ladies."

"Mr. Shaw, there is some exciting news for you!" Miss Waller exclaimed.

"Congratulations," Alice added, extending a message to him.

It was in Clapper's scrawl, but even so, Douglas grinned as he read it. He'd wondered several times over the past weeks whether Carnegie would make good on his promise to meet with him. Well, here it was—his golden opportunity. Douglas took a deep breath, savoring this moment. All other concerns faded. This was the kind of opportunity he lived for.

To see Alice smiling at him, sharing his excitement, made him even happier. "Thank you, Miss McNeil. You should be proud of this, too, you know. You had a big hand in it."

She gave a modest shake of her head. "You are the one who took the idea and ran with it."

"Even so, if you have any other such ideas, please don't hesitate to share them."

She grinned. "I'll do that."

It was a simple exchange, but for Douglas it meant more than words could say. It was a spark of that friendliness they used to have. Perhaps, if he played his cards right, he could keep it.

⁓

"A little locomotive? Your nephew is going to love that," Rose said, as she weighed the package Alice had brought to the post office in order to ship it to Ancaster in time for Jack Jr.'s birthday. Since Rose worked in a post office rather than a dedicated telegraph facility, she had a variety of customer service tasks, including oversight of the newly established parcel post. "You realize this is setting a dangerous precedent, don't you?" she added as she began to write up the bill for shipping. "How many nieces and nephews did you say you have?"

"Just five. The youngest, little Georgie, is only a baby, so I have time before he expects anything."

"Hmm. Don't be so sure about that. I once worked in a tele-graph office attached to a general store. The ladies often came in with their children, and let me assure you that those little tykes always knew exactly what they wanted." She made a face, rolling her eyes heavenward.

Alice laughed. "Thank you for the warning. I'll keep that in mind. How much do I owe you?"

"Advice is always free," Rose said with a wink. "The parcel post is a little more." She turned the bill, which had the fees totaled at the bottom, toward Alice. "Sign here," she indicated.

Alice signed the bill, then pulled open her reticule to search for the coins she needed.

"Emma told me she saw you at the park last week," Rose said.

Alice looked up in time to see a knowing smile creeping onto Rose's face. *Drat*. "What else did she tell you?"

"You know the dear girl can't keep a secret. She said you've been having men trouble."

Alice sent a quick look around, worried other customers might be within earshot. There was only an older gentleman standing at another counter, looking up information in the large book of postal and telegraphic addresses that was kept there. Turning back to Rose, Alice whispered, "Are those your words or hers?"

Rose answered with a shrug. "Emma was doing her best not to say too much, as apparently you'd sworn her to secrecy." She said this with a chastising look. "She also said you weren't too forthcoming on the details. Something about that spinster book. Is that Fred fellow still madly in love with you? Has he proposed yet?"

"What? No! He's overseas at the moment. He—" Alice stopped midsentence. As she pulled out her money, the note from Fred came with it. It had lain crumpled in her bag ever since the night of the tea dance. She looked down at it, her embarrassment rising. "He, er, wrote me a letter."

"He did?" Rose's gaze landed on the letter, now lying on the counter along with Alice's coins. "What did he say?"

"I don't know. I haven't been able to bring myself to read it."

Rose looked at her in astonishment. "You're joking." She picked up the letter. "Suppose I read it for you and let you know if there's anything devastatingly awful."

Alice nodded. Maybe it would be good to read it with a friend. She glanced back at the other customer. He'd found the address he was looking for and was now filling out a telegram order form. It wouldn't be long before he approached Rose to request sending it. "We'll have to hurry, though."

Rose opened the note, scanned it, and gave a little smirk before quietly reading it aloud.

"Dear Alice,

"Please excuse my forwardness in writing to you directly. I feel that, as we have known each other for such a long time, it won't be unforgivable if I send you my personal greetings.

"My new position as cargo master is turning out to be rewarding in every way, if I may say so without boasting. My cabin is right comfortable. Not as large as the captain's, of course, but with three portholes to let in plenty of light and roomy enough that even two people could move about easily.

226

"We have reached India and are now loading up with goods to bring back. I am diligently ensuring that every last crate is accounted for. By all indicators (God willing), it will be a profitable voyage. I shall soon be able to set up a nice home for me and my future wife, whom I hope to be blessed with at some day in the not-too-distant future.

"I hope you are kindly thinking of me.

> *"Your good friend,*
> *"Fred Arbuckle."*

Alice gave a little sigh of relief. That didn't sound too bad. Or at least, it could have been worse.

But Rose said, "He practically proposed to you!"

"Don't be ridiculous."

"It's all here—he's got the money to support you, a nice house, and even a ship's cabin large enough for two!" She gave a suggestive raise of her eyebrows. "Does he know you have a hankering for travel?"

"I might have mentioned it," Alice mumbled with chagrin.

"When does he return?"

"A few weeks, I think."

"You'd do well to prepare your answer for when he proposes in person, so you can let him down gently. You are planning to say no, I suppose?"

Alice glared her reply, to which Rose only laughed. She handed back the letter, and Alice stuffed it once more into her reticule.

Rose scooped up the money and took it to the till. She returned to give Alice the change just as the other customer approached. Because of his presence, they had to keep the rest of their conversation short and formal.

"Thank you for your help," Alice said.

"My pleasure," Rose replied.

The glint in her eye was unmistakable. She clearly found the whole situation with Fred amusing. Alice could only berate herself for the hundredth time for having ever bought that spinster book.

CHAPTER
Twenty-Three

The meeting with Carnegie was going well, if not entirely as Douglas had envisioned. He'd laid out his proposal for a deal to transport grain from Oregon to New York via one of the railways in which Carnegie had a controlling interest. He pointed out the financial advantages to all parties. Carnegie had listened attentively and asked detailed questions.

They were just finishing luncheon at one of the finer restaurants in Liverpool. Carnegie had declined to meet Douglas at the Liverpool office of Henley and Company, stating that he was still officially on holiday and thought this would be a more agreeable place to chat. It certainly was the most elegant restaurant Douglas had ever been in. The food and the service had been outstanding. He could see that Carnegie took pleasure in enjoying the finer things in life, and he could admire him for that. Such luxuries required money, of course, which was why Douglas was here.

"As you can see, this is a very lucrative opportunity," Douglas said. "It would be foolish not to capitalize on it."

"So you have pointed out quite vigorously, Mr. Shaw." Carnegie smiled as he touched his napkin to his lips.

Perhaps Douglas had overstepped, due to his eagerness? "I can't help but be excited about it, naturally," he replied. "I'm sure you see all the reasons why."

"Yes, indeed." Carnegie returned his napkin to his lap. "Oh, by the way, did I mention that our party spent two days in Glasgow on the way here from Inverness? By then we had given up our coach-and-four and were traveling on public transport. Sailing up the Clyde from Greenock was quite pleasurable. In Glasgow we stayed at the Central Hotel. Are you familiar with it?"

Douglas nodded, surprised Carnegie had taken the conversation in this direction. "It was my first glimpse of the privileges of wealth—even if I was only seeing it as a messenger boy delivering telegrams. It made me determined that one day I would be able to afford such things. And here I am." He motioned to the ornate dining room where they sat.

"Yes, here you are," Carnegie agreed pleasantly. "You mentioned earlier that your parents are still in Glasgow. Do you get there often?"

"When I can." The answer was hedging a little. Douglas in fact went there as little as possible.

"And you offer them financial support, I suppose?"

"To the extent they will accept it. They are proud. Especially my father." Douglas was beginning to feel uncomfortable with this line of questioning.

Carnegie leaned back in his chair, toying with his glass as he gave Douglas a long, assessing look. "Mr. Shaw, might I offer a word of advice?"

"Certainly. I'm all ears." If they were getting back to business, Douglas was eager to pick up any pearls of wisdom the millionaire might offer.

Carnegie pushed back from the table. "Perhaps we could take a walk? It aids digestion to walk after a meal, and I'd love to get a better look at the shipyards."

Douglas obliged, rising from the table with him. He wasn't sure how well they could discuss business if they were walking around a busy port, but he wasn't about to second-guess this man, who clearly knew what he was doing.

They left the restaurant and walked toward the wharfs. The day was cloudy and the breeze was high, which kept the temperature comfortable.

Once they were within sight of the ships, Carnegie spoke again. "I think you have gleaned by now that anything I engage in, I do it wholeheartedly. I push myself to be involved in every aspect of the work that I possibly can."

"Yes, sir, I know, and I greatly admire you for it. Your talent for business, and the way you have risen from humble beginnings to where you are now . . . it is an inspiration."

"That's kind of you to say. I only hope I can inspire people in the right way."

Douglas shook his head, not following Carnegie's meaning. "How so?"

Carnegie paused and turned, meeting Douglas's gaze. "Throughout our conversation today, I noticed your emphasis on pursuing certain business deals primarily because of the financial profit."

Carnegie spoke as if there were something wrong with that view. Douglas shook his head again. "Surely this is the goal of all men of business?"

"To varying degrees, I suppose. However, I will warn you right now that you will be a lot happier in the long run if you understand that simply acquiring wealth is not the be-all and end-all in life."

"I don't believe I ever said that."

"Perhaps not expressly. But the idea seems to underlie your words and actions."

Douglas wanted to voice an objection. Did this have something to do with the questions about his parents? It wasn't as though he hadn't tried to improve their lot. It was part of why he was driving himself. With his father unable to work, they would be destitute without his help. But Carnegie's piercing gaze seemed to charge him to consider his words carefully before speaking.

"I believe the drive to amass wealth can be one of the worst kinds of idolatry," Carnegie continued. "No idol is more debasing than the worship of money. If a person is going to spend so much of their life's blood and sweat on something, it should be something that is elevating in character."

"You don't regret becoming wealthy, surely?" Douglas challenged.

Carnegie chuckled and shook his head. "I strive to ensure any business venture I'm involved with is profitable. I won't deny that being successful is hugely satisfying. But I find greater satisfaction in using money for benevolent purposes. Giving back to help others. It was a great thrill for me to revisit Dunfermline, my birthplace. As you might expect, they treated me with high honors. But I didn't go there just to feed my pride. My mother and I laid the foundation stone for a new library. That library will benefit countless people for years to come. I have funded other public works there as well. None of these charitable projects are overtly a benefit to my ledger book, yet I believe my business prospers because of them. More importantly, though, they add to a greater account. One that is more satisfying to the heart. Do you understand what I'm saying?"

Douglas considered Carnegie's words. He was aware of the steel magnate's fame as a philanthropist, but he hadn't thought much about it—at least, not in regard to himself. That was what Carnegie was clearly encouraging him to do. "When I saw you in London, preparing to give your mother a grand tour of England and Scotland, I thought how much I should like to do something like that for my parents."

"I'm glad to hear it. Always honor your father and mother. But it doesn't hurt to look a little further afield, as well. To remember one's fellow man."

Douglas wasn't sure whether Carnegie's advice was meant as just that—advice—or if it was a reproof. He decided it must be the former. After all, Carnegie knew next to nothing about Douglas's personal life.

Carnegie looked out over the crowded piers bustling with activity. "Do you want to know a dream of mine?"

Douglas, sensing this was a rhetorical question, waited quietly for Carnegie to continue.

"I had to give up school when I was fourteen to work full-time. One day, I would love to spend a few years at Oxford and get a proper and thorough education. Then I would settle in London and purchase a controlling interest in some newspaper, giving the general management of it my attention. The paper would focus on covering public matters, especially those connected with education and improvement of the poorer classes."

"You mean you would leave the other businesses behind?" Douglas couldn't imagine walking away from an empire like the one Carnegie had built.

Carnegie shrugged, although he had a happy, far-off look as he thought about his plan. "As I said, it is a dream of mine. I could arrange my affairs to secure a good amount per annum, and use the rest for a project such as the one I just described."

They were silent for a minute as Douglas digested this information. The air was filled with the cries of sea gulls and the shouts of men calling out orders to those loading or unloading cargo. Douglas took a deep breath of the salty air, tinged with the smell of coal fires and the smoke from the steam engines that powered the cranes lifting heavy crates onto the ships. It was the smell of success for those who were in the right position to profit from it. "I have to say, sir, that I cannot picture a man as successful as you are being willing to walk away from it all."

"And why not?"

"Respectfully, sir, I have been poor. I was raised in abject, soul-crushing poverty. I've had to work ten times harder than the average man for everything I've gained. I will never, *ever* be in that position again. Not while I still have breath and the ability to fight for something better." Although Douglas kept his voice modulated, he was clenching his fists as he spoke. The resolution was hard as steel in his soul.

Carnegie's expression sobered. "Mr. Shaw, I would never suggest that you subject yourself to those miseries again. Lord knows I'm thankful to be living comfortably, and I'm especially thankful to be able to provide a good home for my mother. Perhaps it's more a question of balance and priorities. I know firsthand how hard it is to live hand to mouth, barely subsisting. I hope I never forget it. Yet there is always the danger that it will warp your soul to the end that you pursue money to the detriment of all else. That is what I caution you against."

"Ah, money. The root of all evil." Douglas's voice soured as bitter memories arose of the sermons he'd heard as a child.

"No, Mr. Shaw. The *love* of money is the root of all evil," Carnegie corrected. "Why are you acquiring it, and what will you do with it? The Good Book says we are to work heartily so that we may have to give to him that needeth. I strive to ensure that a sizable portion of my money may be used to do good."

"That is admirable, sir." Douglas meant it, even if his heart wasn't entirely on board. There were a lot of things he had to do first, before he could be comfortable with the idea of giving away large swaths of his hard-earned money.

Sensing his reluctance, Carnegie gave him an understanding smile. "You're young and still making your way in the world. Perhaps one day you'll comprehend the truth of what I'm saying."

Douglas nodded, unable to think of any other response. He'd been looking forward to learning from Carnegie, but this wasn't what he'd expected.

"But you didn't come all the way to Liverpool to hear a lecture from me," Carnegie said amiably. "Suppose we get back to discussing that deal."

Being an experienced negotiator, Carnegie seemed to know when he'd made his point and it was time to move on. Douglas admired him even more for that. He was also glad to return the conversation to more familiar ground.

"Perhaps you'd like to visit Henley and Company's Liverpool office after all? It's just a few streets over from here."

"Excellent idea," Carnegie said. "Lead the way."

The next hour was one of the best Douglas could remember. Carnegie was affable and polite, but he also pushed Douglas hard on the facts and details of what they were discussing. *This* was what Douglas had wanted from him. He felt as though he was sitting at the feet of a master teacher.

They could reach no agreement at this stage, as Douglas would have to take this information to Mr. Henley first. After they'd made plans regarding the timing of future communications, they walked outside together so that Carnegie could find a cab to take him to his hotel.

As they shook hands, Carnegie said, "Thank you, Mr. Shaw, for a very stimulating afternoon."

"The pleasure was all mine," Douglas replied sincerely.

"Perhaps you might consider a trip to Glasgow to visit your parents before returning to London? It's not such a long journey from here by train."

"That's a good idea," Douglas agreed, keeping his answer non-committal.

Douglas remained at the Liverpool office for another hour, reviewing the paperwork and thinking over all that had happened. The subject Carnegie had raised about the perils of idolizing money had not arisen again, but it had never left Douglas's mind. Did Carnegie think Douglas was guilty of this? If so, was he correct?

Douglas tried to delve deep into his soul for the answer. He believed in God, although he could not understand his parents' meek subjection to their impoverished circumstances, as though they had been ordained by the Almighty. Surely God was not an angry overlord whose main goal was to test His followers with hardships and troubles. That was something Douglas could not believe. He didn't have an answer for why there was so much suffering in the world. He just knew he would do whatever it took to rise to better things.

Carnegie *had* returned to the subject of his parents. Reluctantly, Douglas decided he should probably take the advice and visit them. After all, Carnegie had been right about so many other things. Douglas had also noticed that the last few letters from his parents sounded different. Less reproachful, somehow. He wasn't sure if this was really true, or if it just came out filtered that way by whoever was writing on their behalf. Whatever the case, Douglas couldn't deny that a visit to his parents was overdue.

He wired the London office that the meeting had gone well and requested leave for another week. Henley sent back his permission, along with a hearty note of "well done." Douglas was pleased that Alice had transmitted that message. She would know this trip had been a success. He knew she would be proud of her part in it.

With plenty of things on his mind to review and consider, he set off to the railway station.

⁂

Douglas checked into the Central Hotel near the railway station in Glasgow. Normally he stayed at a more modest hotel when visiting the city, but the way things were going with Carnegie and his other projects, he decided this time he could spend the money. Besides, he liked the idea of following in Carnegie's steps. He left his bags in a nicely appointed bedroom that was larger than his parents' sitting room and headed out. Without his luggage, he was free to walk to his parents' house. That would at least allow him to economize on cab fare.

He usually dreaded these trips back to Glasgow. The squalid streets in the section of town where he'd grown up always pained him to revisit. He'd been happy to escape and angry at his parents for their refusal to seek something better. In short, he disliked coming face-to-face with the world he'd fought so hard to leave behind.

This time, as he walked the streets toward his old neighborhood, his thoughts took a different turn. He pondered Mr. Carnegie's statements about the joy he'd gotten from giving back to his hometown. During the train ride from Liverpool the idea had begun to make inroads in his thoughts. But Glasgow was not a small town like Dunfermline. It was a sprawling city with endless problems. What could Douglas do? How would it have any lasting impact? He did not have millions to spend, like Carnegie did.

He turned onto the narrow lane that was deeply etched into his memories. It looked much as it always had, with small children playing in the street and lines of drying laundry hanging overhead. Looking at it through the eyes of an adult, it seemed smaller. More confining.

The door to his parents' home was open to let in the breeze, as was the narrow window of the sitting room. Douglas stepped through the doorway and paused, looking around. His father was seated at the small table where they ate their meals.

"How are ye, Dad?" Douglas said, a touch of his brogue returning unbidden as he stepped into his childhood home.

His father raised his head. Seeing Douglas, his face widened in a smile. He called out, "Jeannie! Look who's come to call!"

He pushed back his chair and struggled to stand. A work injury had left him with a bad back that made such movements laborious and painful.

Douglas went over and helped him up. It was an action he'd often performed, but he wasn't ready to find himself subsequently clasped in a tight embrace. His father was not normally so demonstrative.

"Och, I've missed ye, son," his father murmured.

As his father released him, Douglas glanced down at the table. There were papers on it, along with pen and ink. "What's this?"

"Now you've gone and spoiled the surprise," was his father's enigmatic reply.

A clumping on the stairs announced that his mother was coming down. She let out an exclamation of delight when she saw Douglas. She fairly ran down the rest of the steps, and once more Douglas found himself enveloped in a hug.

She pushed back to give him a scolding look. "Why didn't you tell us you were coming?"

"It was a spur-of-the-moment decision. I didn't have time to write a letter."

"Have ye never heard of telegrams, boy?" his father said, smiling.

Douglas blinked, not sure he had heard correctly. His father usually derided telegrams as an unnecessary luxury. In fact, Douglas hadn't sent a telegram because they'd have to tip the messenger,

236

and they needed every penny. Not to mention they'd have to find someone to read it for them. His parents had grown up before the laws for mandatory education for children had been enacted in Britain, and their reading skills were practically nonexistent.

"You'd best sit down, Richard," his mother admonished. "You know you can't stand up for long without bringing on the pains."

"What a worrier you are," his father grumbled good-naturedly. But he allowed Douglas to help him to a chair by the tiny fireplace.

"What were you working on at the table, Dad?" Douglas asked, still curious about what he'd seen there.

His father leaned back in his chair, while his mother beamed at them both. "Well, son, as it happens, I was just tryin' my hand at writing you a letter. It's slow going, though."

"You were . . . writing?" Now Douglas knew there was something wrong with his hearing.

"I'll get us some tea," his mother said happily, "and your father can tell you all about it."

CHAPTER
Twenty-Four

Douglas listened with amazement while his father explained how he'd begun learning to read and write. A lay minister named Mr. Johnstone had moved to Glasgow some months ago. He and his wife saw a great need among the working classes who, for various reasons, had never been able to attend school. They opened a free school with classes on Sundays and some evenings that were primarily aimed at helping adults improve literacy and arithmetic skills. They'd had success establishing a few schools for the miners in Newcastle and wanted to do the same in Glasgow.

"They give the lessons at the little meeting hall next to the church," his father said. "There's no charge, but they ask those who can afford to bring paper and pencil to do so. I used a bit of the money you so kindly sent us for that."

"We didn't think you'd mind," his mother put in, giving Douglas a knowing smile.

"That is . . ." Douglas searched for the word. *Astonishing? Unbelievable?* He settled on ". . . admirable."

"Your father wasn't so easy to convince, though," his mother said. "It took a little doing."

Douglas wasn't surprised. He knew from experience that it was tough to change his father's mind about anything. "What finally won you over?"

"I wasn't sure about this Mr. Johnstone at first, but I guess you could say he grew on me. He said a lot of things I hadn't heard before, and he was reading it straight from the Bible. And I'll be honest: as a man gets closer to his judgment day, he starts to care a little more keenly about what may happen at that particular event. I decided I didn't want to take someone else's word for it and find out too late that I was depending on the wrong information."

"And how is your . . . er, research coming along?"

"Well, it's slow going, as I said. I read from the church Bible that they keep at the school. There's a lot o' words in there! But Mrs. Johnstone helps me find verses that are easier to read. I've copied a few of them down for practice. Shall I read them to you?"

"I'd like that very much."

Catching his wife's eye, his father motioned toward the table. "Bring me those papers, will you, Jeannie?"

She quickly obliged.

Clearing his throat, his father looked down at the pages and began reading. "'Thy word is a lamp unto my feet, and a light unto my path. . . . For the Lord God is a sun and shield: the Lord will give grace and glory: no good thing will he withhold from them that walk uprightly.'"

He read a mix of verses that seemed to come from both the Old and New Testaments. His pronunciation was halting at times, especially on longer words, but was always clear.

Hearing these words from his father's lips, Douglas was unexpectedly moved. So many verses talked of the goodness and salvation of God. He'd never known his father to take much interest in religion, other than taking the paradoxical stances of railing against it while also accepting the precept that people were born into certain stations in life where they must remain, and that somehow God was responsible for that. Something had clearly changed.

His father continued reading. "'Charge them that are rich in this world, that they be not highminded, nor trust in uncertain riches . . .'"

Until this point, Douglas had been focusing on the worn carpet as his father read, afraid that if he watched, he might be too overcome with emotion. Now he jerked his head up. Money had always been a sensitive topic. Was his father reading this as a rebuke to Douglas's pursuit of financial success? He took a deep breath, as he often did when about to go head-to-head with his father on something.

"'. . . but in the living God, who giveth us richly all things to enjoy,'" his father said, finishing the verse. He set down the papers, clearly done with his reading.

"That was wonderful, Richard!" his mother exclaimed, gazing proudly at her husband. She turned to Douglas for confirmation. "Wasn't that wonderful?"

For the moment, agitation had overcome the pride Douglas had been feeling. "I was just wondering, Dad, why you picked that last verse."

"I believe the point is pretty clear—that we are not to trust in riches, but in God."

"I see." This was an attack on him after all.

"However"—his father lifted the paper again, pointing to the verse—"it also says that God gives us richly all things to enjoy. Perhaps He doesn't want His people to be destitute. Perhaps He does want us to take some enjoyment in life."

Douglas thought of the distinction Carnegie had made between having wealth and serving it as an idol. It would seem his father was saying something similar. "Does this mean you're no longer angry with me for fighting my way out of this place?"

His father shook his head. "I was too hard on you. I think I was angry at myself for not bein' able to provide better for you."

They were silent for a few moments to appreciate this newly forged understanding between them.

His mother was the next to speak. "Richard, you've told him

your main reason for learning to read. But it's not the only reason, now, is it?"

His father looked flustered. "It's the only one that matters."

She said gently, "Quit bein' so hardheaded." She tilted her head toward Douglas. "Tell him why you did it."

After a moment, his father met his gaze with a sheepish expression Douglas had never seen before. "I thought, well, seein' as how you're advancin' into the better classes, I wouldn't want to be an embarrassment to you."

Douglas was so stunned that it took a moment to find a reply. Surely it could not have been easy for his father to make such a confession. He would have had to swallow the tiny bit of pride he'd clung to all these years. It gave Douglas a newfound respect for the man he'd so often felt ashamed of. He had to clear the knot in his throat before he could answer. "You're not an embarrassment to me, Dad."

His words seemed to lift a great load from his father's shoulders. He straightened in his chair, the lines in his forehead relaxing as he offered a tentative smile. The wariness that always kept Douglas tense around his father seemed to ease. He supposed his father felt the same way.

"Perhaps you'd like to see the school?" his mother suggested. "I know the Johnstones would love to meet you."

"I'd like that very much," Douglas said. A germ of an idea was planting itself in his mind.

Things had been busy while Douglas was away. The usual barrage of messages over the wires had contained the good news of his successful meeting in Liverpool. Alice couldn't wait until he returned so she could get all the details. At first, the atmosphere of the whole office had seemed brighter. She even saw Archie smiling to himself. She wasn't sure what to make of that, but since he also sent fewer caustic remarks her way, she decided to accept this as a positive thing.

However, within a few days, Alice began to get the impression that something was amiss. The pace of the messages, both going and coming, reached a fever pitch. There was so much traffic on the wires that Alice was unable to piece together the content of the messages with any understanding. The bookkeepers were constantly in Mr. Henley's office, many times behind closed doors. Given that the men kept sending Mavis to the filing room to locate more documents, Alice surmised that something had gone wrong with one of their contracts. A few times she heard Mr. Henley exclaim, "Of all the times for Shaw to be on holiday!"

The day before Douglas was scheduled to return, Alice was just getting back from lunch when she was met at the door by Mr. Henley.

"There you are!" he said, as though she'd done something wrong by taking her normal break. He glowered at her with a red face. "Miss McNeil, come to my office, please. There is something we need to discuss."

"Certainly, sir." Alice threw a glance at Archie, wondering if he had some idea what this was about. But he was calmly tapping out a message on the telegraph. In fact, he seemed pointedly uninterested in what was transpiring just a few feet away from him. For some reason, this set Alice even further on edge.

When she followed Mr. Henley into his office, she was surprised to see his wife there. She was seated in a chair, frowning, and she met Alice with a cold stare.

Alice sensed she was in serious trouble, although she could not guess why. She looked questioningly at Mr. Henley. "Yes, sir?" she prompted. Whatever was going on, she wanted to get it out in the open as quickly as possible.

Mr. Henley picked up a piece of paper from his desk. "This is the message I wrote up on Thursday last to be sent to our agent in New York." He put it into Alice's hands. "Do you recognize it?"

Alice scanned the message. It was a modest-sized order for cotton from one of their suppliers in Mississippi. It contained details regarding price and transport. She handled dozens of such orders every week—sometimes more. She looked up. "I can't say that I remember this particular one. Was there some mistake in the transmission?"

"Mistake!" Mrs. Henley burst out with a shrill voice that caused Alice to jump. "I daresay it was no mistake!"

"Dolores, hold your tongue!" Mr. Henley said in exasperation.

She huffed and said no more but continued to stare daggers at Alice.

"Tell me, Miss McNeil, how should this message be coded?" Mr. Henley demanded, jabbing a finger at the paper.

Alice didn't need to refer to the codebook to answer. This was the kind of thing they did so often that she knew the code words by heart. She took a moment to make the full translation in her head before speaking it out loud.

Her response, which she knew was correct, only seemed to make Mr. Henley angrier. He snatched a second paper from his desk and thrust it into her hands. "Then will you kindly tell me why you sent *this* instead?"

Alice was surprised to read the second note. When decoded, the order was for a shipment four times greater and at a much higher price. She looked up at Mr. Henley. "This message is so different! And that price is unusually high."

"It is devastatingly high!" Mr. Henley barked.

"She admits to it!" Mrs. Henley screeched, rising from her chair and pointing a finger at Alice. "You deliberately tried to sabotage our business! You want to bring Henley and Company to ruin!"

Alice was so shocked by this accusation that she could only stare at her employer's wife, her mouth agape.

"Ha!" said Mrs. Henley, interpreting Alice's silence as an admission of guilt.

Somehow Alice regained her voice. "Why would I want to ruin the very company that is my livelihood?"

Mrs. Henley smirked. "Common sense generally flies to the wind when jealousy is involved. As they say, 'Hell hath no fury like a woman scorned.'"

"Scorned?" Alice repeated, unable to fathom the lady's meaning.

"It would appear you have developed an attachment for Mr. Shaw. Don't try to deny it! You saw his star rising and thought catching him was the perfect way to raise yourself."

"You think I'm some sort of social climber? I assure you, nothing could be further from the truth!" Alice couldn't figure out how Mrs. Henley would even know about this. Not unless Archie had been spreading rumors and they had somehow reached her.

"Do you deny that you and Mr. Shaw have been spending time together outside of work hours?" Mrs. Henley pressed.

What could Alice say? She lifted her chin in defiance. "I was not aware that was against company policy."

Mrs. Henley whirled toward her husband. "You see, Mr. H., this is exactly why I warned you against hiring women. They begin fraternizing with the men, and then the relationship goes south, and the next thing you know, the company suffers the consequences."

Alice could hardly believe she was hearing these degrading remarks from another woman. It was infuriating to the point that her anger nearly overcame her distress at being falsely accused of sabotage. She fought to contain her frustration and calmly addressed her employer. "Are you quite sure this is an accurate transcription of what I sent, sir?"

He gave a curt nod. "Our Liverpool office has confirmed this is what they received, and that your signature was on it."

The message had followed the usual protocol of being sent to their Liverpool office and from there over the transatlantic cable to New York. Still, something had to be amiss. Alice could never have made such a serious mistake—not even when things were busy and she was sending out telegrams as fast as humanly possible.

She boldly met Mr. Henley's gaze. "With all due respect, I can't believe I would have done such a thing."

His face reddened. "Are you contradicting me?"

"No, sir, but—"

"I have received a complete written report of what happened. This is the exact transcription of the telegram you sent."

"Perhaps it was mistakenly transcribed by the receiver. Have we checked the confirmation?" Messages like these were always confirmed—that is, repeated back to the sender to ensure accuracy. Those were kept on file as well.

"There is no record of confirmation on our end. Miss Waller has thoroughly gone through all of our files to confirm this."

"It must have gotten lost somehow. Or misfiled—"

"Or deliberately destroyed!" Mrs. Henley finished. "Hiding the evidence."

"Can the order be rectified?" Alice persevered, ignoring Mrs. Henley's outburst. "Surely we can explain there was an error—"

"We've been working nonstop for the past three days to attempt to salvage things. It's going to take time. We lost a damaging amount of money. Even selling at a loss will be ruinous, because the market has completely bottomed out." He paused to let the weight of his words sink in. "So, Miss McNeil, are you going to continue to insist that you know nothing about how this happened?"

"You had better come clean, girl!" Mrs. Henley added.

"I have told you the truth!" Alice insisted. "I cannot believe I sent that erroneous message."

"Well, then. There is no need for further discussion." Henley spoke with cool detachment. "These events have shown that we can no longer trust you to work competently at your position. Nor have we confidence that you are working to promote Henley and Company's best interests."

His words sent a chill into Alice's soul. "Are you . . . dismissing me?"

Mr. Henley nodded grimly, while his wife stood by, smiling in smug satisfaction. "You are to take whatever personal belongings you have here and leave immediately."

Numb from shock and confusion, Alice left his office. She made her way back to her desk. Archie barely glanced at her as she collected her few personal items. He was pretending to be busy with paperwork, but there was a smarmy hint of a smile on his lips. It was clear he had already known exactly what was going to transpire in Mr. Henley's office.

"You seem quite content to have twice as much work to do now," Alice charged angrily. "And I was so sure you were a lazy lump of a man who never lifted a finger if he could help it."

His infuriating grin only widened. "Well, isn't that interesting? It appears *none* of us are who we first appeared to be."

Mavis, however, was as surprised and horrified as Alice was. "You can't leave!" she protested after Alice told her in a few brief sentences what had happened.

"I'm afraid I have no choice," Alice said.

Worried that if she saw Mavis begin crying, she'd end up doing the same, Alice gave her a swift hug good-bye and left the office.

Moments later she was on the street, walking away from the best job she'd ever had.

⌒◦⌒

It was quite an experience to stand in the back of the simple classroom, watching a room full of older men with their heads bent over pen and paper, carefully scratching out simple sentences. A sprinkling of women were there, too, including his mother. Douglas remembered how angry he'd been at having to give up school so young; he hadn't given a thought to the fact that his father had never even had a taste of that privilege.

Mrs. Johnstone led the class from the front of the room. The bulk of the lesson had centered on words and phrases they encountered most often in everyday life. Now she was having them copy a verse from Psalms that was written in large, clear letters on a board at the front of the room.

Douglas saw his father lean toward the man next to him, who seemed to be puzzling over a word, trying to pronounce it. "It's 'light,' Bill. 'Thy word is a *light* unto my path.'"

The other man scratched his grizzled chin. "Seems an awful lot of letters."

His father smiled in response. In it, Douglas saw the understanding of a man who had successfully surmounted the same obstacle. It made him proud. He'd visited the school every day during his stay in Glasgow, and he'd noticed that his father generally tried to help others around him, eager to share his knowledge.

"As you can see, the purpose of our school is twofold," said Mr. Johnstone, who'd been observing the class with Douglas. "It's self-evident that gaining literacy will vastly improve the students' minds and better their everyday lives, but we want it to enhance their spiritual lives as well."

Douglas was impressed with the work the Johnstones were doing. He liked them, too. They genuinely cared about the people they were helping, often visiting their homes and offering help and guidance wherever they could.

"Over the years, I have found that it's one thing to hear a sermon where Scripture is quoted, but it's quite another to read for yourself what is written," Mr. Johnstone said. "It can have a profound impact on people. Your father is one such person."

"So I've seen," Douglas replied. "I still can't believe the change in him." At the school, his father was as happy as a child in a candy shop. The world of words was unfolding before him, and he clearly relished it.

Even more startling to Douglas was discovering that his father was not the only person whose family relationships had changed since starting at the Johnstones' school. Although several of his father's friends had obstinately refused to have anything to do with the school, being too set in their ways, many others had come from around the poorer parts of Glasgow. After speaking with them and seeing their interactions with the Johnstones, Douglas had the clear impression that most felt they'd been given a new lease on life.

Their joy had opened Douglas's eyes. Carnegie was right about the soul's benefit in giving to others. Because of this, Douglas had decided he was going to help sponsor the school. He could provide only modest help, but he could see it would have an impact. He was also going to search for benefactors who could supply the materials needed to enlarge the school building. He could already think of several prospects among the people he did business with.

"My father even admonished me to spend more time reading," Douglas said, chuckling.

"It's good counsel!" Mr. Johnstone replied. "I hope you'll follow it."

They laughed over the irony of it. By now, Mr. Johnstone knew all about Douglas's background and accomplishments. They had discussed many things over these past few days.

"I've no doubt you are well read on many topics, Mr. Shaw. Might I recommend that you spend more time reading the Bible? You will find it explains a lot about why the world is the way it is. And how God would have us live in it. As it says in the Psalms, 'Thy testimonies also are my delight and my counselors.'"

Douglas thought back to something he'd once told Alice—that he liked reading books that explained how the world worked. He'd never put the Scriptures into that category. He'd dismissed their message, or so he had thought. He now began to wonder if many of his assumptions about them had been incorrect.

He couldn't wait to talk about all these things with Alice, and not only because he thought she'd understand his new interest in philanthropy. It went deeper than that. This trip had changed his life in so many ways, and she had been the catalyst for making it happen. It was astounding how much she had impacted his life in the short time he'd known her. She had taken a firm hold of his heart.

Yes, there were a *lot* of things he wanted to discuss with Alice. When he got back to London, that was going to be his first order of business.

CHAPTER
Twenty-Five

W hy, that's terrible!" Emma said. She filled a teacup and set it in front of Alice. "This will help." Emma's way of dealing with any trauma always involved a hot cup of tea.

Rose's response was more visceral. She stood up from the table, her hands clenched. "I'd like to wring that horrible man's neck!"

"Which one?" Alice said gloomily. As far as she was concerned, they had all mistreated her. She even lumped Douglas into that group. He might not have been there at the time, but he must surely have known about it. That pained her more than anything—that he of all people would doubt her abilities or motives.

"That Archie Clapper, of course!" Rose answered. "Somehow he set this up. He must have done."

"Why would you say that?" Emma asked.

Rose snorted. "It's obvious. Alice was better than him in every way. He could not tolerate a woman besting him in the workplace. It was pure jealousy and spite."

"That's what I think, too," Alice said. "But I haven't any way of proving it."

"Please sit down, Rose," Emma urged. She set a full teacup by Rose's chair. "We must remain calm and decide how we are going to help Alice."

Rose complied, but everything in her posture still radiated anger. Alice could understand this. She'd been angry, too, at first. She must have walked five miles around London, trying to walk off her frustration at the injustice of what had happened. Now her ire was tempered by a kind of fatalistic gloom and worry for her future.

"I believe there is an additional reason he acted as he did," Alice said, and heaved a sigh. She'd come here because she knew she could be completely honest with these friends in a way she could not be with Lucy, given the circumstances. "Archie saw that there was a . . . well, a sort of camaraderie developing between me and Douglas Shaw. We spent time together outside of work a few times—only for friendly discussions. We talked about business, science, all sorts of things. But Archie misconstrued what was happening."

"Did he think you might use the relationship to advance yourself in the company?" Rose asked.

"Well, actually . . ." The last thing Alice wanted to do was admit that she had kindled Archie's attraction to her. But she knew she had to tell them everything. "The truth is, Archie was beginning to fancy me."

"What?" Rose slapped the table in surprise, causing the teacups to jump and clatter on their saucers.

"I applied that technique from the spinster book, you see, of making a complimentary fuss over something he was good at."

"Which was?"

"Sharpening a pencil."

Rose gave a hearty laugh. "What a weak-minded man he is, if *that* made him fall in love with you."

"Be careful, Rose," Emma cautioned. "Alice might not take that as a compliment."

"It's all right. I know what she meant, and I heartily concur." Alice went on to tell them about what had happened at the lecture hall, and how Archie's behavior toward her had been worse after that day than at any time since she'd met him.

"A gentleman scorned," Rose said, shaking her head. "I'm very sorry now that I encouraged you to play that joke on him. I had no idea it would turn out so badly."

"None of us could have foreseen it," Alice said sadly. "Least of all me, and I know him best."

"Did you say Mr. Clapper thought you were developing a *tendresse* for Mr. Shaw?" Emma asked.

Alice nodded.

"Well, are you?" Emma's wide eyes looked almost hopeful.

"No," Alice insisted firmly. "No."

But she hadn't fooled either one of them. Emma smiled knowingly, and Rose murmured, "Heaven help us."

Alice blushed furiously. "I won't deny that I enjoy Douglas's company. We have so many common interests."

"Which trick from the spinster book did you try on him?" Rose asked.

"None of them! I was always completely honest. It was just so easy to talk to him. And after that lecture at Ally Pally, we ended up going to a dance." She went on to describe how they got to the tea dance, and how she'd taught Douglas to waltz. "He was so elated that he kissed me. It was an impulsive act, I'm sure. He is courting another lady. The daughter of a banker."

"Then he was toying with you—which is worse," Rose said.

"No. He was always honest with me in return."

"Was he?" Rose looked unconvinced. "Did he tell you about this other lady he's pursuing?"

Alice dropped her gaze. "No. I learned of her from someone else."

"And was he there when you were ruthlessly dismissed from your job?"

"No. He was in Liverpool on company business."

Rose leaned back and crossed her arms. "What a coincidence."

Alice lifted her head again. "No, wait. He was in Liverpool before the trouble started, but on the day I was sacked, he was on holiday in Glasgow."

"How do you think he felt about it?" Emma asked. "I don't suppose he's tried to contact you since then? You said it has been two days."

"No."

"Now I see why they thought you would deliberately sabotage the company," Rose said. "They think Douglas jilted you. Archie has laid the same blame on you that *he* is guilty of."

Alice straightened. "It doesn't matter. I do *not* fancy Douglas Shaw, and I certainly am not heartbroken in any way. I am simply out of work. Beginning tomorrow, I will search for new employment."

"Will you look for another telegraphy position?" Emma asked.

"I don't think I'll have any luck with that, since I can't expect Henley and Company to provide a letter of reference."

"Miserable, horrible, awful men," Rose murmured, glowering.

"There is also Mrs. Henley," Alice said. "For some reason, she seemed to be leading the charge against me. I can't fathom why, but she has not liked me from the beginning."

"That's despicable," Rose said. "There is nothing worse than a woman trying to ruin the life of another woman. We should all be helping one another get ahead in life."

"You could return to the Central Telegraph Office," Emma suggested. "They know what a good worker you are, so you wouldn't need a letter of reference. Everyone there was sorry to lose you."

"Everyone except Mrs. Lipscomb," Alice said ruefully. Mrs. Lipscomb was the supervisor of the women's section. Her heavy-handed style of oversight was a big reason Alice had decided to seek work elsewhere. "I'm not especially enthralled with the idea of having to take orders from her again."

"Didn't you tell us you thought she disliked you because she was afraid you wanted to take her place?" Emma asked.

"Yes." Alice grimaced. "Anytime I went to her with a suggestion for how something could be done better, she took it as a direct attack on her leadership. I went to her one day to discuss a particular

252

issue and how I thought it could be handled, and she accused me of being 'too solution-oriented'!"

"What?" Rose shook her head. "That makes no sense."

"I know, but that's exactly what she said. She informed me that I was to come to her only with the problem, and that it was *her* job to come up with the solution." Alice could laugh about it now, but the memory still irritated her.

"Well, then, here's some good news," Emma said. "Mrs. Lipscomb is no longer there. She's gone over to the administrative side of things. She's been overseeing the training school for about a month now."

"Has she?" Rose said in surprise. "Why didn't you mention this before?"

Emma shrugged. "It never occurred to me. I try not to think about work when I'm not there." She picked up the teapot and refilled everyone's cups. "It's too bad you couldn't have gotten that position at the training school, Alice. You're very good at teaching telegraphy. If you can teach me, you can teach anyone."

"Who is the new supervisor?" Rose asked.

"Miss Holloway. I like her well enough. You don't know her, Alice, but I can put in a good word for you. So can all the other girls who work there."

"It's worth a try, I suppose," Alice agreed. "To tell the truth, I was sadder about leaving telegraphy work than about all the rest of it. I wasn't sure what I was going to do. I thought I might have to learn typewriting after all and wished I'd had a chance to get those lessons while Henley and Company was ready to pay for them."

Emma smiled with empathy, if not with complete understanding. Alice knew she felt stifled working indoors with office equipment of any kind and only planned to keep the job until she could get married and leave work altogether.

"In any case, you can approach the superintendent, Mr. Powell, about employment," Rose said. "He'll remember you. I believe he liked you, and he's the one who makes the hiring decisions."

"Yes, he was always complimentary about my work." Alice

took a long sip of tea and smiled at her friends. She knew they would offer her just the help and support she needed. "I will go and talk to him tomorrow."

⤳ ⟡ ⤶

"You cannot mean you have sacked Miss McNeil over this. It is unconscionable!"

Douglas had returned to London with the happy anticipation that things at the office, and in his life, were going to be even better than before, thanks to the events of his trip. Instead, Miss Waller had tearfully given him the news about Alice's dismissal the moment he'd walked in the door. Meanwhile, Clapper had remained at his desk, looking happy as a clam. Douglas had immediately gone into Henley's office to confront him about it.

"*My* actions are unconscionable?" Mr. Henley returned with equal fervor, rising from his desk and coming around to meet him. "It's what she did that is truly despicable." He picked up a file of papers from his desk and thrust it at Douglas. "Everything is here. Read it and you'll see. She deliberately tried to ruin this company."

Douglas looked through the documents as Henley explained what they were.

He shook his head, still unable to believe it. "Why would she do this? It makes no sense."

Henley crossed his arms as he studied Douglas. "The fact that you are taking this so hard indicates there is truth in our supposition."

"Which is?"

"There was some kind of relationship building between you and Miss McNeil—"

"No!" Douglas shot back. "We were work colleagues!"

"Don't interrupt!" Henley bellowed. "Perhaps you saw nothing amiss. However, she must have been in love with you and was angered when you rejected her." He gave Douglas a hard look. "You did reject her, did you not? Your intentions are still to keep courting Miss Rolland?"

254

"I did not have to *reject* Miss McNeil," Douglas insisted. He said nothing about Miss Rolland, hoping Henley wouldn't press the issue. "All this information you've compiled against her is no more than malicious, unfounded gossip. I'll wager it originated from certain other persons in this office."

Douglas didn't need to elaborate. Henley knew who he was referring to. The fact that Miss Waller had told him Mrs. Henley was in the office the day Alice was dismissed had confirmed it in Douglas's mind. Clapper had cooked up these charges and fed them to his cousin, who in turn had poisoned her husband's mind with them.

"Watch yourself, Shaw," Henley warned. "You are important to this company, but you are not irreplaceable."

This threat was meant to worry him, but it didn't. He figured it would take a lot more than a few angry remarks to lose his position. He couldn't be dismissed as easily as Alice had been. And in any case, just at the moment, he didn't care.

Perhaps Henley read the defiance in Douglas's face. His demeanor softened. "Look at it this way. In the end, her motives are not important. We have the proof right there that she committed this offense." He pointed to the papers in Douglas's hands. "She's lucky merely to have been let go without notice or references. We might well have decided to pursue legal action against her."

"Surely not!"

"Look at those numbers! I shouldn't have to spell out for you what kind of damage this has done to our reserves, as well as our credit. You know what cotton is selling for at present."

Douglas did know. He sighed. He was not ready to give up his belief that Alice had been unjustly accused. However, Henley was correct that getting past this financial crisis was the most critical thing facing the company. Douglas would have to let the other matter rest—for now.

He took a breath and said evenly, "What are we doing to address the problem?"

"I'm glad you're finally seeing reason." Henley motioned for him to take the chair opposite his desk.

The two of them went through the numbers, discussing possible actions the company could take. Douglas was able to point out what a boon this deal with Carnegie would be for them. It couldn't have come at a better time. His mind still simmered with agitation over what had happened to Alice, but he fought to remain calm, assuring himself he would get to the bottom of it.

Once they'd thoroughly reviewed everything and come up with a plan, Henley looked down at the notes they had made together. "It might work."

"It appears that woman couldn't even ruin the company properly, only damage it." This remark came from Archie Clapper. Douglas turned to see him standing at the door to Henley's office. Evidently he'd arrived in time to overhear Henley's remark.

The mere sight of him raised Douglas's hackles. He wanted nothing more than to throttle him. He shot Clapper a dark look. "I feel quite sure that Miss McNeil would be capable enough to thoroughly complete any task she set her mind to. Unlike some people with lesser ambitions."

It was unwise to lob this insult when he'd only barely gotten back on Henley's good side. Especially since it was a defense of Alice as well as an attack on Clapper.

Clapper drew up as if seriously offended. Addressing Henley, he said, "Sir, I really must object to this treatment—"

"What do you need, Mr. Clapper?" Henley asked in mild exasperation.

Clapper came forward and handed him a telegram. "I thought you'd want to see this right away."

Henley read it and grunted. "It's from the bank. Reasonably good news, as far as it goes."

He handed it to Douglas to read. Their banker had been able to rearrange terms on several of their business loans, which would buy them some time.

"We'll recover, won't we, sir?" Clapper said in a tone that to Douglas's ears sounded unusually ingratiating.

Despite Clapper's family connection and the years he'd been

working there, this was the first time Douglas had ever heard him use the word *we* in connection with the company. As though he had a personal stake in what happened to it. Which, of course, he did. Douglas could not imagine him getting another position as easily as Alice might—even if there was now a black mark placed unfairly against her. She was as capable as Clapper, if not more so, and a lot more personable. Clapper had always been obsequious to Henley and his wife, but he had never acted as though he had any greater interest in the company than his paycheck. For some reason, his pretentious remarks now rankled Douglas more than his toady manner ever had.

"Shouldn't you be getting back to work?" Douglas growled.

"Why yes, Mr. Shaw, I believe you're right. I have *lots* of work to do now—until Mr. Henley can hire a new man to assist me." He gave Douglas a smirk before sauntering from the room.

A new *man*. The new hire would be a man, naturally. Clapper would pester Henley to ensure that happened. He was more than happy to be rid of the woman who had been a thorn in his side simply because she'd been intelligent and highly competent.

And beautiful.

The thought came unbidden, and it only ratcheted up Douglas's frustrations.

He followed Clapper to the door and slammed it shut behind him.

Alice walked into the reception area for the superintendent of London's Central Telegraph Office. When she'd left a few months ago, she'd been so full of hope for the future. She was going to break free of the telegram factory and use her talent and skill in a more rewarding position in the business world.

Now she was returning, hat in hand, to a restrictive workplace she thought she'd risen above. Her pride had certainly been taken down several notches. Perhaps a ten-story building's worth. No one else would be likely to hire her without references. At least at the CTO she could point to her stellar work record, with few sick days and no unexcused absences.

Squaring her shoulders, she walked up to the reception desk. The male clerk was perusing some official-looking correspondence and frowning.

"Excuse me," Alice said.

He looked up. "Yes?"

"I'd like to speak to Mr. Powell. My name is Alice McNeil. I don't have an appointment, and I'm aware that Mr. Powell is very busy, but I used to work at the CTO, and he knows me, so I'm hoping he will forgive my rudeness in coming here without prior notice."

The clerk gave her a critical look. She smiled, hoping to soften his demeanor.

He set the papers aside. "Mr. Powell is not here."

"When will he return? I can wait."

"He had a stroke and is incapacitated. He is not expected to recover."

"How awful!" This was shocking to hear. She did not think Mr. Powell was much above fifty years old.

"Mrs. Lipscomb is acting in his stead for now."

"Mrs. Lipscomb!" Alice repeated in surprise.

"If you would like to speak to her, I can see if she is available. We are very busy, as you can understand."

Alice nodded. "I promise I won't take much of her time."

He rose and went into the adjoining office.

Alice waited nervously. Of all the people to be in this position right now, it had to be Mrs. Lipscomb. The woman who didn't like Alice and had been affronted that she'd left the CTO for greener pastures. On the other hand, perhaps being a woman, she would be able to sympathize with Alice's plight. Alice prayed fervently that the door would open for her to return to work.

The clerk reappeared. "Follow me, please."

Relieved, Alice followed him into the office.

Mrs. Lipscomb remained seated behind the large desk as she

greeted Alice. "Why, Miss McNeil! I could hardly believe my ears when my clerk told me you were in the waiting room. What brings you here today?"

Her words were friendly enough, but underneath them Alice could hear a note of condescension. She had probably already guessed the reason for Alice's visit.

"I came to see Mr. Powell," Alice explained. "I'm terribly sorry to hear of the calamity that has befallen him."

"It is terrible. He is not expected to live. A reminder that we must all make the most of our time, for we never know when it may be up." Sitting back in her chair, Mrs. Lipscomb studied Alice, who still stood in the center of the room, since she had not been offered a seat. "But I don't suppose you came to pay him a social call?"

"No. The truth is, I was coming to see if there were any openings at the CTO."

"But what about your other job?"

"It didn't work out." Alice said this with as much dignity as she could muster. Mrs. Lipscomb seemed determined to make her feel inferior.

"Were they dissatisfied with your work?"

"I believe I was unfairly treated and unjustly accused of wrongdoing. You know my record. You know I worked at CTO for seven years with an excellent attendance record. I am a diligent and conscientious worker."

"And yet somehow your performance at the other company was insufficient." Mrs. Lipscomb was eyeing her with suspicion now.

"You of all people should know how the scale can be weighted against women advancing in the workplace," Alice pointed out. She didn't say it aloud, but she doubted Mrs. Lipscomb would be in this present position of acting superintendent if the emergency with Mr. Powell had not arisen.

Mrs. Lipscomb frowned. "Thank you for your interest, Miss McNeil, but there are no openings at present. Our most recent crop of graduates has proven to be very capable. They are also well-mannered and graciously accept direction."

This was a barb aimed directly at Alice. They'd had their run-ins while Alice worked at the CTO, and now Mrs. Lipscomb was getting her revenge.

How ironic that this woman, who had gotten where she was by being anything but docile, wanted only to hire sheep to work under her. But then, it was in her best interest to keep staff who would not challenge her authority.

Mrs. Lipscomb rose from her chair, signaling that the interview was over. "Miss McNeil, I'm sorry we haven't a position to offer you. I wish you luck in your future endeavors."

Alice left the building, quickly wiping away the weak, foolish tears that tried to form, and questioning every decision she'd made over these past few months. Perhaps even the past several years. Had she been wrong to want the things she did? She couldn't believe it. And yet, it seemed to be true. Everything she'd thought had set her on a trajectory to success had turned out to be a gamble. And she had lost.

CHAPTER

Twenty-Six

"M ay I help you find something, Mr. Shaw?"

Douglas looked up from the filing cabinet he'd just pulled open to see Miss Waller standing in the doorway to the filing room. He had come into the office very early in order to peruse the files before anyone else arrived. In fact, he'd done this for the past several mornings. Today the time must have gotten past him. He'd been through half a dozen drawers already. The saying about a needle and a haystack came readily to mind.

He paused before answering Miss Waller's question. She'd been friendly with Alice and was devastated to see her go. But could Douglas trust her to keep what he was doing confidential?

At this point, he supposed he had no choice. "I was searching for Miss McNeil's personal information. Her address and so on. I assume we have such a file?"

"Oh yes, sir!" Miss Waller said. "Is she going to be reinstated?"

She spoke with such hopefulness that it pained Douglas to give the answer. "I'm sorry to say there are no plans to do so at this time. However, I am doing my best to help her. I would like to speak to her, if possible. There were some questions raised about her last few days here that I'm trying to clear up."

"You don't know where she lives?" Miss Waller asked, surprised.

Perhaps she had assumed a certain closeness between him and Alice, just as the others had.

"No. That's why I'm here." He pointed toward the cabinets. "Can you help me?"

"Certainly." She went immediately to one of the cabinets and opened the bottom drawer. "That kind of information is kept here."

It was one of the drawers Douglas hadn't gotten to yet. He waited with mounting anticipation as she thumbed through the folders to locate what he needed. He'd spent three mornings searching this room, plus he'd gone every evening to the bookshop, just in case Alice should stop by. He'd even ridden the omnibus from work to The Angel on the off chance she might be aboard. That had been the most unlikely way to run into her, given that she no longer had the same work schedule, but he'd done it anyway. Now, at last, he might finally be getting somewhere.

Miss Waller worked her way to the back of the drawer, opening every folder along the way, before shaking her head. "I don't understand. It's not in here."

"Are you sure?"

She closed the drawer and stood up. "I checked thoroughly. It should be there, but it's gone. Someone must have taken it out."

"Why would they do that?" But as soon as he asked the question, he thought he knew the answer. Someone wanted to keep that information concealed. "Do you by any chance remember any of the details that were in there? I assume you typed it up?"

She took a moment, thinking. "I believe we sent her offer letter to an address in Bloomsbury."

Douglas shook his head. That couldn't be right. If she lived in that part of London, she wouldn't have been taking the omnibus all the way to Islington to get home. "Are you sure you're not thinking of Islington?"

She snapped her fingers. "That's right. After starting here, she moved to Islington. What was the name of that street? Something to do with water . . ."

She paused, clearly racking her brain, while Douglas waited on pins and needles.

"Ah! It was Waterford Terrace. Near the canal. Does that help?"

"It's close enough." Douglas prayed the street wasn't too long. He'd have to spend time loitering there, hoping to see her, but it gave him a better chance than constantly visiting the bookshop had done. "And I'd appreciate it if you kept this conversation confidential, just between us."

He searched his mind for some plausible reason for this, but it quickly became clear he didn't need to.

She beamed at him. "If this is to help Alice, you can count on me."

⚜

Alice had finally told Lucy about her situation. It had been more difficult to share this news with her than with her other friends, but she knew she couldn't put it off any longer. She didn't want Lucy to show up unannounced one day at Henley and Company to be told Alice no longer worked there.

Lucy had taken the news with surprising serenity, commiserating with Alice over the unfairness of how she'd been treated. She had insisted Alice come to tea the following day. "We can sort it out together," Lucy had told her. Alice had agreed even though she thought there was little Lucy could do to help besides offering moral support.

When Alice arrived at Lucy's home, the butler led her into the formal parlor instead of the more comfortable sitting room where she and Lucy usually spent their time. This room was much larger, and yet somehow it felt smaller, more stuffy. The heavy mahogany and horsehair furniture produced a stultifying effect. It admirably met its goal of being a magnificent display of affluence.

Lucy was seated on the horsehair sofa. To Alice's surprise, Fred stood nearby, waiting to greet her.

The sight of him brought a sinking feeling to Alice's stomach. "Fred! I thought you were still at sea."

It was a terrible greeting, bordering on rude, but he didn't seem to notice. He gave her a bow—something she'd never seen him do before—and approached her. "Our ship made port several days ago. I was not at liberty until we had entirely unloaded, but now, here I am. I could hardly wait to see you, but I asked Lucy to keep my arrival a surprise."

He and Lucy smiled at each other. Alice knew she was in trouble. "Usually you can't wait to see me leave," she joked.

Lucy stood up. "I'll see about getting us some tea."

She left the room so quickly that Alice didn't have time to point out that the butler's call button was within easy reach. Lucy closed the door behind her, leaving Alice alone with Fred.

He motioned toward the couch. "Would you like to take a seat? Make yourself comfortable?"

"Thank you." But she slipped into a nearby chair instead of the sofa. It seemed safer.

Undeterred, Fred pulled a second chair forward so that it was inches from hers. "I thought about you ever so much while I was at sea."

Alice's throat went dry. "Did you?"

"We've known each other for such a long time, haven't we?"

"I see you are familiar with the use of calendars." Why was she being so rude? It had to be some kind of horrible defense mechanism.

Today, Fred seemed inclined to overlook her remarks. He reached into his pocket and pulled out a slender black box about three inches square. "Because we're such good friends, I brought you something from India." He extended the box. "Go on," he encouraged, when she didn't reach for it.

Alice dreaded to think what might be in it. What if he gave her something expensive? That would signify they had an understanding that went beyond friendship. "You're very kind, Fred, but I don't think I could accept—"

He pressed the box into her hand. "You'll like it, I'm sure. I got one for Lucy, too."

That sounded encouraging. Maybe it was simply a gift between friends, as he'd said. Hesitantly, she lifted the lid. Lying on a bed of cotton wool was a silver brooch shaped like an elephant.

"It's nice, isn't it?" Fred said proudly.

"Yes," said Alice. "It's very pretty." She lifted it out of the box to inspect it and was relieved to see it was not actually made of silver but some cheaper metal. Fred had probably bought it in a bazaar where they were sold by the dozens. She was impressed he'd come up with such an interesting and thoughtful gift. She was still concerned about accepting it, but there seemed no valid reason to refuse. "Thank you."

He looked pleased. "I'm glad you like it. Isn't it good that we made up from that silly grudge we held against each other all those years?"

Alice had never held the grudge, but she would be the worst sort of ingrate to point that out right now.

"It occurred to me that you are quite a reasonable and self-sufficient lady," Fred went on. "And somewhat good-looking to boot."

Just when Alice was beginning to think she'd misjudged him, he came up with a comment that proved she'd been correct all along. Placing the brooch back in the box, she gave a little smirk. "Thank you. I think."

"You have quite the sense of humor, too!" He nodded, smiling. "You know my sister has been going on about me getting married for some time now."

Alice gulped. He was going there after all. "I didn't realize."

"Well, she has." He nodded solemnly. "I'm five years older than she is, although I don't look it." His hand went to that dimple in his cheek. Alice couldn't decide if the movement was intended to recall their conversation about it or if it had been done unconsciously. "There I was on that ship, standing at the railing and staring out over the wide blue sea. And it hit me, just like that, out of the blue. You would be the perfect wife for me!"

"Is that because of my sense of humor, or because I am somewhat good-looking?"

"All of it!" he answered with a laugh, not catching the sarcasm. "I'm away at sea a lot, you know. Gone for months at a time. But I make good money. My portion of the ship's take is very good. But I explained all that in my letter to you, didn't I? You didn't take offense at my writing?"

"Yes—I mean, no." It was hard to keep up with his questions when her mind was scrambling for a way out of this with everyone's sensibilities intact.

He beamed. "I've loads of money in the bank, mostly because I live simply, staying in a boardinghouse or here with my sister."

"And you are looking for someone to help you spend all that money?"

"I wouldn't mind having a home of my own. But I need someone who can steward it wisely and take care of herself while I am away. It can't be a clingy, dependent sort of person."

He was looking at her expectantly, as though he'd asked her a question. She had no doubt that one was coming, but she wasn't going to hurry it along.

"Don't you see, Alice?" He reached out and took her hands. His were big, beefy, and calloused. "I don't have much experience when it comes to courting ladies. But I'll tell you this—I am nothing if not honest. And isn't that better than them silver-tongued fellows? They can lie to you as easy as slipping on an icy pond."

"Don't I know it," Alice murmured. The words slipped out before she could stop them. She took a sharp intake of breath and closed her mouth firmly, worried that Fred might ask for more details. His sister certainly would have asked.

Fred, however, didn't seem to notice. He merely said, "Dear Alice, won't you marry me and make me the happiest of men?"

Alice suspected those last words were recited from a book. Or perhaps Lucy had coached him on what to say. And yet she felt that Fred was sincere. His hands were clammy around hers. She tried to find some way to let him down gently.

"This seems rather sudden," she said as she carefully extracted her fingers from his. "Although it's true that we've known each other a long time, we haven't spent a lot of time together. Not in *that* way—that is to say, not courting. There really is a lot we don't know about each other."

"Pshaw. Plenty of people get married knowing each other less than we do."

"I suppose you've discussed this with Lucy—your idea about marrying me, I mean?" But Alice knew the answer already. That was why Lucy had left the room so quickly and why she was gone far longer than it took to call for tea. She had set the stage for the proposal and was giving them time to make the most of it.

"Lucy and I had a long chat about it," Fred confirmed. "She's concerned about you, you see. What with you being out of work and all, and how you might never find decent employment again."

"Lucy is greatly exaggerating the situation. I'm not—"

"Oh, I know you did nothing wrong," Fred interrupted. "You were unjustly treated. The world can be a cruel place sometimes. Lord knows I've had it happen to me. For years I've had overseers who underestimated my abilities. That just meant I had to work extra hard for promotion. But I'm not bitter about it."

"I'm glad you took the high road." At this point, Alice was saying anything to stall for time.

"When I told Lucy I'd been thinking about marrying you, we agreed the timing is perfect. It's as though it were meant to be."

Fred was talking as though Alice had already accepted him and they had only to set a date for the happy event. "Wait—stop!" she exclaimed. "I don't want to marry anyone. I'm happy as I am."

He looked confused for a moment, but then he rallied. "Lucy says you're worried because you see other husbands telling their wives all the things they can and cannot do. But I assure you, I'm not like that. As I said, I will be away a lot, and you'll be in charge of the house and the day-to-day details of running it. I suppose we might go over the household books whenever I'm home, just to be sure we are in agreement. But I have every confidence in you." He was like a bulldog, never giving up once he'd set his mind to something.

"That's very kind, and I appreciate your high appraisal of me. But I must tell you honestly that I cannot give you an answer just yet. I will have to think it over."

Rose had warned her to be prepared for Fred's proposal. This was the only plan Alice could come up with—to stall for time until she could find a way to change his mind. Given the way Fred had proven he could hold grudges, Alice was worried that a flat refusal might send him back to hating her. In addition, memories of what had happened when she'd pushed Archie the wrong way plagued her. What if something similar happened with Fred?

It wasn't such an outlandish idea. Even now he was staring at her, his brows drawn together, mouth turned down into something between a frown and a scowl, unable to believe she hadn't immediately accepted him.

Oh, what a mess her life had become because of that book!

Alice jumped when the door to the parlor opened suddenly and Lucy came breezing in. "How are you two getting along? Is everything settled?"

⁂

Douglas walked up the hill toward the area of the park where he knew he'd find Miss Rolland. He would have preferred to be anywhere but here—especially now that he had a way to locate Alice. He was desperate to see her again. But he had an appointment with Miss Rolland today, and he knew he had to keep it.

This meeting was not going to turn out as the lady was probably expecting. Douglas knew with clarity what he had to do. Throwing away a prime opportunity to advance himself financially and socially was not something he'd ever thought he'd allow to happen, yet here he was. This decision was the culmination of many things—not the least of which had been Alice's challenge to his honor.

Miss Rolland stood near the butterfly bushes, but she did not seem to be actively stalking the creatures. She was listlessly chatting with her chaperone. Her entire demeanor changed when she caught sight of Douglas. She set aside her net and ran toward him, her face alight with pleasure.

Worried she'd try to throw her arms around him or something equally ill-advised, Douglas took a step backward. She took her cue from his movement, stopping short about a foot away from him. But she was still smiling as she said breathlessly, "I'm so glad you've come."

"Yes, well, I said I would."

She poked him playfully in the chest. "And do you always keep your promises, Mr. Shaw?"

Douglas felt a stab of panic. Had he promised her anything— whether overtly or implied—about the future of their relationship? If so, he'd be honor bound to keep that promise. He quickly raked through his memories but thought he was in the clear.

"Come now, that shouldn't be such a difficult question to answer," Miss Rolland said, crossing her arms as she pretended to chide him.

He'd better get it out quickly. "Miss Rolland, I've something important to discuss with you." Before she got the wrong idea, he added hurriedly, "I fear this may be a difficult conversation. Perhaps we might sit down?" He pointed toward a nearby bench.

"All right," she murmured, displeasure creeping into her voice. Maybe her women's intuition gave her some sense of what was coming.

Douglas was aware that they were still under the watchful eye of her chaperone thirty yards off. He hoped Miss Rolland wasn't the sort to make a fuss if things didn't go her way, for he had no doubt she'd been expecting a proposal of marriage. Some part of him still couldn't believe he was throwing away this opportunity. But the rest of him could think only of Alice. She had ruined him for anyone else.

"What's on your mind, Mr. Shaw?"

"Miss Rolland, I'd like you to know how much I've enjoyed spending time with you."

She turned eagerly toward him. "Those feelings are returned, I assure you."

"However, the thing is, I think it would be best if we stopped seeing each other. In this sort of setting, I mean." He gestured to the park around them, including their private meeting—the distant chaperone notwithstanding.

"It's kind of you to worry about my reputation, but I'm sure you're being overly concerned." She leaned in closer and laid a hand on his arm. "Perhaps you might discuss the matter with my father?"

He tried to move away without being too obvious about it. "Miss Rolland, you are a charming young lady. Any man would be lucky to be the recipient of your affection."

Catching the way he was distancing himself with the phrasing of this compliment, Miss Rolland frowned. "Is there someone else? Is that what this is about?"

"No!" His reply was vehement, but he knew it wasn't true.

The look in her eyes said Miss Rolland knew it, too. She stiffened and pulled back of her own accord. "You may think me a foolish girl, but I know what's at stake here. I know your employer and my father are working on an important business deal. Is that still true?"

"It is. I hope very much that it comes to pass."

"But it can't be the only reason for your interest in me, can it?" She looked at him with pleading eyes, the eyes of someone who loves and longs to be loved in return.

It made Douglas feel like a worse cad than he'd have been if he'd gone ahead and married her without love. "I'm very sorry. I certainly never meant to mislead or hurt you." He spoke sincerely, though it was painful to do.

Then, as he watched her reaction, a very interesting thing happened. She blinked, and it was as if the loving, shining eyes had been blinked away. She seemed to be thinking, her forehead slightly crinkled in calculation. Douglas held his breath, unsure what was coming next.

"Very well, then," she said at last. She stood up, looking down at him with disdain. "You may keep your money dealings with my father. He will get richer from it, too, which will benefit *me*. But here is what you must do. You must attend Lady Gordon's dinner party on Thursday next. I believe you have already received an invitation for that, yes?"

"Yes," Douglas answered, a little confused.

"Good. At that party, I shall—very publicly—give you the cut direct. Everyone must think that *I* chose to end our little romance, not *you*. Is that understood?"

Douglas rose to his feet, hardly believing the change that had come over this woman. "Yes, of course."

"There's one more thing you must do as well. At some point during that party, you will take Mr. Busfield aside and tell him I threw you over because I am in love with someone else. You will allow him to divine that that person is him."

"I see." Douglas had no idea how he was going to accomplish that little feat. On the other hand, given Busfield's high opinion of himself, it might not be too difficult.

She was looking at him with a hard expression, her face flushed with barely suppressed anger. "If you do those things, then I will tell my father that he ought not to hold this against you, nor against Henley and Company."

"Thank you."

"You will be free to seek out another bride, although I feel certain you will have a difficult time finding one in London society after this."

He knew what she was implying. Gossip about what a terrible person he was would do him in, and she would be the one to ensure that happened. Two things that seemed contradictory became absolutely clear to him. He truly had hurt her feelings. In that regard, he could understand her actions. She was trying to salvage her pride. At the same time, he was heartily glad for this disaster, despite the pain it had caused. It allowed him to discover her true nature now, and not after they'd said marriage vows and it was too late. There was only one way to mollify a woman like this when she was angry or affronted: meet her demands without question.

He gave her a little bow. "I promise I will do all those things, just as you requested."

She gave a superior little sniff. "See that you do."

With that, she turned her back on him and set off. Douglas could see alarm on the chaperone's face as Miss Rolland stalked across the lawn. He had no doubt that whatever Miss Rolland told her would not be the least bit flattering to him.

Douglas had thoroughly burned that bridge. He didn't know what all the ramifications would be, but as he turned and walked in the opposite direction, he was sure he'd been right.

⁘

"I think you're being selfish and unreasonable," Lucy declared.

"How can saying 'I will consider it' be either of those things?" Alice placed a hand on her hat as she spoke. They were riding in Lucy's open carriage, and the day had turned out unusually windy. Clouds also loomed on the horizon, which had been clear this morning. So far, the weather was turning out to perfectly match the rest of her day.

"It is selfish to keep Fred and me on the hook," Lucy answered, clamping down on her own hat and resetting her hat pin. "It is unreasonable because you have no other means of supporting yourself. Do you want to end up destitute, with no place to live?"

As if Henley and Company were her last chance at being self-supporting. Despite what had happened at the CTO, Alice had every confidence of finding other work. Lucy couldn't even fathom why a woman would *want* to earn her own living. If Alice didn't know better, she'd have suspected her friend of engineering that dismissal from her job—if only to force Alice into Fred's arms.

The very thought of being in Fred's arms made Alice shudder. "I am not going to make a life-altering decision on the spur of the moment. Even Fred understood that. I said we ought to spend more time together before making any commitments, and he agreed. You heard it yourself."

Alice's real plan was to show Fred enough of her true self to make him see what a mistake he was making in thinking they were suitable for one another. Once that happened, he would be more than willing to steer his ship in another direction. Alice would graciously release him from his offer of marriage, and everyone would be happy.

"He agreed, but reluctantly," Lucy pointed out. "He doesn't waste time endlessly ruminating over things. I believe it's one reason why he's been so successful."

Given that this was the third time they'd had this argument since leaving Lucy's house, the conversation was growing wearisome. At least Alice had managed to keep Fred from escorting her home. Lucy had helped with that, though probably so she could spend the entire trip berating Alice.

Just when Alice thought they had covered everything ad nauseam, Lucy came up with a new and more devastating line of attack.

"You know, Alice, you're wasting your time *and* your life if you think that reprehensible Mr. Shaw will come and rescue you."

"What?" Alice shrieked.

Lucy leaned closer to her. "If that's why you are dillydallying about Fred's proposal, it makes you the worst sort of woman in my book. Mr. Shaw might not have been there the day you were sacked, but you know very well he had a hand in it, and you need to stop denying that fact." She spoke rapidly and forcefully to prevent Alice, who was sputtering in indignation, from cutting her off. "Plenty of time has passed since then, and has he done anything about it? No! Why? He cannot risk having you at his workplace. You might interfere with his marriage prospects. Perhaps he was attracted to you after all and knows he can't trust himself, or perhaps—and this is more likely, in my opinion—he can't risk making his prospective fiancée jealous. In short, he needed you out of the way. Therefore, you need to put him out of your mind and get on with life."

She gave an exaggerated nod to put the final stamp on her words, crossed her arms, and leaned back. Her look dared Alice to find fault with anything she'd just said.

Stunned and angry, Alice could say nothing. Her soul stung from this barrage that managed to be both insulting and to have a ring of truth. The words pierced right to the center of her heart. Was Douglas truly glad to be rid of her? Had he been involved, or at least complicit, in her dismissal? Had she secretly been harboring some fantasy about him coming to her rescue, like the make-believe princes sighed over by the kind of women she abhorred? She was glad another gust of wind forced her to reach again for her hat. It gave her several more moments to gather her thoughts.

Seeing Alice's obvious inability to come up with a rebuttal, Lucy could have exulted in her victory. But she must have seen Alice's distress, too. Her expression softened.

She leaned forward again, this time offering a conciliatory smile. "I'm sorry I was so blunt. You do believe I want only the best for you, don't you?"

Alice still couldn't answer. She didn't want to part on bad terms. She really did love her friend, though they had grown apart in many ways since their school days. Lucy's outlook on life had been greatly affected by her marriage. She was so satisfied with it that she couldn't imagine any better course for a woman to take.

They had less common ground now, but the two women were still very much alike in one particular way. They were single-minded in pursuing what they believed was right. It could be a two-edged sword at times. Until today, Alice had considered it a positive attribute. Whether Lucy's view of the situation was correct or not, she had grown too overbearing. Alice wanted only to get away and find space to breathe.

The carriage rounded the corner onto Alice's street and pulled to a stop in front of her house. "Let's talk again in a day or two," Alice suggested. "As you can see, I'm rather overwhelmed at the moment."

Lucy squeezed her hands reassuringly. "Of course."

Ironically, that patronizing little gesture only reignited Alice's anger. Lucy still believed she had made an unassailable case. Alice turned to accept the footman's hand and exited the carriage before her expression could reveal to her friend just how wrong she was.

Alice didn't know how she had allowed herself to reach this point where men had so horribly interfered with her life—sabotaging her career, damaging her friendships, and wreaking havoc on her peace of mind. But she was absolutely certain of one thing as she watched Lucy's carriage drive away: whatever happened, she was never, *ever* going to allow herself to get into such a position again.

She had about ten seconds to solidify that resolve before she found herself face-to-face with a man coming out from under the shade of a nearby tree.

Judging by the way her heart began skipping with more hops than a schottische, she must have been wishing he would come after all. What a foolish woman she was, to expect a man to solve her problems. Especially this one, who had somehow been in the middle of all of them. She clenched her fists, as though that would give her the inner strength to withstand this man's dangerous pull.

"What are you doing here?" she demanded.

Douglas looked taken aback, but he managed a smile. "Might we be able to talk?"

CHAPTER

Twenty-Seven

I t seems rather late for a chat, doesn't it?"

Her words hit Douglas like the hot breeze that teased the loose wisps of hair around her face. If it was true that Clapper had manipulated events to get her wrongly removed from her position, then Douglas was now seeing a demonstration of pure righteous indignation. Alice probably felt utterly betrayed and abandoned.

He tried to think of a response that might alleviate her anger. "Well, I tried looking for you several times at the bookshop, but I was never able to catch you. I had no luck finding your address in the company files, either. Happily, Miss Waller was able to give me the name of the street where you live."

"You had to search for me?" For a brief moment, she seemed to soften. But then she clenched her fists tighter. "Did you wish to acknowledge that I was scandalously treated by Henley and Company? If so, I quite agree with that assessment. But in the end, it does not signify. I have quite gotten over it and am moving on in other directions. Good day, sir."

She was actually going to walk away! After all he'd done to find her!

Scrambling for a way to stop her, Douglas tossed out the first question he could come up with. "Was that Mrs. Bennington I saw you with just now in the carriage?"

She paused. Her shoulders visibly tightened. She made a sharp turn to face him. "Why yes, it was. I've just had a most excellent tea at her home with her brother. He asked me to marry him."

Douglas gasped. "The sailor?"

She crossed her arms and lifted her chin. "He's a cargo master. It's a position of great responsibility. He has a cabin almost as big as the captain's."

Why was she telling him this? Douglas stood frozen in shock. The satisfied look on her face was probably an indication that this was exactly the effect she'd been going for.

Mrs. Bennington had mentioned her brother Fred that night at Ally Pally. But Alice had never spoken of him. She'd spoken only of remaining unmarried as her life's goal! Was this other fellow going to beat Douglas out for the privilege of winning over the world's most desirable and determined spinster? Surely it could not be true.

He expected her to continue—dreading but at the same time unable to believe she'd announce that she'd accepted Fred. But she was apparently waiting for *him* to speak. Well, then, he would. It was clear he'd fallen pretty far in her estimation. He had to win back her respect.

He swallowed. "I want you to know that I had nothing to do with your being dismissed. I had no knowledge of it at the time, and I protested vigorously to Henley the moment I found out about it. I don't believe for a minute you sent that erroneous message, either maliciously or by mistake. I also want you to know that I hold you in the highest esteem. I would never try to hurt you."

Something flickered in her eyes. Was he getting through? His hope grew as her gaze hung on his for a long moment. But then she blinked. "Actions speak louder than words, Mr. Shaw. Are you still employed by Henley and Company?"

"Yes."

"And are you still—" She paused, sucked in a breath, and began again. "And does the current black mark on my record—the one leaving me without work or references—still stand?"

"Yes," he was forced to admit.

"I see."

There was heavy censure in those two words. Douglas had shown himself powerless to do anything about what had happened to her. He didn't know what kind of man Fred was, but he knew that as for himself, he had fallen very short of the mark. He said in desperation, "You're not really going to marry that sailor, are you?"

She looked at him, her head slightly tilted, as though his question had caught her by surprise. He thought he glimpsed the vulnerability he'd seen moments ago. But then she turned away. "I cannot talk any more today, Mr. Shaw. I've many important things to attend to."

"Alice . . ." He said her name as an entreaty.

She turned back once more. "You might want to go back to reading Morse code off the tape, Mr. Shaw. Your hearing doesn't seem to work very well anymore."

This time when she walked off, Douglas didn't try to stop her. He saw everything clearly now. She wasn't going to accept words, only actions. He'd spent days searching for her when he ought to have been searching for answers instead.

Alice stopped when she got to her doorstep because there was a cat sitting on it, blocking her path. It looked up at her and meowed.

Even though her back was to Douglas, he could see her body go rigid with irritation. Finally, she bent down and scooped up the creature. Juggling it with one hand, she unlocked her door, stepped inside with the cat, and shut the door behind her.

Unwilling to leave just yet, Douglas stood pondering the situation.

Of all the things she'd said, it was the things she hadn't said—or hadn't allowed herself to say—that spoke loudest to him.

"And are you—" she'd begun to ask him. What had been on the tip of her tongue? *Are you still pursuing Miss Rolland?* He happily would have answered that question. But she hadn't given him the chance.

278

He had work to do. He wasn't going to rest until he had uncovered the truth about the events that led to her dismissal. She deserved to have her name cleared, and he was going to find a way to do it.

In some ways, it seemed absurd that Clapper would purposely put the company at risk. If Henley and Company folded, what other firm would hire such a surly, lazy man? On the other hand, Clapper would know the company could take a certain amount of loss and still survive. And in the meantime, he would have gotten rid of the woman he'd clearly resented. He *must* have orchestrated the business with the telegrams. All the paperwork Douglas had pored over had to be lacking some vital clue that could prove who really had done it.

Like a thunderbolt, it occurred to him there was one place he hadn't yet looked. His next step was so obvious that he was ashamed at his stupidity for taking so long to think of it.

He took another moment to gaze at the house Alice had entered, memorizing the number posted in brass letters next to the door. Then he went home to pack his valise.

⚜

By the time Alice reached her flat, her legs could barely carry her. They felt as wobbly as rubber. The stress of marshaling her anger, plus keeping her emotional distance from a man who seemed to have an irresistible magnetic pull on her, had worn her out. On top of it all, the cat had made her attempt at departing nobly look utterly ridiculous.

She dropped onto the sofa. The cat wriggled out of her arms, landing with a light thump on the floor. Alice looked wearily down at her. "Miss T, you were a naughty thing to block my doorstep. Were you trying to keep me out, or were you there to ensure I didn't give in?"

Today, however, the cat was keeping her own counsel. She wandered off to the bedroom to take a nap on Alice's bed.

Alice dropped her head back, closing her eyes and seeing only Douglas.

Lucy had been wrong. He had come back. He had not been complicit in her sacking. He believed in her. Everything in her life had been upended once more.

She'd been determined to give him no quarter, and yet he'd kept pressing, kept looking for a way into her heart. It had taken every ounce of strength she possessed to keep him out. She'd been right to do so, for the biggest problems had not been solved. The workplace disaster hung over them like a dark cloud. Nor had he said anything about Miss Rolland. Alice had been dangerously close to asking, but pride had stopped her just in time.

She couldn't believe she'd told him about Fred's proposal! What had she been thinking—that it would somehow impress him? That it would prove she was getting on with her life, as she'd claimed? Quite likely it had done neither of those things.

It had been worth it, though, to see the dismay on his face. It had, ever so briefly, fanned a flame of hope in her heart. A hope that he loved her. Alice was no longer going to deny that she loved him. Nothing could ever come of it, but there it was. She'd planned her life so carefully, but now she understood that the leanings of the heart followed no rules.

She sighed, bringing her hands to her eyes, feeling the cool moisture of tears. In this depressed state she lay, ruminating sadly over everything.

A knock at the door startled her back to a sitting position.

Although the front door was down a flight of stairs, she heard the knocking through her open window. Pushing herself to her feet, she went to the window and looked out to see who it was.

A telegraph delivery boy stood on the front step. He pushed back his cap as he looked up at her. "Miss Alice McNeil?"

"Yes, that's me. Wait just one moment, please."

Alice hurried to her bedroom to locate a coin for the boy. All the gloom she'd been feeling coalesced into worry. What if the telegram contained bad news? Perhaps her mother's health was more frail than she'd realized. She ought to have heeded her sister's admonitions to visit them more often.

Opening the door, she received the telegram and tipped the boy in return. With a quick thank-you and a tip of his hat, he raced off. Alice tore open the telegram and quickly scanned its contents.

YOU MUST COME TO PARENTS PARTY SATURDAY.
REFUSAL NOT ALLOWED.

AFFECTIONATELY

YOUR FORGOTTEN FAMILY

Even though it was signed as from the whole family, this missive was definitely the work of her sister, Annie. Of that, Alice had no doubt.

Annie had written several letters telling Alice about the party, a celebration of her parents' fortieth wedding anniversary. Alice had been putting off her reply even though she knew, as the telegram stated, that she must go. She owed this to her parents. Such a milestone was not often achieved. Her father was nearing seventy, and her mother was not as vigorous as she'd once been, after bearing seven children. Alice loved her family dearly. She only hesitated because every time she went home, she faced an endless barrage of questions from her mother and sister, trying to ascertain if she had any gentlemen courting her and whether she was considering marriage. At least her brothers and father understood that she wanted and enjoyed this life she'd been living. They'd been happy for her successes.

And now?

Now she was mortified at the thought of going home. Aside from her shame at having lost her job, she would bring worries that would dampen a joyous celebration.

Expelling a deep sigh, Alice plodded back up the stairs, thinking over what to do. She spent a long time trying to decide how much of her troubles to reveal to her family. One thing she was determined *not* to do was mention Fred. Or Douglas.

She sniffled back a few more tears, then prepared to go out.

Although her family's desire to see her was understandable, something in Alice's soul balked at being *ordered* to go. She was half-tempted to keep them in suspense, not even sending a reply before she simply showed up on their doorstep. But then she decided there was no point in being contrary. She would wire back her response, despite the cost, and let them know she'd be arriving on the early train.

Besides, sending the telegram would give her a chance to see Rose. It was only an extra twenty minutes' walk to reach the post office where she worked. The thought of seeing Rose cheered Alice, even though she knew full well what her friend would say about her troubles with men. Rose would insist that Alice was far better off to be rid of them all.

And, of course, she'd be right.

CHAPTER

Twenty-Eight

When Alice stepped off the train in Ancaster, she found her brother Nathan waiting for her at the station. Annie was with him, too.

Annie threw her arms around Alice in a big hug. "I'm so glad you're here! Thank heavens you were able to get away from that horrid workplace and come home for a while."

"I keep telling you it's not horrid," Alice said, forgetting for a fraction of a second that she no longer worked there. "It's the same work Jack and Father do."

"Even so. Now we have you for two days. Mother and Father are so happy you're coming." She wrapped an arm around Alice while Nathan, who was not the sort to give hugs, merely grinned his greeting and put her valise in the wagon.

As they rode toward home, Annie explained that her husband, Roger, had to work that morning but would join them all later in the afternoon.

They soon arrived at the house where Alice had grown up and which was still occupied by her parents; her brothers Nathan and Peter; and Peter's wife, Jane; and their two sons. Today the house was bursting at the seams, because Alice's eldest brother, Jack, and his wife, Minnie, were there, too, along with their three children.

Altogether it was quite a brood, and Alice had no doubt that Annie and her new husband would soon be adding to the number.

Of the five siblings, only Alice and Nathan remained unmarried. Unlike Alice, no one was bothering her brother about remaining single.

Alice was instantly set upon by her sister-in-law Minnie and several of the older children, who subjected her to hugs and kisses. She always enjoyed hugs from the little ones, but today the arms around her neck and the soft hair brushing her cheek felt especially poignant. Perhaps she'd missed them more than she'd realized.

After she'd disentangled herself from the others, her father greeted her with a sound kiss on the cheek. "Welcome home, daughter. I'm glad you could come."

"You know I wouldn't miss your fortieth anniversary celebration! However, I confess I have a hard time believing that number is right." It was true. Her father was still as healthy and spry as a man twenty years younger.

"You are as beautiful as ever, Alice," said her mother, speaking from her chair by the window as though she hadn't seen Alice in years instead of only a few months.

Alice was sad to see that her mother wasn't faring as well as her father. According to letters she'd received from Annie, their mother was having increasing trouble getting around, so she had taken to directing the household from her chair in the main room.

Alice went over to give her a kiss. "Annie is the pretty one," she reminded her mother with a smile. "Not me."

"Correct as ever," said Peter. When they were children, he'd always teased her mercilessly.

Alice gave him a playful swat. "Where's Jane?"

"Upstairs tending to little Georgie. She'll be down shortly to introduce him to you." At just two months old, Georgie was the only member of this growing family that Alice hadn't met yet. "You'll find he's a fine, strapping lad," Peter added.

"Are you sure he's yours, then?" Alice teased.

He drew back, pretending to be offended. "Why, Alice! How dare you insult my wife like that!"

Everyone laughed.

"Come and sit by me, dear," her mother said, indicating the chair next to hers. "We want to hear all about what you've been doing in London."

"Yes!" said Jack excitedly. "I'd like to know more about your work at Henley and Company. I daresay the messages you send are a lot more exciting than the mundane stuff we get at the post office."

The mention of her former workplace instantly brought all of Alice's troubles back to the forefront of her mind. Why had she thought it would be enough simply not to mention work? Naturally they would want to ask her about it. She stared at Jack blankly while she tried to figure out how to answer.

"Jack, she's just arrived," Minnie admonished. "She hasn't even had time to take off her hat, and I daresay she could use a cup of tea."

"That's an excellent idea," Jack said, the point his wife was trying to make going completely over his head. "Can you go and make us some?" He dropped onto the sofa, returning his attention to Alice. "You have to send the messages in code, I'll bet. How does that work?"

Alice could have begged off and delayed this conversation, but it wouldn't be any easier later. Besides, her father was also looking at her expectantly, just as interested in this subject as Jack was.

"A cup of tea would be lovely, thank you," Alice said gratefully to Minnie, who was still shaking her head over Jack. Alice was used to her brother's ways. She knew he would always treat her as a sister and never as a pampered guest.

"I'm happy to make *you* one," Minnie said. "The blokes might need to fend for themselves." But she said this with a smirk, and Alice knew she was only teasing.

Minnie went off to the kitchen, and since that was the land of tea and treats, the children followed in her wake. Alice removed her hat and made herself comfortable in the chair next to her mother.

She did her best to answer her family's questions as neutrally as possible, trying to frame her responses without using the past tense. But discussing her work routine, her tasks, and the many things she'd learned while at the company was hard on her heart, for she missed all of those things already. Above all, she missed seeing Douglas every day. Quite apart from the minor fact that she was in love with him, he'd been the best work colleague she'd ever had.

Jack whistled in astonishment when she told him the volume of messages they sent and received daily. "And you have to put most of them into code first!" he said, marveling. "I'll bet they're glad to have a crack telegrapher like you working for them."

It was a rare compliment from her brother, and hard to accept, given the circumstances. In the short space of time since she'd last seen her family, she had gained and lost the best job she was likely ever to have. Never mind that she'd been forced out by a spiteful colleague.

"Al, you're not tearing up because Jack said something nice, are you?" Peter said. "I can't believe you're getting soft."

Alice shook her head, trying to think of a funny retort, but her throat was tight from holding back tears. Anything humorous completely escaped her.

Annie's sympathetic look told her she sensed Alice's distress. "Ah, look, here's little Georgie!" she said brightly, pointing toward the stairs, where Jane was just coming down with her son in her arms. Annie got up to meet them and began cooing elaborately over the baby. "Come here, my big boy," she said, taking Georgie into her arms. "You haven't met your Auntie Alice yet." Annie brought the boy over to Alice. "He's a beauty, isn't he?"

Alice accepted the little bundle from Annie and looked down into that cherubic face. The baby was pink and plump, with pale wisps of hair and wide blue eyes.

"He looks just like Peter," Annie teased. Their brother was slender and dark haired.

"He'll grow into it," Peter said.

Holding a baby was nothing new for Alice. Aside from her nieces and nephews, there had been her little sister. She'd had practically the entire care of Annie during her first few years, as their mother was often bedridden with problems from subsequent pregnancies. Today, though, as with everything else, Alice found that holding the baby was affecting her in troubling ways. This visit was already taking an emotional toll, and she hadn't even been here an hour.

"Georgie, this is your Aunt Alice," Annie told the boy. "Be nice to her, because she's going to be a wonderful aunt."

A *wonderful aunt.*

A maiden *aunt,* another voice in her head supplied. Of course that was her destiny; she'd known it all along. She'd consciously made that choice years ago, never once expecting she might regret it.

"Here's the tea," Minnie said, arriving with a tea tray and the children still in tow. "I brought just enough cups for the *ladies,*" she joked, sending a playful frown at Jack.

Sometime later, the tea had been consumed, and the family had split into various groups—the men were chatting and watching the older children play, while the ladies were conferring about the details of tonight's dinner.

Jane and Peter's other son, two-year-old Samuel, was staring at Georgie, who was seated in Jane's lap. He was fascinated by this little creature who had joined his family and taken all their attention yet couldn't do anything except simply *be.* Alice had to avert her gaze, because just the sight of them stirred deep longings in her soul.

Annie pulled Alice aside, out of hearing of the others. "Alice, is everything all right? You seem worried about something. Peter was right, even though he was joking. You're not usually the type who's often on the verge of tears."

"Maybe I'm just happy to be here. And I'm concerned about Mother."

Annie searched her face. "Is that really all, dearest? Because I can't help but think that something else is going on. Something serious."

Her sister knew her too well. *Should I tell her?* Alice was torn.

"Let's take a walk," Annie suggested. Without waiting for a reply, she announced to the others, "Alice is looking far too pale from being cooped up in dank, windowless buildings. We're going out for a bit."

They decided to walk out to a meadow on the edge of town where Annie could pick some wildflowers for the table and they could talk without interruptions.

"Now will you tell me what is bothering you?" Annie prompted.

"It's rather a long story."

"We have time."

"I didn't want to say anything in front of the others because I don't want them to worry. So you must keep this between us. This is a special time to celebrate Mother and Father, and the last thing they need is news from me that will worry them. I didn't even want to tell you because you are still in your happy, honeymoon part of life."

"Don't worry about that. I've been married five months now. Roger and I are quite used to one another, and we've already had our share of disagreements."

"Really?"

"Nothing serious," Annie assured her. "Don't look so horrified!"

Alice chuckled. Her sister sounded very grown up.

"This conversation is not supposed to be about me, however," Annie persisted. "Please tell me what's going on with you in London."

Alice let out a long sigh. "Remember, you mustn't tell anyone."

"Yes, yes," her sister replied impatiently. "Out with it."

"I've been let go from Henley and Company."

"What?" Annie looked rightfully shocked. "That's impossible. You're the best worker there. Is the company in financial trouble?"

"Yes, but it's not what you think." She began the tale from the beginning.

"Alice, that's so terrible," Annie said when Alice had finished. "How can they think you would do such a thing? Obviously this was the work of that horrible Mr. Clapper." Annie had never met Archie, but she knew enough about him to draw her own conclusions.

Especially since Alice had focused on Archie's dislike of working with women as the main source of friction at work. She couldn't bring herself to reveal the other details. "Why isn't anyone suspicious of him?"

"He seems to feel he has complete immunity and can never lose his position." Alice gave a resigned shrug. "It appears he is correct."

"Perhaps there is one good thing to come out of this. You'll be coming back here, won't you?"

"Return to Ancaster with my tail between my legs? Certainly not. There are endless opportunities in London. I'll find another position, that's all."

Annie shook her head. "If it's as easy as that, why are you so determined the rest of the family should not know about it?"

"Because they will react just as you did and start badgering me about coming back. Mother, especially."

"I don't know about that. Mother might surprise you."

Alice shrugged. "Even so, I'd rather not tell them until after I have secured a new position. I don't want them to worry."

"*I'll* worry in their stead," Annie said. "But surely it won't be long before you find something else. Any company would be glad to have a worker as talented as you."

"I don't think I can handle so many compliments from my siblings in one day," Alice joked. She didn't point out that, most likely, any other telegraphy job would be closed to her.

As they walked back to the house, Alice reflected that there were many things she couldn't tell Annie, nor anyone else in her family. All dealing with the deeper things of the heart. It was an odd situation, to be able to tell one's friends but not one's family. She decided, though, that it was best to leave things as they were.

⁓⊙⊙⁓

The celebration dinner was a boisterous affair. Alice worked diligently to keep the topics of conversation on everyone but her, asking endless questions about their work and families and the children. She learned that her father, although officially retired from his telegraphy job at the railway station, filled in at the post office telegraph a few days a week.

"I like to keep my hand in," he said. "Keeps my mind sharp." His face lit up. "Say, Alice, I've got an idea. I could telegraph you at your work sometime. Just for a little greeting."

"No!" Alice exclaimed. She took a breath. "That is, they have strict rules about that sort of thing. It's not to be used for personal messages. In any case, the other telegrapher who works there is generally the one receiving the incoming messages." It was mostly true, but it made her feel guilty, nonetheless, to lie to her father.

"A pity," he said with a shrug. "If it's slow, I'll just have to keep up the chess game over the wires with the geezer who works the telegraph in that little town in Devon."

"*Geezer*, Dad?" Nathan said with a smile.

Their father straightened. "Age is simply a state of mind, son."

After dinner, everyone crowded into the parlor for games, which the children particularly enjoyed. Alice watched the interactions between the married couples, which was everyone except her and Nathan. She had always been happy for them, glad for their growing families and contented lives. But she had never envied them until tonight.

It hit her most dramatically toward the end of the evening, as the children were beginning to tire and crawl into the laps of their parents or sit next to them on the chairs. The room was settling into a comfortable ease. Her parents, seated in twin chairs at the end of the room like a king and queen, looked out over their brood with joyful expressions.

Jack stood up and cleared his throat. "Ladies and gentlemen. And little people," he added with a nod to the children. "We are gathered here tonight to celebrate the life of an extraordinary couple."

Alice's mother smiled and shook her head, too modest to accept such a superlative term.

"Indeed you are extraordinary," Jack continued, "for you have produced this family—which, I think we can all agree, is extraordinary."

"Hear, hear!" shouted Peter, and everyone laughed and voiced their agreement.

"It wasn't easy. There have been hard times, but there have been plenty of good times, too. Through good times and bad we have supported, loved, and helped each other, no matter the challenge. That is why I believe this family is so extraordinary. You have been a stellar example to us these past forty years, and you have our undying love and gratitude."

Everyone gave heartfelt applause. It was clear their mother and father were deeply moved. They held hands tightly, alternating between gazing into one another's eyes with affection and looking at their family with equal love and joy.

"But that's enough speechifying from me," Jack said. "*Paterfamilias*, will you give us a few words?"

For the first time this evening, now that he had been put on the spot, her father was speechless. He looked down at the hand still clasped in his. "My dear, we have had quite a time of it, haven't we?" He lifted his eyes again to smile at his wife.

"We certainly have. God be praised that we have been able to see so many years together."

"And you"—he indicated his children—"have been my best life's work." He appeared too choked up to say more.

Their mother, usually the quieter of the two, said, "Well, John, since the cat seems to have got your tongue, perhaps I will add a few more words."

He gave her hand a little kiss. "Say on, my dear."

"To my sons: you have grown into fine men and good fathers. Nathan, your time will come on that last part, I've no doubt," she added with a smile. "To my daughters-in-law: I love you and think of you as my daughters. Thank you for loving my sons, and for the fine children you are raising. To Annie: you are a tenderhearted soul, and I trust you and your husband will take good care of each other in the days and years ahead."

Alice noticed her mother was placing a lot of emphasis on marriage and family. She supposed that was to be expected, given that this was a celebration of their wedding anniversary, and that her mother had always valued her family above all else. But it made Alice a little nervous about what her mother would choose to say about her.

"Alice, come over here," her mother said. She waved Alice toward her chair. Feeling really nervous now, Alice reluctantly stepped forward. "Long ago, your schoolmistress, Miss Templeton, told me that you had many talents and gifts, and that I should never hesitate to allow them to thrive."

Alice looked at her in surprise. "Miss Templeton told you that?"

"She did. I didn't appreciate it at the time. I worried that she was putting impractical ideas into your head, leading you in directions that would ultimately make you unhappy."

Alice stood rooted to the spot, hardly able to breathe. Considering how unhappy she was at this moment, she didn't know what to think, how to react.

"But now I understand," her mother went on. "Over the past few months, as I have read in your letters your excitement for your work and the wonderful things you are doing, I see your satisfaction. I couldn't be prouder of you than I am now."

"You're proud of me because I work at Henley and Company?" Alice choked out.

Her mother shook her head. "I'm proud because you are forging a unique path, being true to yourself. I see how much you value your independence. I pray that God will continue to prosper you in everything you do."

Everyone applauded, and Alice returned to her seat, unable to speak, wiping away tears.

Annie leaned over and whispered, "I told you Mother might surprise you."

This was, in Alice's estimation, the oddest, most upside-down day of her life. Here was her mother, finally praising her for the very things in her life that she was beginning to doubt.

"I worried that she was leading you in directions that would ultimately make you unhappy."

Who was correct? At this point, Alice had no idea.

CHAPTER

Twenty-Nine

I t's a pleasure to see you again, sir," John Griffin said, shaking Douglas's hand.

Griffin was the chief telegrapher for Henley and Company's office in Liverpool. He also oversaw the other telegraphers and clerks who worked there. This was the first time Douglas had come to Liverpool without sending advance notice, so Griffin was bound to be curious. "Everything all right in London, sir?"

He must have heard the rumors of trouble within the company. Douglas wasn't surprised. The comptrollers at both offices had been in constant communication with each other over the past week. Mr. Rosser, who oversaw financial matters in Liverpool, had in fact been called to London and was there today.

Douglas answered, "We've had a bit of a setback, but we're getting it sorted out. The company remains on solid footing." This was overstating things, but Douglas wanted to set Griffin at ease. Besides, he had confidence the company wasn't going to fold. He was doing everything he could to ensure it didn't. "I'm here to do a bit of research, to see if I can locate more details about our communications to America on the matter of a recent order of cotton. I'd like to view your copies of the incoming and outgoing telegrams from that time."

Griffin nodded. "Certainly. I'll take you to our filing room."

They walked downstairs to a room where shelves filled with filing boxes lined every wall. Several rows of tall, freestanding shelves were equally full. At one end of the rows stood a young woman who was placing a stack of telegrams into a box. She paused, looking up from her work as Douglas and Griffin entered the room. She pushed her spectacles up her nose, looking surprised to have visitors.

"This is Miss Davies, who has the unenviable job of filing the telegrams," Griffin explained. "Miss Davies, this is Mr. Shaw from the head office. He wants to review copies of some recent messages."

Miss Davies quickly smoothed back a few wisps of hair and tugged at the cuffs of her shirtwaist. "Good afternoon, sir. I'm sure you'll find everything is in proper order."

Douglas heard the note of worry in her voice. "Don't be alarmed, Miss Davies. I'm not here to do an audit. I simply wish to track down the copy of a telegram that came through this office a few weeks ago. I would appreciate your help in locating it—especially as I can see you have everything so well organized."

Looking relieved, Miss Davies said, "Certainly, sir! Do you know the precise date? Everything is filed chronologically and is separated as to incoming and outgoing. We should be able to find what you're looking for with relative ease."

"I'd like to see everything sent on the twelfth of this month, both incoming and outgoing."

"The twelfth . . ." She turned back toward the shelves. "Those would be located in these boxes."

Douglas followed her down the row and lifted one of the two boxes she indicated. "We'll start with this one."

Griffin returned to his work upstairs, while Douglas and Miss Davies set the boxes on a table and began to look through the telegrams inside. It didn't take long to find the one sent from London regarding the cotton purchase.

Douglas read it carefully. It matched word for word the copy Henley had shown him. As was customary, the signature of the sender was recorded: AM. Had the receiving telegrapher somehow misheard the second initial as *M* when it should have been *C*? It was highly unlikely, given that the codes for *C* (dash, dot, dash, dot) and *M* (dash, dash) were very different. The fact that the message was received at 1:35 p.m., when Clapper would have been at lunch and only Alice would have been at the telegraph, made it even more unlikely.

The telegram included the notation that the message had been repeated back to the sender for confirmation. This procedure was often used when important information was being sent and accuracy was critical. In the outgoing batch, they found the other telegrams related to this one, showing confirmation all down the line. From the transatlantic cable to the final destination in Atlanta, the message had been sent and repeated back precisely as it had been received from London.

Douglas stared at the line of telegrams laid out on the table before him, willing them to divulge some new piece of information. He didn't know what he expected. After all, he'd already scoured every inch of them.

Then, suddenly, the small numbers at the top right-hand corner of each form caught his eye. As with most telegraph stations, these were preprinted forms. At the top was the Henley and Company name, along with the addresses of the offices in Liverpool and London. Below were lines to write in the address of the recipient, the time, and the message, plus spaces designated for other information, such as the initials of the receiver and sender. The seven-digit numbers in the upper corner ran in chronological order. Douglas's eye had skimmed over these numbers before, but now he noticed one significant detail: the telegrams were laid out before him in order of the time received, but the sequential order of the form numbers was off. The number on the telegram purportedly received from Alice was lower than the ones around it.

Galvanized, Douglas sat up straighter, rubbed his eyes, and reviewed the numbers again.

Apparently noticing the difference in his demeanor, Miss Davies said, "Did you find something, Mr. Shaw?"

"Look at this." He turned the forms around to face her. "This telegram is numbered 4931955. Wouldn't you expect the ones that arrived just before and after it to end with the numbers 954 and 956?"

"Yes, I suppose they would." She scrutinized the forms, just as Douglas had. "How very curious."

"In your experience, are these forms ever out of chronological order?"

She sat back in her chair, giving it some thought. "To be honest, I've never paid much attention to the numbering. My job is to file them by date and time so they are easy to retrieve if needed. The telegraph clerks keep a logbook upstairs recording date and time of the message and who the sender is."

"Do they also record this seven-digit number in the logbook?"

"Yes, they do."

"Excellent." He picked up the original telegram again, intending to take it with him.

Something else struck him. The sender's initials were noted as AM. Alice signed as AXM. He'd asked her about it during one of their conversations. She'd told him it was something she developed while working at the Central Telegraph Office to distinguish herself from another telegrapher with the same initials. She'd kept that signature after coming to work at Henley and Company. Other telegrams he'd seen in the archive stack sent by Alice had the signature AXM.

It was a small discrepancy. But Douglas didn't mind grasping at any straw that presented itself.

Returning to the main floor, he went searching for Griffin and located him at a desk near the telegraph machines.

Griffin stood up as Douglas approached. "Did you find what you needed?"

"I believe so."

Douglas asked to see the logbooks for the telegrams. Sure enough, the numbers there were oddly out of order.

Referring back to the original telegram, Douglas said, "It notes here that JS received the message. That's Jimmy Smith, isn't it? I'd like to ask him a few questions. Where is he?" Douglas remembered Smith from previous visits to this office. The man currently seated at the telegraph was someone he didn't know.

Griffin shook his head. "Unfortunately, we had to let Smith go three days ago."

"What was the reason?"

"Dereliction of duty. He kept missing work, on account of being in jail. Kept getting picked up by constables for drunk and disorderly conduct. Fights and such."

"We had such a person working for us?" Douglas found that hard to believe. During his few interactions with Smith, he hadn't noticed anything objectionable, although the man did seem to keep to himself.

"He wasn't always that way," Griffin said. "The problem came on slowly and got worse over the past two months. The last fight was with his landlord, who was trying to evict him. We found out Smith is a big gambler on horse races and owes a lot of money to some disreputable people. I feel sorry for his family—he has a wife and baby. But I'm sure you understand why we could not risk keeping such a man as one of our telegraph clerks, with access to a lot of sensitive information."

"I understand." Douglas sighed. That was a blow. He'd wanted to ask if Smith recalled hearing the X in the signature. Perhaps he'd missed it or simply left it off the transcription. On the other hand, if he had not been performing his work properly, any number of errors might have arisen.

"Smith was a good telegrapher, though," Griffin insisted, perhaps guessing where Douglas's thoughts were going. He pointed toward the paper. "As it notes here, the message was sent back and confirmed by the originating sender."

This was all true, and Douglas couldn't deny any of it. Still, it bothered him. He began to recall other things about Smith, such as the hazing he'd been giving Alice on the day Douglas met her, and a comment Alice had made once about how Smith and Clapper were thick as thieves.

At a loss as to what to do next, he stood watching as the man at the telegraph finished a transmission and set the form into a box marked SENT.

"Was there a particular reason you wanted to talk to Smith?" asked Griffin. "Perhaps I can answer your questions."

"I doubt it. I wanted to ask him about a detail in this message—"

He stopped short as the sounder announced an incoming message. Immediately the telegrapher sent back a "ready" reply. In another moment, the sounder started up again.

So, too, did the Morse printer. This was a device attached to the telegraph machine that contained a roll of half-inch-wide paper tape. The printer recorded the dots and dashes of the Morse code as it came over the sounder. In the early days of telegraphy, operators would read the tape and then transcribe the message. Nowadays, the best operators trained their ears to pick up the dots and dashes, bypassing the tape.

He remembered Alice's words to him: *"You might want to go back to reading Morse code off the tape, Mr. Shaw. Your hearing doesn't seem to work very well anymore."*

She had spoken in anger, yet Douglas wondered if she'd inadvertently given him another brilliant suggestion.

"Griffin, do you always have the printer on?"

"Yes. That was Mr. Henley's direction. It provides a backup in case we should need it, which isn't often."

"How long do you keep the tape?"

"We purge the spools after a few months. We had been setting them out for the dustman, but then we realized some unscrupulous person who knew Morse code could intercept them to gather confidential information."

"So you would still have the spool from the twelfth?"

"Undoubtedly. I'll take you to the storage room."

Once more the two of them went downstairs. In a smaller room across the hall from the filing room were stacks of boxes, each filled with spools of tape.

"There is a paper in each box, listing the dates," Griffin said.

After searching for several minutes, Douglas found the box with the dates he was looking for. He took it to the filing room, where there was a table to work at and the light was better.

Finally, he found the message. Reading to the end, he confirmed that the initials for the sender were AM, not AXM. But then he noticed something. The message immediately following it on the tape was one he could have sworn had an earlier time notation on the transcribed version.

He looked up. "Miss Davies, I'm afraid we need to pull those records again."

Comparison of the tape to the transcribed messages confirmed that this telegram, the one sent by AM, had been transcribed out of order. Based on the tape, it was received between noon and 1:00 p.m.—the time when Alice would have been out of the office at lunch. It appeared that the telegrapher who'd received this message, Jimmy Smith, had deliberately recorded the wrong time. Given what Douglas had learned today about Smith and his money problems, he would lay odds Smith had done it for money.

Douglas and Griffin sat at the table, reviewing everything once more.

"I can't believe it," Griffin said. "I'm sorry now that I've already dismissed him. That means I can't dismiss him for deliberately falsifying our records. But why would he have done this?"

"Do you know whether he was particularly friendly with Archie Clapper?"

"The man at your London office?" Griffin shrugged. "I presume so. Smith always spoke well of him as a telegrapher. In fact, I believe Smith had a letter of reference from someone in London, and that was one reason we hired him. That was several years ago, and I don't remember the details. I'm sorry that I can't say whether Clapper had anything to do with that."

"It doesn't matter," Douglas said. He was elated to be holding the proof that would clear Alice's name. "I have everything I need."

Douglas caught the night train back to London, not caring that he got precious little sleep. He was in the office bright and early the next morning, insisting on a meeting with Clapper and Henley the moment they'd both arrived.

Once the three of them were in Henley's office with the door closed, Henley said, "All right, Shaw. What is this important matter you wish to discuss with us?"

Douglas had spent the train ride working out exactly what he planned to say. He didn't waste any time getting to the point. "I know that Clapper conspired with Jimmy Smith, one of the telegraph clerks at our Liverpool office, to send the infamous telegram that has done so much damage to our company. I know Smith agreed to forge the time the message was sent in order to make it appear as though Alice—that is, Miss McNeil—had sent it."

Using Alice's Christian name was an unfortunate slip of the tongue, revealing just how close his relationship with her had gotten. He'd been hoping to keep any whisper of that fact out of this conversation. He wanted to keep Clapper on the defensive.

Even though Clapper said nothing about Douglas's slip, he did give a sneer before answering. "What gives you the right to make such accusations?"

"Smith also forged Miss McNeil's signature—which, by the way, was incorrect. That was sloppy of you, Clapper."

Archie turned a furious gaze to their employer. "Mr. Henley, do you know of any reason I should stand here and accept insults from this man? You know I am loyal to this company! And you know why." He gave a pointed glance at the photograph of Mrs. Henley that was on Henley's desk. "I would never try to deliberately sabotage it. I had no reason! Whereas Miss McNeil had plenty. She was jealous and underhanded—"

Henley held up a hand. "We've been through all of this already." He looked wearily at Douglas. "Mr. Shaw, I have to ask your reasons for these allegations against Mr. Clapper."

"I've just returned from Liverpool, where I carefully perused the telegrams, the logbook, and the tape from the Morse printer.

300

I found some discrepancies. Mr. Griffin can confirm everything I tell you."

This introduction got the attention of both men.

"Go on," Henley directed. "What were the discrepancies?"

"First, Alice's signature was listed on the telegram as AM when, in fact, it is AXM."

"A mere slip on Smith's part," Archie said with a scoff. "That proves nothing."

"Second, there was an issue with the seven-digit numbers printed on the forms," Douglas continued. "Those numbers are recorded in the logbook. The number of the telegram supposedly sent by Alice was much lower than the ones around it. That would indicate it had been sent earlier in the day—say, perhaps when Miss McNeil was out at lunch, rather than Mr. Clapper."

"You're grasping at straws, Shaw," Clapper said. "It would be very easy for a loose stack of forms to get out of order. Especially on warm weather days, when the windows are open and there is a breeze. Happens in our office all the time." Once more he turned toward Henley. "If you examine our own logbook, you'll see the numbers aren't always in exact order. As I have just pointed out, that is through no fault of our own. Surely you can't believe any of that implicates me."

Archie's tone was belligerent, yet Douglas thought he heard a note of worry creeping into it.

Henley sat silently for a moment. He didn't look happy at being placed in the middle of this thorny situation. Finally, he said, "I have to agree with Mr. Clapper. Those two issues might be put down to mere chance or sloppiness."

Very naturally, Clapper took this statement as proof that his argument had won the day. "So you must also agree that it's evident this man is trying to smear my good name. He wants to make me appear guilty, when we all know it was a craven attack by a woman whose morals were unhinged for love. And over this very man! Mr. Henley, if you really want to see justice done and preserve this company, you'll send Shaw packing, off to join his paramour."

"Nobody's going anywhere just yet," Henley said, although he turned an angry gaze on Douglas. "Would you mind telling me exactly what you are trying to do?"

"Thank you, sir, because I haven't finished telling you everything yet." Douglas spoke calmly, but he could see he needed to finish making his case quickly, lest Henley become angry enough to do as Archie suggested. "You see, there's the matter of the Morse printer. It confirms the time this telegram was received, and that it couldn't possibly have been Miss McNeil who sent it. Perhaps Smith figured no one would think to check it. But I did."

Archie was seething, his fists clenched. "Why you—"

Douglas cut him off before he could complete the epithet. "By the way, I also discovered why Smith was sacked. I even went to see him at the jail. He wanted me to tell you that you still owe him the fifty pounds you promised for doing the job."

"Fifty pounds! It was nowhere near that! He—"

This time, Clapper cut himself off, realizing too late the trap Douglas had set.

Henley's eyebrows rose. "And just how much *did* you offer to pay him for forging that telegram?"

CHAPTER
Thirty

Alice decided to take a roundabout way home. There were questions on her mind. So many questions. So instead of returning to London, she was riding a train to the seaside town in Kent where Miss Templeton lived. Perhaps the woman who had been so instrumental in forming her life's dreams would have the answers.

Seated by a window, Alice watched as the landscape rolled by. Like her life, it seemed. She was twenty-eight years old, and with the recent setbacks, it seemed she had not advanced one step beyond when she'd first left home so many years ago.

What was she to do now? In what direction should she expend her talents and efforts? These concerns filled her thoughts, even as the train came to a halt at the station, and Alice disembarked.

A railway clerk gave her directions to the address she was seeking. Miss Templeton's home turned out to be a tiny clapboard cottage on a short street near the cliffs, overlooking the sea. Heart in her throat, Alice knocked on the door. She hadn't seen Miss Templeton for over twelve years. Was coming here the right thing to do?

A ruddy-faced, unkempt young woman answered the door, looking at Alice in surprise.

"I'm here to see Miss Templeton," Alice explained. "Is she at home?"

"Why yes, miss." The maid ushered Alice inside. She explained that she'd been hired to assist the older woman with meals and cleaning and even helping her get dressed and move around the house. "She's been doing poorly," the maid whispered as she led Alice down a short hallway. "She's a proud one, though. Doesn't like asking for help, but I do all I can."

As they entered the sitting room, Alice's first glimpse of Miss Templeton was disconcerting. She'd been in her midfifties during Alice's school days, which meant she must be approaching seventy now. She was seated in a chair by the fireplace, her slippered feet propped up on a footstool. Although she was swathed in blankets, Alice could see she was very thin. She seemed smaller, too, almost disappearing into the high-back chair.

Her face, however, lit up when she saw Alice. "Merciful heavens! Is that Miss McNeil? My star pupil!" She held out her arms to encourage Alice to approach. "Please excuse me for not getting up. I've been ill."

Alice took her hands. "When your letters dried up, I began to worry about you."

"And you came all the way to see me? That's terribly kind. I'll be a poor hostess, but I'll do the best I can." She called out to her maid. "Grace! Will you make us some tea?"

"Yes, ma'am," Grace said, and shuffled off to the kitchen.

"And see if you can find us some biscuits, too!" Miss Templeton called after her.

Alice had never spent much time thinking about herself at an older age. Looking at Miss Templeton now, though, was sobering. The spinster book had spoken of a quiet home, a flowerpot on the windowsill, and the company of cats. It had not mentioned dust on the mantel and curtains, nor cobwebs in the corners, nor becoming beholden to a housemaid of indifferent quality. Whatever the maid defined as *doing all she could* didn't seem to extend to the dusting.

Alice moved a stack of books off the only other chair, placing them on an already overcrowded little table, so she had a place to sit.

"I'm sorry to say my home does not meet the standards we used to keep at the school," Miss Templeton said. "Grace is not the most efficient maid, but I'm doing my best to teach her some things. As soon as I get back on my feet, I intend to oversee a thorough cleaning."

Alice found these words promising. "Does this mean you're on the mend?"

"I am slowly improving, I believe. Whether it's because of my doctors or in spite of them is a subject for conjecture." She adjusted her glasses and peered fixedly at Alice. "Unlike me, however, you are looking very well—if rather too pale. You must ensure you get outside regularly for walks, girl. It's good for your health."

"Yes, ma'am," Alice answered, feeling like a schoolgirl again.

Miss Templeton leaned back in her chair and sighed, readjusting the blanket around her shoulders. "You must do it while you can, for our physical strength does not last forever."

"Perhaps you need more rest?" Alice said, worried by her mentor's frail appearance and once more second-guessing her decision to come here.

"Nonsense, I'm glad you've come." She reached out to give a brief, comforting pat to Alice's arm. "My mind is still sharp as ever, and I'm in need of good company to occupy it." She wagged a finger at Alice. "Your letters have been rather sparse of late, Miss McNeil." With this brusque comment, she sounded just as she had all those years ago when scolding a poorly performing student. "You must catch me up. What have you been up to?"

"Well, I . . ." Where should she begin? It was a bigger question than Miss Templeton could guess. Alice decided to start with the simplest subject. "I've just spent two days in Ancaster. We celebrated my parents' fortieth wedding anniversary."

She went on to describe her visit, using cheerful, uplifting terms. Given her love for her family, it was easy enough to do, despite the raw feelings her time with them had evoked and the effort it had taken to hold so many emotions in check. A new surge of discomfort rose as she answered Miss Templeton's polite queries about her parents and siblings.

Grace arrived with the tea, and Alice poured cups for her and

Miss Templeton. The tea was weak but hot, and accompanied by some rather stale biscuits.

"I'm glad to hear your mother has come around on the subject of your career," Miss Templeton said. "I'm sure you must have felt great satisfaction at hearing her express her pride in you."

"Actually, I don't know what to think about that. You see—" She paused. From the corner of her eye she could see Grace hovering nearby. The maid was clearly listening to every word of their conversation.

"Grace, these biscuits are unacceptable," Miss Templeton said. "Will you go to the baker's and get us some tea cakes?" She set aside her cup and saucer and began searching for something amid the items cluttering the narrow table beside her chair.

"Please, allow me," Alice said. She pulled some coins from her reticule and handed them to the maid before Miss Templeton could object.

"That's very kind of you, my dear," Miss Templeton said. Once Grace had departed, Miss Templeton fixed her bright, clear gaze on Alice. "Now, my girl, what did you wish to say?"

Here, at last, was the moment Alice could be completely honest. She desperately hoped Miss Templeton could give her the advice and encouragement she needed. "The thing is, I've been let go from my position at Henley and Company."

Even though Alice had shared this information with her friends and her sister, this time it felt different. It felt like a confession, a sorrowful admission that she'd not been able to live up to the vision her schoolmistress had set for her.

"You were sacked?" Miss Templeton looked shocked. "Whatever for? It couldn't possibly be for poor performance. You are too competent for that."

This praise only made Alice feel worse. "They thought I was deliberately trying to damage the company."

"But that's absurd! Why would you do that?"

"I wouldn't, of course! But certain events conspired to make them think so."

Alice told her about the telegram that had done so much harm to the company, and how she'd been unceremoniously let go because of it. She went on to describe her disastrous interview with Mrs. Lipscomb. "I may never work in telegraphy again," she finished sadly. "And that's the worst of it."

"This is terrible, no doubt," Miss Templeton agreed. "But don't lose that plucky spirit of yours, Miss McNeil! Troubles—even those not of our own making—are part of every person's journey. It's how one deals with them that shows true character. I have no doubt you will find a way to triumph in the end."

Alice sighed, wishing she had the same confidence.

Miss Templeton set aside her teacup and leaned back in her chair, her mind clearly working on something. "That business with the telegram doesn't make sense. How could they believe you would *want* to harm the very company you work for? What could possibly be your motive?"

Alice paused before answering, knowing how absurd the truth was going to sound. "Revenge."

Miss Templeton's eyebrows lifted. "For?"

Alice swallowed. She believed that being completely honest was going to be good for her—perhaps even cathartic. But she also knew it wasn't going to be easy. She looked down at her hands and said softly, "Unrequited love."

Several moments of silence followed. Alice looked up again, thinking she might see any expression ranging from disbelief to anger on her mentor's face. But Miss Templeton was studying her with a contemplative expression. She blinked, which, behind her round eyeglasses, gave the impression of a wise owl.

"Was it that assistant director? The conquering hero returned from America?"

"How did you guess?"

"You spoke so glowingly of him in your letters. Nothing but praise. I could read between the lines."

"My opinion of him has changed," Alice said. "I learned he is the sort of man who puts his own advancement above all else."

"How disappointing. That seems very different from the man you described. Do you mean that he joined the other men at the company in this terrible treatment of you?"

Alice shook her head. "He wasn't there. He believes in my innocence, and he objected vigorously when he discovered I'd been sacked."

"How do you know that?"

"He came and told me."

"I see," her mentor replied, nodding.

"I told him that if he truly believed I was innocent, he'd be working to clear my name and uncover the real culprit." Alice jabbed an angry finger in the air as she spoke, as though she were poking an image of Douglas in the chest.

"You set him a task to prove himself!" Miss Templeton said with a smile. "Like the knights of old, who had to strive to be worthy of the lady's hand. If he succeeds, I would say the love is not unrequited—"

"No, no, that's not it at all!" Alice protested. "I merely challenged him to live up to ordinary, honorable, decent standards. And in any case, he is pursuing a very different sort of lady. One who will bring him wealth and prestige."

The bitterness in her voice would be hard to miss. Miss Templeton eyed Alice with skepticism. "Are you sure you're not in love with him?"

"I—I didn't say that," Alice faltered, on the cusp of admitting the entire, awful truth.

"Well, are you?" As in Alice's school days, Miss Templeton's pointed questions could not be shirked.

When it finally came out, her reply was barely audible. "Yes."

With that small, half-whispered word, all the tears Alice had been holding back overflowed, like water over a dam. She was admitting to what was undoubtedly her greatest failing.

Miss Templeton gave her an appraising look. "I suppose next you'll tell me you want nothing more than to have a husband and children. I thought I detected a certain note of longing in your voice when you described your visit to Ancaster."

Alice hung her head. "I'm a weak, foolish, pathetic woman. I've fallen far short of the mark, I know, and made a miserable mess of my life."

"My heavens," Miss Templeton said, sounding highly disgruntled. "I always considered myself a superb educator, but clearly I didn't do a good enough job."

"It's not your fault—it's mine," Alice insisted, swiping at her wet cheeks. "I ought to have done better at living up to your standards."

"On the contrary. From what I can tell, you have lived entirely up to the standards you thought I set for you."

That one word—*thought*—penetrated the fog of Alice's distress, arresting her attention so much that she stopped practically in midsob, catching her breath. Sniffling, she gave her mentor a questioning look. "*Thought?*"

Miss Templeton continued speaking in her crisp, authoritative voice. "If there's one thing I taught all my girls, it was to have confidence in themselves and make the most of their gifts. Even the girls whose primary aim was to make a good marriage. Why do you think Lucy Arbuckle did so well for herself? She had more than mere beauty and more than the so-called 'feminine wiles'— which are nothing but a cheap art practiced by those who have nothing better. She knew who she was, and she knew her worth. Just as you did."

"But—" Alice stared at her, confused at this turn in the conversation. Miss Templeton knew that Alice and Lucy had remained friends after leaving school, but why was she mentioning her now? "I don't remember you saying we should apply those principles to husband-hunting."

Miss Templeton gave her that look that always telegraphed, *Do try to keep up.* "You were in a different curriculum, my dear."

Alice's mind went back to that day in Miss Templeton's parlor. The day her course had been set. Had she somehow misunderstood?

Her mentor sighed. "However, God is the searcher of hearts, not Cornelia Templeton. Perhaps it wasn't the most suitable course for you after all."

"But you said only vapid and silly women allow their lives to be run by a husband." Alice remembered this very well from the many lectures Miss Templeton had given to her pupils.

"Yes, but I never said only vapid and silly women *get married*. If that were the case, where would each new crop of bright young women come from? Granted, there are a few anomalies—"

"But, Miss Templeton!" Alice burst out in shocked surprise.

"Yes?"

Alice couldn't even formulate the question she wanted so desperately to ask. She was perched on the edge of her chair, her entire being thrumming with the desire to understand. To discover that perhaps she hadn't been such a terrible failure after all.

The older woman nodded, as though hearing the unvoiced question. "It would take a special sort of man, of course. They're not so easy to find. However, you must ask yourself a very important question: Do you truly want a husband and children, or does family life suddenly appear safe after these reversals have left your future uncertain?" She held up a hand. "Don't answer right away. Take some time to ponder it."

Alice sat back, dazed, trying to assimilate everything she'd just heard.

Miss Templeton resettled herself in her chair, carefully redraping the blanket covering her lap. She gave Alice a fond smile. "I must admit to feeling slightly envious of you, Miss McNeil."

"Of me? I never thought I'd hear you say that. Especially not now."

"Well, if I didn't raise up young ladies worthy of emulation, what kind of educator would I be?" She extended her teacup toward Alice. "Would you be so kind?"

Alice complied, still marveling over Miss Templeton's words. "Why are you envious of me?"

"You are young. When it comes to marriage and family, you still have that choice to make. I made my decision, and I can't say I regret it. I've been able to live my life on my own terms. And as for children, well, I've had hundreds of them! I ran that school for thirty-three years." She paused, evidently thinking back on those years with satisfaction. Then her lips quirked. "Granted, I cared for some girls more than others, so perhaps that's not the best analogy to motherhood. A mother will love you unconditionally. And yet, a schoolmistress will be more clear-eyed about your faults—and about your abilities. I was deeply concerned that every young lady in my charge should make the most of her gifts and find her place in the world. That's why the best mothers sent their girls to me." She said this with a proud lift of her head that was the epitome of the woman Alice remembered so well. "However . . ." Her smile turned wistful. "There are times when I wonder what might have happened if I'd made a different choice."

To Alice, this was a stunning admission. She couldn't conceive of Miss Templeton living her life any differently than she had.

"Unfortunately, I don't have very many choices at this point," Alice said glumly. "My telegraphic career is over, and . . ."

She couldn't even finish the sentence. She dropped her head and sighed deeply.

"Perhaps you shouldn't completely write off that Mr. Shaw," Miss Templeton said. "After all, he might surprise you."

Alice looked up, startled. Those were the same words Annie had used regarding their mother.

"Mind you, I'm not saying you should wait around, pining," Miss Templeton said sternly. "Don't waste a minute of your life when you could be doing something productive."

Still a little numb, Alice could only nod.

"Ah, I hear Grace coming back from her jaunt to the bakery," Miss Templeton said cheerfully. "We shall have a proper tea now, eh?"

———

Alice just managed to catch the 7:00 p.m. train back to London. She had plenty to think about on the journey home. There was so much she'd misunderstood about her life and so many new things to consider.

Above all, she mulled over the question Miss Templeton had put to her: Was her desire for hearth and home merely a temporary urge that stemmed from her current fears that she might not be able to continue supporting herself? It was an important question. She spent time on it, plumbing the depths of her heart.

No, that wasn't it. Something else had been stirring in her soul ever since she'd heard her father's words at their anniversary celebration. *"You have been my best life's work,"* her father had said.

Family was not to be undervalued. Providing a loving home for children to be nurtured. Raising up a new generation with a loving husband. She smiled as she recalled Miss Templeton's words: *"Where else would each new crop of bright young women come from?"*

This was what Alice wanted. Unfortunately, it was also true that finding the right sort of man would not be easy. Alice couldn't picture anyone except Douglas in the role. Even though he had disappointed her. Despite all that had happened, she still believed he had a core of integrity deep in his soul, even if it had been submerged by his plans for worldly advancement.

Miss Templeton had been right: Alice did hope Douglas loved her, and she'd sought proof that it was so. Proof that he could be the kind of man who would put love and honor above money and security. A man to whom she could safely entrust her heart and her hard-earned independence. That was why she'd challenged him.

If Douglas was not the man for her, perhaps one day there would be another. In the meantime, she would continue to pursue her own path. She must make plans for her life in the here and now.

"Brethren . . . this one thing I do, forgetting those things which are behind, and reaching forth unto those things which are before."

That admonition from Scripture came to mind, and she realized it spoke clearly to her today. It was inspiring, but humbling, too. She had begun to feel as though every door was closed to her. Now she was ready to test the notion that it simply meant new ways were opening up. That something very different was on the horizon.

She might not know exactly where she was going, but she had to believe the right path was out there and that she would find it.

CHAPTER
Thirty-One

Douglas walked into the post office and went immediately to the counter where the telegram request forms were located. He picked up a pencil and began to fill out a form. It took almost no time to complete it. After two hours of walking around the park, he had decided exactly how it should be worded.

Only after he'd begun advancing toward the customer service counter did he notice the clerk was a woman. In this situation, he would have definitely preferred a man. It would be embarrassing to show the contents of this message to another woman. His first inclination was to leave and find a different post office, but the clerk had already seen him coming and was looking at him expectantly.

"May I help you, sir?" she said.

He had no choice but to approach her. "I would like to send a telegram, please."

She must have thought his hesitation was due to a lack of experience at sending telegrams. "It's a simple matter. I'll be glad to assist you. The rates are by the word, based on the destination. I see you've already located a form."

"Yes. I've filled it out. It's going to a London address." Reluctantly, he extended the paper toward her.

As she reached out to receive it, Douglas noticed there was a mourning ring on her hand. It was a very fine one, its tiny pearls and diamond contrasting with a black and gold band. He was surprised and saddened to see it, as she could not have been much older than he was.

She ran a finger over the top of the form, checking that the information for the sender and receiver had been properly filled out. Her eyes widened. Then she blinked and looked up at him.

"Is something wrong?" Douglas asked. "I believe I entered everything correctly." He knew these forms inside and out, although he supposed it was possible that in his distraction he had missed a detail.

She was still staring at him, her mouth slightly agape. He began to wonder whether he'd sprouted a third ear or something. He looked down at the form and then back up at her, hoping the gesture would spur a response.

She closed her mouth. "It's just that, erm . . ."

"Yes?" he prompted.

"The, er, address is in Islington. That's . . . less than two miles off."

He was curious why this would be an issue. Lots of telegrams in London traveled distances shorter than that, although he supposed those were primarily for business. "This isn't the closest telegraph office to that address, though." Douglas had already researched that when devising this plan for contacting Alice. "I presume you'll send the message there?"

"Yes, that's true."

She was still looking at him strangely, and he was fairly certain she hadn't even read the body of the message yet. The thought of how she might react at that point only increased his discomfort. "So, can you send it?"

"Yes, of course."

It seemed to take great effort for her to take her eyes off him and look back at the form. He waited, his embarrassment growing, while she read it. This was why he'd wanted a male clerk. A man might smirk over the contents but then send it and think no more about it. For a woman, it might set off a whole chain of

314

questions—even though she would be forbidden as a matter of protocol to ask them.

The standard practice was that the operator read the message aloud to ensure they had not misread the handwriting. This clerk followed the same procedure, but her voice sounded odd, and she stopped twice for an intake of breath. When she got to the end, she blinked, but there was a gleam in her eyes.

"Yes," said Douglas, "that is correct."

"Very good." She counted the words. "That will be one shilling, please."

Her voice was brisk and businesslike, but she was brimming with unasked questions. He could see it in the way she was looking at him.

He handed her the coin, which he'd had at the ready. "Will you be sending it right away?"

"Yes, sir. Right away."

"Thank you." He smiled, and once more a stunned, almost wondering expression came to her face. Douglas knew he could sometimes have a certain effect on women, but never to his knowledge had it happened with a young widow. He decided it could only be her reaction to the contents of his telegram. Perhaps she had a sentimental streak.

Douglas hurried from the post office, eager for the next phase of his plan. Even though his encounter with the clerk had been incredibly awkward, it had also filled him with hope. If his telegram had affected a stranger so deeply, he could only pray it would do the same for Alice.

Alice sat at her table, reviewing advertisements in the paper and circling a few of them. Tomorrow morning she would go out and pursue the more promising ones. It was a start. She was free to move ahead, and she was feeling optimistic.

Miss T jumped up on the smaller table across the room. Alice realized the spinster book was still on it. She'd forgotten all about it. The cat sniffed at the book for a moment and then promptly sat on it.

Alice couldn't help laughing. "At least that book is good for something, isn't it, Miss T?"

That book had caused her a lot of problems, but she hadn't needed it to extricate herself from at least one of them. Good old-fashioned honesty had done that. Bolstered from her visit with Miss Templeton, she'd decided to tackle her problems head-on. That included not putting off her refusal to Fred. He'd been surprisingly sanguine about it. Lucy had taken it less well, until Fred himself had told her not to worry, that it was all for the best. Alice was still shaking her head over that one, but she was happy to concur with Fred's opinion.

She stood up, intending to make herself some tea, deciding she might as well enjoy the luxury of having her own kitchen. Although she was hopeful, she knew there was a possibility she'd have to give up this lovely place and move back to a boardinghouse.

Through the window, she could see a messenger boy approaching. With no idea whether this spelled good news or bad news, Alice went down to collect the telegram.

As soon as the boy had been tipped and dispatched, Alice tore open the telegram.

```
YOUR NAME IS CLEARED. IF YOU CAN CONSIDER
FORGIVENESS PLEASE MEET ME AT THE BOOKSHOP.

EVER YOURS

DOUGLAS
```

For a moment, Alice didn't know what to do with herself. She laughed and choked back a sob at the same time.

He had done it. He believed in her, and he'd proven it.

Your name is cleared.

Ever yours.

A ten-page letter couldn't have said more.

Alice didn't need two seconds to consider. She had fetched her hat and was out the door before the dust had even settled behind the messenger boy.

⌒⌒⌒

Douglas was beginning to worry that this was a terrible plan.

It had seemed like a good one at the time. He'd felt that by sending a telegram, he could get the most important information to her before she could walk away. Then they would be able to begin the real conversation—the one he'd been wanting to have ever since he'd left Glasgow with an entirely new set of goals for his life.

He'd been waiting in the bookshop for some time now, though, frequently glancing toward the window, hoping to get a glimpse of Alice approaching the shop.

Douglas had done so much to get to this point. First, he'd routed out Clapper's treachery. Henley had been forced to act on that revelation, and the outcome had been supremely satisfying. Not only was Alice exonerated, but the door was open for her to be a part of the company's future, if she wished it. Whether she chose to do so, and in what capacity, remained to be seen.

Then had come the night of Lady Gordon's party, when he'd endured the Charade of the Cut Direct. Miss Rolland had walked up to him, looked him in the eye, and walked away without uttering a word. She had ensured the moment took place when plenty of important people were standing around to witness it. It wasn't as though Douglas had never been humiliated before, although it had been a while. Not since he was a young man, still in poverty. Nor did he care so much what the other guests thought of him. His priorities were different than they had once been. He didn't have to marry into society to feel he was a success. That idea seemed shallow now.

The only bad part—and it had been excruciating—had been putting up with Busfield's superior attitude. Nothing had been required on his part to persuade Busfield that Miss Rolland had thrown Douglas over for him. Busfield believed it instantly. He'd cornered Douglas shortly afterward in the smoking room to share his particular brand of sociability.

"You know she was never going to choose you, Shaw. You were only a passing fling. I indulged her because I am a generous man." Throwing his shoulders back and looking supremely self-satisfied, Busfield had added, "Yes, she's going to be glad she married me." It was only then, for the briefest of moments, that Douglas had felt sorry for Miss Rolland.

But Douglas had kept his mouth firmly shut and allowed the bank officer his moment of glory. He'd kept his eyes on the goal: winning Alice.

For these reasons and so many more, Douglas had spent the afternoon at this bookshop, waiting on tenterhooks to see the results of sending that telegram. He'd put his whole heart into those few lines. Would she accept it?

He was beginning to see the pitfalls to his plan. He didn't know how long it would take for the telegram to reach her. What if she wasn't home? If she didn't show up, how should he interpret her absence? Should he assume she hadn't yet received it, or that she was rejecting his request to meet? Maybe the messenger had gotten lost, or some other delay had occurred. The possibilities were endless.

Whatever the case, Douglas was committed to this plan now. He'd stay here until closing time, if need be. If Alice still didn't come, he'd find another way to reach her. He didn't fancy loitering outside her house again, as that hadn't worked out so well the last time, but he'd do it if he had to. He would talk to her, and when he did, he was going to lay out his case with the utmost care, because this was the most important negotiation he would ever undertake.

He was turning over these things in his mind for the hundredth time when he finally saw Alice walking up the street. She paused at the window to the shop. The warmth in her eyes as their gazes met told him he was starting this negotiation from a very favorable position.

Here, at last, was the opportunity of a lifetime.

It was fitting that he should be waiting for her at this bookshop. Through the window Alice could see him standing in the same place she'd first spotted him: next to the row of shelves where the spinster book had been housed. She hurried to the door, her heart bubbling in anticipation.

He met her there, opening the door for her. They stood in the doorway, looking at one another.

"You came," he said. Simple words, but the joy on his face said much more.

Ever yours.

She wanted to melt into his arms, to stop resisting the powerful draw he'd always had on her. But there were so many things she had to know before she could unloose the hold on her heart.

She held up the telegram. "Would you care to tell me what this is about?"

"Alice, I've *so* much to tell you—"

"Pardon me," a man's voice interrupted. It was a customer wanting to leave the shop.

Murmuring their apologies, they moved away from the doorway. Douglas led her down one of the aisles of books.

"Why are we meeting in the bookshop?" As much as she enjoyed being with him in one of her favorite places, she had to ask.

He paused, turning to look at her much as he had done at the doorway, although this time with a sly smile. "I came to see if there were any books about Argentina."

"Argentina!" she blurted in surprise.

"Yes. I'll be going there in a few months, so I'd like to read up on the place. I've been trying to convince Mr. Henley to diversify for some time now, and there is an opportunity to forge new contracts there with beef exporters."

This was good news for Henley and Company, but why did he look so happy about going away? She couldn't possibly have read too much into that telegram, could she? What was he driving at?

She waved the telegram under his nose. "Douglas Shaw, are you going to explain this to me or not?"

He took her hand. His touch was warm, bringing back so many memories. "Alice, I want to tell you everything. It's too much to discuss here, though. Perhaps we might go somewhere else?"

They left the shop, having decided on the garden behind Alice's lodgings as their destination. It was a pleasant, private spot. As they walked, Douglas told her what he'd uncovered at work. She was furious at Archie's subterfuge and yet filled with awe at the way Douglas had unraveled it.

"You really did clear my name," she said, marveling.

"Henley truly regrets what happened, how he was tricked by Archie and coerced by his wife to do what he did. Over the objections of Mrs. Henley, he sacked Archie immediately. We had to scramble to find a replacement. I've also been helping out, but we still need someone to fill the other position."

Alice pulled up short. "Are you implying that I ought to reapply?"

"Let's hold that thought for a bit, shall we?" he said.

By now they had reached Alice's lodgings. As they made their way to the garden, Alice thought over what Douglas had said. The idea of returning to work at Henley and Company was gratifying, but she wasn't sure it was the right thing to do. Not after all that had happened there. And certainly not if Douglas planned to— No, surely he didn't. Not after the way he'd signed that telegram.

"Are you still courting Miss Rolland?" she demanded, pausing just as they passed through the garden gate.

"No. She gave me the cut direct."

"She did?"

Douglas smiled. "I see you are rightfully horrified. However, you shouldn't feel bad for me. Miss Rolland and I agreed on it ahead of time. It was all staged, in order to preserve her vaunted reputation and give her the upper hand."

"You *wanted* to be insulted? But why?"

"That's a long story, too. Will you indulge me?" He motioned toward the nearby bench.

Alice nodded. At this point, she wasn't about to refuse.

Douglas began by describing his conversation with Mr. Carnegie. Alice listened, riveted, as he went on to tell her about his family. With every word, she understood him better: where he had come from and how it had molded him. By the time he shared the good news from his recent visit to Glasgow, she was rejoicing right along with him. Everything confirmed what she'd always felt must be true about his character, despite how it had looked at times. He was a good man. As Miss Templeton had said, such men weren't easy to find. But Alice was pretty sure she had done it.

"And that is how I ended up getting the cut direct from Miss Rolland," Douglas concluded. "But of all the things that have happened to me, that matters the least. I hope to win the hand of someone much more admirable."

Douglas took her hand again, and Alice's heart began to flutter in that way that had been totally unfamiliar to her until she'd met him.

He looked into her eyes. "My dear Miss McNeil, dare I hope that you turned down that offer of marriage from the cargo master?"

The question was so unexpected that she had to swallow a laugh. "Yes. I did."

"Does that mean you are determined to remain a spinster?"

She gave him the same wobbly smile that had once worked so well on Fred, only this time she meant it. "I don't think that plan is going to work out so well, either."

His hand tightened on hers. "Isn't it funny how plans can change? As our great Scottish poet once said, the best-laid plans of mice and men often go awry."

"So what do we do?"

"Make new plans, of course! If, as the poem says, our little nest has been turned out, we shall seek other pastures. What would you say about accompanying me to Argentina, for starters? You'd be going in an unofficial capacity, as my wife, but—"

"Your wife!"

"Well, naturally. I thought that was understood—"

She stopped his words with a kiss. It was an unusual proposal, but she didn't mind. She'd never had any interest in courtship by the book.

Much later, when they'd had time to catch their breath and she was enjoying the solid comfort of leaning against his chest, Alice murmured, "What were you saying about Argentina?"

She felt his chest move as he chuckled. "I didn't finish that statement, did I?"

She snuggled in closer, savoring the warmth of his touch. She'd had no idea how satisfying it could be. "So I'll be going along as your wife," she prompted.

"That's right. But I'll need your help with our telegraphed communications back to the company. There is a new codebook, with a whole new set of coding to learn. Shipping beef involves quite a few details that aren't relevant to cotton or grain."

"How long do you suppose we'll be gone?"

"About four months, I expect. Long enough for us to become versed in a bit of Spanish, perhaps. But you're likely to feel at home much of the time. I'm told that Buenos Aires is quite the cosmopolitan city, with whole sections made up of people from England, Germany, France, and Spain."

"It sounds wonderful."

"Am I to interpret that as a yes?"

She pulled away from him just enough to gaze into his eyes—those warm brown eyes that had captivated her from the beginning, even if she'd been unwilling to admit it.

His smile broadened as he understood exactly what she was telegraphing with her gaze. Then he kissed her again.

After a time, Alice said, "I don't believe I'll want to go back to Henley and Company after our return. What would you say to the idea of my starting a commercial telegraphy school? There is a high demand for those skills."

"You would encourage women to join such a profession after the experiences you've had?"

"It led me to you, didn't it?"

He grinned. "I can't argue with that."

"I might even expand it into a more general business school. I could teach typewriting, as well, and shorthand for taking dictation. We could even find sponsors to offer scholarships for those in need."

"Yes!" said Douglas eagerly. "I like that part especially. I can help you draw up the financial plans—"

She placed a hand to his lips. "Perhaps we should start by planning our wedding?"

He kissed her fingers. "That's an excellent idea."

"I envision a large wedding with lots of people and an elaborate wedding breakfast," Alice said. "We ought also to have dancing, of course."

At her mention of dancing, Douglas grimaced. "It's too bad we can no longer run off to Gretna Green and be married by the blacksmith."

"True. But I've no objection to going to Scotland for our honeymoon trip."

"Och, you will love the Highlands, lassie. They are beautiful this time of year. Or so I've heard."

She saw a hint of pain behind the laughter in his eyes. He was Scottish, yes, but he knew nothing of Scotland beyond the industrial city where he'd been raised. Alice had never been to Scotland at all, even though her grandparents had been born in Inverness. "Yes, I believe it is high time we both saw it."

"It's a good plan, wouldn't you agree?"

Something on the brick wall opposite them caught Alice's eye. It was Miss T, who had come out to sun herself. She was looking down on them with a placid gaze, as if she approved.

"Yes," Alice said. "It is the very best plan."

He kissed her again, and that was the end of their conversation for quite a long while indeed.

EPILOGUE

That must have been the finest display of professional restraint ever shown by a telegraph operator," Mr. Bennington said, laughing as Douglas and Rose each gave their version of what had happened on the day when Douglas sent the now-famous telegram to Alice.

Her wedding was just ten days away. Even now, as she watched the man she loved smile as he chatted with their friends, Alice could hardly believe it was true. Her heart felt as light as the butterflies flitting over the rosebushes on this sunny afternoon.

They were gathered by an elegant stone fountain that was the centerpiece of Lucy's garden. Lucy had arranged a luncheon to celebrate the upcoming wedding. Douglas's friends Stuart and Hal had been invited, along with Emma and Rose. Lucy was inside, overseeing the final preparations, while everyone else enjoyed a stroll in the garden.

Lucy had finally become reconciled to the fact that Alice was going to marry Douglas instead of Fred. Her change of heart had been helped along by Fred himself—who, as it turned out, already had another marital prospect. While still in limbo after his proposal to Alice, he'd attended a party at the home of his ship's captain. There, he'd met the captain's daughter and had become immediately smitten. According to Lucy, the young lady returned Fred's interest, which was why he'd been so unruffled when Alice officially turned him down. As with so many things, she could thank Miss Templeton's wise counsel for that. By not delaying her talk with Fred, things were now infinitely better for everyone.

Even Lucy's husband, Mr. Bennington, was having a good time today. He generally approved only of parties that fit his social status, but today he seemed inclined to overlook the unusual nature of the guest list. Alice thought he might have another reason for agreeing to this party besides his willingness to accommodate his wife's wishes. He was clearly impressed with Douglas. Her fiancé's growing reputation in the business world was something the successful stockbroker could understand and admire.

He was also having a good laugh over the Telegram Incident. It had quickly become the stuff of legend, especially as Douglas had nearly keeled over from shock the day Alice introduced him to Rose.

Mr. Bennington said, "Clearly, Mrs. Finlay, you deserve an award for meritorious service."

"I'd be thrilled to receive such a recognition from the postmaster general," Rose answered with a wry smile. "Especially if it were to come with a pay raise."

"I still can't believe you managed to keep the secret for so long—even from me!" Emma exclaimed. Rose hadn't breathed a word of her involvement in that telegram to anyone until the moment she and Douglas were officially introduced by Alice.

Rose nodded. "It was probably the hardest thing I've ever done. I was desperate to say something and so anxious for Alice—how would she react to that message? Not to mention, here was my opportunity to examine the man who had turned her head."

Once upon a time, Alice would have vigorously denied that any man could turn her head. It was too late now, however, so she gave a happy, if slightly embarrassed, smile.

"I could see you had plenty of questions," Douglas said to Rose. "You stared at me like I was some sort of mythical creature."

"I halfway believe you are!" Rose joked. "Such honorable gentlemen are as rare as unicorns!"

This cheeky remark brought chuckles from everyone.

But then Rose sobered and added, "However, it wasn't so much that I wanted to pepper you with questions. There was really only one thing that I wanted to say to you."

He eyed her with interest. "What was that?"

She stepped closer to him and stretched as tall as she could in order to look him in the eye. "You had better do right by Alice and treat her well, Mr. Shaw. Today and always. This is the finest woman in the world, and she deserves nothing less."

Her words brought tears to Alice's eyes. They were a high compliment, and they also showed how fiercely protective Rose was of her friends. There was an edge to them, though. Scars from Rose's past sometimes surfaced in this way. Alice guessed that she was voicing her own pain.

Emma touched Rose's arm. "You needn't be so worried. He's not going to hurt Alice—he's *in love* with her!"

This naïve view of love would normally have no power to persuade someone like Rose. Nevertheless, she stepped back from Douglas, and her posture softened. "I didn't mean to imply you would intentionally hurt her. I didn't mean to cause offense."

"None taken." Douglas gave Rose one of his impossibly charming smiles. "You are a good friend to Alice. I hope I shall prove myself deserving of your confidence."

His heartfelt response must have been exactly what Rose needed to hear. Expelling a breath, she gave an approving nod, and the atmosphere lightened again.

As everyone else moved into other conversations, Emma took Alice aside. "I've already got all your cards addressed, ready to post after your wedding."

Emma had eagerly offered to take on several bridesmaid's duties, including sending out the announcements after the wedding. The cards would go to friends and extended family members and would include the new couple's address. Because Alice and Douglas planned to leave in a few months for an extended trip to Argentina, they'd decided to set up their first home in furnished lodgings. It was a spacious set of rooms located not far from where Alice lived.

"We like the neighborhood," Douglas had cheerfully explained to their friends. "There's a bookshop nearby that we are partial to visiting." By then, Alice had told Douglas about how she'd overheard him and his friends discussing the spinster book. They'd all had a good laugh over that, too.

"Just imagine, one day you'll have your own home!" Emma said dreamily. Her gaze was taking in Lucy's house and garden, probably imagining Alice and Douglas owning such a place. "In the meantime, I can help you decorate your new lodgings, if you like. Even though it is furnished, you'll want to add your own touches. And some plants, too!"

Alice nodded. "It has a large, sunny parlor. I'm sure we could put some plants in there."

"Yes! That will make it feel like it's truly your *home*." Emma put loving emphasis on the word. She hugged Alice tightly. "I'm so happy for you! I wish I could attend your wedding. You *must* tell me every detail when you return."

"Agreed," Alice said. "I know you and Rose will be with me in spirit."

Despite her teasing of Douglas on the day they'd become engaged, their wedding was going to be a simple affair. Alice's mother had insisted it take place in Ancaster because the bride's parents had a duty to provide the wedding breakfast. Her mother had once been resigned to Alice's spinsterhood, but the moment she'd learned Alice was to be married after all, everything had changed. Now she was the doting mother of the bride, filled with plans for the wedding. In her view, having the wedding breakfast at the bride's home was the only acceptable thing to do. Never mind that Alice hadn't lived there for nearly ten years. Alice had agreed primarily because her mother was not strong enough to travel to London. Alice felt that made her too frail to host the breakfast, too, but that argument had not prevailed. Her mother had been adamant, and Annie, Minnie, and Jane had insisted they'd be helping her at every step.

Most of Alice's and Douglas's friends would not be able to get away from work to attend the wedding in Ancaster, which was the reason for having this celebratory luncheon together instead.

"Let's rejoin the others," Alice suggested to Emma, noticing Lucy coming out of the house and heading toward the garden. "I believe it's nearly time to go in."

Douglas and Mr. Bennington must have been chatting about business, because as Alice and Emma walked up to them, Lucy's husband told Alice, "You certainly have done well for yourself in marrying this gentleman."

"My thanks to you for the compliment," Douglas said, "but the truth is, *I* am the one who is marrying up." He took Alice's arm, love evident in his eyes as he looked at her. She never had been able to shake the breathtaking feeling that came over her at such times. Nowadays, though, she didn't mind at all.

"You are indeed the lucky one," Lucy told him, arriving in time to hear his comment. She tried to look stern as she said it, but a smile got the better of her. Now that she was no longer stuck on the idea of her brother marrying Alice, she was warming up to Douglas. It helped that her husband, whose opinions she held in high regard, liked him as well.

Alice was glad the Benningtons, at least, would be able to attend the wedding. Her friendship with Lucy had been comfortably restored. Alice had a newfound respect for her friend, particularly when she recalled Miss Templeton's words about how Lucy had done so well because she understood her self-worth.

Lucy's talent for fashion was also proving to be a boon. "Tomorrow we go to the dressmaker's to see how that new traveling dress looks on you!" she remarked to Alice as the luncheon party walked toward the house. The traveling dress was her wedding gift to Alice. Lucy's sartorial flair had never been more evident, nor more appreciated, as when they'd chosen the material and decided on the design of the dress.

"I'm excited to see it, too," Alice said, even though she knew the admission would stoke Lucy's visions of future shopping trips. Apart from her wedding gown, the traveling dress would be the first outfit she wore as Mrs. Shaw. She loved that it would be the gift of a longtime friend—a friend who had always been convinced Alice would marry someday. What came after the wedding might not unfold as Lucy imagined, but then, their plans for travel, business, and the telegraphy school were dreams belonging uniquely to Alice and Douglas. It was a new phase of her life that Alice couldn't wait to begin.

During the luncheon, the upcoming honeymoon trip was a big topic of conversation. Alice and Douglas explained that after being married in Ancaster, they would spend a few days in the Lake District and then go to Glasgow to visit Douglas's parents. In Glasgow, they would be honored at a party organized by the Shaws and the Johnstones before going on to spend the bulk of their trip in the Highlands.

"The Scots are lively folk," Hal pointed out, affecting a very bad Scottish brogue. "I expect there will be dancin' at that party."

Alice looked at Douglas, worried this remark would bring panic to his face, or at the very least, a grimace of pain. Something flickered in his eyes that might have been those things, or maybe just a grim determination to face the worst. But then something interesting happened. He took Alice's hand, and his eyes smiled into hers.

"In that case," he said, "I'll just have to get plenty of private lessons beforehand."

AUTHOR'S NOTE

My interest in the history of the telegraph began when I read a book called *The Victorian Internet*. The book detailed many of the ways the telegraph's impact on the world in the nineteenth century was similar to the internet in the twenty-first. The world got smaller, news traveled faster, and businesses were completely altered. As with the internet, there were even scams and long-distance romances!

Almost from the beginning, telegraphy was an occupation pursued by women as well as men. It was work that both could do equally well. Sometimes they worked in separate departments, but more and more, men and women worked right alongside each other. It didn't escape many people at the time that this setup could easily give rise to workplace romances. That's a fun idea I'll be pursuing in the LOVE ALONG THE WIRES series.

The steel magnate Andrew Carnegie makes a few appearances in this book. His trip across England in a four-in-hand coach actually happened. Much of the advice he gives to Douglas in this book came directly from Carnegie's own writings.

In my research, I discovered a real-life inspiration for *The Spinster's Guide to Love and Romance*, the book which causes so many comical problems for Alice. Written by Myrtle Reed in 1901, *The*

Spinster Book is very definitely tongue-in-cheek in its handling of the subject of love and the ways men and women interact with one another. The guide Alice uses purports to be a straight-up how-to manual, although Alice has plenty of doubts about whether anyone could really take it seriously. Many of the quotes in this novel are taken from *The Spinster Book,* so I'll let you decide! Although written over a hundred years ago, the book pokes fun at many human foibles that are timeless. In future books in this series, Alice's friends will also discover its potential for sparking romance and a few unintended consequences on the road to true love.

I hope you've enjoyed this glimpse into the Victorian workplace. There is a popular saying that "The past is a different country." While that's certainly true, I've enjoyed exploring some of its similarities, too. With the busy pace, the inevitable conflicts with coworkers, and the vital importance of business machines, Victorian offices don't seem so different from many today.

331

ACKNOWLEDGMENTS

My thanks to Claudia Welch for hours of brainstorming on this story, and for the inspiring Friday afternoons at the coffee shop, writing and talking books.

Thanks to Elaine Luddy Klonicki for beta-reading the manuscript and providing so many excellent insights.

Many thanks to Dave Long and to everyone at Bethany House, including Amy Green and Noelle Chew in the publicity department and my wonderful editor, Jessica Barnes, who always makes my writing better (and shorter!).

Thanks, as always, to my husband, Jim, for tireless support and encouragement, especially at deadline time.

Jennifer Delamere writes tales of the past and of new beginnings. Her novels set in Victorian England have won numerous accolades, including a starred review from *Publishers Weekly* and a nomination for the Romance Writers of America's RITA Award. Jennifer holds a BA in English from McGill University in Montreal, Canada, and has been an editor of educational materials for two decades. She loves reading classics and histories, which she mines for vivid details that bring to life the people and places in her books. Jennifer lives in North Carolina with her husband, and when not writing, she is usually scouting out good day hikes or planning their next travel adventure. Learn more online at jenniferdelamere.com.

Sign Up for Jennifer's Newsletter!

Keep up to date with Jennifer's news on book releases and events by signing up for her email list at jenniferdelamere.com.

More from Jennifer Delamere

Brought to London by different circumstances, three sisters are swept away by unexpected love and adventures of their own. Filled with drama and romance, history and charm, this nineteenth-century series brings Victorian England to life.

LONDON BEGINNINGS: *The Captain's Daughter, The Heart's Appeal, The Artful Match*

You May Also Like . . .

Gray Delacroix has dedicated his life to building a successful global spice empire, but it has come at a cost. Tasked with gaining access to the private Delacroix plant collection, Smithsonian botanist Annabelle Larkin unwittingly steps into a web of dangerous political intrigue and will be forced to choose between her heart and her loyalty to her country.

The Spice King by Elizabeth Camden
HOPE AND GLORY #1
elizabethcamden.com

Determined to uphold her father's legacy, newly graduated Nora Shipley joins an entomology research expedition to India to prove herself in the field. In this spellbinding new land, Nora is faced with impossible choices—between saving a young Indian girl and saving her career, and between what she's always thought she wanted and the man she's come to love.

A Mosaic of Wings by Kimberly Duffy
kimberlyduffy.com

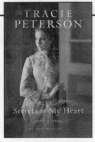

Reunited with childhood friend and lawyer Seth Carpenter, recently widowed Nancy Pritchard must search through the pieces of her loveless marriage for the truth behind her husband's death after his schemes come to light. But as they pursue answers, their attraction to each other creates complications, and dark secrets reveal themselves.

Secrets of My Heart by Tracie Peterson
WILLAMETTE BRIDES #1
traciepeterson.com

◆ BETHANYHOUSE

More from Bethany House

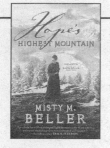

On her way to deliver vaccines to a mining town in the Montana Territory, Ingrid Chastain never anticipated a terrible accident would leave her alone and badly injured in the wilderness. When rescue comes in the form of a mysterious mountain man, she's hesitant to trust him, but the journey ahead will change their lives more than they could have known.

Hope's Highest Mountain by Misty M. Beller
HEARTS OF MONTANA #1
mistymbeller.com

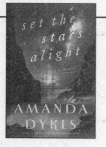

Reeling from the loss of her parents, Lucie Clairmont discovers an artifact under the floorboards of their London flat, leading her to an old seaside estate. Aided by her childhood friend Dashel, a renowned forensic astronomer, they start to unravel a history of heartbreak, sacrifice, and love begun 200 years prior— one that may offer the healing each seeks.

Set the Stars Alight by Amanda Dykes
amandadykes.com

Wanting to do her part in the Civil War effort, Clara McBride goes to work in the cartridge room at the Washington Arsenal. Her supervisor, Lieutenant Joseph Brady, is drawn to Clara but must focus on preventing explosions in the factory. When multiple shipments of cartridges fail to fire and everyone is suspect, can the spark of love between them survive?

A Single Spark by Judith Miller
judithmccoymiller.com

BETHANYHOUSE